SPARK OF VENGEANCE

THE IMDALIND SERIES, BOOK 9

REBECCA ETHINGTON

Published by Market Street Books LLC

Copyediting by C&D Editing
Production Management by Market Street Books

ISBN (print) 978-1-949725-47-6
ISBN (e-book) 978-1-949725-41-4
Printed in USA
This Edition, June 2021

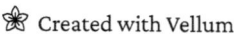 Created with Vellum

THE COMPLETE IMDALIND SERIES

PROLOGUE

The plan was simple. Excavate an ancient tunnel system that zigzagged through Europe and blow the alien's barrier from the outside.

My team and I had found the tunnel years ago when a mission in Poland had sent us underground. Desperate to escape before our cover was fully blown, we took shelter in the mountains, hoping that trees and caves would be our savior before we could be extracted.

What we had found instead was infinitely more valuable.

An ancient man-made tunnel that weaved through mountains, burrowed under cities, and who knows what else. We had traveled through the intricately carved paths for days, carefully documenting the ornate creations that lined the walls and doing our best to mark each turn and fork we crossed lest we get lost. The further we traveled, however, the more the caves became a labyrinth, swallowing us and our hope into the darkness.

We had expected to die in those caves, lost in an underground trove forever. Instead, we found a door.

1

The surface was carved in stone and iron in a scene full of animals and people who all stood together underneath a sky of stars and explosions; fireworks perhaps. It was beautiful, and I ran my fingers over it in awe, desperate to see what treasures a door that beautiful concealed.

But it was sealed shut.

No matter what we did, we could not open it. The massive thing would not budge.

Eventually, we left the door and wandered back into the maze of dark caverns as we tried to find a way out.

We crawled out of the cave a month later, reported what we had seen and everything was filed away in the military archives to be forgotten.

That was until several years later when an explosion erupted inside the city of Prague and the entire metropolis was swallowed by a large red dome.

The massive thing was like a canker. Its scarlet walls stretched to the sky, sealing away the city under an opaque barrier that looked as though a massive sun was rising from within the earth. Within weeks every government had rallied together to conquer this foreign invasion. Every method of attack was used to destroy and banish the aliens.

Nothing worked.

After months of foolishly fighting this stationary enemy, it was determined that the dome, while impenetrable from the top, might be breakable in the depths underground where it extended.

It was clear what needed to happen: a powerful explosion, directly against the barrier, preferably underground where the attack couldn't be monitored.

Although whoever had created the barrier had not attacked us. Despite the dozens of bombs that were dropped on it daily, there had been speculation that because the planes could be seen, whoever was inside the dome could be fighting against the attack. If we attacked where we could not be seen, we might stand a chance. Lucky for them, I knew exactly where to go.

It was this mission that had brought me back to this cave.

After wandering for days, we had finally found it. The same bright red barrier that covered the city stretched over the rough hewn tunnel from wall to wall and ceiling to floor. It was just waiting for us. I could already hear my soldiers begin to retrieve the bombs.

"Klotz!"

I wanted to jump at the loud voice behind me, but I stood still, arms folded over my chest as I stared at the wall of red. The glistening surface sparkled as I stood before it, as if it knew I was here.

As if it knew what we were here for. I stared at it, wanting to touch it, wanting to destroy it, and knowing that somewhere beyond it that door was waiting for me.

This time I would be able to step through it.

"Klotz!" The yell came again as the heavy fall of feet ran up behind; Commander Ramdoir and a few of his men ran up to surround me.

"Sir," I acknowledged his presence with a snap of my heels and a quick salute, but I still did not remove my eyes from the glistening surface.

I couldn't look away.

"Beautiful, isn't it?" The awe was clear in his voice.

I wanted to agree, but I couldn't. As much as the beauty called to me, as much as it enticed me, there was something else I wanted all the more.

"Are you referring to the surface, or to whatever it is hiding?" I finally looked away from the bright red wall to look at the man beside me, his tall frame trimmed perfectly in the deep blue uniform of Ukraine.

Commander Ramdoir had trained me from the moment I had been recruited from my local police in Kiev. I was his pet project so to say, and while I was sure he had interests in me beyond being trained as his replacement, I was not interested in entertaining them.

I had a career I wanted to build. My goal was to take over his position as the head of the Security Service, not take over as his wife.

"You are the only woman I know who sees beyond the surface," he whispered, obviously wanting to keep his voice low enough that his soldiers couldn't hear.

The way he spoke drove nails into my spine.

"And you are the only Ukrainian I know who cannot take no for an answer." I did not hide my disgust and he did not notice it. He laughed and stepped closer, his voice reducing to a low hum.

"Don't play coy, Nastya."

"Don't be..."

Any retort I had left as the barrier we stood beside vanished with a pop. A rush of hot air pressed through the cavern at its disappearance, the sound of what I was sure was a scream weaving through the tepid wind. I lost my balance at the pressure, feet stumbling as the air rushed over us.

"What in the world?" I asked in a panic, stepping toward where the barrier had been a moment before, hand extended in expectation of an impact.

Nothing came.

"It's gone," I whispered to myself as the Commander's shouts began to echo over the dark stone.

"Get back to the surface, see if it is indeed gone," he

boomed from behind me, my focus still narrowed into the dark in complete shock. "You! Build a team and get into the city if it is! You, and you, get into those caves."

Sounds washed over me as everyone jumped into action; orders, cocked guns, the heavy thunder of footsteps. The sound of a prepared war rippled behind me as that scream I had heard before grew louder. The distorted noise sent a shiver through me, the sound growing... growing...

"Silence," I yelled to the soldiers, holding a shaking hand up as everyone froze.

I couldn't even hear them draw breath.

The feral yells thundered down the cave toward us like a pack of animals. The soldiers around me began to shake and step back. They heard it too, we all saw them coming.

At first, I thought they were bats, but everything about that was wrong. They flew through the air in broken lines, their screams dangerous howls that were more human than animal. They looked at us with filthy sphinx-like faces, their teeth gnashing together.

They weren't bats, and whatever had popped the barrier had released them.

"Run!" I yelled, but the command was too late.

The swarm of flying monsters engulfed me, their claws ripping against clothes and flesh as they screamed, as their teeth sunk into the skin on my lower back.

I felt the teeth, felt the acid that followed. It burned and roared and sent me to the ground in a tangle of pain and screams as heat raced through my veins, pressing against skin and skull as though it was going to explode.

As though I was going to explode.

As it changed me.

CHAPTER 1
ILYAN

The handcuffs were cold and painful where they pressed into my wrist.

I tried to ease the pressure and shift away from the hard edge, but I was trapped. Each hand was cuffed to the bedrails of the hospital bed, pressing me into the uncomfortably hard mattress. I was propped on pillows, that same infernal beeping, buzzing in my ears.

The sound that had once been a lifeline was now just a noise that was drowned out by so many others. Voices whispered in the corner, the hushed sounds blending with the shouts from the hall and the endless scratching of the detective's pen. Below it all was the low buzz of the television that had been set to the local news for days, the same scene of some city being bombed playing on repeat.

Detective Bondar, the man who sat closest to me had turned it on, stating that he was hoping that it would trigger some memory, some feeling, something that would lead him to the truth. Truth of a murder, of some nefarious plot.

Something about me.

"It has been days since this terror began and destructive creatures invaded our cities and we are still no closer to discovering anything about them..." The voiceover on the screen was low, but I still heard it, the report all the more terrifying alongside the blood strewn street they were displaying, people running and screaming away from what looked like a flock of bats.

I had no memory of the world before this; but this was the world, now. This place that was full of little winged monsters that ripped men apart and bombs and massacres...

The images twisted in my stomach as I once again looked away, only to be met by the narrowed eye of the detective. He had been looking at me the same way since he had arrived a few hours before.

"Anything coming back?" he asked, a glint in his grey eyes as the scratches of his note taking turned into an irritating tap-tap of his pen against the metal railing I was cuffed to.

"Anything ringing a bell?" The neatly trimmed mustache on his face waggled awkwardly with each syllable. I stared at it as it moved, barely hearing his thickly accented voice as he spoke in yet another language I mysteriously understood. I think this was the third one he had tried.

"Do you remember this? This attack on a city in our region began only a few days ago. It has since spread across the globe. Were you there? Were you there where it began?"

"No," I growled, the feelings of anger and resentment rippling up my spine and pulsing through my shoulders.

I couldn't stop the shake from rumbling over me, any hope of the detective not noticing vanished as he smiled at me knowingly, glancing once at his silent partner behind him before turning toward Dr. Sirko.

The older doctor was perched at the large computer bay nestled into the corner of the room, his aged shoulders sagging as he too watched the replay on the television.

"Are you sure he wasn't bit?" The detective asked, his mustache waggling in irritation as the doctor shook his head dismissively.

"We checked him thoroughly," the doctor growled, not looking at either of us. "We know the rules. We kill them all before they turn and restrain them otherwise. We cuffed him, didn't we? Guilty or not we have done as we have been ordered."

Detective Bondar nodded at him approvingly, but I sat, locked in place, staring between them in confusion.

"I'm sorry," I said politely, trying to keep my voice level, "but what do you mean by 'turn'?"

Dr. Sirko's focus snapped right to me, his dark eyes wide as the wrinkles on his forehead pinched together. I could tell he wanted to say something, but he sat still, hiding behind the large monitor of his computer as if he was using it as a shield.

"Why don't you tell us." This irritating detective really didn't understand when I said I remembered nothing about what happened to me, or why I was in this hospital.

My heart raced as I turned to the detective, my heart screamed of some danger I didn't understand. I kept my breathing under control, kept the anger out of my eyes. He smiled more, and it was then I realized what this emotion, this odd internal pull was.

I wanted to fight him.

I wanted to protect the others in the room from him.

The feelings were both familiar and foreign, and they

scared me. Especially with the replay of the massacre in Prague on the television. Steadying my wild emotions with a shove, I turned to face detective Bondar, and shook my head.

"I don't know. That would be why I asked." My tone was so formal, so.... regal.... commanding.

Regal. Commanding. Protective. Perhaps angry as well? I had hoped that knowing would help me to piece together something about who I was, but my discomfort was only making me more agitated.

The corner of the detective's mouth pulled up in the same annoying grin, the gleam in his eyes telling me that he thought his trap was working.

I wished I could tell him he had set a trap for ghosts, because there was nothing there.

Nothing but scraps of paper that a child had scribbled on instead of memories. Nothing but blood against stone and the faint outline of a woman that my soul was screaming for.

"You know of the attack in Prague, yes?" Dr. Sirko began from where he sat perched at the computer. "The reports on the television have told you enough about that..."

"He knows more," the detective spat, his voice grinding between his teeth. "He will not leave here until he has given his information to the state. To me."

"A single blurred memory means nothing," Dr. Sirko spat, turning from me as he spoke to the detective directly. "No matter what murders you try to frame him for..."

"Enough," the detective growled, voice low as Dr. Sirko turned back to me with a shake of his head.

"You have seen the aftermath of what happened in Prague, yes?" The detective was defiant.

"I know something happened, but they haven't said

what," I shifted my weight a bit, trying to appear less like an invalid. "They keep speaking of a war. Was it an attack or a war?"

"Both," Dr. Sirko pinched his brow between his fingers as if it was a pressure relieving valve. "The city was attacked, and when we finally released the city from the prison the *things* kept it under..."

"It became a war," The detective's companion provided, his comment pulling the focus of both the doctor and the detective.

The detective looked between the two of them, his mustache bristled in anger as he threatened them in silence.

"When Prague was attacked it was encapsulated," Dr. Sirko sighed, tapping his pen against the computer monitor he had turned toward me, the screen no longer filled with patient records but instead with a freeze-frame image of what looked like a bomb exploding.

I leaned forward as much as I could, the handcuffs clanging loudly as I pushed against them in an attempt to see.

A smooth red dome rose above farmland and trees, cutting through ancient buildings and who knows what else. The image made it hard to tell what I was looking at, or even how big it was, until I saw the outline of someone standing right before it, the tiny speck almost lost among the trees and farmland.

It was massive.

"The entire city was covered in what we call the Czech Sun. It was there for months. All the governments worked to remove it, to save the city. If we had known what was inside..." The doctor trailed off, pinching his forehead together as he shook his head.

"We would have done it again," the detective said confidently from beside me, the look in his eyes clear he had given more of a warning than a statement.

"You may say that," Dr. Sirko said with a snap, "you work for the state. You have not watched people die. You have not fought those things. You have not been imprisoned by your country..." The doctor's angry rant faded to nothing as the sound of pounding feet filled the hall outside my room. Raised shouts and screams echoed over the linoleum, rattling the glass in the window pane.

The room fell silent as everyone stood, facing the door as horror lined their faces. As they waited...

"He's got a mark!"

The screams swelled as the door was thrown open, a nurse shouting for help before Dr. Sirko and the detectives rushed out, slamming the door behind them and leaving me alone with the echoes of screams that buzzed through the walls and pressed against my chest in a million thunderous pulses.

I clung to the rails of the hospital bed I was cuffed to, unable to grip anything else, unable to get away. Everything heated as the screams increased in volume, the sound of retreating feet making it clear that something more than 'just a mark' was happening. Eyes focused on the door, I tried again to escape my restraints, being chained here while the world was under attack on the other side of my door suddenly seemed like a very bad idea. The metal underneath my palms grew warm and I jerked, wrists pulling against cuffs as I tried to escape the pain.

"Hovno!" I exclaimed alongside the screams from the hall. The word was yet another language, although this one felt familiar.

I wondered vaguely if that language was mine before

the question faded, my eyes widening at the sight of my hand.

My entire palm was covered with what appeared to be a raw red burn. It looked as though I had burned my hand by clinging to the rail, except that it didn't look fresh; it looked as though it had been there for a while. It looked familiar.

Just staring at the burn pulled an emotion that was hiding in that same painful pit in my heart, a desperation, a determination.

A love.

Her.

I knew it was. This had something to do with her. It didn't matter how long I looked at it though, there was nothing else there. No memory. No flash of her. It was just another injury, like the scars on my chest, that I couldn't remember.

The screams in the hall erupted again, pulling my focus before they began to fade, leaving the muffled sound of the television to take its place.

"The creatures have reached through much of Russia and Africa now, with sighting reports coming in from many Middle Eastern nations. Many countries have also adopted the instant kill policy that much of Europe has taken after multiple reports of victims having exploded."

"Exploded?" I repeated the word to myself, just as a loud bang echoed from the hall, the sound causing me to jump.

Heart thundering as I stared at the door, suddenly afraid of what was going on. Of what this world was full of.

"If your loved ones are bitten by the creatures we urge you to get them help at your nearest facility." The sound from the TV continued behind me as I stared at the door, the reporter's voice deepening into a tone that only heightened the danger in the suddenly quiet hospital. "It may be tempting to hide them, but the Ukrainian government has urged against this due to the extreme risk of death to those around you. We can help. Take them to a hospital or treatment center the moment a bite is found."

The silence in the hall was deafening now, the sound from the television a frightening echo as the image on the screen shifted to a man sitting in a room much like mine, smiling as a pretty nurse looked over his chart. No handcuffs. No detectives. No screaming people.

The lie on the screen was a cruel mockery.

"Those who have been bitten will display extreme pain followed by a sleep that can last hours or days. If anyone around is displaying these..."

Another loud bang shot from the hall, this one accompanied by a scream and a flash of light. I didn't jump that time. I sat still, listening to the deep Slavic voice of the reporter rumbling through the room as the television flickered and buzzed.

"The Chrlič, as they are being called," she continued, the familiarity in the phrase pulling my attention right back to the screen, "travel in packs and seem to be more dangerous from dusk to dawn."

The broadcast shifted to a diagram of the creatures, an image of a dirt brown bat-like thing taking up half the screen, bullet points filling the other as they went through a list of what I could only assume were its traits.

- Venomous
- Venom passed through bite
- Bite appears as a raised brand on skin

A Raised Brand...

The words burned into my skull, they buzzed in my ears, pulling through me as a single image flashed in my memory.

The woman. The same one I had seen in shadow before, but this time she was in brilliant color, the moment so clear I was sure I was there. That I had seen this.

I had seen her.

I was with her. I was certain my heart would explode out of my chest from seeing her there.

Her long dark hair was soft against my fingers as I swept it away from her face, her silver eyes shy as she looked up to me. It was a beautiful color, like the silver light before dawn, the color of water underneath stars. A sweet smile covered the smooth lines of her face, but there was something behind her eyes that made my heart beat faster, made my heart ache with longing.

I couldn't lose that image, that memory. I couldn't lose her. My heart was screaming, begging for more.

My heart felt as though it was going to burst out of my chest when my fingers moved to her neck, moving long dark strands of her hair out of the way to reveal a large raised mark on her neck. A raised brand hidden behind her ear, similar to the ones that were now being displayed on the flat screen.

Circular shaped, raised from the skin, dark and red as though it had been burned there. The woman spoke about them like they were dangerous, but that didn't seem right. She didn't seem dangerous.

As haunting as the mark on this woman was - it was not what buzzed in my head with equal parts of hope and pain.

The woman.

I saw her.

She existed.

15

But more than that, she was one of them. One of these people that they are killing. One of those people that were exploding.

The report shifted again, this time to a bearded man who stood before a table filled with the bodies of the things, "of the few that have been able to be captured and killed we have noticed an overwhelming similarity in their skin. While it appears to be muddy and brown it is actually more like a fungus. That is why the 'run regimen' has been commanded, as it is concerning that their physical touch could also cause infection..."

His words buzzed over me as he pointed out different parts of the little creatures, showcasing their wingspan, displaying their fangs.

I saw him move, I was sure I heard the words.

But nothing stuck.

Nothing seeped in.

I just stared, cringing in pain as my heart seized, that same electric jolt moving over my chest as I put it together.

As I realized what had happened.

This dark haired beauty that I longed for, this woman I loved, she had a mark.

And I had killed her because of it.

CHAPTER 2
JOCLYN

"Close it! Close it now!" I screamed over the roar of the Vilỳs that were following us, the little monsters moving through the tunnel in a wave that looked more like tar than a living thing.

"Move it, Ry!" Wyn's shout broke over mine as she muscled past where Ry and Thom were trying to keep the Vilỳ at bay. A blast of grey exploded from Thom's palm as he sent another wave of them back.

"Wyn! The wall!" I rushed right up to her, muscling my way past the bright blue Vilỳ that was gasping and swearing at all of us.

"I've got this, Jos. Go calm him down!" Wyn glared at Rinax who was trying to stop us from attacking the mob.

He really wasn't making this easy.

"Leave them be! I can save them! Stop!" Rinax was now hitting Ry upside the head as he tried to pull him back.

I rolled my eyes, letting my magic wrap around the cranky Vilỳ. I pulled him back to me, just as the other three attacked. Thom and Ryland fired once, sending the wave back away from Wyn who had pulled off her glove.

Magical fire swirled away from her in a tornado that twisted itself into a wall of flame. It stretched between us and the attacking horde, pinning itself against the walls of stone with crackling fire that might have been beautiful. You know, if we weren't being chased by hundreds of flying rats.

The first of the attacking Vilỳ lunged against the fiery wall to get at us, teeth and fangs ready. Instead, it hit against it with a high pitched shriek, and burned itself into a shower of ash. That was all it took to send the other Vilỳs back, snarling and gnashing a safe distance away.

"That'll do it," Wyn grinned, sliding her glove back on with a victorious smile. Ryland and Thom were both heaving as they leaned against the stone.

"That'll do what? That'll kill them all?" Rinax snarled, wiggling his way out of my grip with a well-placed fist to my jaw.

"Fu--!" For such a tiny thing he sure packed a punch.

"Hey! Watch it!" Ryland shouted, he and Thom jumping to their feet as though they were going to defend my honor from the Vilỳ. I waved them off.

"Why should I watch you! You are killing my kind!" he snarled, looking a bit like his diseased counterparts as he soared toward the flames as though he was going to knock it down and save them all. Luckily, he seemed to think better of it, stopping a few feet short. He stared at them for a moment before his wings sagged as he dropped a few feet.

"I would hardly count them as your kind," Wyn mumbled, luckily I don't think anyone heard her.

"I told you Rinax," I kept my voice soft as I walked up behind him, the sound of my steps inaudible against the continued screams of the monsters. "They aren't your kind. Not anymore."

I had warned him about this after we decided to leave the safe house in France. He had seen a bit of what the Vilỹs had become on the news now, but I don't think anything could have prepared him for what we found in the cave.

Heck, I don't think any of us were prepared for what we found in the caves.

It was a simple plan. Clear out the underground tunnel system so we could get around Europe, get back to Imdalind, and start saving people bitten by the Vilỳ.

The caves, however, had already been overrun.

Thom and I had been here less than a week before, but we had stuttered in and out, we hadn't gone through the caves.

"This is so much worse than what the television showed," Rinax said, his voice as limp as his wings. "What did he do to them?"

"He destroyed them," Ryland whispered, all of us had gathered around Rinax now, staring through the swirling fire to the still gnashing beasts.

"All of them?" Rinax had been hiding in an underground cave for the last eleven years, and it showed. He pressed his hand forward as though Wyn's flames were glass.

I felt my heart crack with the look on his face, my gut twisting uncomfortably. I knew that pain. I knew that pain all too well. I had felt as broken and shattered as he was for the past few days, as though I had been cracked in two. Seeing his posterity was shattering Rinax, just as losing my mate had shattered me.

I turned from them, the large cavernous hall that had once been the entryway to the caves of Imdalind. The only times I had been here was when I was running through towards danger, and running out after said danger brought the cave down. It was supposed to be my home.

I wasn't sure what it was anymore.

With every step I took, the golden ribbon of my crown sagged, and pulled against the stone behind me. It was like the tail of a very sad kite, as though it was mourning its loss too.

It pulled against the remains of the braid in my hair, probably pulling more hair free. I hadn't touched it in the days since the last battle. I didn't dare. It was the last braid Ilyan had given me, for all I knew it was probably sacred now.

Much like this cave.

You could only see a shadow of what had been. Now, broken stone was piled everywhere, ancient frescoes cracked and shattered. What little light made it through the ancient skylights was twisted and refracted in grey strobes as the broken mirrors tried their hardest to amplify it.

"I think he was breeding them to be like this," I heard Ryland say from behind me, the strangled gasp that came from Rinax only broke me more.

I grit my teeth and stopped the cracks before they grew too big. I couldn't let that pain take hold. I refused to let it rule me. I was going to find Ilyan. We were going to get out of this.

I straightened my shoulders and turned back to the group, unsurprised to see Wyn staring right at me. Keeping my jaw tight I nodded at her, avoiding the rundown about how much pain I was in right now; just being here was hard. The quicker we could get out of here the better, it was starting to get hard to breathe.

"Okay, so first things first," I began, cutting off their

conversations, and stepped into the broken cave. "We need to clear out those tunnels."

"Clear them out?" Rinax whirled on me, the sharp little points of his teeth inches away from me. If I hadn't been bitten by him once before I might have been scared. "What do you mean?"

"We need to make this place livable," I knew I was tiptoeing around what needed to happen to 'clear out' the tunnels, but I wasn't sure he could handle it right then. "If we are going to be rescuing everyone who is bitten before the world executes them, we need a place to put them, and we need a way to get them here."

"And logically, you thought of a caved-in tunnel system liable to crush us all." You gotta love Thom's optimism. He gave me a sour grimace, but I just grinned at him.

"Yes, I did."

"Don't be so negative," Wyn said, smacking Thom in the arm as she came to stand next to me. "I can have this cleared out in no time."

I tried to ignore the flutter of hope that had wound around my heart, "Then we can find him."

It was a gasp of hope. I closed my eyes, inhaling so deep I was sure I could smell the scent of him, feel his touch against my arms. When I opened my eyes again, everyone was looking at me. Ryland was giving me that same look he had been giving me the last few days.

Ultimate worry.

"He's alive." I was firm. Ryland's brow furrowed more, while Rinax nodded his head vigorously. We hadn't talked about what had happened at the Wells of Imdalind before the cave collapse. I had given them the bare basics, sure, but I hadn't been able to get us all alone since then.

I guess now was the time. There was zero chance of being overheard.

"I know you think I'm crazy," I said, even though part of me was wondering if they would think I was even crazier after what I was about to tell them. "But I know he's alive. I know, because I told myself that he was..."

I finished lamely, even Wyn was starting to look at me like I had lost it. Okay, there was probably a better way to phrase that.

"I know because the me of the future told me that--"

"Okay, yeah, you sound crazy." Wyn was having a hard time holding back her laugh.

"Dumb as rocks you are," Rinax snarled, landing on the top of one of the boulders to look at us all. "If I hadn't seen you down there..." He wrinkled his nose at me.

"Okay, Rinax, how would you explain it?" Sometimes that little ball of negativity got on my nerves. I had originally been told that Vilÿs were the peacekeepers, but after meeting Rinax I was starting to wonder.

"The Earth. The woman you saw is the magic of the Earth. She created you. She created me. She reincarnated a form of her magic in you so that she could restart the magic." Rinax looked between us all as though he had said the simplest thing. We were all staring at him in different stages of confusion, which only seemed to piss him off more. He swore and flew back to the wall of fire and the Vilÿs behind it, although most of them seemed to have given up their pursuit.

"So, the magic of the Earth created me, and you," I nodded to Wyn, "to end Sain after he tried to kill all of the other firsts."

"So, he was a bastard from the start," Thom interrupted

me with a snarl, his fists clenched against his leather jacket. "He was playing us all."

Thom looked ready to explode; he had known Sain the longest after all, considered themselves friends. Of course, all of that had been blown apart before all of this happened, but it was still salt in an open wound.

"We already knew that. Besides, we got to be the ones to kill him in the end." Wyn was grinning far too much for someone who was talking about murder.

"At least you weren't the daughter of the person you were supposed to kill," I said with a shrug. It probably helped that I didn't really know him. And that he was trying to kill me.

"Yeah, what's up with that?" At least Ry was finding the same humor in it that I did.

"She has a great sense of humor," Rinax said from where he was now perched above us, the towering rock half covered with some painting that seemed to depict dancing animals. "That and she needed you to have his power to end him. But that's what we are saying," Rinax went on before anyone could question him. "The Earth restarted magic. The original firsts were taken from this Earth and replaced with a new line. Drak," he flew down, blue lights falling from his wings as he fluttered right to me. "Trpaslík," he flew right to Wyn, who was just staring at him as everything went together. "And Ilyan is your Skřítek. He has to be alive, because if he is not, then magic falls from this Earth. The four can never die."

All of that pain that had been rattling around in my heart since the last time I saw him swelled until it felt like I was in a pressurized cage. It wanted to escape, to explode. Everything burned as I looked between them all, seeing all of that pity and loss and pain staring back at me almost made it worse.

Except, that I knew it wasn't true pity. They were trapped in the same hell. They had lost their brother, too.

"He has to be alive. I have to find him." The words were so choked I could barely get them out.

Wyn and Ryland rushed toward me, wrapping their arms around me, as Thom's warm hand fell on my shoulder.

"We will help you," Ryland whispered in my ear, his voice broken as his magic filled me, soothing me the same way that he always had. "I will help return your mate to you, Jos."

"Don't count me out of that," Wyn teased, pulling back enough to look at me. Tears were streaming down her face as though they were rivers. "Besides, I'm a freaking first now! I can do anything! I'm so badass."

"If it was hard to keep your ego in check before, it'll be impossible now," Thom was as gruff as he always was, his voice coarse. Except when he looked at Wyn it was with all the pride and joy and support that I had seen in Ilyan. It was enough to break me all over again.

Ryland's arm tightened around me as if he could feel the pain that was dripping off of me, his magic swelling around my heart. Ry said nothing, he didn't even look at me. He just stood there in silent support as I turned to look at the cave, toward the caved-in entrance I knew he was behind. I stared at it, pushing the long strands of hair that had come loose from my braid behind my ear again.

"Okay, so as first of the Trpaslíks," Wyn was already prattling away, her voice echoing off the stone so loud I almost expected Ilyan to just walk toward it as though he was joining the meeting. "I command that we start with clearing the tunnels, then we can clean up Imdalind so we can come home... hey! Wait! If you are one of the original firsts, Rinax, why are you still here?"

I turned, Ryland's arm falling away as he stepped toward the Vilỳ.

"Because all of my people have been turned into poisoned lunatics, or did you miss that? Do you really want one of them to sit with you in high council?" he snapped, eyes glinting as he folded his arms. "I have to reverse that, find the oldest, and save my kind... and here you all are sobbing about an ancient king that I already told you is alive."

"He's my mate, Rinax," I snapped before I could stop myself. And to think he fooled me that he wasn't all snappy comments and insults a minute ago. "We can find him and help the Vilỳ."

"No offence, *your highness*," he snarled my official title with as much disdain as Sain had. "But you only seem interested in killing them."

"We don't want to, but we don't know how to protect ourselves otherwise. We are open to suggestions." It was the truth. I had gotten so used to killing them that I didn't even bat an eye anymore. But looking at the pain in Rinax's hate-filled stare I realized I had clearly lost sight of what they were.

Problem was, even as we stared at each other, I could tell he didn't have any idea either.

"We can find a way to save everyone, but right now--"

"No!" So much for being diplomatic. Rinax cut me off and flew down to me so fast that Ryland pulled me behind him. I gave him a look before wiggling out of his arms and facing the blue faced Vilỳ head-on.

I was going to have to talk to Ryland about how I wasn't some wilting female.

"You are going to kill them."

"I don't know another way."

"Neither do I," he admitted, voice falling as his wings fluttered and took him back from me a bit. "But I have to find it."

"We can help, Rinax," Thom ground out. I hadn't realized how on-guard they all had gone by Rinax's sudden movements.

"No." He flew back again, and for the first time he didn't sound like he was going to rip our heads off. "I have to do this on my own. I will check in. I will help as needed. But I do not think you can help with this, not when you are only interested in killing them."

I opened my mouth to respond, but he just flew off, turning into nothing but a trail of blue glitter as he disappeared into the rock.

"What the--" We all turned as he vanished, staring at the bit of stone that still glowed bright blue.

"Vily are always like that," Ryland said after a moment, running his hand through his hair. I had almost forgotten that he was the one to release Rinax from his father's cage. He probably knew the little bastard better than anyone. "Let him cool off, he'll be back."

I had no other option but to believe him.

"He's hurting as much as we are," I whispered, forcing myself not to look back to that caved-in archway again. "He has to save his people too." I swallowed, ignoring the same sad eyes they were giving me and plowed on. "We need to get down to the last place anyone saw him."

"The blue room," Ry said, just as I said, "The room with the river."

Wyn looked between us, and then shifted her weight to the caved-in hall directly behind me. I turned, hair and ribbon pulling as it twisted around me. I grabbed it, letting the long length of golden ribbon twist over my fingers.

Just touching it pulled at my magic, my memory flared and buzzed with Drak power as it took me back to that moment when he had braided it into my hair for the first time.

Our mating ceremony.

I could use this to direct my sight to him. I had tried to see him when Thom and I were here before, but I got nothing more than what I had seen the first time: Ilyan and Ovailia fighting. Ovailia throwing Ilyan to the ground in some alley as she screamed. Nothing more, But maybe this...

Wyn prattled on as I stood there, twisting the ribbon between my fingers as I stared at the stone, as I thought of every time Ilyan had braided my hair. The way it felt. Every motion. Every bit of love he had left there. I had tried to do the same for him, although my braids were clumsy. None as much as that first time, when I braided his hair after he left it loose for decades. As he waited for me.

"I know exactly where those rooms are. It shouldn't take me too long, maybe a month at most. You guys clear out the tunnels, and I'll get the Orchard cleared so we can move back home--"

"Before we do any of that," I cut in, fingers still twisting around the ribbon. "I need you two to do something for me."

I turned, looking from Thom to Ryland as all of those broken pieces inside of me threatened to break further. I pushed them away.

"Anything," Ryland whispered, Thom nodding once.

Ilyan's brothers. They looked nothing alike, physically. But staring at them now I could see him in them. In their kindness, in their mercy.

I pressed my lips together, refusing to let the tears come as I clenched the ribbon.

"I need you two, as Ilyan's brothers, to unbraid my hair."

Wyn gasped, but Thom and Ryland said nothing, they didn't fight. They didn't try to argue with me. They understood. They nodded in tandem, eyes screaming with sadness as they stepped forward.

"But the crown--?" Wyn started, before Thom cut her off with a look.

"I will wear it as Ilyan did." My words were choked, my heart breaking as I thought of Ilyan's smile, as he showed me where he had kept his ribbon for centuries. As I thought of that first time I braided his hair. "Ilyan wore his hair down as he waited for me, and I will wear mine down until I find him again."

Wyn's eyes dug into mine as they filled with tears, both of us staring at each other as Ryland and Thom flanked me and began to unbraid my hair.

My eyes burned with tears that I refused to let fall. My chest felt as though it might explode. But as I sat there, feeling them unwind the precious strands with gentle fingers I promised myself I would find him.

That I would never give up.

CHAPTER 3
JOCLYN

W aves washed over my toes, the cold water against
hot sand. Sand as hot as the sun that beat against
my back, as hot as his fingers that ran up and down the skin
of my bare back. Seagull claws echoed in my ears and I
jerked up, water moving over me as I blinked into the world
of a Tòuha.

Our Tòuha.

This was our place. He had pulled me here. He was here,
he had to be.

"Ilyan!" I shouted his name before my eyes had even
had a chance to blink away the brightness of the sun.

"I'm here, mi lasko," his voice was that same raspy deep
that I loved, that chuckle light and as joyful as the smile
that spread over his face.

I blinked twice, forcing him to come into focus as I
stared at where he lay beside me, his fingers tracing over
my arms, over my collarbone, across my lips. Everywhere
he touched he left that line of fire behind that I could only
feel here. Only with him.

"I'm here." He said it again and I felt like I was going to explode.

All of that pain and agony that had kept me awake for the past week since he had gone missing, all of those heart shattering tears I had shed, every time my chest felt like it was going to explode; it didn't matter anymore. He was here, and it all fell away as I threw myself onto him. Onto the warm skin of his firm chest, into the mess of his long hair that surrounded him. I burrowed myself into his collarbone as he laughed and wrapped his arms around me; holding me so close I could tell I wasn't the only one who had been looking.

And here he was, I had found him in our Tŏuha. I could find him now.

"You have to tell me where you are," I practically yelled as I sat up, my heart already screaming to lay against him again, as though I had ripped the Band-Aid off a bleeding wound. Maybe I had.

"Where I am?" He parroted back to me, smiling as he tucked some loose hair behind my ear.

"Yes, I have to find you." I captured his hand, pressing it against the dull ache in my heart. "So I can bring you home."

"Home, you are my home." His other hand traced down to my neck, his scarred palm warm as he placed it against my mark.

There was no explosion of power and light as there usually was in this place, no buzz of electricity as our magic blended together. Just that warmth. The warmth of his that felt so right, but was so wrong.

I could have sworn my heart broke apart all over again.

"No," the word was a choked sob as I grabbed his hand, pulling it up to press it against my cheek, to kiss it, to smell it. To soak him up. "You aren't home. But I will find you."

I was firm, confident. I could have screamed the words and they wouldn't have been more true. I could feel them rip from me. My magic exploded through the air of the beach and the seagulls quieted, the waves fell away to nothing. Even the sand faded until it was just Ilyan lying beneath me, smiling.

Smiling, yet his voice was sad.

"I know you will. You are my everything, Joclyn."

His hand was warm against my face, the usual roar of connected magic just a buzz as I looked up to the large manor house in the distance. The one he had built for me. The one I had never stepped foot in, that only Ilyan knew about.

Even when I had mentioned it to Wyn and Thom the other day, they had no idea of its existence. But it was there.

I would start there.

"I will find you, Ilyan."

Before I could even finish the words the Tŏuha was broken apart by three large knocks. The booming sounds rattled in my head and I jerked out of the beach and back into the tiny stone room that had been set aside for me in Imdalind. My magic was already flaring, ready for some attack, or bombs, or worse. But I was still on my mat on the floor, the dim light of dusk spilled over the rocks from a crack in the corner.

Clearing the rock away had been more work than Wyn had expected, and after a week everyone was still camped out in the orchard, only a few rooms having been cleared.

Most were fine with it, there was more space there than in the old townhouse we had originally evacuated too, anyway. Plus most of the trees had survived so there was no risk of running out of food.

"Get up, Jos! We're late!"

I jerked to sitting as Wyn began to pound on my door again. This time I raised a finger as I flicked the door open, leaving her to stumble in as she had chosen that moment to pound against the door again.

"We have got to--!" She stopped as she turned to where I sat on the mat, pushing the tangles of dark hair out of my face. "You fell asleep? Finally."

I shook my head, fumbling for my mug. I needed Water, if only to clear the cotton ball that had moved into my mouth.

"Yes, you did, you look a mess, and your dress..." She pulled me to standing, already patting and pulling at the yellow dress she had pulled from the rubble in Prague.

It was the same one I had worn when Ilyan had presented me to be crowned as his Queen, and the perfect thing to wear as I stepped into the role without him.

At least that's what Wyn said; putting it on had been a stab in the heart. Which was probably why I had fallen into a Töuha. I had tried every night to enter the Töuha, along with trying to see more of where he could be with my Drak sight, but nothing had worked.

There was nothing more than what I had seen the first time, not even when I tried to use the ribbon that was now wrapped tightly around my wrist.

"It was a Töuha," I corrected her as I refilled my mug and chugged some down. "I saw him."

She froze in her patting and smoothing and stared at me, dark eyes so wide that if there had been any light in the room they might have sucked it in.

"You're sure?"

I nodded, "Same place. Same Ilyan. It was a Töuha. He's alive."

Wyn pressed her lips together, and stood back to admire the dress, or in this case avoid making eye contact with me. I knew her too well.

"What is it, Wyn? He's alive."

"I know," she finally looked at me, waving her hand to the side, "I'm not doubting that. Did he at least tell you where he is? We can cancel this and go now."

She was already halfway to the door, but I was frozen, staring after her. My heart tightened and I shook my head, all of that pain rushing back in as I ran through what had happened.

"No. He didn't say much..." Truth was, he hadn't said much of anything. Nothing more than what he would usually say anyway. I turned back to the mat, to the pool of drool by where I had been laying.

"Can you dream Töuhas?" I asked, forcing my voice to stay strong as I stared at the mattress.

"Yes," Wyn whispered, her hands wrapping around mine as she pulled my focus back to her. "I dreamed about where Talon and I used to have our Töuhas for months after his death." I opened my mouth to rebut but she lifted a finger and plowed on. "I know Ilyan is alive. I know how the magic of the firsts works. I know we will find him."

"But you don't think that was a Töuha?"

She shrugged, "What do I know? I used to dream of Thom and my daughter when I couldn't remember them, and then dreamed of Töuhas with Talon after he died. You used to get sucked into Töuhas with Ryland. So, for all I know... anything is possible."

I nodded, letting that feeling that I had felt when I had laid with him on the beach grow, every moment of that dream or Töuha or whatever it was cementing itself into me.

"It may not have been a Töuha," I said, straightening as I flattened my dress, "but it did tell me where I needed to start."

"Oh yeah? Why do I feel like this is an adventure I need to go on?" Wyn was already bouncing on her toes as she opened the door for me again.

"Because I know how much you love beaches and finding massive estate houses hidden on the French countryside."

"Ooo! A scavenger hunt. Count me in," she grinned and pulled me into her, practically dragging me down the hall. "We'll go as soon as we finish with this."

She turned the corner toward the main hall, where everyone had gathered, all of them turning to Wyn and I.

"They've already voted," Wyn whispered as she stepped away, leaving me standing alone in the stone hallway; hair down my back, ribbon on my wrist, wearing the dress that Ilyan had chosen for me. His mother's dress.

I stared at all of those faces, all of the pain, and sorrow, and hope. For the first time since I lost him, I felt that too.

I felt hope.

Hope that I would find him. Hope that we could rebuild. I gave Wyn a nod before I stepped into the hall, and right to the center of the room as Ryland's voice rang out over everyone.

"I present to you, Joclyn! First of the Draks, mate to Ilyan, the first of the Skříteks, our Queen."

I had only just stepped into the center of the space before everyone clapped their hands above their heads, and I turned. I turned right to that hollow cavern that was only partially cleared. Into the dark that was the last place that I had seen him alive, and I could have sworn he was standing there, smiling at me.

'I will find you. I will lead this people. I love you, Ilyan.' I screamed the words into our connection as I stood before his people... our people, and took his place.

CHAPTER 4
ILYAN

A flash of blood against stone was the first thing I saw every night as I fell asleep in this hospital room that had become a prison. The image had become comforting somehow, this memory of having lived.

It reminded me that everything wasn't handcuffs and flying bats that caused people to explode. Although, I still wasn't convinced that staring at blood against stone was much better.

For weeks I had stared at the blood-drenched wall, at the streaks of red that cut into the black until I fell asleep, until the dreams that I really wanted took its place.

Until I saw her in the only promise that my memories still existed, even if they were locked inside of me.

Sparks of my life filled my dreams, the color distorted as she danced with me under a million twinkling lights, the sound broken as she laughed in my ear. Even with the crackle of static, the sound of her laugh was still intoxicating. It breathed into me, lingering as the image shifted to the two of us walking down a beach, the sun hot against my skin.

It was there I got to talk to her. I got to feel her hand in mine. Sometimes those moments, on that beach with her, everything felt too real. It felt as though I could just turn to her and ask a question. I had tried, but I never controlled my dreams. So, I was forced to watch, forced to breathe her in until the beach dissolved into light and air, leaving me with the memory of her laying on a messy bed, her dark curls spread around her like a halo.

She was beautiful.

Although I had learned nothing of her, one thing was clear: I loved her and she loved me.

I held onto that every night as I slept, every night as I watched flashes of memories unfold before me.

Her head on my shoulder.

Her tears on my fingers.

Her laugh over canned sausages.

Her blood covered fingers on my face.

Her scream as she ran.

Her smile as she died.

My heart jumped, screaming as I was pulled out of sleep and back onto the hard hospital bed and the hand-cuffs around my wrists. The beeping of the machines and monitors escalated in my panic, that image of her blood streaked face pulling my pulse to dangerously high levels.

I still did not know if I had killed her because she had a mark or not, I had no way of knowing. Besides, if she had a mark, and if all the reports on the news were correct, she would have died because of it anyway.

Laying still, I tried to pull the joy I had felt in the dream back into me, I tried to prompt it to fill me, to bring those memories back.

But nothing came; only the blood against the stone,

against her face. Tears rolled over my nose as I lay still, desperate for the dream to come back.

I didn't want to return to a reality of monsters and war; where a guard stood outside my door and the low mumble of the news was a plague in the background. The never-ending sound was only broken up by a nurse who was speaking to my guard about her rounds.

I let it all wash over me; they didn't have any new information from what I could tell. I already knew that asking them about the monsters would get me nowhere, the detective only demanded information about a city I had never been to, and a war I didn't understand.

While they were focused on cities, and bites, and wars, and some photo I had yet to see; I was only focused on her.

On remembering her.

On remembering me, my real identity, not the alias I had been tagged on my new hospital records.

Jan Kowalski.

My new name. A placeholder until the day I remembered my own.

"I know you are awake."

The perpetual mechanical beeping of my monitors accelerated as a voice whispered from somewhere to my left. The quiet little hiss was obviously younger and distinctly feminine. I jerked, turning, but nothing or no one was there. Was I still dreaming? Or perhaps hallucinating? That one seemed more likely; I hadn't heard her voice after all, although that voice seemed too young to belong to the woman.

"Your breathing changed a few minutes ago. Not that I am judging, it's probably the only way you get any information about your case, huh? By lying still and listening..."

The voice faded off, the girl obviously doing the same thing. Listening.

I twisted, again nothing.

I was going mad. Not that I was surprised given that I was restrained to a bed, endlessly watching the same report.

I clung to the rails as my hands grew warm, that same shudder of electricity moving through my skin as the emotion did. I pushed it away, last time I had felt that, my palm had burned. I had no interest in burning the other one.

"You don't have to pretend," the girl continued, the tone softer even though the volume was louder. "They aren't in the room anyway. I am the only one here... Well, and you. But, it's not like you are going anywhere."

I twisted fast, chains rattling as I turned back to the voice and a girl who sat in one of the hard plastic chairs that the police had brought in. She was leaning so close to me that all I saw was her nut-brown eyes, the fringe of her dark curls barely noticeable.

"Wow. You do have blue eyes," she gasped, leaning back a bit and sending the ends of her curls swaying against her shoulders. "My mother said you did, but I didn't think they would be that... blue."

"Where did you come from?" I snapped, pressing my lips into a tight line. I tried to be calm, but my voice roared anyway. Something she only smiled at.

"I'm Katenka. Everyone calls me Kaye. I have been waiting for you to wake up... or at least stop pretending to be asleep for hours. And that dumb cop won't let me change the TV. As interesting as what happened in Prague is...." She prattled on, obviously uninterested in waiting for me to introduce myself, but with the way she was talking I had a feeling she already knew who I was. Or at least who they thought I was. "They say you were there... Were you?"

She finally stopped, leaning in until all I could see was her eyes, the eager orbs wide atop a bed of freckles. She was eager, her brown eyes sparkling, but it was nothing compared to the beauty I had seen in my dreams.

"Who are you?" I asked, thankfully not sounding as angry that time.

"I told you," she sighed, obviously irritated. She couldn't be any older than her mid-teens, with how she whined. "My name is Kaye."

"That tells me nothing." I rephrased in hopes of getting an answer. "What are you doing here?"

Her eyes narrowed as if she was gauging if she could trust me. Silly seeing as she was the one who had invaded my space. Then again, I was the one that was handcuffed to the bed. I guess between the two of us I was the one that was least trustworthy.

"My mother is Yana, your nurse," she finally said, obviously giving as little information as possible. "I have school off because everything's exploding in the world and here is the safest place for me."

"Here with a man who is handcuffed to a bed? Who might be bitten? Who may have killed someone..." The words erupted, the confusion over my situation bumping and twisting uncomfortably inside of me. Kaye, however, couldn't care less.

"Those things aren't in here," she clarified with a roll of her eyes. "I can't get bit. I can't explode."

"Explode. Do they really explode?" It was the same wording from before, although it didn't make any more sense. The news had conveniently left out any more than that.

"It happens when you are bit. I've only seen one. He slept for a long time... and then when he woke up he screamed that everything was hot, and then... stuff... started to fly out of him... " She shuddered at the memory, her eyes gaining a haunted quality before she looked away from me to the television. "It was like the air around him was on fire."

The world on fire.

I jumped as a single image smacked hard, a memory of the woman smiling at me with her silver eyes before she ran into flames - dark hair streaking behind her. The handcuffs pulled against the railings as I jerked against them, reaching for the memory as it slipped away.

Kaye shifted at the motion, her eyes wide as she glanced to the door.

"I would try to tell you that you are safe, but I doubt you would believe me as I am currently handcuffed to a bed."

"That could be taken many ways," she snickered, a devilish look in her eyes before she smothered her mouth with her hands in an effort to stifle the giggle.

It was then that it dawned on me what this giggly teenager was really afraid of.

"Ahhh," I sighed, my own smile leaking through. "You aren't supposed to be in here."

Just like that, the smile slid from her face and disappeared only to be replaced by defiant anger. "My mother knows where I am," she hissed between her teeth as she folded her arms and slammed back into the chair.

Part of me wanted to believe her. Even if I didn't know her mother, I had seen her enough, heard the worry in her voice. She didn't think I was dangerous, or she did and she didn't care.

The guards on the other hand...

This time we both looked toward the door, her defiant sneer digging through the fogged glass and into the slightly oversized bottom of the officer who had been assigned to guard me.

"And what would he do if he found you in here?" She stiffened at my question before shaking it off, turning toward me with a look in her eye.

"They would probably freak out a little bit." I opened my mouth to respond, but before I could say anything she lifted her finger to silence me, smiling wickedly as she flopped back in her chair with a clunk. "But only until I told them what I heard."

She continued to smile, and my blood turned to ice, dripping through my veins.

"What did you hear?" I was surprised at how level my voice was, how diplomatic I felt. Even though I could feel the icy panic running through me, and my muscles were tense, taut, and ready, I was calm.

Kaye's grin expanded as she leaned in again, resting her chin on the rails just inches from my hand.

"What did you hear?" I asked again, my voice growing strained as I forced the tension from my muscles.

"Who is Joclyn?"

Three words and my heart ached and thumped and bounced. Three words and everything around me froze in place.

But I wasn't sure why.

I wasn't sure why my chest felt like it was about to explode.

"I don't know," I said, the pain in my chest growing if only because I knew the admission was true. I should know... because I did.

The feeling of her name was the same as the woman.

The woman I dreamed about. Just putting the name with her face made everything heat, my skin felt alive.

"You don't know who she is?" She was shocked, but I just nodded. I wasn't about to share this tiny bit of knowledge with anyone, least of all with a girl who seemed more interested in the gossip than in the mystery of my past.

Whether Kaye recognized the threat in my eyes, however, I wasn't sure. She only smiled wider, leaning closer to me until her body was practically dangling over the railing of the hospital bed that separated us.

"You don't have to say it," she said with a smirk. "I can tell. You either don't know who she is, or you do... and she is the one that you killed."

"I didn't kill anyone," I growled, in a snap that ripped through the still air of the hospital.

Kaye flinched at the loud octave of my shout before ducking down beneath the bed before I had even finished speaking. Weird reaction for a kid who snuck into a room with a possible murderer.

"Sorry for--" Any apology I had been about to give was cut off by the quick footsteps and the squeak of a door hinge.

My glare was still in place as I lay back on my pillows when the door opened, the heavy-set police officer peering in with a look on his face that was a cross between irritation and fear.

"Do you have something you want to say?" he snarled, the threat clear.

Clenching my teeth in agitation, I shook my head once, refusing to do more in case the emotions that ruled me found a way to explode. I seemed to be a very volatile person. I wasn't sure that I liked that.

The officer's eyes pinched together at my silent

response, obviously having expected more. I could practically read the battle on his face, the question if he should egg me on clear. He seemed to decide against it and clicked his tongue before he turned on his heel and exited the hospital room.

I stared after him, watching as he settled back into his chair, the echoing sound of the television heightening in the silence.

"We have just received word that Moscow has been overtaken..."

"Well, that was close," Kaye whispered as she popped up from underneath the bed. At least I knew where she had been hiding before, and that I hadn't gone mad.

Her chair scraped against the floor as I sat, rigid and uncomfortable against the scratchy sheets, watching the back of the officer as he took a sip of his coffee before turning to what I could only assume was a nurse, the mumble of his voice softer and kinder than it had been with me.

When I didn't respond, Kaye turned up the television, the announcer's quick dialect barely loud enough to counteract the sounds of the war behind her.

"We are live in Tokyo as an extremist group has taken control. They seem to be using some kind of weapon to gain access. There are reports of explosions, and things flying around..."

The distorted sounds of screams and explosions bathed the room. I watched the screen, desperately hoping that something would click, that some familiar sound, or noise, or word would pull me into memory. Even if I didn't want them to.

At least, if they did, I would understand why the sounds of war were familiar and why I had felt that I could incapacitate the guard without lifting a finger. My volatility also seemed to go hand-in-hand with a ridiculous amount of confidence. No one could incapacitate someone by just staring at them.

An uncomfortable heat returned at the thought, the handcuffs clanking loudly as I shook my hands in the air, desperate to alleviate the heat, to scare away whatever danger hid just beneath my skin.

"Are you okay?" Kaye shifted her chair away from me again.

"I'm fine."

I settled back into the bed just in time to see her shrug and lean against her chair, the feet grinding against the floor with the shift of movement. Everything was so echoey here, every hard surface amplifying every sound to twice what it would have been.

Every noise made me jump: the sound of the screams, of the chair, of the police officer as he clicked his tongue in impatience, the clock as it thrummed away my life, the machines as they echoed the beat of my heart.

So loud.

I couldn't understand why this child beside me didn't seem so overwhelmed by it.

Why she didn't seem to hear.

Forcing the sounds out of my mind, I turned back to the girl, her focus off the television and on the yellow polish on her nails.

She was picking at it impatiently, her bottom lip clamped under her teeth. I wasn't sure if she was ripping it off or trying to fix it.

It didn't matter.

I just sat there, watching her, staring at the polish on her fingers as a flash of a dark room hit me. The memory was so quick that I couldn't make anything out. Just darkness shrouded by the hulking shapes of furniture, or people, or who knows what else.

"Do you think it was her?" Kaye said suddenly, her voice pulling me out of the memory.

"She *was* what?" I closed my eyes, trying to pull the shadowed room out of my memory again.

"The one you killed..."

"I didn't kill anyone,"

"I don't think you killed anyone either. Least of all her... with the way you say her name. I want someone to say my name like that. Joclyn..." She sighed, a love-sick mockery in her eyes. "You can tell you love her. I mean... I guess it could have been a lovers' quarrel; I've heard of those before. But no, not with..."

"Stop," I commanded, the single word taking the wind out of her sails.

She gasped and glared, but I ignored her, watching some high rise tumble on the screen. I didn't like being questioned by the detectives day in and day out as it was.

"I don't think you killed anyone," she repeated as she turned away, as if saying that made it official, and cops and everyone else had to believe her. "It's not why you are chained to the bed anyway, or why they are still monitoring everything about you. Everyone is dying? You think they care about one murder?"

"No. It's the bites."

"No," she scoffed, her focus still on what was now a map of Europe, a bright red blob spreading over the continent. "Bite or not, if it was that, you would already be dead. They think you came from Prague. They say they saw you..." She stopped abruptly, giving me a quick glance before she returned to the TV, her focus a laser on the screen.

My heart rate monitor sped up, my chest tightening as I shifted toward her, muscles aching at the distorted movement. I had already pieced that much together, what with the ridiculous questions they liked to ask. But there was something about the way she said it. She knew something.

"How do you know this, Kaye," I whispered, trying to stay calm.

"My mom thinks you were part of one of the massacres around here, though. There have been so many. She thinks you escaped." The perky girl that had both irritated and intrigued me for the last few minutes was gone as she leaned in, all business and conspiracy now. Her lips pulled into a tight line as all the light was sucked out of her. "Those things fly in hordes. Hundreds of them moving in little black clouds through the sky. You never know when they will dive, when they will suddenly plunge toward the ground and strike. Killing, biting... The Chrlič don't stop. They try to shoot them out of the sky but they scatter, or worse, attack. No one can stop them. That's why she has me in here..."

"In here?"

"In the hospital," she clarified, finally looking away from the television, her eyes boring into me for one thunderous moment before they were gone, leaving me imprinted with her terror and panic.

In that moment I think I truly saw her. Not this bubbly, go lucky girl - but this terrified teenager that knew her life was in danger. That knew her life could end if one of those swarms of black winged beasts decided to plunge from the sky, right to her.

"A year ago I was in school," Kaye continued, still looking at the TV as she wrinkled her nose and folded her arms over her chest. "I wanted to be a nurse like my mom. A year ago everything was different."

"I wish I remembered what was before." My heart was aching again as I tried to pull up more memories, something good. There was only blood smeared on stone.

"If you were there," she said, gesturing toward the city of Prague on the TV, "it's probably better you don't remember."

She was looking at me out of the corner of her eye, but I didn't turn. I was frozen, my monitor suddenly going crazy as the TV shifted to a reporter giving a tour of what looked like the remains of a church in Prague. You could still see the shadow of what I was sure was a steeple in the background.

Beds and tents were littered over the space making it clear it had been some kind of camp for those who had been trapped there. Everything that was left behind was burned and destroyed, telling a haunted story.

A familiar story.

"What do you know about my case?" I pulled my focus away from the TV to stare at her, not enjoying the way the images were making me feel.

Kaye did the same, heaving a big sigh as she flopped back in her chair again, the old metal and melamine giving a grunt.

"I only know what my mother knows..."

"And I know nothing," I interrupted with a slight smile, "so between us you know more."

"All the more reason for me to share, I suppose?" The light was back in her eyes in an instant, glowing and vibrant and hungry. Eager, even.

I had to admit, the girl was sharp, I could already tell by the excitement that was pouring off her that she was ready for what was to come. She already knew, she expected it. She wanted it.

"If I have any hope of figuring out who I am, then yes." I looked at her, trying to make my intent clear without saying it.

I needed an ally, and even though I knew nothing of this girl, even though I wasn't sure I could trust her, there was something about her that made me want to.

Something that needed to.

"You want me to solve the mystery of the girl? Of Joclyn?" She was practically bouncing in her chair. I hesitated, I hadn't told anyone about my memories. About the connections I made. But I guess, if I had to choose anyone, a teenager hiding in a hospital with an assumed murderer was a good place to start.

"I want you to help. I need to find her. I need to know if she's alive."

"Or if you killed her?"

"That too." I sighed. "First, I need you to tell me what you know."

CHAPTER 5
ILYAN

They had found me in an alley not far from the hospital, covered in blood. It was dried to my long blonde hair and plastered to my chest. I was covered in a layer of the dried fluid, but more - much more - of it was wet. It glistened as it dripped from my skin, as it ran through my hair, saturating my pants. It absolutely covered me.

Someone, a woman, had screamed for help from within the alley, and luckily a police officer had been passing.

'Most people ignore screaming.' Kaye had said, 'They run from it... just in case it's the Chrlič.'

Even though the officer had heard the woman scream, by the time he had gotten to where I was, the screaming woman was nowhere to be found.

The blood that I was covered in was not mine, at least, not most of it. My own blood was what was dried and caked against my skin, that layer covered by the fresh blood of another, a woman. Tests had shown she was 'a close relation'.

Why my own blood was plastered against my body,

however, made little sense. I had no wounds when I had arrived here, and although my nose, jaw, and left arm bore signs of having been recently broken, there was no cut, no wound - nothing that would have released that much blood.

I did have quite a few scars on my chest, large raised crisscrossed brands that I had told the doctor hurt on occasion. They had been healed for some time, however, and therefore not the culprit.

The injury on my hand was another possibility, the skin raised like a burn that covered my entire palm, extending up my wrist. The injury was very similar to the scars on my chest, although it looked somewhat fresh and was scabbed and marred in places, like it had healed in unclean circumstances. Even if the wound was fresh, there was no way that so much blood could come from it.

So the blood remained a mystery.

I remained a mystery.

The way I had arrived, the symptoms I displayed, the fact that no dental records could be found despite the straightness of my teeth promising a past of dental work.

There was nothing.

I was no one.

Kaye sat back in her chair with a deep sigh, all information seemingly relayed.

Mission accomplished.

Too bad it was only the beginning.

Kaye barely knew anything more than I did, but it didn't matter. When combined with the information I had, it was precious. When you add it with what little I had been able to remember, the possible murder, and the accusation of having been in Prague; little pieces of the puzzle were starting to come together.

First, there was a woman. Her image came to me without effort now. I could see her clearly, the dark hair framing her pale face, eyes so bright and clear that they were almost nothing. The shimmer of a pearl against silverlight. I didn't think that such a color could exist. Yet, they were here, trapped in my mind; glistening above a smile so shy that it melted my heart. Through all that heart-aching beauty was one thing that made my stomach twist in agony: one of those marks hidden behind her ear.

The moment I had mentioned a woman the police had assumed it was her blood that covered me, that I had killed her. However, if the blood was a close relation as they had said, then I was going to need a serious psychological evaluation.

My memories, the way my heart swelled at the very thought of her, these were not the emotions one should have for a sister.

So the blood remained a mystery, one more thing I did not know.

What I did know, however, was that the girl and I had been together in Prague. I didn't know when, and I didn't know for how long. I didn't know if we had been rescue workers, or if we had been trapped there - but everything I had seen on the news had felt familiar somehow.

"So what do *you* know?" Kaye said, her tone slightly accusatory as she grew impatient.

She tapped her toe against the hard floor in a tempo that I was sure was meant to get my attention, her eyebrow arching as she waited for my response.

"I know more now than I did before," I said, careful to keep my voice even. "I do, however, think you are right."

She perked up, a smile twitching around the corner of her mouth.

"Oh, am I?" She beamed, obviously pleased with the fact that she was correct at something.

"Or rather, I think the detectives are right," I clarified, her smile faded instantly. "I think I came from Prague. I think I was there."

Her momentary disappointment was sapped at the admission, a new kind of eagerness taking over the light in her eyes. I moved away instinctively, handcuffs clanging against the metal.

"Do you think they wiped your memory, then?" She looked like she might explode with excitement. I was lost again.

"They? You mean those flying things?" I was careful how I chose my words.

"Yes, or the aliens. One or the other..."

"The aliens?" I interrupted, I had been watching the news for a while, and not once had they mentioned aliens. The idea was laughable and I tried to keep my laugh at bay.

A small chuckle escaped on its own, however, and she shot me a glare. If you could call it that. She looked like a baby tiger ready to attack. I laughed harder.

"You saw on the news about that dome thing that covered the city, right? The Czech sun?" She plowed on, although slightly ruffled she sure wasn't going to let that get in her way. "They say they don't know what it was, but most of us know it was the aliens. And those flying things, those creatures... whatever they are. They were sent by the aliens to destroy us. Maybe they *are* aliens."

She grew more excited as her hypothesis grew.

"That seems a little bit excessive, don't you think?" I said, even though I was aware that part of it made sense. Something very loud was nagging that she was very, very wrong.

"No," she said without hesitation. "It seems like what it is."

I tried to understand what she meant, tried to find some sort of truth or sanity in what she was saying. Who was I to judge sanity, though?

"I don't…"

"So did they wipe your memory, or are you one of them?" She continued to chatter, her focus back on the TV as if that settled it. "Maybe Detective Bondar thinks you are one of the aliens. It would make sense why you are here, why you still have all those wires."

She turned back to me with a jump, exhilaration flooding off her as a new idea took hold.

"That's it, you are the alien, and they are doing their own experiments on you!"

The heart rate monitor jumped in confusion and shock, my chest constricting in the blanket of real emotion.

"No." I was firm. I couldn't be an alien. The entire notion was ridiculous, yet I knew I was there. I knew…

My focus drifted away to the before and after images that were now flashing over the television screen. There was something familiar…

"We are just starting to understand the destruction Prague has seen… "The reporters quick Ukrainian cut through the silence as more images made their debut.

A once ancient bridge now plunged into a river that was stained red. A tall building of white stone was now nothing more than a heap of rubble. A clock that had been built into the face of a building generations before was ripped and twisted to the ground.

One after another I saw them, and one after another they peaked in the back of my mind, they pulled and they tugged.

It was familiar.

It was all familiar.

Just like those tents that I had seen.

Although I already knew that I was in the city, these little familiarities that flew into my mind made it all the more clear.

And what was more, I knew she was right.

These little flying monsters were sent to kill everyone. Except I didn't know by who, and I didn't know why; but something told me it wasn't the aliens.

"So," she said, turning back to me, the matter settled somehow. "Should we start looking for Joclyn?"

I stared at her, knowing it was the logical first step, but having no idea how this was going to be possible.

"She could be dead..." The words physically hurt to say, each one burning against my chest as I forced the probability out.

Kaye stared at me, her hand wrapping around the heavy handcuff on my wrist, as if the action was a comfort.

"If she was... There is normally a body," she said, the statement stabbing deep and I turned toward her, hair swinging in shock. "There wasn't a body. There wasn't anyone but you in the alley."

I wish that settled it. But there was so much I hadn't told Kaye. So much I wasn't ready to. Like about the mark behind Joclyn's ear. I didn't know what it meant other than that she was surely dead.

I swallowed again.

Kaye couldn't know that. I didn't know enough about the world, I didn't know enough about her, and I had to protect them. Both of them.

"I suggest we look online first," she said as she pulled a thin box out of her pocket, pressing the flat surface as if she was controlling it. *A phone*, my memory provided although it didn't seem right. "There are message boards set up for survivors to contact loved ones. Although, it's a long shot with only one name. Do you know her last name?"

This time I couldn't help but laugh, the light chuckle out of place against the pain of loss. I knew nothing about myself. Nothing at all. How in the world could I know her last name?

"I'm not even sure how to spell Joclyn..." she mumbled as she tapped on her phone, shifting in her seat as she settled in, thumbs moving on the screen that was now only inches from her face.

The rhythmic tapping of skin and nails against glass blended into the beeping and hissing of the machines as the newscast picked up again.

"The Government of the United States has released images from their troops' body cams." The report on the television shifted as the voice did, a male speaking fast as the images of the city faded to a news desk. "The images, while not clear, are being evaluated as a worldwide search has begun..."

I leaned back, handcuff clanging as I twisted my wrist to turn up the volume ever so slightly. I had no interest in alerting the guard again.

"I heard about this," Kaye whispered from beside me, pulled from the 4x5 inch world and back into reality. "Your detective's partner was talking to Dr. Sirko about it last night. The first images from inside the Czech Sun or something."

I had heard them talk about it, too. Or rather I had heard one sentence before everyone had rushed out of my room in panic.

"A single blurred image means nothing," I repeated Dr.

Sirko's words in a mumbled haze, my focus now absorbed in the gallery of images they had filled the screen with.

They were fuzzy, obviously pulled from a video or a bigger image they weren't interested in sharing. Even through the hazy lines and faded colors you could still make out people.

"The Americans have released a report along with these images saying that the five people shown were inside of Prague prior to the implosion of the Czech Sun and were then found in the Svarov ruins moments later…"

The reporters semi-monotone reading of his script was interrupted by quick tapping from Kaye, the sound of thumbs against glass joined by her toe snapping against linoleum.

"Jan," she said as she scraped her chair towards me. "It kind of looks like you."

My heart ratted against my ribcage as she turned her phone toward me, one of the blurred images the news was showing expanded to cover the entire surface of the screen.

The image was pixelated, the colors light enough that they were blending together - but even through the washed out grain of the image I could see it. There, in the middle of a few filthy tents, was a man with long blonde hair that trailed behind him as he ran. Some of it appeared to be tangled in a yellow string that was trailing behind him, disappearing in the pixilated tents. Although most of his facial features were washed out, you could clearly make out the blue of his eyes, the color bright as he looked behind him for something.

She was right, it did look like me. It had been a shock to stare at myself in the bathroom mirror the first time, and this was no less shocking. From the hair to my lanky frame, right down to the faded color of my eyes it was familiar.

I stared at it, wishing I could grab the phone to get a better look. Before I could even try she snatched the phone away, leaving me trapped against the bed, heart thundering in my chest, the image burned into my mind.

"No wonder Detective Bondar is so determined," I said in a whisper.

Kaye nodded once in agreement, but she had already gone back to her phone, mumbling about how she thought there was another one with me in it.

My chest was growing tight as I looked back to the television, the screen now cycling slowly through the whole set of images as the reporter dissected each one.

"This man," he began, a wide red circle drawn on screen to encapsulate the figure that looked like me, "is seen in quite a few of the images. The French Embassy has reported his supposed capture as of just a few days ago, but no evidence to back that up has been provided. He is still sought after as well as many others seen in the photographs..."

"Here it is," Kaye interrupted, her fingers tapping faster as she sat back in her chair.

I didn't even turn to her, I was glued to the screen, everything tense in preparation for what was going to come next.

For what I knew had to come next.

"Called 'The Oheň' by many countries, his female companion..."

Kaye turned her phone to me, just as the television zoomed in on the exact image she was trying to show me.

The same lanky blonde man ran through the tents, his image a blur as he reached behind him, his hand wrapped around that of a woman much smaller than him.

She stood only to his shoulder, her dark hair bound in a

tight braid, the same string of fuzzy yellow trailing from her. I only saw her profile, the image so distorted that she could have been anyone.

They could have been anyone.

Except it was her.

I could see her; see her determination as she ran through those tents, sparks of fire similar to what I had seen in my dream popping in the air around her.

Erupted from her.

"It's her."

The memory was gone with a gasp from Kaye, her focus back to her phone as I was left staring at the TV, the memory fading as fast as it had come.

"Great. We are looking for the same woman the rest of the world is..." Kaye said as the image shifted to another one of her, of Joclyn. The image was so blurred I could barely make it out.

"Are there any more images of her?" I asked, unsure if I was speaking to Kaye or to the TV directly.

"I'm seeing a lot of them," Kaye said, her eyes growing wide as she continued to tap against her phone. "When the Czech Sun vanished, people were everywhere. She was everywhere in Svarov. There is a picture of her killing the Chrlič. Do you think that's why they want to find her, to find all of you... I mean, if you can stop them..."

"Find the picture." I interrupted her with a snap. "The one with her killing the Chrlič."

She grumbled so low I was sure she thought I couldn't hear her. "Whatever you say, your highness."

Your Highness.

The word stuck to my bones, it twisted in my stomach and restrained my already tense breathing. I could feel myself react to it, but it wasn't in recoil, it wasn't in disgust.

It was in familiarity.

The recognition twisted my stomach further.

"Why do they call her The Oheň?" I asked, reading the info bar at the bottom of the screen as I pushed the feeling away.

She looked up at me from behind her phone, her perfectly groomed eyebrow raising toward the long pin curls that made up her hair.

"I told you," She sighed, tapping once more before she turned her phone toward me. "Because she can kill the Chrlič."

Everything grew heavy. My bones felt weighed down as I struggled to move, struggled to breathe at the sight of the picture Kaye now showed me.

It was her. It was her face, the gentle lines of her jaw that I had caressed over and over in my mind. It was her lips turned up into a wide smile. It was the colorless sliver of her eyes, her focus determined as she looked past the lens and into me, into the cluster of those little bats that were flying right toward her, the little things snarly and frightening.

I couldn't look away. Her determination. Her strength. She was spectacular.

I understood at once why Kaye was so frightened of these little flying creatures, frightened of the warzone this world had become.

I understood why this picture mattered.

The things were terrifying. The way they flew with teeth and claws bared, they wanted nothing more than to destroy everything in their path.

And this woman, this amazing woman, could stop them. She wasn't afraid of them.

Darkness erupted from the palm of the hand she held

toward them, a spark of dark fire igniting from her and sending the monsters to the ground.

Dark Fire.

The Oheň.

I saw that moment. I lived that moment. This time, for the first time, the memory lingered.

Her and I, running through tents, fighting with light and fire that came from within us.

It could have been frightening, but it filled me with nothing but pride, nothing but a smothering love that I knew was for her.

That I knew came from her.

"Do you think it's really her? Joclyn?" I barely heard her.

I couldn't hear her.

All I heard were the pops of the explosions in my mind. All I saw was Joclyn running through tents, running through fire, through stone.

All I felt was warmth as the same fire I saw in my mind tried to consume me.

Tried to explode out of me.

The sensation was so strong, so powerful, that for a moment I was afraid I would. Just like Joclyn was in those images.

The Oheň.

Everything was becoming muddled as the memory left, only for my vision to blur as Kaye stood over me, staring down at me.

"Hey? Jan?" Even her voice sounded constricted.

"No." I tried to get the word out, but it was only a groan, the sound restrained by the growing pressure and heat.

Kaye's wobbled worry faded as the heat grew, pressing against me as the sound of waves and the smell of the sea assaulted me

I gasped at the sensation, panic growing as the warmth did, the image of her returning as she danced with me on a sandy beach.

"Are you okay?" Joclyn asked with Kaye's voice, her fingers soft against my lips.

"You will be okay," she said with her own voice, her smile stretching as she laughed.

I laughed along with her, laughed at the memory, laughed at the world. The sound of my laugh buzzed in my head, growing and replicating until it was all I could hear.

"Hey, can you hear me?" Kaye asked as the beach left, the world still swimming in laughter and static.

The sound rippled through my skull as it multiplied, the screams on the television mutating with it, blending in a mutilated orchestra of painful sound. Cringing, I turned to Kaye, curious if she heard it too. But one look at her face and I could tell that she had not.

"Jan?" she asked, the sound of the fake name I had been given adding to the cacophony.

I cringed against the name, grimaced against the sound in irritation, pain and fear.

"That's not my name," I gasped as the room around her began to shake, as the sound duplicated. I suddenly found myself unable to catch my breath, unable to breathe; it was all I could do to force out one single word before everything went black.

"Kouzlo"

CHAPTER 6
WYN

The town was small, just a few shops and small hotels nestled against the beach. A perfect destination. Well, it would have been a few months ago. Now, it was horrifying with how the officers moved through the buildings with brutal precision. It reminded me of a million other soldiers in a hundred wars before this one.

They were killing people just as brutally, too. Or they would, if they found what they were looking for. I made sure they hadn't.

"Open up! We are the guard!" They yelled the words in French the same as they had at the last few houses; the door instantly opened, shaking hands gesturing them in.

"If they put one toe out of line I'm going in there," I snarled, laying flatter against the sandy rise of the beach that Jos and I were currently camped out on. I could just make out the front door to the house through the long beach grasses. Luckily, my magic could make out everything.

The soldiers were demanding everyone strip before they checked them all for Vilỳ bites. They wouldn't find any in that village; I had cleared the two with bites out before they could reach them. Everyone that was left was human, not that they could tell.

Or cared.

France was just another nation that had deemed the Chosen unfit and ordered their capture and execution. Only the UK was left as a safe haven, and those who had survived the bites were running. That made Ryland and Thom's job of finding them easier, but it made everything else so much more dangerous.

After the French government made the announcement a few days ago, Jos and I had been following this band of soldiers as we made our way down the coast in search of Ilyan's beach house.

They hadn't put a toe out of line yet, but when they did...

"I thought we agreed on no murder, today?" Jos mumbled from where she lay on the sand behind me, her eyes closed as she faced the sky.

"I can follow them and wait to do all my killing tomorrow." My fingers curled around the long grasses as my magic flared. It let me see the soldier get a little too close to the young woman who was now being forced to take off her clothes at gunpoint. Luckily he didn't do any more than check her skin. They left a few minutes later, but just the look he had given her was enough to make my blood boil.

"The world has gone to hell," I snapped as I plopped myself down on the sand next to Jos.

"I don't know what you expected after what Edmund did." Jos finally opened her eyes to look at me, giving me a scowl before she turned back to the sky and the seagull that sounded a bit too much like a Vilỳ. We both jumped.

"Not this. I dunno. Maybe I was foolishly hoping that

this would welcome in a new age of magic and we could all sit hand in hand and listen to Styx and roast marshmallows..." I had to stop at the look she was giving me. She was clearly trying not to laugh, and her cheeks had puffed up like a squirrel.

I pushed my hand against her forehead, shoving her away. and leaving a weird ring on her skin where my boiling skin had not touched. Thank you hole in the hand.

We both lay back, listening to the waves and the retreating army as the sun slowly began to set.

"Well, we better get going if we are going to save them all," I announced, jumping up after the last rumble of their Jeeps faded.

"What are you talking about? We aren't going to save them all," Jos answered, blinking against the sun as she stared at me. She didn't even shift from where she lay in the sand.

"Excuse me? We have to save them all, it's like our divine journey." I was fully aware I had my hands on my hips in some kind of superhero pose.

She opened her eyes again, the silver orbs dark as she pushed herself onto her elbows.

"You are taking this way too seriously. You do realize that we *can't* save them all, right? I mean, don't get me wrong, Wyn, we are going to try, but there is actually no feasible way we can save them all. We can't be everywhere in the world and there aren't enough of us to try. Not to mention that the bastard who was supposed to help us heal the Vilỳ disappeared..."

She sighed and laid back on the sand. I was left standing there, staring at her, knowing she was right. There was no way the twenty or so of us could do everything, especially against murderous governments and wherever the last of Edmund's army had ended up; they had disappeared as thoroughly as Rinax had.

We hadn't seen or heard anything from the little bugger in the two months since he vanished. For all we knew he could be dead. Well, except for the whole 'the firsts can't die, thing'. So, I guess, not dead, just a bastard with an attitude problem.

"You sure are cynical today," I said as I settled back into the sand, facing the water that Jos had sworn was a perfect replica of the coastline in her Tòuha.

We had been here for a few hours, trying to discover any shield that might be there. We even walked around where the house should be in the hopes of running into something.

Nothing.

"Just being realistic." Or depressed, judging by the sound of her voice, not that I blamed her. We had been searching the coastline for weeks, and nothing. She sat up, wrapped her arms around her knees and stared into the incessant waves.

"Are you giving up?" I asked, ready to give her some lecture about why I would kick her ass if she did that, but she just quirked a brow at me and laughed.

"Finding Ilyan? No. Fighting the government? I gave up on that before we started. I'm just saying we can't save everyone, but we can sure as hell try to save as many as we can. We need to stick to tracking down those bitten by the Chosen before the government does."

"Okay... so what are you saying?"

"I'm saying we need to go home. His house isn't here, and I've got Chosen to heal and a people to lead. We need to clear out the cave." She was firm, I would even go as far as to say commanding. The curve in her spine, however, gave her away.

"We will find him," I whispered, pulling her into me as I sat beside her.

"I know we will. He's just not here. On to the next place to look." She gave me a forced grin that almost broke my heart. She was trying so hard to be brave, even though she was cracking inside.

I had felt that far too many times to count.

"It's okay to cry. It's a much better outlet than killing people. Trust me." I was trying to be supportive, but she just chuckled, shook her head and pushed her hair out of her face.

"Trust me, I cry. But crying isn't going to get me anywhere. I have to keep moving forward, kicking ass, and changing the world." The calm finality of her voice washed over the waves as she looked into them.

I would never tell her, or at least not for a few years, but she was kinda a badass. She had become who she was born to be, and who Ilyan had always known her to be. She might be my hero.

I threw my arm around her, and kissed her very wetly and very loudly on her temple.

"Hey! What was that for?" She tried to pull away, but I wouldn't let her.

"Just showing my devotion to my most favorite Queen ever." I grinned at her, knowing I was pushing her buttons and pulled her back against me so that both of us were sitting on the French beach, watching the waves.

"So, speaking of changing the world," I began after a minute, my heart growing heavy and nervous for the first time in decades. "I have a place for us to start."

"Mmhmm?"

"Thom and I would like to be mated, so, as my super badass Queen, I am asking your permission." I said it all very quickly, knowing that this would either slice deep or break through. As she turned toward me, though, with a wide smile on her face, I felt all of that nervous energy fly away.

"That," she began, tears that I was sure she had been choking down forcing themselves to the surface, "is the best news I've had all month."

She grinned, which made this next part that much harder.

"Good, because as Queen, you get to be the one to teach Thom the wedding braid."

"Shit."

CHAPTER 7
WYN

"May the Wells of Imdalind follow your union!"

The words swelled through the Orchard, everyone raising a glass toward Thom and I. We stood on the platform Ryland had made for us last night as a gift to his brother. Ry had presented it to us before the two of them had gone off with Joclyn and all the other married men to try to figure out the braid that was usually taught by Ilyan on the night before a mating ceremony.

Now, we stood, all of our glasses raised as the party wound down and the beginning of the ceremony began.

"If I have to wear this dress for one second longer than needed, I'm going to shred it," I hissed to Thom, displaying the purple 50s cut dress that was more suited for a house-wife than a centuries old fire wielder. Thom just raised his glass a little higher in an attempt to hide his massive smile.

"Wynifred, darling, I have every intention of ripping that dress off you tonight, but I would rather not do it here in front of all these people."

I instantly blushed, the champagne in my glass beginning to boil. Leave it to Thom to be the one person on Earth who could still make me blush.

"We accept your blessing, and seek the blessing of our sister, and our Queen, Joclyn Krul," Thom's voice rang out as I reined in my blush and brought my drink down to a temperature that wouldn't scald my throat.

Any thought of drinking it, however, was gone as Joclyn stepped out of the crowd. Ryland was right beside her as though he was afraid she might pass out. Given how pale she looked it might have been a possibility. She was smiling, joy clear on her face even though her eyes were bloodshot from shedding tears for a different reason.

"I give you my blessing, it is my joy..." she began, reciting the words as Ilyan usually would. Ryland stepped closer as her voice caught. It was only a second of pain, and then she straightened, standing like the Queen she was. "It is my joy to see you wed."

"Finally!" Someone yelled from the back, and all of the Skřiteks chuckled. The poor Chosen looked very confused, but they would have to stay that way. Good thing they had far too much champagne to soothe their confusion.

Joclyn's eyes locked with mine, all of her pride and joy reflecting back at me. They were all so happy. People that I had assumed hated me, didn't trust me... they were smiling.

All of a sudden, I didn't know what to say. Hell, I didn't think I could say anything past the rock in my throat or the warm weight of my heart which was now so full I thought it might burst.

The feeling only grew worse as I turned from the Queen to my future mate, to his wide smile, to his soft hands as he grabbed mine, to the tears that were welling in the corner of his eyes. Emotion that he had locked away was flooding out, just like mine. I had locked away so much.

But we didn't need to, not anymore.

"Finally," Thom repeated the word, the first tear trailing down his cheek as he lifted his voice. "I have waited for centuries for this moment. To be able to take the hands of the woman I love in mine, to tell her of my devotion, of my desire for her. But after all we have been through, it is so much more than that, now. Now, it is a partnership and a love that has grown into something deeper, that has been tried, and tested. A love that will never falter. Wynifred, first of the Trpaslíks, carver of your own path, holder of the fire magic, and mother to my child... will you take me as your mate?"

Every word he said brought that bubble of joy closer to exploding. But it wasn't just his declaration of love, it was how he saw me. Not as my father's daughter, not as Edmund's assassin. Just me. It was how I saw him, too.

"Finally." I had meant it as a joke, but the word was choked. We were both crying now, and it was taking everything in me to say the words I had spent all last night memorizing and not just throw myself in his arms and demand that he rip this gaudy dress off.

"Thomas Krul, brother of the King, son of a beautiful French Princess, and all around badass." My voice caught as he smiled, as a few people chuckled. But it wasn't their laugh I cared about, it was his smile. "You are my first love. Hell, you taught me how to love." I was already deviating from my script, but I didn't care. I just let it all explode from me. "You taught me about life, and joy, and beauty and I spent years dreaming of this moment, wishing for nothing more than to share all of that with you as my mate. And now, here you are. What do you say, will you be my man?"

More laughter, but Thom and I just stood there crying,

our hands warm against each other as we asked for hands and hearts before the Queen, and before our peers.

"Finally," Thom said, or at least I think he said that. It sounded more like he was choking.

"As your Queen, I bless this union," Jos said as she walked up to the edge of the dais. Only then did I realize just how much she was crying.

Her chest was heaving, her face streaked with tears. Thom's hands tightened around mine as though I was going to rush to her. I might have too, until I realized why she was crying, and what she was holding out to us.

"I gift you with this for joy in your union," Joclyn held her hand forward, a tattered brown ribbon on her palm. One of the ribbons Ilyan had woven through her hair on their mating. If I remembered correctly, it was the ribbon that had been woven through Ilyan's mother's hair on her mating to Thom's father.

While not the happiest memory, and not a direct line to Thom and his magic, the connection was clear.

"May it bless you," Joclyn finished as Thom kneeled to her, pressing her hand and the ribbon to his forehead as he whispered something I couldn't hear. Joclyn only nodded once and turned, still crying as she stood with Ryland, who was also crying.

We were suddenly a bunch of crybabies. I would have chastised us all if I wasn't crying just as hard.

"May the Wells of Imdalind follow your union!" Everyone repeated as Thom stood, ribbon in hand and pulled me from the dais and through the large door that would lead to our room.

Our room.

I mean, it had been our room since we had gotten here, but now it was going to be officially our room. It was weird how much of a difference one little ceremony made. So no, it was *our* room.

Gods, it felt good to say that.

The crowd cheered behind us before returning to the party that had been going for the last few hours. They would party all night, as would we...

"Can you please rip this dress off me now," I hissed the second the door closed behind us.

"So impatient," Thom's gruff voice was back, although he did pick up his pace into a run.

Guess I wasn't the only one who wanted to get this thing off.

We ran through the few corners of the once massive cave until we bolted into the tiny room that had been set aside for us, and Thom promptly slammed and bolted the door.

"Okay. Now?" I held my arms out, ready for him to have at me.

Thom's lip twitched, his eyes dragging down my body before travelling up to my face. He just stared at me, that mischievous grin fading again.

"I love you, Wyn," he whispered, so hoarse and deep that I swear I felt each word ripple up my spine.

"I love you, Thom. I always have."

Anything I had been about to say about the dress was lost as I stepped toward him, reaching for him, needing him.

Instead he held up the tattered ribbon Joclyn had given him.

"I wish to bind my magic to yours, to bring us together under one mind, one strength, one heart."

And I was crying again. We had waited so long for this. For the chance to be together, to be truly together. My heart ached for the one I had already performed this ceremony with, but it was a beautiful ache of memory now. Just another part of me. Just like Thom was, like he was going to be.

"I wish to be part of you."

Neither of us spoke as we moved to the bed, as he braided my hair in silence, pulling everything perfectly. This tradition was part of Thom's past, it was who he was, and I felt those motions as he weaved hair and ribbon together in perfect harmony. I felt the love, and the care, and when it came time for me to weave his dreads together in a similar fashion I put all of that into him.

We may never wear our hair up again, he may never braid my hair. But this night, with this ceremony, everything was perfect.

It was only once the braids were done, that we shifted from Thom's traditions, to mine.

When I was mated to Talon, I hadn't had enough of my memories to know what was required of me. But now I remembered. I remembered the stories of my parents' mating when I sat at my mother's hem as a child. I remembered her telling me of the tradition when I came of age and Trpaslíks were flooding our door in a hope of marrying me.

I remembered, and as I knelt before Thom on the stretch of bare stone, I wanted it.

"The magic of the Trpaslíks is different," I whispered, explaining this just the way my mother had. I swear I could still smell the wood in our old house... "It comes from the earth. It moves through the stones. It does not move through the air like the Vilỳs or through the dark like the Drak. It does not dwell in hope as the Skříteks. It is firm. It is unmoving. It is strong. Joining my magic with yours is a powerful thing."

Thom kneeled on the stone before me, eyes wide as he listened, watching the way I had begun to move my hands over the stone that stretched between us.

"It is through stone that the Trpaslík mating ceremony is conducted. I let my pure magic drop onto the rock, just as you do, and the magic of the earth will bring us together." That part had never made sense to me, but sitting here, feeling the power of the earth rattle underneath me, I knew what to do.

As my fingers moved, I pressed against the well of my magic in my heart, I prodded it out, I let it out to find that perfect other half that it was always so desperate to reach. As though it could feel Thom, as though it knew what to do; it flooded through my veins, pulsing right to the tip of my fingers and dripped into the center of the stone in a color just like fire.

The stone rippled as though it was made of water, the hard rock waving between us as I dropped my hand, and Thom's took its place.

His eyes never left mine as he chewed on his cheek, doing just as I had done. Or trying to. His teeth were grinding, his panic evident. Maybe this wasn't meant to be done by Skříteks...

Just as I opened my mouth to voice my concerns a single drop of gold fell from Thom's finger. It dropped into the center of the stone, the rock wavering just as it had done with mine.

We both watched the stone as the ripples grew, and then from the center two perfectly round marbles emerged, each one resembling the magic we had dropped into it. He recognized them as I did.

I nodded, "Yes, it is partially where they come from. But these are different, these are the pure cores of our magic."

I grabbed the two stones, handing him one of them. He held it as though it was precious, almost as gently as he had held Rosaline right after she was born. Which either made what happened next hysterical or horrifying.

Eyes locked with his, I lifted my hand, and ate the bead. He looked at me like I was crazy for just a second before he did the same. We both swallowed, then the warm power of his magic flooded me.

I gasped as he did, his magic twisting through me just as mine did him. It stretched to every cell before it settled in my heart.

His magic, right against mine.

For the first time in my very long life, everything felt right. Thom's magic inside of me was a warm light that stretched through every inch of me. It was like liquid gold, and cooled my fire so that it was nothing more than a comforting heat and not a raging inferno. I had been mated before, but I had not felt this before. I had not felt as though my magic belonged. A perfect fit.

"I should have known that you were my perfect match," Thom choked out, his eyes wide as he clung to my hands.

"You took the words right out of my mouth." And then I threw myself at him. I pushed him to the floor as I lay over him, turning that awful dress to nothing with only one snap of my magic.

"Hey! I thought I was going to tear it off you," Thom teased between kisses, his lips trailing over my neck and ear and driving me mad.

"I got tired of waiting, and I've waited for you long enough." I kissed him again, pressing every inch of me against him as he moaned.

"Finally."

CHAPTER 8
RYLAND
3 YEARS LATER

The water that had pooled in the street from last night's storm splashed over my pant leg as I ran. Cold dripped through my jeans and down into my sneaker as I raced through the cobbled streets toward the sound of screams, toward the spark of vile magic that was flitting between buildings as my father's monsters chased down the few humans that were left in this part of Genoa.

Most humans had left the city years ago. It wasn't safe to be this far into the city, into any city. The country was safer, if only because you could see them coming.

A scream sounded again and my earpiece crackled to life; the Bluetooth that connected my brother and I buzzing with static as his gruff voice sounded over the line. We couldn't see or hear each other otherwise, despite running side by side, thanks to the magical shield that was a requirement in big cities like this.

"That sounded like a bite to me," Thom said, his foot smashing into a large puddle with such force that water sprayed further up my leg.

"Yeah," I nodded once, not that he could see. We were

nothing more than shadows and phantom splashes as we ran down the ancient alley.

The already dark stone buildings were hung with layers of yellow and grey, the dim ribbons of forgotten lamplight washed with the light of the moon as it peaked out from behind silver lined clouds.

It could have been beautiful, instead, it was eerie as hell.

It was a scene from a million vampire movies, and video games. And it was horrifyingly real. It was life.

My back tensed as another scream ripped through the night, the sound seemed to make everything grow darker. I half-expected a vampire to burst from the shadows.

"That makes two of them," I responded, turning from his phantom and back to the street, "How many Vilỳ do you suppose there are?"

"Not so many we can't kick some ass," I heard the laugh in Thom's voice but I couldn't force mine to join him.

It had been three years since my father had unleashed millions of poisoned Vilỳ onto the world and everything had shifted into this war on magic. I hadn't gotten used to the daily rescue missions, used to a world that would sooner kill me than understand me.

Of course, the majority of the globe was more apt to label me an alien than the Prince I had been raised to be.

That hadn't stopped them from splattering my picture on every news broadcast in the world, however.

Wanted. 1 Million Reward.

The first time I had seen the picture had been a slap. I should have been honored that they wanted me so badly, but it was the broken, crazed boy in the picture that had shocked me most.

My father had created more demons than the ones that

flew around the earth ripping the crap out of humans, he had created them inside of me.

Luckily, when my father died so did the monster he had let fester inside of me.

"Ryland!" Thom snapped in my ear and I ran faster, pushing the memory of my 'old west' reward poster from my mind.

"I'm here, Thom." My voice was hard, but more in my own disappointment at having lost focus on what we were doing.

"Good," Thom said, his tone making the glare he was throwing my way obvious. "Then stay with me. I'm going to soar high and arrive from the north, you stay on this path and hopefully we can kill a few more of these monsters today. But not so many that Rinax throws another hissy fit"

"Perfect," I responded, picking up my pace just as I felt a rush of wind by my side.

The powerful torrent of Thom's magic tugged at the shaggy curls that hung over my ears as it picked him up and sent him soaring over the buildings.

The white-hot heat of my power rampaged through my veins as the screams came again, followed closely by the sound of ripping flesh. I was closer than I thought.

"One corner," I hissed to my brother, falling into the code we had built in the countless of other rescue missions that we had conducted.

"One roof," he returned, giving his distance as I had. "Do you have a count?"

I slowed to a walk, careful to maneuver around the last few puddles as I stepped into the intersection of alley and street and turned to the carnage-ridden scene before me.

I would be concerned that the little monsters could see through my shield, but there was only one person who could do that, and she was sequestered in a makeshift hospital more than three hundred miles away.

The Vilỳs looked like deformed terriers. Their deep brown skin flaked and peeled as they hovered on twisted wings that fluttered awkwardly in an attempt to keep them airborne. They snarled with inhuman screeches as they flitted through the remains of their feast.

Crumpled bodies were curled in doorways, hands still stretched toward what they had hoped would be an escape. They lay twisted over garden boxes, bright red drops of blood discolored the white tulips that had begun to bloom a few weeks before. Limbs were tangled, wide vacant eyes stared into the dark for a savior that came too late. And, through it all, were the winged monsters that ripped at their flesh.

Gnawed.

Chomped.

Destroyed.

My stomach twisted, my heart constricted, and I felt my magic rush through me in a wave of anger. As much as I wanted to turn away in horror, I wanted more to destroy the little mutts and make them pay.

"Seven, maybe eight," I said after a quick count, careful to keep my voice low, lest the little beasts hear me over the sound of their meal.

They may not be able to see me, but they could hear me. Luckily, not one lifted its head.

"How many survivors?" His voice was as dejected as I felt; he must be above me.

I looked from body to body, desperate to see even one sign of life, but I couldn't even find where the screams had come from. It was only tangles of lost life set adrift in the dark.

"Unknown." I hated the answer the moment I gave it, although both he and I knew that didn't mean they were all dead. We had found survivors in worse.

It didn't make our job any easier.

Thom sighed in my ear piece, the sound blending with the devouring of flesh and bone in an awkward orchestra that brought my blood into a deeper boil. My magic begged me to step in and kill them all. One explosion is all it would take. My fingers were already sparking. I was ready to release the wave until the soft muffled sob of a woman somewhere in that mess turned my blood to ice.

"One," Thom said, he had heard it too.

"Unplug in five," I responded, already lifting my hand to my earpiece as I crouched down, my other hand stretching over a puddle that lay just below me.

"Four," Thom returned, his suddenly labored voice making it clear he was moving into position.

"Three," I said, and turned the volume up on the earpiece. Continuing the countdown in my head, my outstretched palm hovered over the pool of water, the surface beginning to ripple as my magic surged.

Two.

Magic roared under my skin, bristling over the puddle in a wave of the faintest purple. Just enough light broke through the shield that one of the creatures perked up, his ugly sphinx-like eyes narrowing as he noticed me, as he recognized what was coming.

"Too late."

Before the thing could even open its mouth to scream, one silver line of fire shot through the air behind it, hitting it dead in the back and sending it flopping over its prey and tumbling down to the wet puddle below.

"Nice shot, Thom."

My magic broke free with a roar before the creature hit the ground, the spark of power mixed with the water as it ran over the ground in an electric wave that zapped two of the little monsters who were feasting on one of the victims. The Vilỳs' bodies twisted as they screamed, gaining the attention of the other two.

Watching the shock on the little monsters' faces made all of this worth it.

They looked around in confusion as Thom took out another, the line of light that shot from him did its job, and while it hit the fourth Vilỳ square in the chest, it also gave away his position.

The screams from the others increased as they rushed toward him, the air shimmering as his magic burst through his shield, giving him away even more.

"Nice, Thom," I grumbled, trying to hit one of the monsters that was now following him and missing. "Now the pack will be here..."

"Well then you better hurry," Thom yelled, loud enough that his voice pushed against my earpiece and exploded in my mind.

"Damn it!" I screamed, ripping the still buzzing piece from my ear, my own yell pulling the attention of one of the demons, and the dozens more that had begun to flock toward the sound of a commotion.

"Now who is calling to them," Thom chastised as he spun in the air, his shield falling from him completely as he kicked off from the large brick building beside us.

The Vilỳs' excitement exploded as my brother materialized from nothing. They turned in a pack, snarling and screaming in eagerness to attack. Thom, however, laughed.

"Come on you ugly pixies," he taunted as his lanky frame flew through the air, sparks of light streaming from him to his demonic pursuers. "I'll give you ten points if you can catch me!"

The strength of his magic carried him flawlessly as he continued forward, long brown dreads swinging as he shifted position again and shot straight up into the inky black night.

"Focus, Thom," I chastised, pushing my sagging curls out of my eyes.

How did I end up being the adult in this situation?

"Find her," he called after me.

The Vilỳ screamed after him in a torrent of brown and grey. The sound was meant as a warning, as intimidation. Thom, however, just yelled something in French and cut through the air like a superhero.

I would be shocked, but it wasn't the first time he had done this. Luckily this time Wyn wasn't here to egg him on in competition.

Slamming the earpiece back onto my ear, I rushed toward the piles of corpses that were spread over the tiny alley and wished that this was a video game. This was the part of these rescues that stuck with me, sorting through the dead to find the living. It had been the same for three years. Time had not made it any easier.

It still wrenched at my soul like a rusty knife.

Placing my hand on the first grey tinted body, I let my magic press into the once vibrant man, desperately searching for any sign of life, for a pulse, for the tiniest breath.

There was nothing.

Heart tensing, muscles tightening, I moved to the next one, a young man whose skin was still warm with life, but none of it remained inside him. Even if we had arrived minutes before, we still couldn't have saved him. I counted at least ten bites, no one could survive that. From him I stepped to a middle aged man, and then to a young woman, to a child... nothing.

Moving faster in my desperation, I placed my palm against the forehead of a young blonde woman, her blood still dripping through her veins even though her heart did not beat. The last bit of life was slipping away.

"Signora?" I hissed, knowing that I would not get an answer, knowing that I was too late. Even as I waited, I felt all signs of life in her stutter to a halt.

She lay next to what I instantly recognized as one of the hired soldiers that worked in these parts, and my anger flared. Families paid men like this for safe passage out of cities, to extract them from the red zones. Their journeys were rarely successful.

I had pulled hundreds of survivors out of the remains of their ransacked camps. I had returned days later to bury their dead. I tried not to be mad at the soldier, they were just as desperate to escape the world my father had unleashed, desperate to find their next meal. As I moved to each of those that littered the alley, however, moved to each lost life, I felt the anger swell.

My heart was like a vice, stomach twisting in an agony that at least reminded me I was alive, no matter how much everything hurt.

He had done this. My father...

"I've almost lost them," Thom's voice buzzed in my ear, the quiet voice making me jump. "Have you found anyone? Have you found the woman?"

I exhaled, the wordless sound making everything clear. "Not yet."

"Check them all," Thom growled, his own brand of

anger rumbling in his frustration. "I am sure some will start cycling back. I would hurry."

I nodded in response, fully aware that he couldn't see, and went back to work, my magic flooding through the next two crumpled bodies before I stopped short, eyes narrowing into one of the many stone doorways that lined the alley.

A man's large body slumped against the doorframe, blood smeared over an already stained white shirt. He had clearly been bitten multiple times. The image was just as heart-wrenching as the others, it still punched against my stomach. It was clear the man was dead, but it wasn't the man that had caught my attention, it was the hand that wrapped around his side, clinging to the stained shirt.

Clinging.

Gripping.

Reaching.

The fingers were moving.

The man's stance made it clear he had been trying to protect something. He had succeeded.

I rushed to the hand, feet slipping against wet cobbles before smashing into a puddle with a sound that shattered the silence like fragmented glass. My fingers wrapped around whoever was huddled behind the man and I let my magic flood them. I found every injury, every scrape, and the two bites.

Two.

She didn't have long.

"I've got one," I hissed to Thom, his gasp making it clear he hadn't expected it either. "I think it's the woman we heard. She's been bitten twice..."

"Can you extract her on your own?" he interrupted, a low grunt hinting at some other battle he was fighting.

"I can," I said with a grunt as I shifted the much larger man off of her frame. "Should I check the others?"

"Just get out of there," Thom hissed, his tone full of a tension that wasn't usual for him. "I'll meet you at the checkpoint."

The sound of a Vilẏ hissed through the earpiece. The high-pitched snarl made me jump, sure the tiny thing was right behind me. Heart thudding in my chest, I turned, expecting to see gnashing teeth. There was nothing but the dark alley, the shadows of blue dipping into darkness as the bright moon hid behind a cloud. The creature was miles away, flying through the air beside my brother, not that it made it any better.

The image was frightening and I restrained a shiver that rolled down my spine, knowing full well I was acting like a baby.

I was not interested in letting that trait continue.

Fighting the shiver, I turned back to the woman that lay dying near an ancient wooden door, her hand still clinging to the man's shirt. Her hair was a mess, her body barely moved. If it wasn't for the desperate tension in her hand, I would have assumed her just as dead as the rest of them.

"I believe that one belongs to me."

I jerked up, ice rolling through my veins. The voice was an unfamiliar drawl, each word spoken with a slow confidence that screamed of danger. There shouldn't be anyone here, not with screams so recent, not with the danger that the night ultimately provided.

There were never mortals here.

But this person, this woman, was not a mortal.

I could feel the faint whisper of her magic roll through the air. Magic that was just as rotted and deformed as the Vilẏs'. The poisoned magic my father created, the raw unhealed magic of those who were bitten and survived on their own. The magic of the army my father had built. It was that possibility that scared me.

I was sure she wasn't from his horde, most of them had sworn themselves under Joclyn. Many more had died, and some had been captured by governments, only to be tortured to death. There had been many factions that had risen up, but as far as we knew no one used magic. Everyone who had been bitten was simply executed too quickly. It's why we had rescued anyone with a bite, we had scoured the earth looking for survivors.

But this woman was very much alive, and very much not human.

I wasn't sure where she had come from, and why her magic was tainted, but everything about her screamed danger; right down to the way she was tucked into the deep purple shadows of the alley. I was sure she had been watching me the whole time. The hood of her jacket was pulled so far down that I could only see the tip of her nose, the tiny bit of flesh as dark as the night that surrounded us.

"I'm sorry, do you know her?" My voice snapped with the same heat of my magic, the roar screaming both inside and out.

I stepped between this stranger and the injured woman, my wide stance a clear barrier between them.

"Do I know who?" Thom's voice buzzed through the earpiece.

Good, he could still hear me. Maybe I could get him over here before everything went south.

"No," the voice said, as it stepped away from the shadow and into the alley just enough that I could make out the dark lines of her face.

Unnaturally green eyes peered at me from pools of

smooth black skin, the high cheekbones and painted red lips beautiful even in the carnage.

She was beautiful, and she knew it. Something she was trying to use. Unfortunately for her, I had lived with Wyn for long enough to know all of those tricks.

"Well," I began, playing into her games. She smiled more, clearly thinking she was playing me. "If you don't know her, I don't see how she can belong to you. I believe the term we humans use here is 'finders keepers'."

The woman smiled at that, a long twisted grin raking over her face as Thom's growing frustration vibrated through my eardrum.

"Finders keepers? What are you..." He paused, swore so loud I fought the need to rip the earpiece off, and then went off in a ramble that made me smile.

"Crap Ry, I keep telling you we need a code word just for situations like this, but no, Mr. 'Second-in-command' insists that there is no need. Of course, we could learn from my centuries of experience..."

My grin grew with every word, the idea that I had backup, even if it was the surly sarcastic kind that made me smile even more. Luckily, the woman took the grin as her successful seduction, and not the ridiculous humor it was.

"Humans," she mused, pulling her hood down to reveal a closely shaven head. "I do not suggest that you take her. You do not know what will happen if you do."

I could hear the threat, I could see it in her eyes. It barely fazed me, as much confidence that danced through her, I was sure she knew exactly what she said. Judging by the way she continually stepped closer, however, she didn't know who she was facing.

She didn't recognize me. Weird.

"I'm pretty sure I got this, thanks." I knew I was stalling, although chances were high that I could take her even without Thom here, I wasn't foolish enough to risk it. The shadowed woman's magic might be broken and fragmented, but there was a power in her that promised she knew how to use that fragmented magic. I didn't know if I should be interested, or terrified.

Refusing to let my focus drift from the stranger, I released my magic through the air, searching for anything else I might have missed. Anyone that could be hiding in the shadows. There was nothing, poisoned or otherwise.

"ETA Three minutes," Thom's voice buzzed.

"Do you really wish to fight me?"

The short answer to her question was no. The long answer was something more along the lines of knowing that we needed to find out who she was first. I only knew of one sure way to accomplish that.

"I will fight you if I have to," I said with a sigh and stepped closer to the hooded woman, fully aware I was putting the dying woman in danger, something that was possibly not smart considering the time she had left.

"Don't do anything stupid," Thom said, but it was not in a plea, it was a flat-voiced reminder that he knew was falling on deaf ears.

"I can't make any promises," I responded to him audibly, letting my magic flare in a spark of energy that rolled over my skin like white flame to congregate in the palm of my hand in a flaming orb of the brightest blue.

Her eyes widened, staring at me and the magic that she couldn't hope to accomplish. She looked scared, her eyes widening just enough that the bright green of them was swallowed by a bloodshot white.

"Well, at the very least don't get yourself killed." Thom was even more disinterested that time.

"She reminds me of your wife," I said under my breath, the jab getting a grunt from Thom as the woman's magic sparked, the crackle of the diseased power rushing to her hand.

Instead of the perfect orb of power I had conjured, however, her magic flickered and sparked like a firecracker. It dripped from her hand to the ground in globs of what looked like mucus where it fizzled against the water in a hiss of smoke. The damaged magic flared in a spiral of colors, the power cycling in and out as she attempted to keep it alive.

"Scared?" she asked, jaw tight as the magic sparked again, one bright ribbon flying toward me before sliding to the ground.

"No." I didn't even try to restrain the smile, the crooked thing twisting my face as I hardened my jaw. "Do you align yourself under Joclyn Krul?"

I asked the question, needing to know, needing to make sure that I wasn't about to kill one of our own, but the woman smiled, the wide grin revealing bright white teeth.

"Ah, now I know why you look so familiar."

I guess she did recognize me. It was then she attacked.

The heavy magic soared from her hand, making a beeline right for me. I swore loudly and put up a shield, the powerful wall rippling dangerously under the impact.

Great. Her magic may look like a diseased swamp rat, but it packed a punch. I was going to have to be careful.

I growled between clenched teeth, letting my magic pulse through the air in a snake that attempted to wind around her. She batted the counter-magic away, one motion turning the long snake of iron to grey ash.

I swore again, this time it did not go unnoticed by my brother.

"One Minute, Ry," Thom growled in my ear, the strain making it clear he was pushing himself as fast as he could. "Do we need her?"

Now it was my turn to growl, "Unfortunately, we do. Jos is going to want to see this."

My frustration erupted as my magic did, the attack hitting the woman square in the chest with a single pulse of the brightest white. The woman gasped for air and stumbled back, but I wasn't dumb enough to leave it there, even at full strength that attack would only wind her.

"I don't want to kill you," I growled, hitting her with another attack before trying to bind her with my magic again.

She screamed at the impact of the second hit, little specks of blood covering her bright white teeth as she smiled against the wide white bands of my power that were wrapping around her.

"Oh, but I want to kill you," she said, her voice strained even though she seemed to be enjoying herself. "We want to destroy you, and your brother."

The world slowed at her words, at the harsh tones of her laugh, at the sensation of wind as Thom came up behind me, at the realization of what she had just said.

We.

It took one pulse of magic to find them, standing in the shadows, restraining their magic just as my father had forced me to learn so long ago. Hundreds of people, her people, hiding on the rooftops.

I hadn't looked deep enough. I had been too focused on her, too focused on finding the weak magic, and now we were surrounded.

"No," I hissed, tightening the bands that ran through her and sending a surge of magic right into her flesh. She screamed at the power, screamed at the pain, but I didn't stop, I let it grow, let it pulse as my mind desperately tried to find a way out of this.

I needed a bomb...

"Get down," I yelled to Thom.

Pressing my magic away from me, I lifted the bound woman into the air. Her body twisting as she soared up into the dark night, until I pulled her to a stop twenty feet above, perfectly in line with the army she had hidden on the roof.

She looked down in horror as I smiled, my magic pressing one last surge into the bands that surrounded her.

With a flash of the brightest green, the bands exploded, sending an arsenal of shrapnel into the hidden army and her tumbling back down to where Thom and I stood below.

The screams of her backup echoed as I caught the limp and damaged body of the woman, throwing her over my shoulders as I nodded to the crumpled survivor, hoping that she was still alive.

"You get that one. We need to run."

"What just happened?" Thom growled, fixing me with a look as he made his way over to the one human who had survived the massacre.

"I think our father's army just attacked us."

We had lost track of them after the dome had popped, part of me desperately wanted it to be impossible, but something in my head was laughing that it wasn't.

CHAPTER 9
RYLAND

"Where is Joclyn?" I yelled the moment Thom and I touched down in the small clearing hidden in the forested hills outside of Prague.

The young man that stood guard jumped at our sudden appearance, his body shaking as he turned toward us. Eyes narrowing, he looked ready to chastise me for scaring him. His mouth was already opening when the moon cleared the trees and a ribbon of light fell through the leaves illuminating all of us. The image of the King's brothers standing side by side in the clearing snapped his jaw shut and sent the boy into a blubbering mess, panic lining his face.

So much for having a guard, if that's all it took for the man to freeze we were all dead by morning.

"I... am... I..." He began to stammer, looking from me, to Thom, to the women that we were each carrying; Thom cradling a blood soaked woman and I with a mass of fabric with arms and legs slung over my shoulder.

We probably looked like Vikings bringing booty home to our kin. The thought would have made me laugh if the situation wasn't quite so dire.

"For cripes sake," Thom growled, shoving the poor man out of the way as he rushed toward the solid wall of stone. "We don't have time for this, Ry. I will rip this cave apart if I have to."

I gave the man one last look before following the swinging dreads of my brother through the clearing and right through the intricately carved stone of the mountainside.

A man riding a headless horse, surrounded by Skříteks, Draks, Trpaslíks and Vilỳ who were all standing side-by-side with the mortals.

The granite had been carved by magic centuries before, the scene one from before magic had been forced underground.

For the first year that I had called Imdalind my home I had stared at the beautiful scene in absolute awe. The detail of each face, of the man on the horse. I had even tried to repair the horse's head, which had fallen off when the cave collapsed. Now, I barely saw it. Now, I no longer reveled in the past when man had seen magic and stood in awe of it.

Now, I had my feet firmly planted in reality, as frightening as that reality was.

The haunted twilight of the clearing fell away as we stepped through the beautiful stone tapestry and the deathly silence of stone surrounding us.

Once, the magic that made up the wall had denied passage to any enemy who tried to break through and kept the inhabitants of the stone city below safe. After the siege in Prague, Joclyn had shifted the magic to allow the still changing Chosen passage, like the woman Thom carried. The ones who survived the bite of the Vilỳ.

We knew the change had weakened our defenses, but as we walked through without issue, the unconscious woman who had attacked us still slung over my shoulder, we realized just how weak it was.

She hadn't been sucked into some oblivion or burned to a crisp. She was very much in one piece, and very much alive.

"So much for being safe," Thom said with a sound that was more like a bark.

"How is she?" I asked Thom, gesturing to the injured woman he carried.

"Still alive," Thom growled, "but we still need her. Joclyn!"

He screamed the last word into the massive foyer of the cave, letting his yell echo through the spider webs of hallways and caverns that made up our home.

The tapestries that had been hung over the high walls of deep grey stone shivered under the power of his yell, even the tall chandeliers began to shake. Slivers of multicolored light danced over the room as heads turned, many of the people in the massive hall rushing forward to greet us.

Great.

"Is that really necessary?" I asked Thom as I weaved around a truly frightened middle-aged man to catch up to him.

His quick pace was already leading us down the wide cavern that led toward what was once a farm, but was now a makeshift infirmary.

"I will find her, and if she is not in the infirmary...."

"Joclyn!" He cut me off with another shout, the sound sending the Chosen who had been lingering in the hall scampering away from us.

"You're scaring the children." I tried to keep my voice low, knowing they were paying far too close attention as we rushed past them. Thom, however, laughed, sending a glower toward two younger girls who were obviously trying to hide themselves in the partially cleaned out opening of what once had been a hallway.

"If I am scaring them then they need to grow a bigger backbone," Thom said with a sly smile before he turned toward a man a few years younger than my twenty-two years and growled at him. "Either that or I am not doing my job."

"It's your job to terrorize newly awakened Chosen?"

"Yes, Ryland. Yes it is."

I pushed my curls out of my eyes with my free hand, and this time I was able to cover at least one ear before he roared again.

"Joclyn!" The wrought-iron sconces that lined the stone hallway rattled as he yelled. The multi-colored flame that each one held shivered as his shout was joined by a much louder, a much angrier sound.

The footsteps of a giant. Or rather, a very angry Queen.

She roared around the corner, tangles of her dark hair streaming behind her. Blood was smeared on her blue hoodie and streaked over the faded grey of her jeans, making her look like she had just won a fight. Her silver eyes were screaming danger at both of us, but I couldn't help but smile. She looked just like the girl I had grown up with, the girl I had loved so long ago.

"Now you have done it," I said, not even trying to mock as I shifted the weight of the woman I held. "You had to wake the dragon."

Thom gave me a sidelong glance as he continued toward her, "If you think Jos is a dragon then you clearly need to spend more time around my wife."

Normally I would laugh, but Joclyn had reached us, her eyes widening as she registered the scene.

"How many bites?" she asked as she shifted her hand behind her, one faint sliver of magic flying back into the room she had just come from.

"Two," Thom answered, shifting the woman he carried onto one of the cots that came tearing out of the massive stone hall. Several of the Skříteks who worked with the Chosen followed behind, long hair falling out of their intricate braids as they ran.

Joclyn moved to the woman Thom held, placing her hands on her exposed skin. The air suddenly warmed, everything feeling as though it was vibrating under the strength of Joclyn's magic.

"You barely made it," Joclyn sighed as she closed her eyes, one last surge of power flowing into the injured woman as she sealed bites and locked magic, or whatever she did to the Chosen we brought.

With a sigh, she turned to me, already ready to help and heal the woman I carried.

"She wasn't bit. Well, not recently anyway," I provided, slamming the woman onto a second cot with a bit too much force. I hovered my hand over her, snakes of magic winding over her and the cot in an attempt to hold her in place. "This one attacked us."

Joclyn looked from me to the woman, before her eyes narrowed. "Is she with one of the government factions? We haven't heard anything about Ukraine after that broadcast. Or what about that uprising in Australia, one of the captains heard a rumor they had magic users."

I cringed. I hadn't heard about Australia, my mind had gone to my father, and for obvious reasons, but that option potentially created a much more dangerous situation.

"She better not be," Thom growled, turning from the cot the bitten woman laid on as the Skříteks whisked her away to the massive infirmary, "those dictators don't know enough about the world to have a Chosen working for them."

Thom scowled as he ran his hands over the blood on his shirt as though he could just wipe the stains away.

"She has pure magic?" Joclyn's voice was strained as she looked past us toward the solid rock entrance that led into the cave, probably thinking the same thing we were about our sudden lack of security.

"Her magic is that same poisoned sludge we saw in Prague." My own anxiety rose as I pulled her focus back to us, her silver eyes sparkling dangerously.

Her jaw tightened as she stepped toward the woman, shaking the sleeve of her hoodie back and revealing the long lengths of the golden Délka Vedení Královsk ribbon that she had twisted over her wrist.

The golden line caught the glimmer of every lantern, the surface shimmered with her subtle motions as she reached toward the woman, placing her hand against the smooth ebony of her jaw.

The woman sighed with the contact, a soft moan escaping as Joclyn's magic plunged into her. As Joclyn's magic began to ignite.

There was no whisper of her power, no spark of color, but just as before, I could feel her magic everywhere. It permeated the air stronger than before, pressing against my skin in a warming weight.

Then, Joclyn closed her eyes.

In one blink, the silver in them vanished, the beautiful color swallowed by a black so dark that it reflected nothing. She stared forward with eyes the color of night, seeing nothing. Seeing everything.

"If you ask me to get you your mug Jos, the answer is

no," Thom barked, leaning against the wall in his usual gruff irritation. "You can order a minion to do that."

A small smile played around her lips, but Joclyn said nothing, she shook her head as the black faded to the silver I had loved so much.

"I would rather not invade her privacy too much. Well, at least not yet," Joclyn said, the woman grunting again as Joclyn's magic continued to work its way through her. "I would rather give her a chance to explain who she is, and why she attacked you."

"And who she works for," Thom clarified, Joclyn nodded.

As powerful as the girl thought she was, she was no match for Joclyn. No one was.

That's why she was Queen.

My brother had chosen her as his Queen.

"Maybe when she wakes up and realizes her magic is completely inactive she might be singing a different song."

"Did you bind her magic?" Thom asked, suddenly eager, "because if you did I would like to be here for that awakening celebration."

"In the simplest terms, yes," Joclyn said with a nod, looking back at us with a smug grin.

It took all my efforts to stifle a chuckle, something I was sure she noticed given the intense side-eye. I softened the sound to a cough and leaned against the wall of the long hall, the smooth stone a comforting cool through my blood streaked shirt.

"Actually, I healed her magic," Joclyn continued, her gaze drifting from me to my brother, the stoic man chuckling darkly. "No more poison, just pure chosen power."

"That will be even better," he mumbled like some sort

of cartoon villain. "Her magic will have to be centered when she wakes up…"

"Which means she won't be able to use it," I said as I pushed off from the cold stone to rejoin them. "No risk of attack. At least until she gives us answers."

It was simple logic, but it made perfect sense.

When a human was bitten by one of the tiny dragon-like Vilỳ they could easily die if the poison in the bite was too great, or they would slip into what humans could only describe as a coma for weeks or even months. The trance-like state was essential while the mortal body became immortal, and recessed power was awakened.

It was a simple process of a mortal human becoming an immortal Chosen, the most inclusive branch of magic.

It was all so simple.

Unless the Vilỳ that did the biting was one of the poisoned creatures my father created.

The tiny vultures had hunted around the world for the last three years, and millions of humans had died because of it. If the bitten humans weren't ripped to shreds, then they were at risk of being killed by other humans out of fear. Every government, with the exception of one, was scared of the uncontrollable magic eruption that would occur when people would awaken with poisoned powers. It took training to control newly awakened magic, and the magic built by my father's creations was particularly unstable. Thousands died from those eruptions alone.

The way the mortals saw it, the Vilỳ turned people into bombs and the Vilỳ were spreading whatever alien disease was taking over the planet. So, they issued a kill order for anyone bitten by the tiny creatures. Kill them before they explode. Kill them before they could take over.

Joclyn, however, could heal them, and stop any magical explosion from occurring upon awakening.

Joclyn could take that poisoned magic and turn it into the perfect light of a Chosen. She was the only one. It's why the hospital was bursting, and it's why Thom, I, and so many others spent practically every waking minute attempting to find survivors and save them from what had become certain death.

It was dangerous work, especially with faces as wanted as ours. Someone had to do it, however, and it certainly wasn't going to be Jos. The only person more wanted than us was her.

The mortals had even given her a nickname based on the pictures they had released.

The Oheň.

The Woman on Fire.

"I really need to be here for her awakening, then," Thom mused, his bright blue eyes glittering dangerously as two of the other hospital workers began whisking the bound woman away, Jos giving very quick instructions in Czech as they did so.

"Does that actually mean you are going to work a shift?" Jos asked, giving him a sidelong glance, before casting me a knowing look.

I didn't even attempt to restrain my smirk.

"Oh yes, because you want me in there, greeting the newly awakened into our home..."

"Don't start," Joclyn interrupted him with an outstretched palm, the action stopping his words, but not his smirk. "We don't have time for this anyway, considering we now have an enemy out there somewhere..."

Thom and I swallowed in unison, our bright blue eyes

exchanging a glace as I ran my hand through my hair in agitation.

"Well," Thom said, tying his dreads behind him with the leather band he always had around his wrist. "Seeing as she shouldn't be alone when she wakes up, I volunteer..."

His words were cut short as a deep groan rocked through the cave, the floor beneath us shifting slightly as the walls screamed in a low roar of agony. My muscles knotted, eyes lifting to the ceiling as a shower of dust and sand fell over us.

The roar of the walls was followed by another shake and the echoes of a dozen screaming voices a mile down the cave where Wyn was working. It didn't take much effort to pick out her voice amongst the panicked shouts of the others that were filtering their way toward us.

"I'll sit with her," Jos said, her voice taking on the authoritative tone she had adopted a while ago. "You two go help Wyn."

"I don't see why I have to be the one to..." Thom began, but Joclyn interrupted him with a grin.

"She is your mate, Thom." She was clearly teasing, and Thom hated it.

"Aww, come'on Jos," Thom began to protest, his arms tightening over his chest, "you know she neither needs nor wants help."

"Then go give her moral support," she sighed, although the spark in her eye gave her away as to how much she was really enjoying this. "And at least double check that we aren't all going to die in a cave collapse."

Usually, Thom would fight her but he just sighed deeply, stepped toward the shorter woman and softly said, "you got it, boss."

Jos looked like she was about to say something else

when she shook her head and walked back into the hospital, where soft screams could now be heard through the dull roar that continued to vibrate the walls.

We both knew she wasn't running toward the hospital, however, she was running away from us and the accidental reminder of the day her mate, her husband, my brother, the King, had vanished.

CHAPTER 10

RYLAND

"It's coming down!"

The shout struggled to rise over the rumble of stone as everything shifted, the mountain of rock that made up the underground city groaning as the roof of the cave tried to give way. Screams followed the shouts, hundreds of footsteps echoing through the stone tomb as the rocks shifted further and those who were supposed to be helping Wyn clear the cave attempted to make their escape.

A plume of dust and dirt pushed out of the winding tunnel as something ahead of us collapsed.

Thom hit the deck just as the bath of dirt swallowed us and the hundreds of others in the cave.

"Damn it," I grumbled, spitting the dust out of my mouth so I could breathe. All I was able to do was move it around, however; there was too much, and it kept coming.

Shouts echoed around us as the dust finally began to settle, everyone coughing and spitting up dust with looks on their faces that said just how familiar this all was. Only a few of them flinched as the ceiling began to groan again.

"Damn it," I repeated, spitting more dirt out of my

mouth as I pressed my hand against the stone wall, letting my magic flood into the hard rock.

"Don't do it," Thom warned, but it was too late. The heavy ribbon of my power rushed through the rough rock that we had been working to excavate, searching desperately for whatever crack or break had happened to cause this latest collapse.

Instead, I found an angry woman.

"Get your hand off the freakin' wall, Ry!" Wyn's yell echoed through the dark cave, matching perfectly with Thom's chuckle. "Don't touch it! I can handle it!"

"Warned you."

I gave Thom a look and stepped away from the wall as everyone else around us lifted themselves off the ground by a foot or two, already knowing what would come next.

"Get off the ground!" Wyn screamed, her voice strained as a hot breeze circled through the caves. Heat radiated off the stone, turning the stone tube into a sauna. Sweat was beaded against my hairline as the warmth seeped through my sneakers and roasted my feet, my shoes feeling very heavy as the rubber soles began to melt. I lifted myself into the air just as the heat rushed over everything in a wave.

One more second and I probably would have lost my toes.

Veins of minerals illuminated through the stone in spines of glowing lightning as her magic melted and reformed the rock. Lights popped through the stone as though we were trapped in a galaxy. Floating here, it almost felt like one.

If my skin wasn't threatening to melt off my bones.

"It's beautiful. I'll never cease to be amazed by--" Any compliment I had been about to give Wyn was sucked from my throat as light was sucked from the cave, replaced with a rush of scorching air that sent us all back only to be wrapped in another wall of dirt.

Tiny particles pelted us like a tornado, filling the seams of my clothing and coating the spirals of my hair. I would be picking it out of my teeth for the next few weeks.

I really needed to start bringing a bandana or something down here.

After a moment, the wind stopped, the dust assault slowed, and even the temperature began to even out.

"Can we get down now?" Someone asked through the heavy silence, their still growing magic barely able to keep them airborne. The poor guy was flailing and flapping his arms like a baby bird.

"Clear!" Someone yelled and they all dropped to their feet before scuttling away. If I didn't already know that Chosen couldn't sense magic I would guess that they could sense the wall of power that was coming this way.

"I told you to leave her alone," Thom chuckled as he shook the dust from his dreads.

My feet hit against the ground softly, the stone still hot through my shoes, although it was quickly cooling as her magic left it.

"If we let one more incompetent person down here I am going to lose it!" Wyn's yell rattled everything as she stormed her way through the still settling dust, her dark eyes raging as she hunted me down.

Her auburn hair was pulled up as much as her short cut allowed, leaving her face framed by frizzy strands that accentuated the crazed fury that was barreling toward me. The emotion made the remains of a tattoo that covered her face and left arm that much more prevalent, even though the deep black swirls that cut into her skin were so faint most people missed them completely.

The scars of an unsuccessful death sentence. Magic gone bad.

"Everyone who is cleared to work in the caves passes a test..." I tried to keep my voice diplomatic, but I could already feel the frustration that rumbled under the surface, my own scars threatening to rip through.

"Then we need to make the test harder!" she roared, dusting her hands off on her equally dirt covered Fleetwood Mac t-shirt.

I clenched my fist.

Sometimes, I wasn't sure how my brother dealt with her. Most of the time she was a bubbly care-free spirit. You get in the way of her and her magic, however, and it was like dealing with a whole different person.

I turned toward Thom but the traitor bounced on his heels as he watched the fireworks pop in front of him.

We were obviously better than TV.

I gave him a warning glare, but he laughed anyway, the sound unmissed by his wife, although she didn't turn to look at him.

Traitor was right.

"You are the one who created the test, Wynifred. If you want to change it then we can certainly do that."

As calm as I was, you could still hear the cracks of irritation in my voice, still see the tension as my muscles flexed through my crossed arms. It wasn't meant as posturing, but Wyn certainly took it that way. Either that or she was pissed I was staying as calm as I was.

"Or you can just let me do it myself." Her voice was low, the seductress she always attempted to keep hidden peeking through as she tried to sway me.

Not interested.

Thom just laughed.

I sighed, resisted an eye roll, and placed my bulky hands on either of her arms as I forced her to take a step back. My hands and arms looked massive against her tiny frame, the rugby muscles I had built over the years having grown with the added work of rebuilding a cave city.

Wyn sighed through clenched teeth as she reluctantly allowed me to remove her from my side.

"I've already told you why I am not going to let you do that."

"Safety wouldn't be a concern if it was just me down here."

She tried to rebuff my usual reasoning as quickly as she could. The response made my anger bristle more, but this time I wasn't the only one. Thom stepped between us as if he had been sling-shot into place, the humor on his face disappeared behind a scowl so deep that even Wyn couldn't raise herself to match.

"Wynifred," he began, his voice soft as he took her hands in his. "I know you can do it on your own, we both do..." She opened her mouth to retort, but Thom raised an eyebrow, silencing her. "And Jos knows too, so there is no reason to go running off to complain to her."

Thom smiled, Wyn didn't, and I suddenly found myself taking one quick step back.

"I'm not complaining," Wyn said, her tone a cross between a whine and a diplomatic statement. "I just know I can go faster alone, and these Chosen can't learn Trpaslík magic overnight..."

She faded off, waving a hand toward the rocks as if that explained it. Trpaslík's magic centered around the earth, around the elements, and while it wasn't necessary to melting and moving stone, it certainly helped.

"You are the only one who can teach them, Wyn."

"I'm the only one with fire magic in these caves, not the only Trpaslík," Wyn corrected, "And you and I both know I can't teach them that."

"True," Thom conceded, taking a step toward her. I was more than happy to leave this all to him.

"But you are the best at rock manipulation."

"All the more reason to go alone. Go faster. Get it done."

"Joclyn has asked…"

"I'm not going to find him, Thom."

Their banter froze as I did, my slow retreat cut short as her few words hit against me like ice and iron. I shivered, Thom breathed, and Wyn looked down to her stained Converse dejectedly before she looked between both of us. Just the look in her eyes made me feel like I had been stabbed again.

"We all know it's true."

Every breath reverberated off the stone as we fell into silence, leaving only the faint sound of Wyn's favorite band, Styx, that whispered through the still settling dust somewhere down the tunnel behind us.

"It's been three years," Wyn continued after no one said anything. "I know she wants to find him, I know you all want to find him. Hell, I want to find him, and that's saying something."

She paused, sighed, and shifted her feet. All were actions I wished I could replicate, but I was trapped in place, breath stuck in my chest.

"He's alive, Wyn. We have to find him." I didn't think I would ever believe what they say, about loss getting easier with time. It still stings the exact same way, still makes me just as angry.

Wyn shook her head, "I need to show you something."

Thom and I exchanged a look before he glanced around

the now empty outcropping of the hall, as if checking for eavesdroppers. They had all left the moment Wyn had rampaged out of the dust, however.

Perhaps they had more sense than we did.

"Lead the way," I responded, holding my hand out like a tour guide.

Normally Wyn would smile and give some snide remark at that. Instead, she pressed her lips together, bounced on her heels and turned toward the dark maw of the cave she had emerged from.

The chill air smelled of dust and water, the aroma comforting after having spent so much time down here. Of course, I hadn't been down this far in a while. Wyn had made some serious progress in the last few months.

The deeper into the cave we moved, the more the light faded into a deep black smear of ink. It made the echoed songs of Styx a bit creepier than you would think.

"Would you mind telling us where we are going?" I queried.

Instead of answering, Wyn's magic sparked into an orb of fire, the shimmering dome hovering in the air as it bathed us in rays of orange and yellow.

Great. That was always a great sign.

Muscles tensed, heart pounding, my magic rumbled under my skin as my own multicolored lamp drifted into the air, bobbing above us as we moved deeper, as the anxious tension in my shoulders grew.

"We were finally able to dig it out a few days ago," Wyn finally said as we were completely swallowed by the dark, leaving us walking in a shimmering pool of liquid light.

"Wyn," I hissed as I took a few quick steps to catch up to her. "I'm Jos' second in command, I took an oath, you do realize that anything you tell me I have to tell her."

She slowed her step, flashing me a look that was half guilt and half maniacal plotting. My stomach dropped instantly.

"That's exactly what I am counting on, Ry," she joked, prodding me dutifully in the side, "Then she can kill the middleman, not me."

Thom chuckled from somewhere behind me and I almost turned to deck him. He would have deserved it.

"Gee, thanks, Wyn," I grumbled, my voice flattened by my growl, "I am so glad I could be of assistance to you."

"It's part of the job description, Ry," Wyn said. "You chose it, it's time you get used to it."

She was right of course. When the council had chosen to put Joclyn in as our acting ruler, in the hope that we would find her husband and mate, the true King, it had been between the three of us to take the place of her 'second-in-command'.

Wyn had removed herself from the equation, stating that her magic didn't react well with Joclyn's, which was true.

That left Thom and me.

I volunteered before Thom could even open his mouth. Not that he would have.

They should have disqualified me, I certainly couldn't pass for stable at that time. Besides, we had too much history. Too much time with me trying to kill her, obsessed with her, possibly in love with her.

It certainly didn't make me the perfect candidate for protecting and supporting someone as they became Queen of an entire underground nation of magical beings.

I should have never cleared the first round of votes.

"Yes, I chose it," I admitted. "That doesn't mean I chose

to be manipulated by her best friend who is too scared to give her news."

"I don't see any difference," Wyn said, as she turned to me with a grin that always spelled mischief to her. "And I am not too scared to give her news!"

Chuckling darkly, I chose not to respond and continued down the dark tunnel, as if I knew where I was going. Wyn's exasperated groan rippled off the stone as we turned a corner, right into a wide cavern that was bursting with light and the sounds of Styx.

The room was lined with the broken mirrors that Wyn had attempted to return to their original hangings on the high ceilings. The once intricate designs were now no more than sagging memories against chipped stone. Shards of reflective glass sent prisms of the brightest blue over the walls, the glittering light shifting and dancing against the dark stone in a wave of water.

Light illuminated the circular gathering space, the dozens of still caved-in hallways circling the walls and closing us in, trapping me with the familiarity.

My blood turned to ice as realization hit.

I had been here before.

It was the last place I had seen Ilyan alive, before I had raced from him to kill Míra. The now teenage girl who stood in the middle of the massive clearing as if she had been here the whole time, waiting to continue our fight.

I would have believed it too, except so much about her had changed.

The stony-faced kid was gone, replaced by an angsty sixteen year old that was all limbs and freckles.

Míra had sprouted up at least a foot, while her blonde hair had stretched the same in the opposite direction. She was every bit Wyn's little sidekick. From her ripped and knotted band shirt, obviously a hand me down, to her faded jeans that were just as covered with dirt as Wyn's. She was draped in hanging necklaces and bangles and wore lipstick so red it might as well have been the only color in the place.

"Ryland!" Míra's voice was the joyful bubble I had come to expect from her. Hearing it in this room, however, was bringing about all the wrong emotions.

A low buzz of long-forgotten laughter rumbled through the back of my mind in a haunting melody, the sound of explosions punctuating each heart beat like it was a stab wound.

"Hey, Míra." My voice choked in my throat.

"Can you believe we found this place?" Míra prattled as she vaulted over a large boulder and ran to my side. "It's like our special place. We almost killed each other here, you know?"

Her voice was light, airy, but I could hear the deep undertones behind it, see the danger in her eyes. She was haunted by the memories just as much as I was.

"Look there," she said, standing beside me as though we were gazing at a beautiful sunset. "That was where you threw me into the stone. And there," she gestured toward one of the caved-in openings, "was where I sliced open your side."

"Those don't strike me as positive memories. And while I am not sure we have a 'special place' I do not think this qualifies." I was suddenly having trouble breathing. My chest was too tight. I was only twenty-two, I should not be having a heart attack.

The side of Míra's mouth tweaked into a distorted smile as her eyes sparked with wickedness.

"I almost got you. All that blood, it was everywhere,"

she hissed, stepping closer to me. "At least tell me you still have the scar."

Her voice was low, dangerous, and I flinched at the assassin that looked at me. The familiarity made me uncomfortable, not because I could clearly picture the heavy line of raised skin that she scarred me with, but because right then I was seeing the same beast I fought.

"Míra," Wyn scolded, her voice a motherly snap as Míra stepped away from me, shaking her head.

"Be bigger, Míra," I said, the voice low and under my breath as I caught her eyes. "Don't let him take up space."

I wasn't sure if I was talking more to her, or to myself, but that always seemed to be the same thing when it came to us. The same monster lived inside our heads. The same torture. The same demon.

She stared at me, the brown specks in her green eyes lightening slightly.

"Being here is…" she began, her words fading away as she shook her head.

"She's doing great," Wyn provided before Míra could say any more, which was probably for the best.

I squeezed Míra's shoulder, sending her lanky limbs jostling as I pulled her into a side hug. The momentary darkness seemed to pass, her eyes smiling as she looked up at me. Her shy smile was infectious and I let it chase the remains of madness away, the muscles in my back relaxing.

"We all have scars," I reassured her, soft enough that only she could hear, and wrapped my burly arms around her tiny frame. "Inside and out."

"We just have the biggest battle scars from the biggest battle of all time." The smile smothered her voice as she pulled away from me.

"Exactly. While some hide inside, some make you look

like a zombie," I said, fully aware that my face was criss-crossed with tiny scars, but those were nothing compared to the line of raised skin that ran the length of her face.

Reminders of torture.

I shivered, and Míra smacked my arm, a tiny spark of her warm magic moved into me with the touch. "Ry! You aren't nearly a zombie. I'm still missing a toe! That's gotta count for something."

"Can we not break out in a scar measuring contest," Thom said, already attempting to hedge himself out of the conversation.

He probably already would have if Wyn wasn't playing with the ends of his dreadlocks.

"Agreed." Wyn stepped away from her mate to give Míra a warning glance. The girl was good at derailing conversations, and she knew it, a fact that was emphasized by her smug look.

I had to give it to her, at least she played to her strengths.

"Besides," Wyn said, lifting her hand to showcase the giant ping pong sized hole that was there. "We all know that none of you can beat me."

Míra opened her mouth to say something, thought better of it, and instead broke out into a wide grin. "You win. I know better than to get into a fight with you. My arm is still recovering."

Thom laughed, Wyn scowled, and Míra burst into giggles, the sunny teen having accomplished her task with ease.

Demon conquered. Sanity returned.

For both of us.

I'd have to congratulate her later.

Although much of the control my father had retained

over me had vanished with the destruction of his soul, it was this girl who had become the greatest sidekick in the battle for my mind.

She helped me defeat the voices and regain my sanity. I helped her find herself through her own crippling guilt and anger.

Somehow it worked. Somehow we had gone from attempting to kill each other, to killing our abuser, to defeating our dragons.

"So what brings you down here?" Míra asked, looking from all of us, to Wyn, before her words faded away, only to be replaced with a soft 'O' and the widest eyes I had seen.

My heart sank.

"If that's the reaction we get, I am suddenly very concerned about what you have found," Thom growled, his eyes narrowing at Wyn before she sighed and turned from us to the only tunnel in the room that had been cleared out. The dark opening was a haunted yawn inset into the grey rock, the mouth circled with jagged stone that Wyn hadn't taken the time yet to smooth out.

The shards of stone cut into my soul and I shivered, muscles tensing at the memory of which opening this was, and the blonde hair I had seen run down it.

Ilyan.

I clenched my hands against my jeans, the dried blood making the fabric stiff and uncomfortable.

"I told you he's not down here," Wyn whispered, the dead sound in her voice shifting my nerves.

This whole thing was only getting worse.

"If you don't start moving I am going to lose something," I warned, the strained lines of my emotions feeling like over plucked guitar strings.

"Like a hand?" Wyn waved at me with her hole again

before she walked confidently toward the excavated tunnel. I followed Wyn with my head held high, the shuffling feet of the others not far behind.

"Don't suppose you can tell us what is down there?" Thom whispered from behind me as the wide mouth swallowed us, welcoming us into the dark.

There was no answer, but it didn't matter, I wouldn't have heard anyway. I was too focused on the dark bob of Wyn's head as she darted further and further into the dark.

Everything smelled of damp earth, the aroma so strong that I could feel it against my skin. With each step, the cave began to fill with the sound of thunder, the low roar ripping over the rock. It grew until it was all I could hear, it was all there was; the sound of thunder and the smell of earth.

I forced one shallow exhale out as the dark tunnel opened up into a wide cavern, a river roaring through the middle and splashing icy water over the rough bank of stone.

It was as I thought, the cave where Joclyn had fallen into the waves, dragged to the heart of Imdalind moments before the war had ended. I had heard her relay the story multiple times, and now I was standing here, staring at the rushing river in the partially cleared out cave.

"I used to do my laundry here," Wyn yelled over the roar of the water.

Míra rolled her eyes at her and placed a flat hand to her side, a wall of muted yellow swimming through the air between us and the rapids, muting the sound until I could hear the pulse of my own heart. Something that wasn't particularly surprising with how hard it was pulsing.

"It took time to get here," Wyn sighed, her jaw tightening. "But it didn't change anything. He's not here. Not anymore."

I raised an eyebrow at her curiously, "Anymore?"

Wyn pursed her lips and popped her hip before taking a step toward the section of the cave that hadn't been cleared out all the way.

"I stopped when I found it, when I sensed the residue of their magic, but there was nothing there. Nothing but this."

She waved toward the wall and took a step back, as if giving Thom and I more room to see, but I didn't need more room. I could already see it from here.

The color was faded, the red not quite as bright after having been hidden for years, but it was still there, it still painted everything in a shade of pain and heartbreak.

Blood.

It covered the wall, the splatter large enough, thick enough, full of enough flesh and remains that I was sure no one could have survived it.

"Whose is it?" I asked, hating the desire to reach out and touch the dried scarlet streaks.

"I can feel both of their magic in it. Ovailia. Ilyan." I turned to her, eyes wide, but she just sighed and continued. "It doesn't matter, though. Neither of them are here."

"But they were," Thom said, stepping closer to the massive splatter of dried blood. "One of them survived."

"And the other got out, taking whoever was injured with them." Míra was far too bright, hopeful given the giant smear of blood on the wall.

"Or they fell into the river, there is only one way to know." It was then that Wyn looked at me, and suddenly all of this made sense.

"She's not going to like this," I growled, my jaw clenched as I took a step back, eyes darting over the cave as a deep part of my mind attempted to plot an escape. "She's been holding onto him being alive. New first four and all that."

Everything in me wanted to escape this place, to forget this moment and this twisted smear of death. There was nothing I could do, however, nowhere to go but right back to Jos and tell her what happened. What Wyn had found.

She had tried many times to use her sight to relive this moment, but something was blocking her. Wyn and I knew what, and the massive splatter of blood was either going to help her, or destroy her.

I don't think any of us were ready to pick up those pieces.

"Well, Thom," I hissed, pulling his focus away from the red-stained stone that he was still absorbed in. "I guess you get babysitting duty."

"Fine by me," he said, his focus still intent on the stone, even though he took a step back. "You know I don't like to get in the middle of Jos and…"

His words dropped off, body frozen mid-step as he stared at the blood. It was as though he had been put on pause. If it wasn't for the curious look Wyn gave me and the incessant rumble of waves through the sudden silence, I would have assumed the whole world would have stopped.

"Do you have another quarter, Wyn, because I think your mate is broken." Míra deadpanned beside me, but I couldn't find the humor, I just stared at Thom, the image of him framed by the blood stopping my heart.

"What if it was her?" His question was a snap of anger that shot through me and I jumped. Wyn gestured in confusion, but he didn't even look at her, he just spun to face me, his eyes wide and screaming. "What if she is alive?"

"Ovailia?" I asked, fully aware of why he would want that.

And what he would do if it turned out to be true.

"Yes," Thom said, the single word drowned in his anger. "What if she was the one who made it out?"

"We don't know that for sure," Wyn said, her anger boiling up right beside her husband's, the same animosity for the woman we were supposed to call sister still raging.

Except this anger went past three years. It was centuries old. Most of the time I forgot how old they were, but right then it was screaming from the festering anger that glared in their eyes.

"Then you can track her down..."

"No," Thom cut me off. "What if Ovailia is alive? What if she sent the woman Joclyn is currently guarding? What if we let Ovailia back in?"

"What woman?" Wyn and Míra said in unison, but I barely heard them, I couldn't take the time to answer them.

I was already running out of the cave and back toward the woman I was supposed to be guarding with my life, wishing my legs were faster.

Wishing I had learned how to stutter.

CHAPTER II
RYLAND

S tuttering was nothing more than moving between two points in the universe in an instant. Disappearing from one, reappearing in the other. Or, at least, that's what Joclyn had tried to explain when she tried to teach me how to do it almost a year ago.

She had gone on about some world underneath ours, and how you had to move through the ribbons of memory to reach your destination.

It was all mumbo-jumbo.

I had learned two things from those lessons, and neither of them was to Stutter.

Wyn and Míra, however, had mastered it. Something I had clearly forgotten, seeing as I was surprised to see both Wyn and Míra already standing in the hospital with the woman in question, tucked into a far corner near a cluster of beds that were currently unused.

Resisting the urge to take off into the air and soar toward them, I instead weaved and dodged through the two hundred or so people who occupied the massive space. Most of the newly bitten were still restricted to their beds, but many others were milling around with the Skřítek hosts that had been assigned to them for 'training and intro- duction'.

As busy as the room was, and as much as it dripped with the smell of antiseptic, it had an air of excitement around it that made it infectious.

Well, it would have if I wasn't shaking in panic.

I pressed my way through a cluster of five Chosen as I made my way to the back of the room. A hush fell over them as one explained who I was. The others, all girls, were quickly reduced to a huddle of whispers and giggles, the words 'smoking' and 'hot' spoken clearly. I smiled in what I hoped was an 'I'm not interested' way, which unfortunately sent them giggling and blushing more. Clearly I needed to work on that.

Jos looked up as I collided with a small boy who was running through the crowd, sending him into an empty bed with a noise that ripped through the bustling hospital like a whip. The kid looked about to erupt as he turned, eyes wide as he recognized me. His apology was swallowed in a mumble as he scampered away, giving me one last look of both awe and fear before he ran head first into another bed.

"You would think I am a god with the way they react," I sighed as I finally reached them, dragging my hand through my hair in an attempt to release some of my anxiety.

"You are a God, Ry," Wyn said with a grin. "Did you see how those girls looked at you? They are still twitterpated."

"Twitterpated?" I asked, looking back at the girls who did in fact squeal when I made eye contact with them.

"I bet they would tear your poster out of Teen Bop magazine and hang it above their bed," Wyn continued on, ignoring my confusion.

"Teen Bop magazine?" Míra asked, as confused as Jos and I.

Wyn stopped short, her eyes darting between the three of us with a mix of desperation and frustration.

"Gah!" she exploded, throwing her hands into the air. "How old am I? Those aren't even old references! You all are babies!"

"Yes, they are," Thom's voice rumbled behind me as he edged his way into the circle. "Have you told her yet?"

He asked the question to Wyn, his eyes locked onto his mate's as he nodded once toward Joclyn. The answer was unmistakable and judging by Joclyn's reaction, no, she hadn't told her.

"The woman is still unconscious," Wyn said with a shrug, "She's not hurting anyone. Besides, I am pretty sure we are going to need more moral support than I could give..."

She faded off, throwing her arm over Joclyn's shoulders in what I was sure was supposed to be a supportive way. It had the opposite effect, however. Any joy in Joclyn's face faded as the mood of our little corner of the hospital faded into a deep grey weight.

"I'm not sure this is the right place..." I attempted to hedge, nodding back toward the crowd.

Jos looked at me with wide confused eyes before she exhaled with the tiniest of growls, pulling away from Wyn and stepping right up to me.

"Fine, meet me in my room," Joclyn said, placing her hand on my forearm just as the pop of Míra and Wyn leaving sprouted in my ears.

I didn't even have time to protest, although I had heard Thom mumble about not wanting to 'run around all over the place' before Joclyn's magic pushed into me in a rush.

The strength of her power slammed against every nerve, it pressed against my skin until I felt as though my bones and muscles would escape my body and turn me inside out. I wanted to scream, but the sound was locked inside as the strength of her power pulled me from the hospital and dragged me through the uncomfortable dark. Pain and pressure slammed against my skull until we re-emerged in the bright white cavern that was her room.

I gasped as the pressure left, air returning as the world regained a floor again. A floor I found all too quickly. Everything spun and heaved as I fell to my knees, my magic rushing through me in an effort to ease the dizziness and nausea that was now attempting to find its way out.

Three years of her doing that to me and it hadn't gotten any easier.

Luckily, she didn't say anything about my 'weak constitution' anymore.

"Spill," Jos commanded before I even had a chance to catch my breath. I couldn't even stand up yet, I just sat curled over on the floor, watching Wyn's black chucks and Míra's jeweled flip-flops shift against the shag rug as they appeared.

"You don't want me to do that right now." I barely got the words out, concerned something else would come out alongside.

"Now."

There wasn't a moment's hesitation.

"We dug out the room with the river. The walls are covered with blood."

Well, at least Wyn didn't mince words, I would give her that.

"Geeze, Wyn," I chastised, "you could have been a bit gentler."

I stood just as Jos began to waver, her body tensing as she stared forward, jaw clenching in a slow pulse.

"There was a reason I wanted you to do it, Ry."

I ignored her and instead focused on Joclyn, everything about her stiff as she stared straight forward. Her eyes were glazed over, a dark sheen smothering them as sight threatened to take her, just as it did every time we mentioned her mate. She was trapped inside her magic, as memories of that night, of Ilyan, swarmed her.

"Breathe, Jos," I soothed, standing up to gently brush some of the long tangles of hair away from her face as she came out of the fog.

"I'm fine," Jos said, her voice hoarse, although not in the deep heady sound of sight.

"Did you see anything?" I asked, dreading the answer as much as everyone else in the room.

"No, it was the same. There was nothing." She closed her eyes, took one deep breath and turned to me and Wyn, her wide eyes already blazing with confidence.

"Okay," she said after a minute, obviously still steeling herself for what was coming. "Whose blood was it? Who-" she hesitated. "What did you find?"

"We don't know whose blood it is, Jos," Wyn said, casting me a side glance. "Nothing else was there. No bodies. Nothing."

Jos jerked as though she had been slapped, the same shock piercing through everyone else.

"So, we reached the room, but nothing was there?" Jos stepped away from me then, her fingers pulling and tugging at the golden ribbon at her wrist.

"Nothing but the blood."

"Crap, Wyn," Jos snapped. "You could have led with

that, you know. So, you're saying there's a chance he could still be alive?"

"It was a lot of blood," Míra whispered, refusing to make eye contact with any of us. "I'm not sure anyone could have survived that."

"What do you mean it was a lot of blood?" Joclyn's question punched the air and we all looked to one another, the look on Wyn's face making it clear she wasn't going to spearhead this one.

"Jos." I took a deep breath and ran my fingers through my hair, the dirt and grit still clinging to the damp strands. "It was more than just blood. There was..." I hesitated, there was no good way to phrase this and just thinking about it was making me uncomfortable. "There were bits... flesh..."

Her eyes widened as her nostrils flared, a devastating pain smothering the silver of her eyes as she reached out to me, her hand winding around the fabric of my sleeve. She knew what was coming as much as I did.

"No." Her voice was little more than a whisper.

"It's enough for you to see."

"No." She was more forceful that time, but it didn't make any difference.

That same painful wave washed over me, the muscles in my back tightening as I tried to find a way to comfort her.

"I'm sorry, Jos." I knew the words were not enough. They could never be enough.

There was no easy way to say 'Can you put your hands on the possible remains of your mate and try to find out what happened?'

My stomach spun just thinking about it.

"I wish you didn't have to, but as Wyn said, there was no one there. Not even Ovailia." I hesitated, giving her anger just enough time to jump from one to one thousand.

"So she took him," she snapped. It wasn't a question.

"Or he took her," I clarified, although we all knew the possibility of that was slim. If Ilyan was alive he would have been back by now. No one wanted to say it, however. "Either way we won't know until you use your sight."

She swallowed and let her hand slide down my arm, her touch soft as she bit her lower lip.

"You won't be alone," Wyn said, stepping beside us and weaving her arm around Jos's waist. "We will all be there. We all feel the same pain. We are in this together, remember."

Jos opened her mouth as if she was going to say something before she snapped it shut, a tiny smile playing on her lips.

"And we thought this would have ended with the war," she whispered before pulling us into her, our arms wrapping around each other in a tangle of loss and hope, just like we had been since day one.

The tangle wrapped around my heart and constricted it, pulling my breath out of my chest. I looked up, desperate for air, only to lock eyes with Míra.

She stood about five feet away, arms wrapped around herself as she watched us, her normally sunny eyes shining. Before I could extend my hand to her, the circle broke, the girls stepping away in varying degrees of disarray.

"Okay," Jos said with a shaking confidence. "As much as I want to rip this off like a Band-Aid... I think waiting-"

"We can't wait, Jos," I interrupted, already hating myself for adding this extra layer of dung to the already smelly pile. "As much as there is a chance that Ilyan is alive, there is also a chance Ovailia is still alive. We were just attacked by a woman with magic just like my father created."

"If it was Ovailia who escaped..." Wyn began, doing her best to soften the blow, but Joclyn held up her hand, stopping her mid-sentence.

"If there is any possibility that the two are connected," Joclyn said as she stepped over to the long ornate dresser that stretched over much of the long walls in the chamber, "we need to know."

Joclyn moved from item to item on the dresser, stopping when she reached a small carved box that stood apart from everything else. Her fingers hovered above it before she turned, putting herself between us and whatever precious thing it was hiding.

"Okay. Here is what we are going to do," Joclyn's voice was strong as she looked from Wyn to me. "We need to call a council. I think Etma and a few others are still overseas on rescue missions, I need you to call them back and get everyone together by tonight. Wyn, you and I are going to go down there and see what we can see."

She was confident, sure, even though the light in her eyes was cracking.

"Jos," I stepped to her, my hands already extended toward her; she didn't take them. "I really don't feel comfortable with you going down there without me. I want to be there..."

"I know," she cut me off with a wave of her hands, "but I don't know what is going to happen. I don't know what I am going to see."

She nearly choked on the last few words, the emotion she tried to keep at bay before beginning to break free.

"I know, Jos," I breathed, gently placing my hands over hers. I tried to grab them, to calm her, but she pulled away, stepping back to the dresser and the little wooden box.

"I need to do this on my own." She was firm. Confident, and stubborn as hell.

I swallowed, knowing I couldn't say anything more, knowing she was right. Sometimes being there for her was being as far away as possible.

Exhaling with a shake, Jos turned to face me and Wyn, looking between us as she said, "Call the council, Ry. Wyn, show me what you have found."

Everyone nodded once in agreement, Míra however bounced once on her toes, clasped her hands together and looked Jos right in the eye.

"My lady," Míra began, she was laying it on thick, using Jos's official title and trying to sound like she had stepped out of an old fantasy movie, "may I attend council?"

While Jos and I were able to restrain matching smirks, Wyn's eyes rolled so far into her hairline they might as well have disappeared.

You gotta hand it to the kid. She had guts.

"No, Míra," Joclyn's voice was kind, but Míra's shoulders still sagged dejectedly. "You aren't old enough, not yet."

I knew at once that Jos shouldn't have tacked on that last part. The sag in Míra's shoulders straightened, her head snapping up as she began to fume.

"I am sixteen years old, Joclyn!" Míra said, her voice a calm storm. So much for formalities.

Joclyn gave her a look and while the exaggerated disdain faded, the girl did not give up. "My birthday was months ago! Besides, you know I have seen and done more than anyone else! All these 'Chosen'," she growled the word with disgust, "don't have the ability or power that I have. Edmund would let me..."

"Enough," Joclyn roared in Czech, the single word

rumbling through the air on the back of her magic. I felt it press against my skin in warning, a warm heat prodding me to obey.

I wasn't stupid enough to question it.

Neither was Míra, thank god, which was good because she was already dumb enough to bring up my father. Even with that, it was hard not to be proud of her. With as much emotion that lived inside that girl, she didn't explode this time.

I tried to catch her attention and tell her as such, but she was stubbornly looking away from everyone, her focus on her curled toes as she mumbled something to herself.

My heart dropped. No.

"Míra," Joclyn began, she didn't get any further.

"I won't listen to you!" Míra raged before storming away, each step a slap of rubber against stone before, with a tiny pop, she disappeared into thin air, a strong residue of her magic floating behind her.

"She wasn't talking to me, was she?" Jos asked, looking at the place Míra had been in bewilderment.

"No," I answered, trying to ignore the plunging need to just run after the girl. "I am fairly sure she wasn't talking to any of us."

"I wish she *would* talk to me," Jos sighed, tapping her fingers against the dresser loudly, the sound pulling my focus toward the others.

"Or me," Wyn said, raising her hand beside her. "It's not like we all haven't been mentally manipulated by the same man. It's not like he hasn't killed all of our families, too."

"Well, she is not going to talk to anyone else until we can stop her from doing that," I groaned, turning back to Míra's last known destination right as Thom wandered through the door behind where she had vanished.

He obviously hadn't been in any hurry to get here.

"You're just jealous you can't Stutter..." Wyn prodded, shoving her elbow into my arm.

"While I am not denying that," I said from between clenched teeth, returning the prod and sending her stumbling, "as far as magical teenage breakdowns go, Míra might be winning whatever race she is running."

"I take it I missed another meltdown?" Thom asked coolly as he took a seat beside Wyn.

"One of the best," Wyn said, throwing herself onto Jos's bed and taking Thom with her. "I don't remember you ever being this bad, Jos."

"I don't remember ever being able to string more than four words together, especially in front of an authority figure," Jos said with a strained laugh, her hands tightening over the ridge of the dresser.

"Even at sixteen you weren't as much of an emotional mess as that girl. But, you always had a fire in you," I said, turning toward the stretch of white washed stone that Míra had all but walked through. "But Míra, Míra is a god damn hurricane."

"A hurricane I am not sure we will ever control," Thom said. He didn't have to be here to know what happened. He had witnessed enough. "She would almost give Rinax a run for his money. You know, if we could ever find the bastard."

"Right now, we need to let her fizzle herself out." Jos sighed, dark hair waving as she shook her head. "I can't have either of you running to her aid right now."

Jos looked from Wyn to me, her dark eyes full of a million warnings, all tailored right for me.

"I don't want to wait on this. You have your assignments. Ryland fill your brother in, will you? We don't have much time."

I nodded as Wyn peeled herself off the bed, planted one kiss on Thom's cheek, and took her place beside Jos. The two of them looked as though they were facing a gruesome execution.

Maybe they were, I realized with a painful pinch. With one touch the two disappeared, right back to the cave and into the center of the heartbreak.

"I take it they are going down to the cave," Thom snarked from beside me as we both moved toward the heavy door. "I don't see this ending well."

"Thom, I would have to agree with you."

Thom chuckled darkly, sounding like the old man he really was. "Well here is to a much better, and hopefully a much shorter war."

"You say that like we lost the last one."

He shot me a look.

"A thousand year war, Ry, and we won by the skin of our teeth and with only six people." His humor was turning acrid, the bite on his words cringing in the pit of my stomach.

He was right, yes, but I knew his anger was seeded in something darker. He lost his daughter in that war. He was used by our father in that war, just as I was. He just had an extra hundred years of healing time on me.

"I have no interest in doing it again," he said with a shake of his dreads, his voice rippling with snark. "I came out of the last one with all my limbs and not looking like I got in a fight with hedge clippers," he motioned to me, "I have no guarantee that my rugged good looks would remain intact for a second go around."

He said it so deadpan that I could only shake my head and followed him right back out the door and into a group of young women who instantly broke out into giggles.

"Be careful, or they will start pinning your picture in their bedrooms." Thom teased, breaking out into a chuckle. "Aww... Teen beat."

The joke was still lost on me. The women were pretty, I had seen one of them, Shayla I think, a few times before, and she was gorgeous. But I was nowhere near ready to put my heart back on the line.

I had not had the best luck.

One I had loved since I was a child, but she grew up, married my brother, and became a Queen.

The other I was just starting to build something with when Míra had killed her.

My magic had reacted to another, but I could never have her. There was only danger there.

The thought was a stab to my heart and I swallowed, knowing there was more to it than that and wishing that it somehow made it hurt less.

"You are going to go check on her, aren't you?" The subject of Thom's question couldn't have come at a worse time and I cringed, trying to ignore the way my whole body seized.

"Yeah," I sighed, ignoring the shadow of a laugh that was playing at the back of my mind, ignoring the way my heart was breaking for the millionth time. "If I don't, she is going to destroy her bedroom again."

This time it was Thom's turn to laugh.

I didn't join him.

CHAPTER 12

JOCLYN

W alking into that room was like walking into a nightmare.

Everything had been fuzzy when I wandered in here years ago, following the shadow of myself. It was only after I had thrown myself into the river that I had known Ilyan had followed me. That whatever had happened between him and Ovailia had ended here.

Now, staring at the smears of blood and flesh on the wall, I no longer had any question.

"You okay?" Wyn whispered from somewhere to my left, her voice as hollow and distant as I felt.

I only gave her a low nod, my eyes still focused on the smears of red so dark they were almost brown.

I had spent the last three years scouring the French beaches with Wyn, falling asleep wrapped in blankets thick enough to hide my tears. I had spent three years pushing the pain away, being the strong perfect Queen. Which was fine, it gave me something to focus on.

I could feel all of that crack as I took a step toward the wall. I could feel the pulse of his magic moving through me, my own magic screaming for me to find his, but there was nothing beyond the wall.

I already knew whose blood it was.

"This is really going to suck." My voice cracked as I lifted my hand, my magic pulsing around me as though it was trying to find him. I wanted to tell it that he wasn't there, but I didn't think I could find the words.

"Yep. It is."

I chuckled hollowly at that and held my hand out, my heart skipping a beat as Wyn placed my mug into it.

"Don't worry, if you pass out I'll be here to catch you."

"Gee thanks," I said, finally turning toward her. "What about if I fall to my knees and start sobbing uncontrollably?"

"I'll make sure everyone knows how much of a big baby their Queen is." She grinned, but I just rolled my eyes.

"And then threaten to beat them up if they ever use it against me?"

"You know me so well." Wyn's smile faded as she stepped beside me, arm over my shoulder as she pulled me into her and we both stood, staring at the wall.

"I'm going to see him again," I whispered, that hope that I had clung to all these years blossoming to life again.

"And then we are going to find him." Her words were like a firecracker in me and I nodded. Damn. I was so ready for this. "Let's bring Ilyan home."

I nodded, and practically jumped forward, placing my hand over the mug as I filled it.

I had tried to see it so many times, but I knew this time was different. As the mug filled, as I moved closer to the wall, my magic pulsed and screamed in joy at having found him; I knew I would see. I was going to find him.

"Come home, Ilyan," I whispered, before I threw the

contents of the mug over the wall and the world dipped to black.

Sight hit me like a battering ram. Harder than it had in years. I gasped, sure that I was in fact falling to my knees as the voice I hadn't heard since that night by the Wells of Imdalind filled me.

"He lives."

The words came as the smothering blackness of sight began to flash with white lights. White and black moved in a strobe, the flashes accelerating until everything became a wall of white. The white buzzed in a single high pitched tone before a shout rang in my ears and my sight shifted to an army.

Although I would hesitate to call them an army. They were dressed in rags, covered in blood as they ran. I recognized them at once, the Trpaslíks and Chosen that had fled Edmund's tent city after the dome popped. We had assumed they were captured, killed, or worse. There weren't many, but as I watched them run they began to march, their numbers growing as broken guns and tattered uniforms appeared between them.

"The world is scattered," my own voice began as the army marched forward, their numbers growing, and their tattered uniforms turned into a sleek black emblazoned with an eight pointed star, the top and bottom points looking almost like daggers as they extended beyond the rest. Their guns grew bulkier as they sparked electricity from the tip.

One of the soldiers aimed, firing as he screamed. As lightning shot from the tip of his gun, my sight pulled back, showing me an unfamiliar landscape dotted with fires and battles.

"Before the next rise there will be a shift, catch the

fallen star." The words made little sense as the vision shifted again, back to the army that stretched over Europe as whatever army I was watching blended with another and another.

"Only when unity has been found will an end be in sight." The flashing light came back, this time mixed with a steady beep and a scream that I recognized at once. The Vilỳ.

They swarmed through my sight, chasing something that I could not see as they raced through a white tile hallway toward shards of glass in a frame. They tore through it, only to be ripped apart by the same lightning I had seen in the guns.

Lightning against blood soaked walls.

Lightning shattering glass.

A brown haired girl yelling in panic.

The images moved faster. It took me a second to realize that each image had begun to move in reverse, back to the steadily flashing lights and then to darkness.

"He lives." The voice of the woman, of Earth, said again, the syllables echoing in my head as I saw what I had been haunted by for years. Ilyan and Ovailia in the room with the river. Except this time, the sight didn't end at their fight. It didn't end as Ovailia begged for mercy. It didn't stop until Ovailia stood behind him with a scowl as red spread over Ilyan's chest, as I watched his eyes grow sad, and blood was everywhere.

NO!

I wanted to pull out of the sight. I needed to. I didn't want to see. But I was trapped as I watched him fall, as I watched bits of him paint the wall I now stood before, as I watched Ovailia laugh.

My heart screamed as I saw that alley again, as I saw

her drop him there before running away. My soul was being cleaved in two as everything went dark, and he was only a tangle of limbs. Everything was too broken. I barely saw Ovailia as she walked through a city I had never seen before, as she sat in a diner with a woman with a stupid purple star on her ugly black uniform, as she ran across a broken square in what was clearly Moscow.

I didn't see it. I didn't care.

I screamed as I shoved the sight away. I was still screaming as I opened my eyes to the ground and the warm weight of Wyn's hand on my back. I gulped in air, letting the last of my scream echo against the stone fade away.

"Jos!" Wyn yelled and I gasped, locking everything back up as I focused on my breathing, focused on my tears as they fell and darkened the stone. "Jos, are you okay? No, you're not okay. Why am I even asking?"

Wyn was gentle as she helped me back to sitting, thankfully pointing me away from the wall. Although facing the trickle of water that was once a racing river wasn't the best choice, either. Seeing how wet Wyn was, and how damp the stone was, only told me one thing.

"You saw?"

Wyn nodded, her lips pressed into a tight line. "He's not dead, Jos, he can't be."

My body felt numb as I nodded in agreement. "I want to believe that. But I am really starting to wonder if he is. Even with this, I've never seen anything after his... after... it's like nothing is there."

It burned to admit and I leaned back against the wall and my magic reacted, flaring toward what was splattering the wall above me. I cringed away from the wall, Wyn following me as I crawled toward the river like a child.

"What if it is showing you what happened after, and we

138

just don't know it," Wyn said from behind me and I turned. She sat on the ground, legs folded beneath her as she stared at me, looking nervous.

Wyn looking nervous was never a good sign.

"Those lights," Wyn explained when she tired of our staring match. "It could be a hospital, or a jail. It would explain why you aren't having any true Tŏuhas, and why you can't find him. What if he is unconscious somewhere and there is nothing to show?"

I swallowed, my hope buzzing until one quick thought silenced it.

"What if all those alien believers have him, and are dissecting him or something." Just saying it made me all kinds of ragey, my magic was screaming to attack whoever hurt him. I wasn't the only one, Wyn looked ready to go on a murder-spree.

"I think I like the idea of a hospital better." It made sense; I had a sight with lights like those years ago, long before Ilyan went missing. "If only because there would be less murdering."

"Way to take away all my fun." Wyn stuck out her lower lip, I pushed her away from me, but she came right back.

"Okay, so let's say it is showing me after. Where is an army with lightning guns, who may or may not have a three thousand year immortal under lock and key?" Saying it out loud made it seem impossible. But even I knew that with the world we lived in anything was possible. And there it went again, all of that hope was building again.

"I dunno," Wyn shrugged and looked back to the door we had come from. "But I know someone who might."

"The girl," I turned, letting my magic fly back to the hospital, and the woman in the corner bed who still hadn't woken up. Yes, chances were high that she would know, or would at least be able to point us in the right direction.

"We need to send out some teams. We've been so focused on saving people and keeping the Vilÿs at bay that if someone is after us, we need to know what we are fighting," Wyn said, she was always a better war planner than I was. "We know about a few factions, but I think it's time we stop avoiding them, and start learning about them. See where those that survived Edmund's tents ended up."

"Agreed. Let's keep the council about that. Information. I'll show them Ovailia, and keep it about her. Let's not scare anyone quite yet with armies until I know what I've seen. For all we know those armies are a decade away." I stood, wiping the dust off my jeans as I faced the wall. Thankfully my heart didn't feel like it was going to rip itself out of my chest that time.

Turn to stone maybe...

"I'll be back before the council," I said, still looking at the stone. "Can you and Ry hold everything together until then?"

"Oh, you bet, starting with keeping Thom on babysitting duty. He's good at it." I could hear Wyn's smile in her voice, but I didn't turn. "You going to see him?"

I nodded, "Let me know if the girl wakes up, but otherwise I'll meet up with you in Vienna."

I reached toward the wall, not quite ready to touch it, before I let my magic flare and pulled myself into a Stutter.

CHAPTER 13
JOCLYN

I reappeared only feet from a perfectly made bed, in the center of the room that I had shared with Ilyan when we had been trapped in Prague.

The room looked the same as it had then. Everything was in the same place, the bed made the same way Ilyan had every morning. The only thing that was different was the yellow light of the sun that poured through the window instead of the red glow of Edmund's dome.

I closed my eyes and breathed in, trying to ignore the scent of dust that now lived in the room, and plopped myself down on the bed. I usually tried to be quiet, but today the old springs on the bed were not having it. They squeaked loudly, and I was sure one of the anthropologists that were studying the place looking for more clues about all of us would have heard. Not that they would be able to see anything anyway, we had all come through after those images had been released and either took or sealed anything that would be too incriminating.

There wasn't anything in here that would really qualify for that, but I didn't want them in here anyway.

I rolled over, springs still squeaking and wiggled my way under the covers. I lay in a ball, my head on the pillow that had stopped smelling like him years ago, and closed my eyes.

It took nothing to pull myself into the Tǒuha anymore, although Wyn and I still debated on if I was awake, sleeping, or hallucinating.

I didn't know, and I *really* didn't care.

The warm sun of the French seaside welcomed me and I exhaled, Ilyan's arms wrapping around me as he pulled me into him.

This was utter bliss. I could be the badass Queen every day of the week as long as I found times for these moments. Little moments where everything was perfect and I didn't have to pretend.

"I was hoping you would come back." Ilyan's breath was as hot as the wind as he whispered in my ear, his teeth nipped at me.

"I always come back," I gasped as his teeth moved from my ear to my neck.

"I know..." His tongue flicked against my collar bone and I shivered, pressing myself into him.

I could get lost in him for hours, spend days tasting him, holding him, feeling him.

His hands were chasing a trail down my spine, pressing against the soft flesh as he held me against him.

Gods.

It had been years of me coming here, although I hardly ever asked him for information on where he was anymore. It was clear he, or whatever version of him that my subconscious cooked up, didn't know.

And yes, I was aware I was probably making out with

and ripping the clothes off of a figment of my imagination, but I really didn't care.

"Ilyan," I moaned, his name full of all the agony and longing that I had bottled up as I released it. He chuckled, his hand flattening over the scar on my stomach as he lifted my shirt, tracing circles on my stomach as he kissed a line down my chest.

He was being wonderfully distracting, especially seeing as I did actually have something I wanted to talk to him about.

His teeth pulled at my bra, and I suddenly didn't care about all the things I wanted to talk to him about. They could wait.

"Ilyan..." That time his name was a moan, a gasp, and a plea as I arched my back, practically begging him for more.

"That's not my name," he hissed, his voice low as he moved up to kiss my neck.

I shivered, but that time was for a different reason. His voice had changed, the low rasp of him was the same, but the tone was different. The look in his eyes was different, as though he was afraid.

Fear tickled up my spine, all of that warmth turning to ice. I could have sworn even the sun in the Tȍuha had stopped shining.

"That's not my name?" he said again, although that time it was a question, his eyes dripping with panic.

"Yes, it is." I gripped his shoulders as I pulled away, my fingers pressing into his skin as I watched that face, his face. "That's your name."

"What is? Tell me. Tell me how to find you," his voice shook, his eyes wide as he looked back into me, begging for an answer. The answer I had begged him for for years.

It was him! It had to be. Something had changed, and

now I could find him. I opened my mouth to answer, but at that moment his hand slid from my cheek to my neck, his scarred palm cupping my mark.

For the first time in years, the true force of his magic and our connection flooded me. Electric bolts twisted over my skin, ripping apart my muscles as my back arched. White lights exploded around us as my breathing caught, and I opened my eyes again to him.

But it wasn't the scared, pleading man of a moment before; it was to the Ilyan of my memory. Whatever had happened a moment ago had gone.

"Ilyan?" I touched his face gently, expecting another explosion of power, but there was only that same warm tingle again.

"Yes, mi lasko?" he whispered as he captured my hand and pressed it to his lips. "Is everything okay? You look as though you have seen a dead man."

Talk about the wrong phrasing at the wrong time. I think I might have just been stabbed in the chest.

Which was also the wrong phrasing. I winced, pushing the sight away before it could replay itself.

"Maybe I did." Those few words were all it took for all those tears I had forced away to explode out of me.

Yep, I was crying like a baby, into the shoulder of my ghost mate, in a dream masquerading as a Tŏuha. Real Queenly of me.

"What is it, my lasko. Tell me." He kissed my hand again, his other hand firm on my back as he pressed me against him.

So, I did. I let it all explode out of me like it was a flood. The dam had broken and whatever this version of Ilyan was got all my blubbering, sobbing, over-dramatic explanation of everything that had happened. Of finally seeing more of him in sight. Of the armies, and being attacked, and the blood and everything. The truth exploded out of me as all of the fears and pain and frustrations that I had been bottling up for years finally bubbled to the surface.

And he listened. He listened and he kissed my tears away, and held me close, and didn't say a word until he was sure I was done.

"You know that your sight is not a perfect representation of the future, it is just a guide to what could come," his voice was a whisper, his hand back to rubbing up and down my spine as he chased the last of my tears away. "So where is the guide taking you?"

"I want to find you. I *need* to find you, even if you are dead. But if we are going into war, I can't do that. I have barely been able to do it before now." I had been playing Queen for years, and I might even admit I was good at it. But we hadn't gotten any closer to finding him, Wyn and I hadn't looked in France for ages, and most of my time was spent in meetings or healing people as they were rescued.

"What do you have to do to do that?" His question was simple, and I opened my mouth to answer, and then froze, jaw sagging like a fish as something I think I had known from the very beginning fell into place.

"I need to talk to Ryland."

"You're leaving already?" The disappointment in his voice could break me all on its own.

"I'll be back soon, look for shapes in the clouds until I get back." I kissed him once, my heart aching as I pulled away and back into our room in Prague.

For one breath, I could have sworn the pillow smelled like him.

CHAPTER 14
ILYAN

The skin of my back twisted and burned as it was cut and torn in a line that stretched from the nape of my neck to the arch in my back. The line of fire grew worse as my own blood poured from the acidic gash, the warm fluid pouring over my back, drenching my hair, flooding the floor, filling my mouth as I screamed.

My scream grew louder, desperate to expel the pain, to just pass out, to escape the prison and let death or whatever came after this take me.

But he wouldn't let me.

Because this wasn't real, no matter how real the pain was. It was just a memory trapped in a dream. Even as it began to fade into a burn that criss crossed over my chest in lines.

This pain was familiar, I realized. This was the same as in the hospital, the same as my hand...

Pressure swelled over my chest as the world in my dream swam, everything shifted as my hands flew to the pain in my chest, only to peel away covered in droplets of the brightest red.

I stared at the blood, my confusion swelling as the hollow tone of a hundred voices echoed through the dark around me.

"It is only when she is with you that she will be able to accomplish all that she must..."

The haunted tin of the voices faded out, replaced by the abrasive sound of static as the same image of blood and stone screamed its way back into my mind.

The image flashed bright before the voices returned, the blood-covered stone expanding into a wide cavern. The space was massive, the high ceilings twinkling as multi-colored lights drifted through the dark, dancing over smooth hewn walls and a wide pool of glass. My soul jumped at the imagery, something deep inside of me pulling me toward it, toward the pool, desperate to be swallowed whole.

I didn't move.

I stood still as the pool shimmered, a hundred figures standing along the edge. Dark capes were pulled over them, obscuring face and limbs until they were nothing but grey masses against black stone.

"This child is power." The voices were a song as one man stepped through the wall of monks.

His features were weathered, although he appeared to be no older than the late-20s that I was. His green eyes were on me, staring into me as he continued his advance.

"Power that is strong enough for you," the voices hummed in unison before they began to chant, the same static as before rampaging through my memory.

"For you. For you. For you."

The memory of the wide cave vanished in a swirl of smoke. Although the voices continued, the green-eyed man didn't move. The room around him shifted, leaving him standing in the middle of a room from several centuries before.

Brilliant paintings covered the walls, the murals leaving everything bathed in flowers and trees. The room was a garden, but I had a feeling that was the point, seeing as the massive four poster bed had the same motif. The hand-carved flowers that decorated the wood mirrored in every other piece.

It was beautiful, and I had a feeling it was supposed to be calming. But looking at the anger that had overtaken the man, was smothering it.

I felt only dread.

"For you. For you." The chant continued from somewhere in the distance as the man stepped toward me, his eyes growing harder as he rushed me, hand clenching my face as he shook me.

"You filthy whore! You think you can flirt and I won't notice. You think you can stare and I won't see?" The grip of his hand against my chin increased, dirty nails digging into my skin as I called out in a tiny yelp.

"For you. For you."

"You are mine." He spat, specks of wet littering my face.

"No," a weak feminine voice croaked, the sound rattling from my chest, although I was sure it had not come from me.

It was not from me.

"You are nothing to me. I already have your magic. You give me nothing else." His hand shook me with each word, each syllable ripping my heart apart before he threw me on the bed, his hands clawing at my clothes.

At my dress.

"For me. For me." The chant increased as my heart rate did, my confusion growing as whatever hell I had found myself trapped in moved faster. This was not my memory. This was not my life.

It couldn't be, no matter how real it felt.

I gasped as a hand pressed against my back, the pressure acting like a switch as everything faded right back to that cave. Right back to the man that had thrown me down on the bed. To the man who was beating me.

He stood calmly, no trace of a smile present as the chant continued to drown the air.

Something wasn't right. Nothing about this was right.

"You will love her." The man from the bedroom said calmly as he stepped forward, his green eyes shifting to black as he stared through me. "But you cannot have her."

"You cannot have him!" The same man's voice hissed in my ear as a different memory took hold. The same man, this time haggard and broken as he screamed at Joclyn and I. She stiffened as we clung to each other, her hand clenching against my back as her own anger sparked.

"The length of the royal line was not in the sight," his voice roared as Joclyn stiffened against me, her hands growing warm.

The memory faded back to the cave with a snap, my tension growing as the truth behind the green-eyed man slowly began to unravel. I didn't know who he was, but this pride I felt toward him in this memory was wrong. It was all wrong.

"You will fail." The monotone voices pulled me back into the cave, the tension in me growing. Another flash of the same ornate room as before, the sobs of a woman obscuring everything as I stared into a mirror, stared at that same man as he assaulted me, pulling me away and throwing me onto a bed.

"Do you feel her?" The flat voices of the cloaked people

beside the glass pool spoke over the horrifying image as I lay trapped under this man, an unseen pressure locking me in place. "Do you see her?"

"I do." My own voice pulled me from the horrors in that room as a weight pressed against my chest, pressed into the painful scars in such a way that I wished I could call out.

Wished I could scream.

No sound came, only pain and the smell of smoke and flowers. The combination was familiar as it mixed with a swell of joy so acute I never wanted to let it go.

So I held it closer.

I held her closer.

I held her in my arms, pulling her into me, breathing her in as I placed my cheek against hers.

"Do not be afraid, Mi Lasko," I whispered as everything began to calm. The huskiness of my voice filled with an accent I did not recognize, laced with a language that I did. "I know you have seen everything..."

A flash of the room, of the mirror as the same man plunged a fist onto my back. The impact blossomed down my spine as the image evaporated, the pressure of Joclyn against me never leaving.

"I know you are scared, but do not be..." I continued in a hushed whisper, the words whispering through the tangles of Joclyn's hair. "Know that I am here to protect you, to save you, and to love you."

The mirror again, the room reflected back to me as the image shifted, the mirror moving closer as I stepped toward it, everything burning, everything numb. The numbness left as the mirror did, the panic of the room seeping into the calm memory of the cave.

"Even if you will never love me, I will still be here, right by your side."

I pulled her to face me, my touch gentle as I cupped her chin, her dark curls framing her face in a long tousled mess as she looked to me, the bright silver of her eyes glimmering.

"You're beautiful." I could barely get the words out, even in the dream my heart was so full it was restricting my breathing.

I leaned toward her, needing to feel her, needing to taste her lips against mine. I could feel the hunger, feel the need multiplying. But instead of pressing my lips to hers, I turned, pulling her hair back and gently kissing the raised mark I had seen before, the red brand hidden behind her ear.

A jolt of electricity moved through my body, the feeling the same that I had felt in the hospital bed, the same as I had felt so many times before. This was the moment I knew...

"I love you, Joclyn." The ghost of my voice echoed as I held her, as I lost myself against her.

My heart beat louder as her name cemented in place, no more just the whispers that Kaye had heard while I slept.

This was her.

This was the girl that I longed for.

This was my Joclyn.

"I love you, my Joclyn," My voice came as the memory shifted, Joclyn now laying in my arms, her shirt covered in blood, her face smeared with it.

She smiled at the words, her blood drenched fingers soft against my face, "I love you, my..."

"You need to run!" A scream broke through the memory, turning her last moments into smoke as a new panic cut through me, the scream pulling past memory and plunging me back into reality.

"I'll be fine," Joclyn whispered in my mind, her voice echoing in my head as I saw her again, wearing the same blood soaked clothes as she sat in a cave, hand over her stomach.

"Run!" The shout shattered my dreams, the single word erupting as the girl in the mirror returned, her mouth open in a scream before she punched the glass, shattering it.

The tinkling of broken glass rang loud, mixing with the sound of rubber shoes against linoleum as more yells broke through my memory.

"Now, Kaye." A voice, a woman, yelled. "He has been in a coma for years. You are wasting our time."

I felt a hand on my shoulder, the rough touch different from my memories. It shook me once before it was gone, replaced by footsteps that pounded in my skull. Blood spread over the wall of rock, before it faded to black, before whatever memory-driven hell I had been trapped in faded and the sounds of footsteps melted into the sound of screams.

The sound of guns.

The bangs pressed against my skull like a hammer, they shook my bones as a flood of pain swelled over me and the hard hospital mattress and beeping of monitors returned.

"Run!"

The shout came from the direction of the hall outside of my room, the sound mixing with screams and sounds of retreat.

Terror slapped me so hard that I gasped in air, only to find the passage blocked. Everything was blocked. My mouth was open in a silent scream as something snaked down my throat. My eyes snapped open to the pitch black, eyelashes fluttering against dark fabric.

"Kill it! Stop it!"

The beeping increased with my panic and I clutched at my face, at the heavy fabric covering my eyes, at the stubble that was all that remained of my hair. With shaking fingers, I traced the lines of my face to my mouth and the massive contraption that was attached there.

Muffled sounds of panic exploded from me as I clawed at the tape and pieces of plastic that held the thing in place. Everything shook in my desperation to escape whatever had been done to me, fear and panic bringing only a moment of hesitation before I pulled the tube from my throat.

My chest screamed in pain, my throat burning in agony as I yanked, every inch of the massive tube clearly felt as I removed it.

Rough ridges scraped over soft tissue, a scratchy scream breaking free as the tube did, leaving my throat sore and gasping. Bile poured from me as I ripped the heavy cloth from my eyes, needing to see, only to be blinded.

"Give me that gun!"

Overhead lights flickered in my skull as I looked around in a panic, trying to find the door - to focus on anything. I slammed my hands onto my head, palms wide over the uneven remains of my hair as I attempted to focus past the blur.

"Get back, Kaye!" Someone yelled, the shouts rattling in my skull as multiple shots of a gun bounced off tile and linoleum as it echoed in the hollow hospital.

What horror had I awoken in? Something was terribly wrong.

I needed to move.

I needed to move now.

Rushing to exit the bed, I fell over the railings, the lack of restraints making the motion quick and painful as I collided with the floor. An agonizing pain blossomed in my hand as blood began to cover it, the red fluid pooling over my skin at the unceremonial removal of an IV.

Breathing tubes and an IV. I had no idea what was done to me, what had happened, but the absence of my restraints made sense.

You don't restrain what can't move.

I wrapped a napkin around my hand, yanking at the tiny white pads that covered my chests until the never ending beeping shifted to a high pitch moan. More cables, more tubes. I pulled them all, nose and throat burning as yet another tube was unceremoniously removed.

I would have screamed, would have yelled, but I grit my teeth, desperate to keep the sound inside, and to keep myself hidden from whatever nightmare was happening just outside my door. As the screams began to fade, yet another gunshot rang against the linoleum, only to be replaced by a sound more confusing and more frightening than the tormented dreams I had just woken from.

A snarl.

A gnashing of teeth.

A flap of wings.

The Chrlič.

They were in the hospital. Those things that make people explode, they were here.

I could hear them scratch and screech and scream. The sound cut into me, the scars on my chest heating as that same burn buzzed under my skin.

Trying to get out.

I pushed it away, the electricity adding to the fear that just hearing them was igniting. The more I heard them, however, the more the heat grew. The heat ignited a power and confidence deep inside me, that before the dream, before holding Joclyn in my arms, before watching her die- I never would have thought to be mine.

Staring at my hands as they burned, I tried to stand, knowing that I had to do something.

Knowing that I could.

My knuckles shone white as I gripped the bed rail, legs shaking as I pulled myself to stand. Shaking, dressed only in a hospital gown, I faced the door, eyes wild as I waited.

Screaming rang in the halls, another bang of a gun followed by the squeak of shoes as the door swung open. The sounds of screams and wings grew louder before it slammed shut, leaving the room in muffled silence as I stood facing the door and the back of the woman the door had spit out.

She stood with a knife in her hand, the weapon awkward against her leg as she waited, her long dark hair swinging down her back.

My heart jump-started, screaming that it was Joclyn, that it was her. Any hope was dashed as she turned, brown eyes widening amongst a wall of freckles as she saw me standing there, shock lining her face.

"Jan! You're alive!"

It took me a minute to recognize her. I had only known her for minutes after all. Even with such a small amount of time, it was obvious that something had changed. Was she taller? Were her freckles darker?

I hadn't remembered those.

I wasn't sure.

"Kaye," I asked with the same accent from my dream, my voice scratchy from the harsh removal of what I now saw as an intubation tube. "What happened? What is going on?"

"We need to go," she continued without waiting for any

response or offering any explanation as to what had happened to me.

"Where?"

"Not here." Her voice was stronger than I remember, the giggly girl hidden away behind the blood that covered her fingers, smudges trailing behind her cheek as she moved her hair out of the way. "Anywhere but here."

My heart jumped at the bright color, at the mirror of Joclyn bleeding in my arms. I stared at her, waiting for more memories to come, waiting for more of an explanation. There was nothing but gunshots.

Bang.

Bang.

Silence.

The last gunshot lingered in the halls, filling the void of screams and steps that had rampaged for the last few minutes. Everything was tense as I waited for them to return, every weak muscle throbbing painfully. There was nothing.

Nothing but the sound of Kaye's ragged breathing as she turned back toward the door, the look in her eyes sending my pulse skyrocketing as the heat in my soul began to boil. The silence dragged on, only to be stabbed with a high pitched screech as a tiny dark figure slammed into the fogged glass of the door.

Kaye backed away from the door as she gripped the knife, stepping before me with an obvious intent of protection.

She should not be protecting me, I should save her. Yet, I could only stare at the door, stare at the glass as the same dark figure hovered there, hitting its body against the pane until it cracked.

The pane split from top to bottom, cracking like lightning over the surface. With each hit the cracks spread further, long electric fingers stretching to each corner.

"No," she gasped, moving the knife before her. The tiny thing looked ineffective as she began to shake. "No. No."

The rhythmic bang ended as a high pitch scrape smothered the silence. A shadow of a single claw dragged down the glass. It sounded like nails on a chalkboard as it chipped apart the pane, one piece after another falling to the ground.

Slow.

Deliberate.

As if the monster knew this game.

"Kaye," I gasped, the raspiness of my voice making it almost unrecognizable.

I motioned her toward me, knowing that I could protect her from the flying demon, although I didn't fully understand how. Foolish, really. I could barely stand, and unless there was a gun hidden under my bed, the knife that Kaye was struggling to hold was our only weapon.

Together we jumped as the thing smacked against the glass again, the screeches multiplying.

The Chrlič was no longer alone. More dark shapes began to join the first, each addition twisting up my spine.

"Kaye," I hissed again, but this time she listened, knife still held before her as she rushed to my side.

The hospital bed was between us and the door as though it would somehow protect us from the creatures that were moments away from breaking in.

"Don't let them bite you," Kaye said through streaks of angry tears that were staining her face.

We jerked as the things rammed into the glass, more mud brown claws beginning to work their way through. The air rained with the pops of cracking glass, each break snapping through me in a flare of electricity. Power ran over my skin, twisting in my bones as a twisted sphinx face peered at us through a quickly widening opening. Its fangs dripped with venom as it screamed at us, blood-red eyes looking between us. Calculating who to bite first.

Electric sparks flew over my skin, a vivid memory of the same monsters, the same creatures bursting through my mind. Thousands of them raining over us, flooding through the streets of an ancient city. Destroying everyone in their path.

Prague.

My home.

The memory left as the Chrlič screamed again, the heat rumbling through every muscle as its arms began to pull itself through.

"Don't let them bite you," Kaye said again, repeating the instructions to herself. "Don't let..."

The glass exploded in hundreds of shards, the pieces scattering over linoleum as the tiny monsters burst through, their brown skin streaked with the blood of those they had already killed.

Kaye screamed as they did, the sound echoing in my head as she swung the knife wide, sending two of them tumbling into the wall.

The heat in my body erupted, my yell joining the others as the heat pulsed. Trying to break free.

"No!" Kaye screamed, the knife continuing to swing as more of the things pushed through the shattered opening in the door, rushing right toward us in a swarm.

One of the flying bats dodged Kaye's incessant swings, claws and fangs bared as it soared right to me.

I reached up to stop it, to grab it, to do something. Anything.

Instead, the electric heat exploded.

A ripple of red and yellow soared from my fingers, exploding through the room like the sound of a gun. The Chrlič's calls echoed before two of them fell, their bodies limp as I destroyed them.

As whatever was inside of me destroyed them.

Kaye let out a soft scream as she fell to the ground, looking at me with a combination of fear and shock as she shuffled underneath the hospital bed.

It was a look I returned, our eyes meeting for just a moment before I turned back to the creatures, everything around me exploding as the heat continued to pop and swell.

Dressers exploded. Creatures were thrown away from me by an invisible hand, only to slam into walls and fall to the ground in a lifeless heap.

And the light, the light continued to pour from me.

Just like in those images.

I wasn't sure what was happening, but the creatures did. Their eyes had grown maniacal from the first spark, their screams increasing as a new danger I hadn't expected began to brew.

They knew what this was and they weren't scared of it.

They were ready for it.

And they weren't going to hold back.

Ribbons of color erupted in the air as three more of the creatures fell to the ground with a soft thud. Five more moved to take their place, their bodies soaring fast as claws and teeth gnashed in preparation.

I moved my hand, still trying to understand what made the power come or how to control it, when it died.

"No! Nonononon!" I stepped back as the creatures flew at

me faster, my assumed success now promising doom before a tiny moment sparked in my heart.

A memory so faded it was more emotion than moment.

Joclyn and I, fighting the same creatures, light erupting around us as one after another they fell. As she laughed at the game. As she slid her hand into mine.

The power exploded at the rush of emotion, more than a dozen falling to the ground as a ripple of light moved away from me. It slammed into the walls, cracking plaster and sending portraits tumbling to the ground.

"Vilÿ," I gasped, the memory sparking the word deep inside of me.

I knew them.

I had fought them.

More of the things burst through the broken glass, called to us by our screams and the screams of the others. They soared around me in a spiral, moving closer in their preparation to end me. I heard Kaye scream in fear, but the sound was faded against wings, against my shouts, against the explosion that burst from me.

Light and power surged from me as I tried to control it, it wasn't enough. Wings brushed against me, claws pulling at my skin and clothing. I grabbed the beast closest to me and threw it away from me. Red sparks flew behind it, the bright pops of light that erupted from my fingers as the heat that ran through me dissipated.

They kept coming, so fast and so many that they were little more than a wall of grey, blocking out the light and any hope that we had. I tried to fight them, tried to let the explosions out.

As I tried to save us both.

My fight pulled in memory as the same dark alley swam before me, lines of the monsters heading right for me.

Instead of a spark of light, however, instead of releasing the power that was inside of me, there was only a single word.

"*Zdechnout.*"

My head rattled as I dropped to the ground, hands overhead as I waited for the bite to come, amazed it hadn't yet.

"*Zdechnout*" a woman spoke from somewhere in my memory, this time louder, the snap of a voice I had heard before following right behind.

It was that same man, that green-eyed monster who had beaten the woman in my dreams. He looked right at me as my memory approached him. The sarcastic voice of the woman he had mauled, slapping at my nerves, "*One down, ten million to go.*"

Claws pulled me from the moment as they ripped at my hair, my hands moving fast as I continued to swat the little monsters away while stubbornly refusing to accept that this could be the end.

"*Zdechnout*" The word came again, practically screaming in my head as the memory I saw before repeated itself, a Vilỳ hitting the ground like a lead weight at the sound.

It didn't make sense. But nothing did, not light from my hands, not little monsters that would rip you apart.

So I yelled. I screamed.

"Zdechnout!"

The word exploded out of me as the claws left, the gnashing stopped, and dozens of little thuds hit the ground around me.

I uncurled from my protective position as Kaye did, the two of us sitting on the floor, looking around at the bodies that now surrounded us, the things twisted as if they had never had life in them at all.

As if that one word had sucked it all out of them.

CHAPTER 15
ILYAN

The smell of blood was everywhere.

It hung in the air in waves of acid and salt as I sat amongst the bodies, the limp things rolling off me as I stood. Arms and wings of the tiny creatures moved as though possessed before they hit the floor with a lifeless 'thunk', joining the piles of the others.

They were everywhere. Hundreds of them. They covered the floor, they hung from the television and the hard plastic chairs, they sagged over the rails of the hospital bed that Kaye lay under.

Her eyes were wide as she stared at me, the brown flooded with fear.

"Are you okay?" I asked with that same heavy accent I had in my dream.

She breathed heavier, letting out several soft screams as she scuttled out from under the bed, ripping off her jacket as she jumped to stand.

"Kaye," I said in an attempt to get her attention, but she continued to pour over her body, ripping off shoes and jeans as she stripped.

"Katenka," I said again, using her full name as I rushed toward her, stepping on a Vilỳ in my attempt to get to her.

She still did not turn.

"Kaye!" I yelled grabbing her forearms as she finished removing her shirt, the fabric wadded in her fist.

Her focus shifted back to me, eyes wide in panic as she stared at me. She stood in only her underwear, chest heaving behind a bright red bra.

I didn't look away from her eyes, I forced myself to maintain her focus, to breathe slowly so as to help calm her down.

But I still saw.

I saw what I had seen before but in the panic hadn't understood.

Her hair was longer, her face was thinner, her body matured.

She was older.

Older than the girl who had giggled in hiding on the side of my bed.

I could feel my own panic growing, but I pushed it away.

"What happened?" I demanded, my accent thick under the power of my voice.

Angry tears welled behind Kaye's eyes as she attempted to jerk away from my hold, the panic that momentarily ebbed flooding right back.

"I have to check..." she growled, continuing to push me away. "I have to know if I was bitten."

"You would feel it if you were. It would burn like fire in your veins. You would already be screaming."

The words were confident, self-assured, and I knew that they were true.

It was only then that Kaye looked at me. The fear of a

bite left, the panic of what had just happened subsided and she froze under my hands.

"I need you to answer me, Kaye. What happened?"

"You're alive," she panted, taking a step closer as though she was going to rush into my arms. Luckily, she thought better of it.

"Yes." I kept my voice calm even if inside I was panicking as much as she was. "But I need to know what happened Kaye. What happened to me? What is going on?"

"You're ..." Her awe vanished in a snap, her focus twisting from me to the Vilỳ, and back again. "What happened?"

I wanted to laugh at the absurdity of it all. Instead, I let my hands drop from her arms in the hope that she had calmed enough to at least talk to me.

"That would be what I need to know..." I hunched my back so I could look her in the eye. It was only now, as I stood beside her, that I realized how tall I must be.

Joclyn only came to my chest. Right to my heart. Kaye stood to my shoulder.

"Last I remember we were discussing how to track down Joclyn," I continued, "Last I knew they showed her picture on the television..."

"You were in a coma," Kaye's deadpan voice smacked against me, sucking the wind out of my chest.

"A coma?" The response was as unexpected as the war zone I had woken up in.

"All of that..." She hesitated, looking away in obvious agitation. "The pictures. That was more than three years ago."

"Three years?"

She stepped away from me then, careful not to trod on the things with her bare feet as she retrieved her pants.

I knew how this scene would go. I would roar in shock over the time and she would retell a story of woe and triumph.

None of that happened. I just stood, staring at the wilted bodies and twisted tubes that I had pulled from myself. Tubes that had kept me alive.

"They thought you were brain dead." She shook her head as she threw a shirt over her shoulders, the threadbare shift stained with blood and dirt. "They kept you alive, kept you here..."

She kept fading in and out, everything she said was more like a half-thought than information I could use to piece together the last three years that I had missed. It was more than that, I realized. It was more than the uncertainty. It was the discomfort. It was protection.

"What did they do to me?"

She froze in place, a sock and shoe dangling from her fingers as she uncoiled to face me, her jaw tight as she looked right into me.

"They tried to figure out what you are, Jan."

What. Not who. It seemed fitting somehow.

"What did they do, Kaye?" My voice was harder, the demand for information clear.

Kaye looked away, turning back to the bodies as though determined to look anywhere else.

"They still think you are the man from the photo," she kicked one of the Vilỳ, it's corpse flopping over with limbs and wings twisting end over end. "They know you were there. They want to figure out what you can do. They aren't wrong though, are they? About who you are. About what you can do."

Eyes wide, she faced me head on, standing half-dressed amongst the corpses. She looked ready to go back into battle, even as scared as she was. Her jaw tightened as she waited for a response, determined to get it.

"You know they aren't." I refused to look away from her, I didn't think I needed to say anything more after what happened. "Will you tell them?"

Her eyes narrowed at my question, her focus floating back to the garden of corpses.

"What did you tell them, Kaye?"

She shook her head, her lips pulling into a tight line before she finally turned to me.

"I told them nothing and that will not be changing. The SSU doesn't know I exist and I plan to keep it that way. I'm not registered and that means death. But now that you are awake, and now that you can do..." she hesitated, gesturing around her as she struggled to find the right word. "What did you do, Jan?"

"That's not my name," I bristled, a single brow raised in question. I said nothing, I had nothing to replace it with. I still didn't know who I really was. Not entirely.

"It doesn't matter what your name is. I'll call you what-ever you want," she snapped as she pulled pants and socks back on. "All that matters is getting out of here. Can you do that again?"

We faced off, the air was heavy with the question, my body heavy with the thick implication of it.

"I don't know." It wasn't a lie. The heat was gone, and I didn't know how to bring it back. I had thought of Joclyn before, but that didn't seem to be working now.

"We need to get out of here," Kaye said as she slipped her shoes back on, stepping over carcasses as she retrieved her knife. "Can you get me out of here?"

"I'm not sure." I lifted my hands, trying to will the heat

into existence, pulling every memory of Joclyn I had to the front of my mind. My fingers felt numb. Clearly I wasn't doing it right.

I tried again, grunting when the silence exploded with a bang.

"Did you do that?" Kaye hissed, although both of us were staring at the door, and the hallway through the broken glass where the blast had come from.

Another bang echoed through the hospital from somewhere in the distance, the loud thud followed by a stampede of footfalls.

"I don't think I did."

"They are here," she whispered as she began to look around, desperate for somewhere to hide.

"Who is here?" I rushed toward her, trying to pull her focus, but she didn't stop her search, although I was sure she already knew it was hopeless.

"The Cleaners," she gasped as if that made sense to me. "The state police."

The clarification didn't change much for me, but it didn't need to. The look in her eyes told me everything.

"Can we hide?" I asked, my eyes joining her in her search.

"I can," she spat, the words a growl "I don't exist to them. You are supposed to be brain dead... and this..." she gestured around us, the panic in her growing. "What did you do?"

"I used my magic."

I was aware of the absurdity of the word. It grated on me, it twisted in my stomach. Not because I didn't believe it, but because I knew that she wouldn't.

"Excuse me?" She froze in place, all thought of

searching for a weapon gone as she stared at me. "I'm going to pretend that made any kind of sense..."

"I used my magic, Kaye," I interrupted her, the same heat rising to consume me as I walked toward the corner of the room, pulling the computer table toward me.

The metal feet scraped loudly against the linoleum, the sound sure to lead them right to us.

"No, Jan," she stuttered, at a loss for words. "That's not possible. You may think that... but magic isn't real."

"But Aliens are?" I didn't even try to hide the smile on my face. "You have seen the images. You saw the one... of The Oheň, of Joclyn. What did you think it was?"

Her jaw hinged in shock, but I just smiled, shoving the computer off of the table with such noise that if they hadn't tracked us yet, they had now.

"Look, you don't exist and I am supposed to be dead, right?" She only nodded in response. "I can fix one of those things, but we don't have time for this. We can argue the reality of magic and aliens later. You need to hide."

"How do you suggest..."

She didn't get to finish before I lifted my hand above my head, closing my eyes as I brought the moment of Joclyn to mind. The touch of my lips as I kissed her mark. That time it worked. That same electric buzz flooded from me as the ceiling tile shifted, revealing a large open cavern.

"The ceiling will be reinforced along the walls and near the televisions. Stay along those lines and you won't fall through."

I could tell she wanted to fight me on it. I could see the disgust mixing with fear for one split second, but it vanished as the sound of footsteps began echoing toward us, the clear voices of military orders echoing right behind.

With one last look toward the door, she rushed toward the desk, only giving me a single sidelong glance before she was gone, lifting herself up into the rafters.

The ceiling tile slid back into place as I dragged the desk toward the bed, collapsing on the ground between them.

The floor began to shake as the footsteps grew louder, the bodies of the dozens of Vilỳ I was surrounded by shaking and flopping around at the vibration. I lay still, the buzzing of my magic growing as the sound of their stampede did.

I restrained it. As much as it wanted to explode, I did not know what would happen if it did. I did not know if I could control it or how long it would last. Even then, I now had a reason to wait. I needed to get Kaye out of here.

I needed to know what 'here' was before I tried to blast my way out of it. In the meantime, I could piece together the puzzle that was my life.

I slumped against the bed just as the door opened with a bang, the rhythmic sound of combat boots coming to a quick and sudden stop as the expletives began.

Their shock was quickly followed by fear, many rushing to get someone as a few ventured further into the room, their heavy footfalls rippling through me in a countdown to an inevitable end.

To me.

To them.

I looked up to the first soldier as he saw me, the man shrouded in heavy riot gear, a smear of yellow paint on his chest.

The Cleaners.

I didn't know what they were, but judging by the anger in his eyes, he was expecting fear.

Forcing my eyes wide as I put all the panic into my face that I could, I reached toward him, letting my hand freely shake as I locked the tiny sparks of magic inside.

"You have to help me," I said clearly in Czech before I collapsed to the ground in a heap, very much alive.

CHAPTER 16
WYN

"Hit me!"

"Those aren't words a wife usually says to their mate, but okay!" Thom's laugh echoed through the small room that we had cleared for sparring as he sent an attack towards me, the ribbon of light giving away both his position and his intent.

The fool!

Once again, he was not aiming to kill. He always went too easy on me.

I rolled my eyes and countered his attack, sending his magic to the ground and mine right into his chest. It hit him with a bang and he soared right back into the stone wall. Luckily, I was ready and caught him before he slammed into the stone.

That would have hurt.

Okay, so maybe I was as soft on him as he was on me. Something to work on, but not yet. First, I had some celebrating to do.

"I win!" I yelled over to him before taking off into the

sky and landing right before him. He pushed himself back to standing and straightened his leather jacket.

"You win? Nah, technically I'm still strong enough to fight," he let his magic flare, the golden light casting mesmerizing shadows over his face that made him look all grungy. Mix that with his dreads and a leather jacket and he was the bad biker boy that fathers were scared of. Gods, he was hot. So hot he was sending all that fire in my blood into a boil.

"Why, because I saved you?" I couldn't help it, I was hitting on him. Swaying my hips as I stepped closer and leaned in. I was well aware that my low cut shirt was going to drive him wild.

"Yes," he choked out as the magic in his other hand flared. More shadows. More hotness. "Mercy will get you killed."

"Mercy." I rolled my eyes. "Don't flatter yourself. I saved your ass for purely selfish reasons."

He looked confused for half a second before I shoved him against the wall, ignoring the sparking magic in his hands as I pressed myself against him and lifted myself on my tip toes. He foolishly tried to say something before I kissed him, my lips pressing to his as I gripped his hips and brought myself as close to him as I possibly could.

It wasn't close enough. I needed more. I needed all of him.

His lips devoured me as he groaned, as his hands moved down my spine to lift my shirt and begin their trek up my skin. I followed suit, palms flat against his back as I lifted his shirt.

He moaned as I pulled away, those blue eyes nearly golden as he tried to kiss me again and I dodged.

"You are no good to me if your back is broken," I teased,

giving him the tiniest kiss before I pulled away.

"You say that like I am only good for--" I slammed my hips into his at that moment, teasing him. Toying with him.

He loved it just as much as I did, judging by the pressure that was growing against me. I gripped his hips, letting my fists clench around the waistband of his jeans.

"I didn't say you were only good for that. I said I *want* that. NOW." My magic surged through the jeans as I pulled, fabric burning in two as I ripped his pants from his body.

"That's better." I kissed him again, his hands everywhere as he pressed me against his boxer shorts, as our magic surged between us, flaring and mixing a wonderful elixir.

"I swear to God, Wyn, if you hurt my jacket..."

"Then take it off," I helped him out of his leather jacket just as I turned my pants to ash. The smell of smoke was everywhere as I looked at him, his eyes bright as I smirked.

"Better?" I asked and he gripped me, lips tracing hungry lines over my skin only to pause as he stripped my shirt, and then his.

"Maybe I'll let you win more often," he growled in my ear, nipping at my earlobe right as his fingers hooked on the lacy band of my red lace underwear. I hadn't exactly had this moment in mind, but I was glad I had worn them.

God, I was going to explode. I needed him everywhere, I needed...

"What in the world?!" We both froze as light filled the training hall, the door having opened in silence to the two of us, standing in our underwear. Making out.

Okay, more like dry humping, but who's really keeping score.

"Holy Fu--" Thom grabbed his jacket before I could

finish and threw it over my shoulders. He was so chivalrous, trying to cover me from the horrified expressions on the three Chosen that stood there. My stomach spun at the awkwardness of it, but I just laughed, the sound the only thing in the hall before Thom began to sputter, clearly trying to make excuses and failing.

The three Chosen knew full well what they had walked in on.

Thom and I had been walked in on before, after all, and he had reacted the same way when it was Rosy.

Pure terror.

The poor Chosen looked as horrified as Thom did. They looked between Thom and I as they recognized who they had just walked in on, and promptly looked as if they were going to throw up all over everything.

"Well, I'm glad we are still wearing our underwear," I mused, throwing Thom's jacket over my shoulder like I was some kind of swimsuit model. "Come on, Thom, we have unfinished business."

Thom swore and mumbled something as he grabbed the jacket from me, wrapping it around his waist in an attempt to hide his excitement as I strutted out of the hall, and into what I had assumed to be the empty stone corridor.

I had instant regret.

I had walked us right into a wall of Chosen waiting to come in for an advanced sparring class. They all turned at our arrival, a myriad of emotions swimming on their faces as they realized who we were, and what we were wearing.

Yep, there was no way we were going to live this down.

"Wyn, you owe me."

A laugh couldn't even disguise my horror that time. Yes, I owed him big.

CHAPTER 17
RYLAND

Explosions rattled the floor and walls before I even turned into the long hall that housed her bedroom. With every step the explosions grew, and with every step my frustration rose to match. I picked up my pace as the floors shifted, rushing past Karl, who lived in the room next to hers. The frazzled old man was peering out of a crack in his door like a gossiping old woman, except his hanging jowls and bulldog eyes looked like he was ready for a battle rather than a juicy bit of news.

"You have got to control that girl," he growled in Russian, a language I was still trying to master.

"Yes, thank you," I sighed in return, letting my magic flare and slam his own door right in his face.

The older man howled angrily, a string of what I was sure was profanity filtering past the heavy slab of wood.

I didn't look back, I didn't even care, I just rushed forward and let my magic throw her door open with a loud bang. The girl inside turned toward me from where she lay face down on her bed, limbs dangling over the edge.

"What are you doing?" I yelled, slamming the door behind me and braced myself to enter the disaster zone.

The only disaster, however, was Míra. The room was clean.

Not one of her knick-knacks and treasures were out of place. They lay in their places on her dresser, perfectly arranged. The drawers were closed, clothes in place. Even the rug was in one piece.

"Am I in the right room?" I asked in bewilderment, turning in place as I searched for something, anything that she had destroyed.

But she was it. The mess in question groaned heavily at my confusion, the sound choked by the out of control emotions and the mattress she was currently facedown on.

"Yes, Ry." Her answer was just as muffled as her sobs.

"Sure about that? Because I clearly heard explosions..."

Without a word she lifted her hand above her head, turning her shoulder awkwardly as a burst of magic exploded from her palm. With the loud bang of a cannon, fireworks filled the air in a barrage of red and yellow. As the smoke from the explosion began to dissipate a soft scream hissed into the air. It was a nice addition and complicated magic. I wasn't in the mood to be impressed, however.

"I didn't want to clean up the mess," she admitted, flopping over on her bed dramatically, arms spread wide. She glanced through the long strands of hair that fell over her face to stare blankly at the skylight that was carved into her ceiling. "I don't want to do anything."

"Except be overdramatic. Are you going to tell me the world is going to end soon?" She glared at me, but I only laughed. The whole situation was more than ridiculous. I was suddenly very glad that I had never been a teenage girl.

"So what if I am," she snapped, sitting up and looking at me disastrously.

The heavy emotion was clear in her eyes, the dangerous look a warning that her emotions were teetering right on the edge. This time, however, I didn't heed the warning. I couldn't, not with the way her long hair tangled over her face and her crazed eyes stared at me like she was some kind of wild thing. The image was too ridiculous. If I had more than a silly flip phone I would have taken a picture.

"This isn't funny," she roared, her magic sparked as she caught sight of my smile.

"Míra," I began, careful to wipe the smile from my face as I came to sit down next to her.

I would like to say she made room for me, but she more just curled into a ball of teenage angst, wrapping her hands around her legs from where she sat in the middle of her oversized bed.

"Tell me." My voice was soft, and even though I knew she heard me, she didn't respond right away. She just stayed curled in a ball, her bright green eyes never leaving mine.

"Tell me," I prompted again.

"I am bigger than what he did to me," she finally began, her voice shaking as she forced the words past the wall of stone she had built to keep herself safe. "I am bigger than what he infected me with."

She sighed again, her voice shaking more and more as the emotion she was hiding came tumbling out. I listened carefully, nodding with each affirmation, never looking away from her. Waiting for her to finish it.

"I am stronger than I think," her voice broke that time and I nodded once in acceptance, holding my arms open in support.

Míra stared at me for a moment, her eyes wide as she silenced the voices in her head, before she crawled over and curled into me the same way she had for the last few years.

"I don't see how that matters, Ryland," she said quietly, holding onto me tighter. "I just want to go to council..."

"Did you hear him?" I interrupted, pulling her away just enough that I could look at her.

She hesitated, eyes wide as she pressed her lips together into a tight line. She didn't give me any more of an answer than that.

"Then it matters," I said, pulling her back to me.

"He said I was smart enough to go, that I was better than them all..." I tensed at her admission, my own memory filling in the gaps of what she was telling me.

"And that you were stronger than them," I continued for her. She nodded once, her fingers gripping my t-shirt. "And that you could end us all."

Her nod turned into a tremor of fear that shook through both of us as she clung to me in an attempt to escape it all.

"Is that why you ran away?" I asked, even though I already knew the answer.

I knew it because I had lived it my entire life. I had been told all of those things. I had been manipulated into something bigger, until I was torn down into something worse. The only way I could escape it was to run.

The only difference here was that Edmund had infected her with his magic so as to control her. I had never had a Štít of his magic in my chest, and when the Soul's Blade was removed and his soul destroyed, his voice left my mind. When Edmund died, the magic that he had placed in her infected her, filling her with the same demons I had fought.

"I didn't want to hurt you all," she said, her voice

broken by threatening tears. "I don't want to hurt anyone anymore."

"I know," I said, trying to smooth the tangles of her hair for a moment before I gave up. "How do you brush this?"

"Same way as you do," she said with a chuckle, the spell seemingly broken, even though she didn't move from my side. "With a comb."

"Must be some big comb."

Chuckling at the ridiculousness, she pulled away, folding her legs under her as she turned to face me with a wide grin.

"Tell me," I prompted, although this time the request was met with a shy smile instead of a scowl.

"I am bigger than what he did to me. I am stronger than I think. I am braver than he ever was. And..." she paused, her face twisting up as she thought through the list of affirmations we had built, "I am in charge of my mind."

"I like that combination. Ready for mine?" She nodded at my question and I hesitated.

While I knew it went both ways, there were times that sharing these deep insights, especially with her, made me feel too raw.

I still hadn't forgotten how my magic had reacted to hers on that first day.

"I am in control of my mind. I am worthy of my magic. I am stronger than my past."

She nodded once, "I like those ones too. I would say you need to add 'I am sexy enough for my fan club'."

I couldn't stop the groan. She really needed to stop hanging out with Wyn so much, and judging by the stretch of a smile that now covered her face, she knew it.

"That's enough of that, kid," I said, shaking her

shoulder as I stood from the bed, already making a beeline for the door.

"Off to the fan club?" she asked, taking the prod one step deeper.

I turned to her with a forced chuckle, fixing her with a look that was half humor and half irritation. She saw right through it and smiled broadly.

"Off to follow my Queen's orders. You should do the same." I fixed her with a look and she groaned, throwing herself back on the bed in full dramatic flair. "Training awaits you. And school. Off to the world of the Chosen you go!"

"Do I have to?" She was in full whine now.

"You gotta leave the big baddies to the adults sometimes. Being around kids your age is a good thing." I was really getting good at this adult thing.

"I'm only five years younger than you, Ry."

"Still a kid. Still need school."

Míra groaned and threw herself back on the bed again.

"This is the worst."

"Goodbye, Míra."

"At least tell me what happens at council," she pleaded, not even sitting up to face me.

"As much as I can," it was the answer I always gave her, and the one she hated the most considering she knew what it meant.

Closed door councils. Closed door conversations. She wasn't getting a peep from me, although knowing her she would find out other ways to get the intel she wanted. She always did.

"Whatever," she said after me, the angst seeping from under the door as I closed it.

CHAPTER 18
RYLAND

My bones ached with the chill from the rain, my skin burning with each drop of the cold water that hit against my skin. The tiny droplets soaked into the jeans, beating against my already soaked back and dripping from the ends of my now sagging curls.

It was a miserable feeling, but it fit the miserable city that spread before me. Charred remains of houses dotted the landscape, even more burning in the distance. The fires sparked against the horizon as though the stars had fallen from the sky. It was beautiful, and somehow it made the night seem safer, as if the beacons would keep the Vilÿ away. Perhaps that was why the fires were left to burn, and not just because there was no one left to fight them.

Screams echoed through alleys a few blocks over and my muscles tensed, but I didn't move. I stood on the rooftop of the safe house where council was to be held, watching the city burn, watching the world burn, and letting the rain wash it all away.

With a sigh, I closed my eyes to the sky, toward the cold rain that fell onto my face, and tried to block out the sounds of the screams. Reminding myself that I wasn't on duty; that I couldn't save everyone.

"I had a feeling I would find you up here." Joclyn's voice was almost a whisper from behind me, her emotions pulled to the tension of a single thread.

"Have you come to join me in my shower?" I tried to keep the tone light, but my tension betrayed me, twisting the words into a growl.

"No thank you, you just aren't my type," she chuckled as she came up beside me, leaning against the brick ledge as the glowing barrier of a shield shimmered above her like an umbrella, the disk keeping the rain away.

I glanced at her, but she wasn't looking at me, she was staring at what had once been the city of Vienna.

The beautiful city had been a favorite of mine for years as a child, the old European style reminding me of the books I would get lost in. Of sword fights and magic back when mortals weren't terrified of them. Even with the facade of the city that we lived in, I didn't care. Now the city, much like the memories, was in ruins. Every shop window broken, ancient buildings crumbling, centuries of history burned away. Just like the rest of the world.

Jos sighed and pulled the thin sweater she wore tighter, her shoulders hunching over as more screams broke through the night.

This time both of us turned, that one was close.

"Is it worth it to go?" she asked, the hope evident, even though we both knew the answer. Knew what she was avoiding.

"We have three Chosen patrolling this area," I sighed. We were both running away from what was coming, it seems. "Aliger will be arriving from Australia soon, and then we can begin council."

She sighed and leaned over the brick barrier, as though she was one leap from soaring away. Her long hair swung down either side of her face, obstructing her from view. The rain that ran off the edges of her shield began to drip over her, the tiny drops creating a conga line in her hair.

I stared at her, knowing what I wanted to ask, knowing what she wanted to say. Neither of us could find the words. So we stood in the rain, cold droplets running down our skin as the clouds rolled and the wind swirled and the world was filled with the calming aroma of the damp sticking to our skin.

It took me a moment to realize she was crying.

I said nothing. I stepped closer, letting her know that I was there, hoping that she knew I wanted to help. The most I could do, however, was smooth the tangles of hair out of her face.

She looked up at me at the motion, her bright eyes tinged with red.

"I saw him," she finally said, her voice broken with tears. "My sight... It finally let me see him. But all I saw was his death."

My voice choked at her admission, words lost behind a rock as large as the city we stood in. I swallowed it away, forced myself to speak, desperate to say something.

"And the blood?"

She flinched and sagged back down to the tiny brick wall, her tears returning in earnest.

I didn't think I needed more of an answer, but she gave one anyway.

"It's his. I'm not sure how anyone, magical or not, could have survived that."

I couldn't just stand there, I needed to do something. I needed to be there for her. Letting my hand drift over her sweater and down her back; I let little pops of my calming magic flowing into her as the tension in her back melted away.

"Why do I keep losing people, Ry?" she whispered through the rain, still looking ahead.

The question burned at my soul, it dug into my heart in a painful agony that I hadn't felt in years.

Fingers still rolling over her back, I looked at her, and for the first time in a long time saw a scared little girl that I only barely remembered.

"Hey now," I said, prodding my fingers into her back to get her attention. Her silver eyes blazed as she looked at me. "That sounds suspiciously like a mopey teenager I left behind a few years ago."

The corner of her mouth twitched and I plowed on, the heaviness in my heart lifting.

"You know the one I am talking about, hiding behind hoodies and complaining about her dad."

My father might have started this war and carried it on for centuries, but her father sure as hell finished it. The irony that the children of the men who had begun the end of the world were now putting it back together was not lost on either of us.

"You haven't lost me," I said softly, deflecting as quickly as I could, although I was well aware that I was shifting from one pain point to another. "And we all know how easily that could have gone the other way."

"I know," she grinned at me, even though it was forced. "You haven't tried to kill me in at least two years."

"I even volunteered to be your second, Jos." I continued, neither of us looking at each other. "I wanted to protect you. I said I was willing to give my life to save yours. How crazy is that?"

"And here I was thinking it was a ploy to murder me faster." She turned to me, grinning with the broad smile of hers. Beautiful even as she was breaking.

"It'll be okay, Jos."

"Thanks, Ry," she whispered, her focus drifting back over to the burning city, "but you know what I mean."

"I do, but he hasn't left you either."

She said nothing, she just stared at the burning city as her silent tears mixed with the rain in a dance of devastation.

"I'm your second, Jos," I whispered, bending down to bring my burly body closer to where she leaned over the brick and looked her right in the eyes. "I'm also your best friend. I've been your best friend since you were five and scared of shrubbery."

She laughed at that, the joy finally breaking through.

"I want to be there for you, Joclyn," I said, resisting the urge to reach out to her. "Tell me what you saw. I need to know what you saw so I can support you. So we can figure this out together."

Jos looked at me with eyes so wide and clear that she didn't look at me like she was seeing into my soul like she usually did. She was just Jos.

"I don't want to be Queen anymore."

It was an unexpected punch to the gut, and the flinch that rolled through my body made that very clear. Jos said nothing however, she just breathed deeply and sank to the hard roof, curled up against the puddles where she sat, leaning against the wall. I didn't hesitate to join her, her shield stretching to stop the icy drops of rain from soaking our already damp frames.

"I never did, you know," she continued without

prompting. "I just wanted to hold his place. He chose me to rule by his side, not rule in his stead."

"No Jos," I said, giving her a look before I leaned my head against the uncomfortable stone. "He chose you because he loves you. You becoming Queen may have been fate, yes, but that is not why Ilyan chose to bond himself to you. You chose him because you love him. Being Queen is just a title you may not have planned on, but it's yours because he loved you."

"Loved," she repeated softly, the pain in her voice making me instantly regret my word choice.

"He still does, Jos."

"If he is alive." The sound of her voice echoed that of a lifetime of heartbreak.

It seeped through me and rattled my bones.

"What did you see?" I asked, ignoring the devastation for the answer that I knew was coming.

Joclyn's shoulders sagged as she began to tug at the ribbon on her wrist.

"I saw them fighting. Ovailia and Ilyan." Her voice was a low whisper as she kept her focus on the ribbon, her fingers twisting and turning through the strands. "Their attacks were so fast I could barely make them out. Their magic was so fast... it was everywhere... I saw the blood. I know it came from him, I have seen that before..."

"But we know now that visions of the future do not always have to be true," I tried to soften the blow. I wasn't quite sure it was working.

"Yes, but only for the future. This is the past and I saw the blood spread over his chest." Her voice caught, the sound fading away as the tears dripped down her cheeks. The glittering drops of water rolled over her pale skin before they fell on her hands, mixing with the droplets of rain that still lay there.

"Did you see his death?"

She shook her head.

"Then you don't know, Jos..."

"I may not know if he is alive, but I know that Ovailia is. I saw her, in sight. She was in Moscow. I could see the Vilỳs in the sky."

"So it was after Prague fell." Saying it aloud was a stab and I flinched, the truth that she was alive digging deep into my soul.

I could hear the sound of the rain, I could feel my heartbeat in my chest, but it was as though the world had stopped. Everything had stopped. There was only an intense pressure that rippled through every muscle, twisting and turning as my stomach spun.

Joclyn turned to me, an almost identical anger to what was controlling me peering through the nearly colorless spheres of her eyes.

"She killed him, Ry." Her teeth were clenched so tight that the vowels were swallowed with emotion. "And now she is wandering the world... Sending an army after me."

"So it's her then?"

"The council will have the final say on that, but from what I saw," she breathed, "I have no doubt they will come to the same conclusion you did. The same one I have."

She leaned her head back against the stone, her eyes drifting to the sky just as a low roar of thunder echoed from the distance.

"I need you to find her, so I can find him."

She was determined. As her second I was in no place to argue, as her friend I knew I had to.

"Jos," I began, the knot in my throat making my plea a constricted mess. "I don't know how smart this is. I don't know what I will do if I am face to face with her. I don't know..."

"Ry," she said, her palm warm against my damp bicep as she turned to me. "You are the only one I trust. You and Wyn. I need you to track her down. I need you to find her. I need to know what happened to Ilyan. You find Ovailia. I will find my mate. He is alive. He has to be."

I could only nod. We all knew about the four new heads of magic. Rinax had been her greatest advocate for Ilyan's survival. If he had died, then magic would be ripped apart. Seeing as it wasn't...

I let out a shaky exhale and nodded my head once, the knot that stretched from throat to gut constricting.

Jos gasped and threw her arms around me, pulling me against her. I let my arms wind around her, desperate for the contact to take away some of my trepidation.

"Thank you, Ry," she whispered as she pulled away. "Now we just need to convince the council that this is the right choice."

And that right there was the crux of the problem.

CHAPTER 19
RYLAND

W hen we had established the massive townhouse in Vienna as a safe house we had made sure it had enough rooms for those assigned to the area to rest. It also functioned as a makeshift hospital for those that were injured or bitten, before they could be transported safely to Joclyn, or before Joclyn could arrive. It was a beautiful home, built sometime in the midst of the 18th Century. It still had the oil lamps and a kitchen fireplace that made it ideal for life in a world with no electricity.

With as many rooms as the massive home had, however, it had been built in a different century, and it showed. With small rooms and narrow hallways, it was not really fit for more than a dozen people to reside in the space for long, which made the current organization of the sitting room somewhat of a claustrophobic disaster. I was beginning to feel more like we were sardines packed into a can.

More than fifty of us were crammed into a room the size of Joclyn's living room in that tiny apartment she and her mother shared years ago, back before everything started.

The ripped and torn sofas that were normally arranged in the center were pushed into the corners, each spare armrest and cushion occupied. Nothing was exempt as a chair; Elena, the leader of the Russian zone, had even claimed the mantelpiece for herself, her bare feet dangling toward the still flickering flames. The floor was full, with Skříteks and Trpaslíks sitting in little circles of hushed conversation.

The elegant room was full of whispers, the hushed sounds flickering alongside candles and lanterns. The heavy red draperies that covered the windows drowned the walls with an ominous weight that made everything feel like it was closing in.

I swallowed, and turned toward where Wyn and Thom had sequestered themselves beside the door.

They looked ready to stage a breakout. I already knew I would be right behind them. There was too much apprehension in the air for me. I did a quick count, everyone was here, no turning back now.

"I present to you, your Queen, Joclyn Despain-Krul, brother of Dramin, and ruler of the Draks. Mate of Ilyan Krul, who sits as Lord of the Skříteks and King of our kind. Do you accept her?" My voice was bold as I introduced the woman that stood beside me. She actually looked nervous for once. Weird, she hadn't been nervous about council since she had been declared Queen.

As one, everyone in the room lifted their hands above their head and in one fluid motion, they clapped; the sound and motion unified as they accepted her

"I, Ryland Krul, son of the first Chosen Child: Edmund LaRue, half-brother to Ilyan Krul: Lord of the Skříteks and King of our kind, present our Queen and offer myself as her second. Do you accept?"

Again they clapped, the sound a hollow reverberation as the nearly ancient tradition rang clear in the tiny safe house, reaffirming both Joclyn and I in our positions.

"I thank you for your trust, and for your faith in me," Joclyn spoke in smooth Czech, addressing everyone. "I will do my best as I rule and keep the needs of my people in line with those of man. Ryland and I are proud to serve you."

"And I to you, my Queen." My own voice carried with a deep magic, everything rumbling as my response matched her own.

I turned to her, taking her hand as I had always done and bowed down to my knee.

The actions, the words, the traditions were all from a culture that neither of us grew up in; yet, in every council we danced the same dance, made the same promises. Just as Ilyan had done for centuries. Now, we paid tribute to a culture we ruled, a culture that had almost died.

It was beautiful in a way.

As I took her hand in mine, she gripped it tightly, the bright yellow ribbon around her wrist glinting over the tension in her muscles. The fabric was as strained as she was, the deep rumble of her magic stronger than it usually was.

Normally I was to keep my head down until she had accepted me as her second, but this time my head snapped up, panic rushing through me.

"I accept your commitment." The magic from her voice was gone, the power of the ceremony faded into a painful whisper as she pulled me to standing and placed my knuckles against her chest, right over her heart.

This wasn't right. This wasn't how this was supposed to go.

Of course she would do this in a place that I couldn't call her out. I would say something was wrong, but I knew better. I knew her better.

Something very bad was about to happen.

I stared at her, trying to find some sort of answer, some hint as to what was going on, but I only felt the heat of her magic between our skin, and saw the breathtaking sadness behind her eyes.

Joclyn squeezed my hand before, with a nod, she dismissed me from the makeshift platform she stood on. Her fingers immediately moved to fiddle with the ribbon.

Leaving the tiny cleared space in the middle of the room was the last thing I wanted to do right then. Stupid thousand year old traditions.

Giving her one last look, I stepped to lean against the door frame opposite of Wyn, who had noticed everything. Wyn's eyebrows attempted to vanish into her hairline, her silent question growing louder with every step I took. I dismissed her with a nod. I didn't have an answer to give her. Playing eyebrow charades was not really my thing anyway. Especially not when everything was exploding in worry. Crap. Crap. Crap.

Wyn's face filled with the same concern as she bit down on her lower lip. Luckily, no one else in the room seemed as concerned as we were. Even Thom seemed oblivious.

Leave it to her two best friends to notice the thunder before the lightning.

We exchanged a worried glance before Joclyn's powerful voice pulled our focus, the tone strong and steady despite the tension that was rippling off of her.

"This week Wyn and her assistant Míra uncovered the room that was thought to be the last location Ilyan was known to be." Joclyn's voice caught with emotion, the last word swallowed as the room began to explode in murmurs, everyone glancing from Joclyn to Wyn in new found interest.

Wyn's brow furrowed. Normally she would bask in the added attention. I pressed myself against the doorframe, as if I needed a launch pad, or perhaps something to hold me from lunging myself at her.

"Ilyan was not there," Joclyn bellowed, pulling the focus back to her as the question was answered and the murmurs died down to nothing. "What was there allowed me to gain sight of Ilyan and Ovailia for the first time in many years."

Joclyn stopped and sighed. I leaned forward, everything tight and tense as I watched her, as I attempted to figure her out.

"I would like to share that sight with you now."

Wyn glanced at me in confusion, my own bewilderment reflected back, before with a flash of the brightest white and a powerful gust of wind, we were both forced back against the wooden door frame. Cringing against both wind and light, my focus pulled to the woman who now stood in the middle of what looked to be a pillar of water and smoke.

The strength of Joclyn's magic drowned the room, it whipped around us and pulled hair, clothes and any loose bit of paper and fluff into disarray. A powerful gust of wind tugged at everything as it circled around her, circled around the pillar of magic that she stood in. The room that surrounded her was caught in a storm, yet she stood perfectly still, her hair and clothes not even so much as showing a twitch of movement.

Yells of shock and panic carried on the back of the wind, the sound almost swallowed by her voice as it boomed over everything in that deep tenor that identified her as a Drak. "Share my sight."

She looked up at all of us with eyes the color of night, all color sucked from her face as without even a whisper of sound, everything froze.

The wind stopped, papers and feathers and dust and everything else that it had picked up, suspended in place as though they had been glued in the air. The momentary panic drained from the council's faces as they turned to their Queen, awe taking over as the wall of water and smoke she stood behind began to move, images forming over the shimmering surface.

Wyn gasped audibly as Ilyan emerged in the water, his normally bright blue eyes clouded with agony as he yelled at something we couldn't see. Long blonde hair fanned around his face as he turned, as he yelled in agony. Seeing him, seeing the look on his face was a painful burn against my heart.

I had spent an entire life being raised to kill this man, but when the time had come, I instead found an ally. I had found a family for the first time.

I had lost it just as quickly.

My head fell back against the door frame as I tried to ignore the pain, only to wish it would come back when the image changed, swiveling to show who Ilyan was yelling at.

Ovailia could have been Ilyan's twin. Out of all the Krul siblings they were the only two to share the same mother, and it showed in their long sheaths of blonde hair and powerful tall frames.

Just seeing Ovailia sent a ripple of anger through me and I wasn't the only one. Thom flinched and took a step forward before Wyn spread her arm over his chest, her face as twisted with anger as her mate's.

I clung to the door frame as if it was the only thing keeping me from rushing forward, grateful when the image changed, only to feel a different twist of agony at the sight of a splash of blood and deep red waves rolling over the stone of that tiny room.

"The end may be a beginning," Joclyn's voice rang out, the deep haunting quality of sight only fueling the anger that shivered over my spine. "A loss may be a gain and what is seen is not always what is given. A heart beats out of place and the end is a twisted web that you cannot yet see."

The image swirled back to Ilyan's face, distorted in a scream that was equal parts pain and heartbreak. But the image was different. Something in the background was off, the cave seemed to be gone.

Before I could get a good look, however, the image shifted to Ovailia's blood-streaked face, her eyes wild as she laughed.

"Follow the river of blood to find that which is lost," Jos' deadpan voice was nearly swallowed as the wind began to pick up, the images in the fog became muddled like a television with bad reception. "Follow the tracks before the attack comes."

Everyone shielded themselves from the increasing wind, but I stared straight ahead, looking through the swirls of wind and magic to the Queen who was looking right at me.

Her silver eyes were wet with tears, the streaks staring at me in a pleading warning.

"Joclyn," I whispered, knowing there was no way for my voice to reach her. No way for me to ask her what was going on, to help her.

She smiled sadly as the wind fell, leaving the room, and everyone in it, cluttered and disorganized.

"You have been briefed on the woman who attacked Thom and Ryland earlier today," Joclyn began, her voice loud and diplomatic after the haunting tremors of her sight. "As I spoke to many of you on your arrival I heard of other stories, similar encounters that when placed with the words and images that we have just seen can point to only one thing. Ovailia is moving against us."

The room instantly broke out in a panic, the window draping's shuddering at the pressure of angry magic that rippled off everyone. Many looked horrified at the assertion, but many more nodded and instantly began agreeing with their Queen.

I said nothing, I did nothing, even though multiple heads had begun to turn in my direction. I had already spoken to Joclyn, she knew where I stood. I would stand by her. Besides, after seeing her sight it was no wonder she was so shattered on the roof. No wonder she was barely holding herself together here.

"Silence," Joclyn roared again, her magic rumbling over everything as they were all forced to quiet.

"There will be time to argue the validity of this statement later," Joclyn continued once all the eyes were focused back on her. "But right now it is imperative that we move against whoever it is that is targeting us. Ryland and Thom were attacked, nothing can change that. I propose that we send Ryland Krul and Wynifred Krul, mate of Thom Krul, to the faction that resides in the UK. Based on the interaction, the woman hailed from England. Michel Diaden leads the faction there, perhaps he will have more information, perhaps he will know whoever is moving against us."

My stomach knotted as everyone began to murmur in agreement, the clap of approval coming almost instantly.

"Looks like we are going on an adventure, Ry," Wyn beamed from beside me.

I didn't look at her, I barely heard her, my focus was still on the frayed Queen before me.

"Thank you for your agreement," Jos said to them all, her voice kind even behind the formality of the words. "They will be leaving at first light tomorrow. Thom will remain here to assist in watching the woman who was captured, to act as my second in Ryland's absence, and to use his skills to gain any further information we need."

"Great," Thom growled, loud enough for everyone to hear. "Babysitting duty."

I chuckled, the soft sounds of a few others blending with my chortles.

Joclyn pulled my focus as she signaled for me to come over to her, the request a clear break in protocol. She never broke protocol. Of course, she never looked as nervous as she did now, either.

"Will you serve me in this?" Jos asked the moment I reached her, the words regal and familiar.

She reached toward me, her fingers wide as the unspoken request hit me. Taking her hands with only a slight hesitation, my magic rushed to my palms as I nodded silently in response, unsure of what else to do.

"Will you serve me in all things, as you have vowed?"

I looked back to Wyn, almost begging the girl to clue me in as to what was going on, but she stood as wide eyed and confused as I was, her hands twitching as she stepped away from the door frame, ready to bolt to us.

"I will," I could barely get the words out, they were little more than a squeak, choked by the giant nervous rock that had taken up residence in my throat.

"Then in that, I would command, with the council's

approval, you to take up the role of King, and rule in my stead, until Ilyan can be found."

I heard Wyn gasp behind me, and she wasn't the only one.

I guess when Jos said she didn't want to be Queen anymore, she meant it.

CHAPTER 20
RYLAND

I stared at her, a million things screaming at me to be said, but not one of them making their way out.

Not one of them was allowed to. Not here in council, and definitely not in front of all of these people.

First among them, *'what the hell are you doing?'*

I swallowed my demand as the murmurs of question grew into the buzz of a million bees; the nasty things swarming around my head. Wyn said something in French to Thom behind me, their low voices only adding to the cacophony that Joclyn had erupted. I didn't dare turn. I had a feeling that seeing the look on Wyn's face was only going to make it harder for me to keep my outburst locked inside.

"Silence," Joclyn said for the third time, her strong magic smothering everyone and plunging the room into silence.

Instead of being filled with anticipation, however, the calm of the room was filled with dread and irritation. The emotions drowned me in my anger, pressing against my soul like a dead weight.

I wasn't wrong that she had been hiding something, but

I hadn't expected this, even though she had spelled it out to me on the roof.

I was a fool, a blind fool.

"I present this sight, this request for the future leader of Imdalind to you in confidence that you will all come to the decision you feel is best for our people. Once Wynifred and Ryland have returned from their mission we will reconvene to speak of Ovailia, of war, and of the state of our King. I ask you to be vigilant and contemplative until then."

Joclyn spoke to each and every one of them as she circled around me, her voice sounding like it was a miles away from where I stood, frozen in the middle of the room, rage and confusion distorting both sight and sound.

"With these words, I release you," she continued, her voice hazy and distant before it was shattered with the sound of a singular clap that erupted through the shocked hush with a boom of a cannon.

I jumped at the clap, the sound ricocheting through my spine as it rattled my aggravation, only to have a wall of sound slam against my chest as hundreds of questions exploded around us.

"I will return tomorrow morning to answer any questions you may have," Joclyn attempted to yell over them, her hand wrapping around my wrist as she pulled me toward her, the heat of her magic pressing against my skin. "I ask that you all remain in this house until then. Wynifred and Thom will be here with you until my return."

The two of them groaned audibly from where they stood, but Joclyn ignored them, looking at me expectantly. I could only shake my head, she did not want me to say all the things that were buzzing around my mind. She did not want me to open my mouth. The wide smile that covered her face twitched knowingly, but remained in place as she turned toward her subjects.

"I must prepare Ryland for the task that is ahead of him. There is a sight I must share and duties that must be relayed."

The questions returned in an onslaught, the faces of those around us mirroring a rainbow of emotions, most of them tilting toward the angry side.

Joclyn mumbled a few apologies, a few pleasantries, but her voice was wavering, her grip on my wrist was tightening.

I looked toward Wyn for the first time, unsurprised to see her anticipation for our adventure replaced by confusion. Thom looked angry, but knowing him it was more for having been put in charge of an angry mob than for whatever changing of the guard I had just been thrust into.

He didn't want to be in charge of anything larger than a gerbil.

I didn't either.

Before I could say anything to Wyn, to Jos, or to any of the angry and possibly betrayed people around us, Joclyn's hand pressed against mine, her magic pulsing into me in a wave.

I tried to say something, I tried to stop her, but any protest was lost in the black between dimensions as she pulled me from the safe house into the black tunnel of hell.

The demonic suction of the void pressed against me as my own scream rattled my skull, little pops of light hitting the backs of my eyes as I tried to stay conscious.

"Damn it," I groaned as the pressure of the torture she liked to call a Stutter left, leaving me folded over and trying to keep the contents of my stomach intact and not spread over the ancient cobbles that I recognized at once.

Prague.

She had brought me to Prague. Not the underground caves of Imdalind that twisted beneath the city, but the ruins that the mortals had only recently begun to rebuild, or rather begun to clear away. Most would still not set foot back into the ancient, and once vibrant, city. Which, ironically, made it one of the safest places to be. This cluster of houses, however, happened to be where a few brave settlers had decided to make their return.

With faces as wanted as ours it was obvious why she brought us here. More visibility, less yelling. Screw that! I didn't care who saw, or who heard.

"What in the hell are you thinking?" I roared, my question escaping in a burst of sound that rippled over the white stone buildings that towered over us.

It took all my strength to speak and not collapse, but I held on, clinging to the wall as I tried to see past the shifting world and gasped in a desperate breath.

The air was heavy with the smell of dirt and rain, Prague must have been on the edges of the storm that was still tearing through Vienna. Judging by the clouds that smothered the setting sun, there was a chance it would hit us.

"Sending me on a mission to find Ovailia is one thing... but this, Jos! Have you lost your mind?"

Joclyn turned to me, fuming, "I'm quite sane thank you, and I have been thinking of this for quite some time."

"You have been thinking of volunteering me..."

"No," she interrupted with a snap, the glare from her stony eyes forcing me to take a step back, pressing me against the wall as everything continued to spin. "I have been thinking about how I don't want to rule without him. How I won't be able to find him if I'm stuck in meetings and healing people. Wyn and I haven't been to France in over a year. If he's dead he's dead, but I need to know. I need to stop pretending he's just going to come waltzing back in here."

Even with the anger behind her words, the pain inside of them still struck me to the core. My chest seized as I relaxed into the wall, sagging against the stone as the last of the spinning left.

"I know, Jos," I sighed, reaching for her before thinking better of it and dropping my hand. "I heard you on the rooftop. But do you really think that this was the best way to do this? We could have talked about it. We could have..."

"You know you wouldn't have talked about it," she scoffed, her smile wicked as she leaned against the wall opposite from me. She looked like something out of a magazine the way she stood there in torn jeans and a tight fitting leather jacket, the color nearly matching her tall boots. It was something she wouldn't have been caught dead in growing up.

"Yes we would," I was stubborn, but she was too used to me and rolled her eyes.

"You would have shot me down before I had a chance to even explain."

"No, I wouldn't. I would have heard you out, Jos." I lied, I knew the answer to that as much as she did.

"Not about this," she said softly, touching the ribbon on her wrist before stepping away from the wall and walking down the cobbled road that led to the Vltava River.

"So you figure, volunteer first, ask questions later?" I gasped as I caught up to her, trying to keep my voice down as we passed a cluster of reporters taking pictures of what was left of the Charles Bridge.

"It's always worked with you before," she said, beaming at me with a toothy grin.

"Nice, Jos." I didn't even try to stop the grumble from escaping that time. "So, now that you have brought it up, do we at least get to talk about it?"

"Yes, we can." She stopped short, sending me stumbling a few steps beyond her.

She stood on the blood-stained cobbles on the edge of the riverbank, the chain that had once kept pedestrians out of the water curled around her feet like a noose that would surely catch her if she fell. The breeze that danced over the murky waters tangled through her hair, sending the strands over her pale face like long black ribbons. She didn't seem to notice any of it. She just stood there, staring into the city that had once trapped us, seeing something I could never understand.

It would have been beautiful if her eyes weren't so sad, if the world behind her wasn't as destroyed as she was.

"You heard what I said on the rooftop," she said, her voice powerful over the faint lapping of water. "I don't want this anymore. I don't want to be Queen. Not without Ilyan. But you... Ryland... your father was raising you to be King."

"No," I quickly corrected, straightening my shoulders as the muscles flared in agitation. "He raised me to be an assassin. He never expected me to rule."

"But you sat in on meetings, you led teams..."

"On assassination missions," I cut in, she ignored me.

"You know how to rule. At the very least, you were the captain of the Rugby team, weren't you?"

"That hardly counts," I grumbled. She didn't even smile, she knew that she was reaching.

"True. But the last three years you have shown that

you care for these people. All of them. You have helped me lead, you have solved problems. They trust you. You have come from the same place as more than half of them. Tortured by your father, created as a weapon..." Her voice faded off, leaving us to drown in the whisper of wind and shutter clicks from the reporter's several yards behind us.

With every word, every click, every pulse of my heart; my body constricted as though it was being swallowed whole. This couldn't be happening, this couldn't be a real suggestion, could it?

"That is all the more reason that I shouldn't be allowed to rule, Jos," I interjected, not even trying to restrain my growl anymore. "I was raised as a freakin' weapon. A weapon that was trained to kill pretty much everyone in my family, Ilyan, you! There is no guarantee that all of that will not come back!"

It came out in a rush. Every fear. Every reason I worked so hard to support her. Every reason I wanted to be better. All of it. The words tripped over each other as they grew louder, spewing out of me in a web of anger and fear.

"There is no promise that I am safe, I may never be."

Although it had been years since I heard my father, I still had moments where I was at risk of losing control. Jos knew it, which is why I was sure she wanted me to go after Ovailia. She knew where the weapon could be valuable, which is why her suggestion made no sense.

Nothing about me, besides my bloodline, had the making of a King.

"Joclyn," I said, pushing my fears to the back of my mind, to hide amongst the madness. "I am not fit to rule them. I am not my brother."

"Neither am I," she continued, her voice soft as she

threw the sleeve back on her jacket. "But none of that matters now. They trust you, Ryland. I trust you."

The long golden ribbon that was wound around her wrist slid into her hand with the smallest of tugs, the impossibly long string of gold looking like a glittering bird's nest in her hands.

My heartbeat sped up, the pulse a heavy rattle against my chest as I stared at the ribbon.

"They are as much your people as they are mine."

Joclyn stood there beside the river, hair whipping around her, hand stretched toward me. The long golden ribbon lay in her palm, ready for me to reach out and take it. As if it was just as simple as that.

If only it was.

Seeing it awakened the monster, awakened the years of training, cruel punishment, and inevitable torture. Awakened the greed.

I didn't know how to rule. I knew how *he* ruled, and that was a path I would not follow.

"I will not be like my father," I snapped, roughly pushing her hand away from me. "I cannot do this, Joclyn. I will follow you in everything, I cannot follow you in this. I can't."

I was too loud and the reporters looked up from their incessant picture taking, their confusion at what they were witnessing melting into horror as one after another they recognized us.

"Damn it!" I roared as a grey-haired man lifted his camera, moments away from capturing us in the city that in many ways was our only sanctuary.

Magic bubbling to the surface, I lifted my hand. A wide wall of glittering red magic rushed out of me, pushing the reporters back in a wall of wind. They stumbled as though they were caught in a strong breeze and gave us just enough time to escape.

Joclyn stood a few steps away from me, her focus still across the river, her jaw set as she stood seemingly oblivious to what just happened.

"We have to go!" I wrapped my arm around her waist, pulling her into me as my shield wrapped around us, my magic bubbling in preparation to explode into the air.

"No!" She yelled, pushing her hands forward, stretching toward the river in what I was sure was an attack.

Panic grew, confusion ripping through me as I looked up, right as a single line of magic exploded from the other bank and smashed into the side of my shield with the force of a tsunami.

Tightening my arms around Joclyn, I wrapped my body around her protectively as we were thrown into the wall of the building behind us. The crack of brick, and I was sure a bone or two, snapped in my ears as we were showered with debris, bits of rock and dust raining over us as we slid to the ground.

I strengthened my shield just as I felt Joclyn's magic flare in a blast that streamed over the surface of the water like cannon fire. Wind rippled away from her as she stood powerfully before me, the force of the gust sending the reporters scrambling. The sound of shutter clicks was a haunting score behind a second explosion, this one impacting with Joclyn's extended hand with the boom of a thunderbolt. Fire rained over us, the sparks of magic sprinkling right over our heads.

"Great. Just freakin' great," Joclyn growled as her magic pulled her into the air and she vanished from sight. I stared into the heavy clouds that dripped from the sky, trying to find any sign of where she had gone, but her magic had swallowed her, smudging her out.

"Damn it!" I yelled as I followed her motions, exploding into the air over the river and heading for the bank where the explosion had come from.

Instead of cloaking myself, however, I left myself visible, purposefully soaring in a wide arc away from where I had assumed Joclyn to be. I let my magic spark in the twilight, the color catching against the sky as I turned myself into a living decoy, determined to get Jos to her destination safely. The danger surged through me, pulsing adrenaline into every muscle, fueling my magic in exhilaration. Excitement. This was different than facing the poisoned monsters, this was child's play.

And not just for me.

As powerful as Jos was, she could not only see through shields, but also feel where magic was hidden with scary accuracy. I expected the eruption of a quick kill. Instead, I got a single line of bright yellow magic soaring right at me, the powerful line sagging and sparking just like the broken magic from my father's army.

From the woman in the alley.

The cancerous infection dripped through the air before I spun away, the attack narrowly missing the edge of the shield that I had cast around myself.

Well, whoever was over there was sure going to make this fun.

I changed directions, soaring right to where the attack had come from. Attack after attack cut through the air. I spun and dodged, sending my own magic toward theirs in purposefully flimsy counter attacks. I missed both the twisted attack and the bank where I assumed the attacker to be standing. As much as the desperate need for a good fight taunted me, I never once retaliated against them. I couldn't risk it. I knew where Jos was heading, and if they hadn't figured out what I was doing by now, they were already dead.

A blast of bright green erupted from nothing, the riverbank was so close now that I could see right where they were, the air around their poorly cast shield shivering as the assailant moved. Carefully dodging the attack, I finally sent one of my own. One well-aimed streak of grey ripped through the air, swallowed by the wall of the attackers shield as it disappeared. The air shimmered like oil as a scream broke through the silence, the shield around the man displacing in pops of light as he came into focus. His red hair was the first thing I saw, the color matching the glistening spot of wet that was flowering over his chest.

Hand flaring, I sent another stream of magic into him, the white-hot heat ripping another scream from him as my power instantly cauterized the wound and sent him to his knees. He tried to attack as he collapsed, but his magic only sputtered in useless sparks that ignited in his palm before falling to the ground in lifeless drops of liquid color.

Cobbles rattled underneath me as I landed right before him, the snakes of my magic wrapping around the man as I restrained him, binding his magic further. Every muscle strained as I rose up to my full height, my shoulders stretching wide as my shadow moved over him, blotting out the stars like ink against the road.

"Who are you?" I roared in Czech, looking down at the man as I carefully stretched my magic away from me, letting it wander as far away from me as I dared.

I knew I was pushing it. I needed to control this man, but I also needed to find the others. There was no way he could be here alone. Not after the ambush from the alley. More than that, though, I needed to find Joclyn.

She was here somewhere. The fact that she hadn't already attacked this man herself was making me uncomfortable.

She loved a good fight as much as I did.

I resisted the urge to call out for her and kept my focus on the would-be assailant, knowing that Joclyn could take care of herself, even though it was technically my job.

"Who do you work for?" I snapped.

The assassin gave me a blood-stained smile, his eyes boring into me with a look of pure hatred. The look in his eyes was familiar, too familiar.

It was the look my father gave me before he would 'teach me' something new. It was the look my father's guard, Cail, would fix before he took a life. It was the look I saw in myself every time the sleeping monster took control.

I flinched at the glare, at the memory and emotions that rippled over me, and stepped back, torn between escaping this man, or restraining him further.

I never got to make the choice.

"Ya stoyu z Tykha Shist´!" He practically screamed the words in a language I didn't understand, before he began to convulse, a bright white foam spewing from his lips and dripping down his chin.

"No!" I yelled as my magic pressed into him in a rush, but the man didn't even seem to react. He just continued to shiver and shake.

I had seen this exact moment in movies a hundred times before, seen the way the fast-acting poison would kill a man. The man convulsed as my magic rushed to every organ, stretched to every muscle as I sought to counteract the effects of the cyanide, to scrub the poison from his system.

As fast as I moved, as much power as I used, it did not seem to be enough. Nothing was, and even though I fought, I watched him slip away.

"Damn it!" I roared as I felt the last beat of his heart, my large frame shifting away from him to crouch against the rough cobbles of the road.

I sat there, staring at the now lifeless body as Joclyn appeared a few yards behind him. Her eyes wide and staring as she looked from me to the man and back again, the panicked lines in her face deepening into furrows. I couldn't even look her straight in the eye, any relief at seeing her was smothered by my frustration.

"Ry?"

"I'm fine," I managed to get out, although the sound was a rumble.

It didn't stop her. She still collapsed to her knees beside me, her hands pressing against the bare skin of my forearm as her magic surged into me in a warm wave. I restrained a gasp at the strength of the invasion, instead gritting my teeth as she checked me for any injuries.

Satisfied, she sat back, her focus pulling to the crumpled man, her long black hair swinging over her back.

"He's dead." The words sounded hollow on my tongue.

"I know," she whispered, crawling toward him cautiously, as though he was going to reanimate into something frightening.

I didn't blame her. The way he was tangled up in his twisted limbs, white foam still dripping from his mouth was reminiscent of all the terrible Grade-B horror movies we used to watch together. The similarity was only made more disturbing by the way his eyes stared right at us, looking into us, seeing nothing.

"You know?" I asked, something about her phrasing off to me.

Joclyn only nodded and settled back onto the cobbles beside me, the dust-covered stone pin-pricked with dark as the storm arrived.

I sat, staring at her, a single drop of cold hitting against my arm.

She hesitated, "I watched you fight him, Ry."

I instantly began to fume. Sometimes I wondered why she needed a second at all.

"You watched me?"

She nodded, "I knew you could handle it, that you could be the leader."

"You stood right there..." I began, waving my hand toward the now dead man.

"There was nothing I could do to save him," she interrupted, as if that somehow made it all better. I only glowered deeper, I didn't trust myself to say anything. "Cyanide attacks the brain. I have tried to stop it before, but I'm not strong enough for human poisons."

The anger at her theatrics began to subside, although I could still feel the ebbing wave lap against my subconscious.

"You've seen this before?" I asked, she nodded once, a single drop of rain hitting her cheek as the storm began to pick up, the dark spots multiplying against our shoulders.

"When I was trying to find Ilyan last year... I didn't think the group was any more than humans who didn't want to be murdered by their own kind, not understanding that they were safe," she said as she stood, stepping to the man as the rain created a checkerboard of glistening leather on her back. "You were the one who told me there was an uptick in cyanide pills on the black market about a year ago. Remember?" She shook her head, sending her long hair swinging. "I never would have assumed the ones who were buying them weren't human."

"Or that they were part of an army building against us?"

Speaking about distant armies and enemies didn't sound as ridiculous now that we were standing above the empty corpse of a Chosen sent to attack us. To attack her. The thought made my insides twist and I stood up, stepping toward Joclyn as she turned to me, her silver eyes fading to black as she stared through me.

"You need to go, Ryland," she said dully, her eyes fading back to silver and reaffirming the fear that was bubbling inside of me. "It has to be you. Thom has taken your place before."

I hated when her Drak magic took control, not that she could often control it, but it didn't make it any less freaky.

"Yes, he has," I said, rubbing my hand over the back of my neck, gripping the skin as though it was a release valve for stress. "But never when someone is actively trying to take your life."

"Isn't someone always trying to do just that?" she said, a smile dancing in her eyes as the corners of her lips turned up. I couldn't find it in me to join her and instead I scowled, a look that only made her smile more.

"I'm serious, Jos."

"So am I," she said, all business now. "I am The Oheň, or whatever name they have given me. Every country wants me. Every scientist dreams of dissecting me. And now a group, a group with magic mind you, wants to kill me. If Ovailia is behind it, then this is more dangerous than all of those countries and scientists put together."

"All the more reason for me to..."

"All the more reason for you to find them," she interrupted me, taking a massive step forward until not even a drop of rain could sneak between us.

"I need you to track them down, I need you to find her."

"I thought you needed me to take Ilyan's place?"

She flinched as though I had slapped her, that time I did take a step back.

"We all need you, Ryland," Joclyn said, her voice soft even though the look in her eyes was anything but. "Right now, however, we need to be safe. Any change will take time, right now I need you to find them."

I flinched as lightning cracked overhead, the flash of light riding on the back of the thunder in a boom that rumbled in my bones. Joclyn stood still, her eyes digging into me with a look that reminded me so much of my brother's that all breath seemed trapped in my chest.

"I need you, Ryland." Her voice was nearly a whisper, my best friend peeking through in a flash of vulnerability that cut right through me.

As she stood before me, I knew she was different. She was stronger, braver, more confident than she ever had been.

Right then, however, I only saw the girl I had grown up with. I saw my first love. I saw the shy little girl that hid herself from the world.

I saw my Joclyn.

"You know I am always here for you, Jos," I said, my voice a low promise that ripped through my heart, shredding the already mutilated organ. "You're still my diamond girl."

"Always."

CHAPTER 21
WYN

Flowers swayed in the breeze, tickling my feet as I lay with my head in Thom's lap, the sun beating down on my face as Thom ran his fingers through my hair. It was times like this I wished I never had to leave.

Thom and I had gone back to this hilltop shortly after our bonding, and found only miles of apartment buildings and disheveled streets. It was kind of heartbreaking to see it like that, and not like how I would always remember it, not how it had been in my dreams for years, not how it was right now, in our Tòuha.

Here, it was rolling hills that stretched all the way to the ocean, the long green grasses littered with so many flowers that I couldn't even name them... it was beautiful. All that was missing was her, her laugh, her incessant flower crowns. But just being here was being close to her. That wound may never go away, just like the hole in my hand; but if it has gotten so much better, also like the hole in my hand.

"How long do you think we can avoid reality?" I mumbled, turning in Thom's lap so that I could see him. He looked like a hunky god as he loomed over me, back lit and grinning. I half expected an angel choir to begin singing.

Instead, my stomach clenched, everything growing warm.

He had that effect on me too.

"As long as you want. You already got rid of all the questions after Joclyn's announcement?" He was still grumpy about it.

"Mmhmmm." I curled into him more, burying my face in his lap and he gasped.

"Then I would say we have some time." His voice was half a laugh as he gripped my shoulders and lay back on the grass, pulling me with him so that I lay on top of him. Every inch of me pressed against every wonderful inch of him.

My stomach flipped again, my core tightening as I flattened myself against him and moaned.

"It seems that you have the same thing in mind..." Thom's voice was a husky growl as he pulled me down, his lips capturing mine as his hands fanned over my hips.

"Stop talking, more kissing."

He laughed at that, and shoved my hips against his with a grunt that made my stomach tighten as I kissed him. His lips were that same soft wonderfulness that they had always been. He growled like some kind of animal as I teased him, biting his lower lip before I tasted him... instead of sugar and coffee, however, he tasted like day old cheese and rotten bread.

Suddenly, my stomach tensed for another reason.

"Oh my god!" I pulled back quickly, which only made my stomach twist and flip more. This was trouble, the feeling was real. "I'm going to be sick!"

The clenching, dizzying, terribleness that was happening in my stomach was now moving up my throat.

My tongue felt so big and heavy that I couldn't even swallow properly. If I didn't move quick I was going to hurl, and I had a bad feeling that I would do so in the real world too. Which means I would vomit all over Thom who was laying right next to me.

Nonononono.

"Are you--" I didn't even give Thom the chance to finish before I pulled us out of our Tӧuha and back into our tiny cramped room. I practically flung myself off the bed and through the open door to our bathroom.

I barely made it to the porcelain throne in time.

"Wyn?" Thom was right behind me, hand on my back and neck as he helped to pull my hair out of my face. "Are you okay?"

"I..." I gasped, focusing on my stomach as it thankfully began to calm down. "I'm fine. I ate some canned food that one of the Chosen brought me yesterday, and I clearly should have read the label better."

My head felt slimy and hot as I leaned back against the cool stone wall of the bathroom, letting the stone counteract the fire that was boiling through me. It was really lucky that I didn't vomit fire or all those would have been a whole lot worse.

I took a deep breath and turned to Thom, who was still feeling my head and neck from where he sat on the edge of the tub. He fixed me with those big ol' puppy dog eyes that I always loved, except this time they were full of worry and matched with that signature 'what the hell are you talking about' frown that was so him.

"What, did I sprout two heads while I was puking my guts out?"

"You're my mate, you never get sick, and you are supposed to go off with Ryland to chase down the bastard who murdered our daughter..." He lifted a finger for every reason he gave me, the furrow in his brow growing with each one. He could be so overdramatic sometimes. "So yeah, I'm going to look at you like this. I'm worried, Wyn. Are you okay?"

His eyes were dark as his hand moved from my neck to the side of my face. I would have been sure that he was about to kiss me. You know, if I hadn't just been vomiting.

But that wasn't why my stomach was twisting. That wasn't why I was staring at him with an expression that was just as horrified.

He was right, I never got sick. Magical people didn't get sick because our bodies were pretty much self-healing. The only time I had ever been sick like this...

"Rosaline," I whispered, now staring at the toilet.

"Wynifred? Are you okay? The toilet looks nothing like our daughter." I couldn't be sure if he was frustrated, or laughing, but it didn't matter. I could only stare at the toilet as my mind buzzed through the last few months.

I had been so focused on clearing the caves that I hadn't even noticed.

"I'm pregnant." The words were a gasp as I finally looked away from the toilet to Thom, to the worried face that had twisted into something closer to joy before it was overtaken by the same feeling I was sure was now twisting up my spine and making my stomach flip-flop again. Pain.

Fear.

"Wyn... are you? I mean... how?" He sputtered and gasped until the last word exploded from him in something closer to a growl. I should have been worried, but right then everything was too numb. I wasn't even sure if I was sitting up straight anymore.

"Well, I mean, you were there... but when a man and a

woman love each other very much..." I lifted my hands up, ready to act out how all that works, something that was going to be so much easier thanks to the hole in my hand, but Thom shoved my hands back down into my lap.

"I know how it works, Wyn."

"Good, cuz I was worried."

"I mean... how did this happen?" He was serious, and I lifted a brow at him. I was trying my best to keep my laugh in, but only because I wasn't one hundred percent sure that only a laugh would come out.

"I stand by my original answer," I said as dead pan as possible.

Thom rolled his eyes, and thankfully chuckled at himself. "Okay, fine. How can we be sure you're... pregnant?"

"Find a pregnancy test, that's not expired, in a drug store that hasn't already been cleared out. Or we just wait for my stomach to swell up." I shrugged, but even as I said it all of that panic that I was feeling fell away to excitement, the joke and the word possibility that it had been before became reality. As real as the memory of my belly as it had swelled up before, as it made room for our daughter...

I still felt like I was going to throw up, but as I sat there on the bathroom floor, I cried. I freaking cried. Tears fell over my cheeks as I gripped my hand around Thom's and pushed our hands against my stomach. Right where Rosaline had grown, right where this baby was going to grow, too.

"I'm sure," I whispered, tears pouring from both our eyes now as I stared at him. "I haven't been tracking my cycles very well. But I'm sure. I'm more than a few weeks late, Thom. We are going to have a baby."

If we were crying before, it was nothing compared to

right then. To that beautiful cathartic moment, where this thing that we had wanted so much became real. Even before Rosaline was two we had known we wanted another, that we wanted a family. But Edmund wouldn't allow us to be mated, he wouldn't allow us to create more children that he couldn't use. And even then, why would we want to bring a child into that? Not that this crazy world was better, but it was *better*.

"Another baby," Thom corrected, that same pain as before taking over his features. "I just... I get to be a father..."

"Again." I added on.

It was so hard, to miss her, to know this wasn't our first child. It was a hard thing to grapple with, and I don't think either of us were willing to acknowledge that pain more than we were right then. So we sat in silence, our hands pressed against my abdomen as though we were going to feel something.

"Wyn..." I knew that tone. I had heard that tone before and my head snapped up to the same worried expression as before.

"I'm going with Ryland, Thom." I was firm and his brow furrowed more. "I've gone on missions pregnant before, I'm not an invalid, pregnant ladies can be badass fighters, too." I held up a finger for each of my points, just as he had done. "Plus, I am not sure I want anyone to know yet."

Thom blinked, "Anyone? I have to tell Ry, he's my brother. And Jos..."

"No one. Not yet." I was firm, well until my stomach spun and I closed my eyes in an attempt to calm my stomach down again. "I just... I mean... after Rosy I don't want to tell anyone for a while. I want this to be just between us."

"But you leave in the morning--"

"And if I had started throwing up tomorrow night instead of today I would already be on a mission and neither of us would know." I had a point and he knew it. His brow wriggled as though he was going to fight me, but even he knew he was going to lose. He sat back against the wall next to me, his thumb caressing my stomach where his hand was still wrapped around mine.

"Okay, but you have to promise to take care of yourself. Nothing reckless."

"You say that like I'm going to go in and tear down a building or collapse a cave," I grinned at him, knowing full well that was something that I would do. "Okay, no cave collapses. I think I've had enough of those to last a lifetime."

I tried to smile at Thom, to prod him the way I usually did. But the sharp turn of my head sent everything into a twisting tumbling mess again and I only barely made it to the toilet.

"You know, I'm glad that Ryland is young... or else even he might figure it out."

CHAPTER 22
RYLAND

I could never sleep during thunderstorms.

My body couldn't rest from the sound of the world splitting apart, from the flashes of light that ripped through the sky. It reminded me too much of the dungeon.

One flash of lightning and I was back in that dark cave, the boom of thunder replaced by explosions of magic against my bones.

Normally I could keep it at bay, keep my focus on anything else and ignore the terrors that were always threatening. But laying in the dark, watching the strips of light cut over black rock, it only made it worse.

I contemplated rolling out of bed and making myself busy until the storm passed, but Wyn and I were supposed to be leaving in just a few hours. I needed rest.

Although, ideally, I needed to be stronger than these ridiculous memories.

The dull rumble of thunder shook the heavy stone of the cave, the sound echoing through the large chamber just as the light that filtered in through the skylight exploded in a pop of white. I jumped, cringing at the sound and closed my eyes, carefully counting out my breaths as my hand wandered up to the nest of crisscrossed scars that littered the skin over my heart.

A token of torture. Just like the scars that covered my face, or the massive web of barely healed knife marks on my back from where he had cut out the brand that marked me as a Chosen. Even though I wasn't, not really. I was born with magic. But my father was obsessed with power, and injecting the poison of a Vilỳ directly into my body was just what he needed to make me the powerful weapon he wanted.

I cringed, pressing my fingers against the white t-shirt that covered the raised skin and resisted the need to curl into myself as another roll of thunder charged the air in my room.

Come on, Ry. Get over yourself.

I rolled over, fully intending to force myself back to sleep only to freeze at the sound of my door opening.

"I am surprised you used the door."

"I didn't want to scare you," Míra's voice answered, her soft whisper riding on the back of yet another roar of thunder.

"Was it the dream again?" I asked, the tension slowly leaving.

"Yes," Míra gasped, her voice shaking with fear. "I saw him again. I saw his eyes."

My stomach twisted and my muscles tensed, trying to knot themselves into a ball.

"You know you are supposed to go to Wyn for these things, Míra." I still couldn't bring myself to turn to her, even though I could hear the soft sniffles that bled through the gentle wash of rain.

"I know," she said, her voice deepening as she stepped closer to me. "But her and Thom are talking. And the rain..."

She faltered as another roll of thunder echoed over the stone, the sound causing her to jump as a wave of tension ran through my already knotted muscles. I groaned softly, just wishing it could be over already.

"I can't talk about them, Míra," I whispered as I sat up to face her, sending a spark of my magic up into the ceiling. The golden light hovered amongst the crevices there, sending the light over us in ripples in gilded waves.

She stood amongst the shadows, hair pulled into a messy braid that snaked over her shoulder. Long strands of blonde had pulled from the weave, leaving her face framed with tangles of frizz. She stood in her too-small pajamas with a look so gut-wrenching that for a moment I forgot the storm.

"You know I can't."

She nodded once, wiping her nose on the back of her hand. Her red blotchy face illuminated as the accompanying lightning lit up the massive room.

Míra stood there, shuffling her feet as she nodded once more, "I know. I don't want to talk about them, though. We always talk about them..."

Every word was a downward stab. She didn't have to say their names for me to know who she was talking about.

Jaromír, Risha, Dramin.

All the people she had killed.

It was a minefield of emotion, but one that I seemed to be trapped in.

"I don't know why I always have to go to Wyn..."

"You have to go to Wyn because that is a demon you share with her," I said, motioning toward the overstuffed chair that sat near the foot of my bed.

The chair had always been Míra's. I moved it in here specifically so she had somewhere to sit when she needed to talk.

Míra looked at me curiously, clearly not understanding the connection before she moved to the chair, wrapping herself up the large patchwork quilt that was draped over the side. She had pulled the blanket out of the remains of her home in Prague after the war had ended. It had been her brother's.

"You mean because she killed for Edmund?" She stumbled on his name, flinching slightly. "Or with the Drak?"

"Yes," I said, answering both questions as I pulled my own blanket around me and leaned against the headboard. Another loud rumble of thunder sent both of us jumping. "How much do you know?"

"I know that Jos is the only living Drak. And that Wyn killed a lot of them at Edmund's command."

I exhaled as I crossed my arms over my chest. While, to me, this was something I had grown up with, having heard it from my father, Sain, and later from Wyn's, correct, perspective-- it was not common knowledge.

"Yes and no. Yes, Jos is the last living Drak. But Wyn killed more than just 'a lot' of the Draks. With the exception of Sain," she flinched, "and Dramin," another flinch, although this time she curled into herself, practically disappearing beneath the blanket as her guilt smothered her, "she killed them all."

Míra jerked up out of the burrow she had made in her blanket, her eyes wide and perplexed. Her jaw dropped as she emerged, but I didn't wait for her to formulate whatever question was buzzing in her mind. I plowed on, far too tired and cranky to be pestered by questions.

"Edmund knew that the Drak would be gathered at the

main well of Black Water for an annual celebration. You have seen Jos drink the stuff, you know what it is, and what it can do," I hesitated, hating the feeling of guilt that was twisting in my stomach. I hadn't even been born then, but just being the son of the man who had given the order was enough.

"They were in a cave near what is now Mongolia to celebrate the children who had come of age, and have them use their sight for the first time. They were vulnerable and all in one place. My father sent Wyn to kill them, to do away with the Drak and with their powers of foresight. And she did. She didn't even question it. Why would she, he was her master."

Míra didn't look away from me, even as her agitation increased with every word, with every flash of lightning that reflected the moisture in her eyes.

"That's what Edmund had me call him." I barely heard her, but it didn't matter, I already knew. Cail, his guard, had called him that for centuries before I was born. It was what he demanded. A title and unwavering loyalty.

I swallowed and leaned toward her, the blanket that was draped over me falling down to my waist.

"Yes," I said, resting my chin on the tips of my fingers, "and she killed all of those people because she had to. Because her master commanded her. Just like you killed Jaromír." And Risha, I kept that one in my head.

I couldn't say her name to Míra and keep the waves of hostility that were drowning me inside. So I kept it restrained, knowing that just her brother's name was enough to make my point.

It was all it took to release the wall of tears that had built up in her eyes. They poured from her with a gasp and she buried her face in Jaromír's blanket, the sounds of her cries a wrench to my heart.

I sat there, torn between wanting to yell at her, and needing to soothe her. But I couldn't even move. There was too much connection there, too much anger. It wasn't safe.

There was a reason she was supposed to go to Wyn.

"I didn't want to!" she wailed, her words muffled through the fabric. "I didn't want to hurt him. I asked him to move. I just had to kill one person. No one else had to die! I could have kept everyone safe."

"Do you really believe that?" I asked just as a loud burst of thunder rumbled through the cave.

Neither of us jumped.

"Do you really believe that if you had succeeded and killed Thom like Edmund had asked that everything would have been fine, and everyone would be safe?"

It was not the first time I had asked her the question and she responded exactly the same. Her eyes drooped as if in prayer, shoulders sagging before she looked back up to me.

"At the time," she admitted, "which is why I did it. Which is why..."

Her voice caught and faltered, plunging us into a stony silence that was only broken up by the rumbles of thunder as it began traveling into the distance.

"Wyn did it for the same reason, Míra," I said in a hoarse whisper. "She killed people she loved. She watched people die. That is why you must talk to Wyn. Because she killed for the same reasons. You know this, Míra. But what you don't know, and what you are still learning, is how to get out of it. How to forgive yourself. Wyn and Thom are your best teachers for that."

She nodded once, curling the blanket around her tighter

and leaning against the arm of the chair as though she was fully intending to fall asleep there. Knowing her, she probably was.

I leaned back against my headboard, relaxing into the silence as I looked from her to the long strips of skylights that were cut into the rock. The lightning was only a dull flash now, like a light left on down the hall after a nightmare. I stared at the comforting glow, wondering if I should kick her out or not.

Normally I didn't and I had a feeling tonight would follow that pattern.

"How did she get over it?" Míra asked from the nest she had made against the worn fabric of the chair.

"That's something you need to ask her, Míra. I know for me, and for Thom, coming back from Edmund's control began with knowing that we could be forgiven for whatever we had done. And, for many of us, that started with Ilyan."

Mentioning him, remembering his unwavering kindness and understanding only made the pain of losing him that much harder.

"But he's gone," she sighed, the loss dripping from her voice, but not for the same reason I was, it was the loss of a chance. Of acceptance. Of forgiveness.

"Not entirely," I said, the confusion on her face deepening. "Joclyn is still here. And Joclyn forgave you for what you did, she knows what you did in the end. She knows what you helped me do. She knows that there is good in you."

I stared at her, my eyes boring into her as I tried to drive the point home. I wish it was as simple as saying it aloud once and 'poof' magically it was all better. But it was more like a Band-Aid, you had to keep reapplying it until the wound had healed.

And in many ways, her wound was still bleeding.

"And Joclyn is enough?" The trepidation in her voice was clear.

"You have to decide that Míra; at some point you are going to have to tell yourself you are enough too."

She blinked, her lips pressed into a hard line as she slowly dissected what I was saying. I wanted to look her in the eye and tell her that, tell her that she was enough.

But I couldn't. I couldn't because I wanted that too at times, and I knew it didn't fix anything.

"What if Ilyan doesn't agree?" she finally asked, diverting back to my brother. "What if he wants to kick me out?"

"He wouldn't do that," I tried to explain but she cut me off, nearly hysterical.

"But what if he would?"

"He wouldn't," I snapped, pinching the bridge of my nose between my fingers. "Even if you don't understand it, he has already forgiven you, he has already welcomed you home."

"If you are going to say he is 'still with us'..."

"He is still with us, and in more than just memory, Míra."

She narrowed her eyes at me and I faltered, suddenly questioning how much of this I should tell her. As much as she hung around with me and Wyn, she was still an outsider. She was not part of the royal guard, and more importantly, she was still young.

"Edmund placed his magic in you in a Štít," I whispered. "When he died some of that power was left behind."

"What does that have to do with Ilyan?" she asked, her voice trepidatious.

"When a couple is bonded, when they are mated, their

magic is fused together for eternity. When Joclyn and Ilyan were bonded their connection was even deeper, seeping right down to their souls. It's why Joclyn's loss is so deep, she lost more than her mate. She may as well have lost part of her soul."

Míra's eyes grew wide, the bombshell rocking through her.

"No wonder it always makes her so sad," she said quietly. "Is that why her sight can't see him?"

My lips pressed into a tight line as I looked at her, nodding my head once in a move so slight that I wasn't sure she caught it. It didn't matter, however, it wasn't something I was willing to elaborate on, especially with her.

"It also means," I continued on, veering the conversation away from her question, "that Ilyan is still here. I see him in Joclyn every day."

"Just as Ilyan gave me a chance, and gave Wyn a chance, Joclyn is here - doing the same for you."

She seemed to like that, the sadness in her eyes leaving as a tiny spark of hope colored the bottle green orbs. She sunk down into her blanket, and I felt the tension in the room relax. My body leaned into it, the roll of thunder not sounding quite as ominous as it had before.

"Do you think the dreams will ever end?" she asked after a moment, her voice quiet in the dark.

"You know I don't have an answer for that," I said, wishing that I could tell her yes, but I had no answer. I wasn't free of my own terrors, I still saw him every night. Saw the things that were done to me. I didn't know if she would ever be free. But I hoped she would be, I hoped we both would. "I want you to remember that what happened all those years ago wasn't the end, and even though you made those choices, even though we all made those choices, it doesn't make us bad people. There is always time to change."

"I feel like I am bad people." Her voice had darkened, the tone the all too familiar rumble from the moments before my father's magic attempted to take control. I straightened, catching her gaze and holding it in place as I leaned toward her.

"Is that you saying that, or is it the darkness inside of you?"

She pressed her lips together and curled up into a tighter ball, her eyes focused on me with a heavy intensity.

"You are bigger than it, Míra," I whispered, the sound of thunder like a whisper over the rocks again. "And you are a good person. I see it every day, and I saw it when I first met that little girl in the hospital. It was deep inside you then, we just had to let it out - and we will continue to do that."

My magic sparked at the memory, at how one touch from her magic had filled me. I could feel it press toward her now, but I pulled it back.

"Do you think *he* would forgive me?" she asked quietly, her tone making it clear who she was talking about.

"I know he would," I said without hesitation, my heart tightening. "I forgive you, Míra."

She smiled, lips pressed together as she curled up in her blanket, silence falling between us.

The air was cloudy with exhaustion and humidity as I settled back down onto my bed, pulling the covers around me as I curled into myself, sleep finally ready to take me.

The distant sound of thunder was more like a lullaby now, a gentle sound that pulled at my sleep deprived mind, prodding it into the forefront. I listened to the low rumble of thunder and the slow depth of Míra's breaths; instead of the sounds of screams, I heard the power in the earth. Felt the calm.

"What am I going to do while you are gone?" Míra said into the dark, her voice a sob-filled whisper that pulled me from the brink of sleep.

My heart tensed at the question, but I didn't move, I didn't turn to face her.

Of course, she knew what was decided in council, she always found a way.

"You are going to get to know Thom and Joclyn a little better." I knew she wouldn't like the answer.

She sighed, shifted her weight, and I let myself drift away.

CHAPTER 23
RYLAND

The morning came too early, and Wyn's pounding on the door came far too loudly.

I groaned, rolled over, and yelled something mostly inaudible toward the large wooden slab that was inset into the stone.

"Just get your butt out of bed, Ry!" Wyn yelled in reply, the slaps of her shoes echoed from the hall. "I don't want to wait anymore, and I don't want to drag you..."

Her voice faded away as she walked, even though she was yelling just as loud, intentionally waking everybody up. Great.

Another groan escaped me and I punched my pillow, trying to dispel my morning grumps like they were nothing but a bad dream. I hadn't gotten enough sleep to give this day the chance it deserved.

Stupid thunderstorm.

The thought ran through me like a live wire and I jerked, turning toward the large red chair.

Míra had gone, although the large blanket was still

clumped over the faded upholstery. The chair looked far more dilapidated, and far more lonely this morning.

I vaguely wondered when she had left, how long she had stayed, before I threw my own blanket away from me and rushed to my dresser, pulling on fresh clothes and throwing a few extra pairs in a battered backpack I had found in Prague when we were still trapped in the city.

The green canvas was tattered, one of the straps had been sewn back on a few times and was once again threatening its removal. It was, as Wyn liked to point out, dead. But I couldn't bring myself to let go of it. I didn't even know why.

I had picked it up on one of the raids Ilyan had taken me on in Prague, the strap on the bag I had been using to store what little food we had found, broke. In my haste, I had grabbed the first thing I saw. It wasn't new then and was full of school notebooks that I hastily dumped to make room for cans of tuna, beans, and peaches. But one item had stayed lodged at the bottom: a zebra print wallet.

It was still there, but now it was more in memory of the girl who had once owned the pack, who had once lived.

Aliana Olivier

Pack over my shoulder, I bolted out the door, slinking down the hall as a few of my grumpily woken up neighbors watched my hasty retreat. Luckily only a few of them were bold enough to let their displeasure shine on their faces; most were still too scared of me.

As Joclyn's second I was almost as close to royalty as she was. The thought made me uncomfortable, especially given the odd reverse coup that Joclyn was attempting to stage. At least it kept them away this morning. I was in no mood to field a snide comment, especially when they got to go back to bed.

The storm of my mood had not decreased by the time I made it to the entryway, scowl firmly in place as I walked in on Thom, Wyn, and Jos standing in a huddle of whispers.

"Break it up," I grumbled the second I was within earshot; it was always too early in the day to be trapped in girl talk.

The three of them jumped, turning toward me in one fluid motion. The looks on their faces were such an array of emotion that they looked like one of those posters they hang in elementary schools, the ones with little pencil drawings of a boy 'feeling' things. I almost took a step back.

Jos looked so excited she might as well have been floating in mid-air, Thom looked pissed, and Wyn... Wyn looked like she was about to throw up.

I decided for that step back. I liked these shoes.

"Do I want to ask?" I guess if there was any cure for morning grumps this was it.

"No," Wyn growled before anyone could answer, shooting Jos a warning glance that clearly screamed at her to 'back off'. "I ate something sour last night, and Jos is obviously just excited to get rid of us. Maybe we smell bad or something."

Jos' good mood faded away at that, the girl frowning toward Wyn before she rolled her eyes. Thom chuckled, threw some of his renegade dreads over his shoulders and stepped toward me with his hand outstretched.

"Can we get this over with?" Thom asked, looking from me to Joclyn. "I was up late dealing with the backlash from Joclyn's announcement and I want to go back to bed. Take it you were just as surprised?" he added when he saw the look on my face.

I nodded and shot a look at Joclyn. I was nowhere near done fighting her.

"It's too early to do this," she said, reading my foul mood and setting a line in the sand.

"Too early in the day, or too early from when you volunteered me for a life of indentured servitude." I couldn't stop the words, they just seeped out, igniting that scowl from Jos I had expected before, her silver eyes smoldering.

"Give me your hands," Jos snapped, holding out her own with a little more force than she would have a minute ago.

Thom didn't hesitate to put his large calloused hand into Joclyn's. I, however, froze, staring at the silent request and my frustration melted into anxiety.

This isn't wise.

The thought roared through me and I barely restrained the growl of disapproval.

As much as I wanted to fight her decision I had already exhausted my attempts. I knew her reasoning, and she knew my objections.

Gritting my jaw, I placed my hand into hers, instantly feeling her magic rush into me.

"Ryland, you are my second and it is your duty to protect me," she began, her voice was calm considering the magic that laced the inside of her words. "Today, this duty will take you away from my side, to seek a danger that is not yet known."

She paused, the warmth of her magic spreading through me as her gaze dropped to the ground. The sound of her breath rattled through the quiet of the cave and as I gripped her hand, the constraint pulled her focus back to me, her eyes hard as they bored into me.

"As you leave me, so does your protection. Who shall stand by my side in your stead?"

It was not the first time in the last few years that I have

served her that I had left Thom in my stead, that we had stood in this foyer and made this promise of transfer. I didn't know if it was the lack of sleep or the weight of the conversation I had with Míra last night, but something about this time was off. Something was different.

Perhaps Joclyn's random pronouncement from last night was just making me twitchy.

I looked from her to my brother before responding, scrutinizing everything about him, trying to place where this odd renegade emotion was originating from. But he only smiled with his usual, side-mouth twitch and inclined his head, prompting me to continue.

"Thom, my brother by blood and yours by marriage shall take this role while I cannot be by your side. He shall take the oath until I return, and keep you and the Délka Vedení Královsk you wear safe from anyone who would attempt to remove it."

Even as I said the words, I couldn't shake the thought away, my magic reacting to the mood with a wave of cold as I turned to Joclyn.

"Will you accept him into this role?"

"I will," Joclyn replied, her voice strong even though she looked at me quizzically.

"Do you accept this role while my second is gone?" she asked, turning to Thom.

I heard Jos asked the question, I heard Thom's mumbled reply, but I wasn't looking at either of them. I was staring at Wyn, who stood just a few steps away, her eyes glistening with tears as she watched the exchange.

Wyn was crying and I was freaking out over emotional premonitions. Had I woken up in the twilight zone?

"Then, I transfer these duties for a time, giving each of

you the strength to perform your vow. One near, and one far."

With each word she spoke, the warm heat of her magic increased until it filled every part of my body. The heat was a fire pressing against my bones, spreading over my chest as Joclyn's grip on our hands tightened. With a gasp, her eyes widened, dark ink spreading over them until there was nothing but a liquid ebony, her focus looking into us.

Sight was not part of the ritual.

"The path before is covered in lies," she said, her voice lengthening into the deep tone of a Drak. I flinched and tried to move my hand away, but she held on tight, her thumb clasping over the back and locking me in place.

"Follow what little light you see, and save the one who was made for you," she continued, Thom and Wyn watching her intently now. "This is the path that will lead to the truth."

Her last word lingered in the air as her eyes slowly began to fade to their normal silver sheen.

Wyn stepped forward in clear interest, even as I was trying not to freak out. Phantom sights right before we left on a dangerous mission were not helping the panicky apprehension I already felt.

"This sounds like a bigger adventure than I expected," Wyn said, bouncing on the toes of her ripped up kicks. "This is going to have more excitement than smuggling an illegal shipment of radios... or hams... or horses."

"Except without that flyswatter spaceship," I said, purposely messing up the name of her favorite show.

Everything about Wyn went from eager to playfully dangerous in a flash. Everyone else, however, just laughed.

"It's a Firefly class ship, Ry." The warning was clear on her face.

"Firefly, flyswatter, doesn't really matter if we don't have one," I said with a shrug, Thom chuckling darkly from beside me.

Wyn opened her mouth to retort, but I held up a finger, turning to Joclyn with a look that was all business.

The laugh that lined her face faded almost instantly.

"What did you see?" I asked, my stomach twisting at the question.

"Follow what little light you see..." she began to repeat, but I shook my head, shaggy hair tickling my neck as Wyn took a step closer.

"No Jos," I asked, every muscle in my back winding tightly together, the way her jaw was tensing was doing nothing to ease it. "What did you *see?*"

She swallowed, Wyn and I exchanging a look as Jos stared us down, something dark hidden behind her eyes.

"I saw the world," Joclyn's voice was hollow as she stared at us, clearly seeing. "You will see the world. There will be death," Thom rushed forward at that, almost as though he was ready to grab Wyn and rush away, but Jos held up a hand, freezing him in place. "But I do not see that death lying with either of you."

The statement didn't seem to calm Thom down at all, he just stood there, fuming.

"It was more that following the death leads you where you need to go," she finished, the lines in her forehead deepening again.

"But you also said to follow the light," Wyn said in confusion.

"I know." Jos shook her head as though she was trying to jostle around whatever she had seen so as to make sense of it. "There was light there, and a girl with long blonde hair that was always running away..."

"Like Míra?" I asked, not liking the image that my mind was putting together.

"The hair was similar, but it wasn't her." She closed her eyes briefly before they snapped open again. I expected the orbs to be completely bathed in black again, but it was only the spark of bright silver that looked back at me. "I think *she* is the light."

"Míra?" I asked, really not understanding now.

"No," Jos said with the tiniest of smiles playing around her lips, "the blonde girl."

Thom nodded once, as though that settled it, but Wyn and I exchanged a look that clearly said she was as confused as I was. If I had learned anything about Joclyn's sight, however, it was that that they weren't 'doomed to be' as Sain had said, and sometimes they were just downright too vague to make heads or tails of.

Like this one.

Jos sighed in frustration and scrunched her face at us, nose wrinkling as her eyes clamped shut.

"All of it still helps. Plus, now we know for sure that going to London is the right choice," Wyn said brightly, throwing her arm around her best friend's shoulders. "Oh, and that we won't die."

"Am I supposed to be celebrating?" Now Thom looked like he was going to puke.

"I've already called Michel in The Draíocht," I said, pulling the conversation back to where we were headed; the magical faction that lived underground throughout the UK, or what was left of it. "They are expecting us."

"Great!" Wyn said, sarcasm dripping off her as she picked up her backpack and slung it over her shoulder. "I love getting hit on while simultaneously having to soothe

the guy's ego. If I have to hit on him again, you owe me twenty dollars."

"You say that like money is good anymore." I rolled my eyes. "Last I heard most of the food in the UK is rationed and electricity is at a premium."

Her face fell instantly.

"Do I need batteries for my stereo?" She looked like someone had just taken her most prized possession. "I only have four left and I'm saving them."

"Nah. I am sure someone can sing Renegade for you while you drift off to sleep," Thom began with a smile, his arm drifting around her shoulders. "Either that or you can go kidnap Dennis DeYoung, didn't he survive the bite?"

I wasn't sure if Thom was prodding her or calming her, but it didn't matter, I laughed all the same, Jos joining in as Thom's smart-ass smirk melted into a soft smile as he pulled Wyn into him for a far-too-emotional-for-my-tastes goodbye.

Avoiding emotions was my specialty. I stepped away as Thom and Wyn moved closer, Jos following me in my retreat. She walked silently, sipping Black Water from a large brown mug that I assume she had placed on the floor by her feet during the ceremony.

"Are you okay?" she asked before drinking again.

"I don't know," I responded, glancing back at Wyn and Thom. I half expected them to have turned into a two-headed monster with the way they were kissing. "Something feels off. During the transfer ceremony, I kept getting a feeling... I don't know how to explain it, but it was like something was telling me to run." I stopped mid-sentence, running my hands through my hair. "Never mind. It sounds ridiculous."

"You are talking to someone who sees into the future

and telling me your feeling sounds ridiculous?" She raised an eyebrow at me and I couldn't help but laugh.

"Point taken," I conceded. "Doesn't make it sound any less bizarre."

She shrugged, thankfully not choosing to pick that fight. She knew that her sight made me uncomfortable.

"Well, I don't think you are that far off," she said, taking another drink. "Thom is all out of sorts too. Nerves. Maybe neither of you want to go."

"You know I never do," I sighed, purposefully kept my focus as far away from her as possible. Staring at the stone cave was as good a choice as any to conceal my emotions. "I don't like not being here to protect you."

"I know, but this time, maybe you can focus on protecting Wyn." Staring contest with the rock wall forgotten, I turned back to her, her silver eyes flashing with something I didn't understand as she smiled at me from behind her mug.

"You have met her, right?" I chuckled, "she doesn't need anyone to take care of her, and you know that even if I try I might come away without a finger... or worse."

Joclyn's smile deepened, her own chuckle escaping as Wyn's exasperated response echoed over to us, "I heard that."

"Well, maybe just make sure she doesn't get into too much trouble," Joclyn amended, careful to keep her voice low.

"That sounds closer to what this mission will be like," I said, knowing full well that if it was anything like our last one we would have more trouble not blowing our cover than getting work done. Wyn wasn't really great at 'laying low.' "That, and making sure she doesn't annoy too many people with Styx."

"I heard that, too!" Wyn roared, her voice half-full of humor as she broke away from Thom and steamrolled toward where Jos and I had migrated to across the hall.

"I'm not taking it back," I said, as I turned toward her, the tension in my chest finally dissipating. "We all know it's true, and as much as you fight us, you and your classical music may not be welcome in these trying times."

"I will fight that until the day I die," Wyn said with a stoic vow, her hand held over her heart as though she was pledging allegiance to the obsession that is Styx. "It is not classical music. It is not even classic rock. I lived through the 1950s, the 1850s and a few hundred years before that," she said, rubbing her index finger over her nose as she faded off. "Styx is not classical music. They are gods among musicians."

Thom's eye roll was so extreme I was surprised he didn't lose control of the muscles altogether.

"I'm suddenly feeling very threatened," Thom deadpanned. "How can I ever compete with Dennis DeYoung? He is just too sexy. That mullet... me-yow."

Thom made the sound like a tiger and Wyn turned on him, her skin rolling with flame as her magic flared. Thom laughed. Although the sight of Wyn's fire magic igniting on her skin was quite frightening, he had obviously seen it enough to not step back as Jos and I did.

"Maybe I do need to keep her under control," I said under my breath to Joclyn, the Queen giving me a smug side eye just as Wyn whirled back around, flame and fury extinguishing all at once.

"Whatever," she said, checking her faded band shirt for scorch marks. "Five hundred years of manhandling this puppy. I think I've got it."

She winked at me, gave Jos a massive hug and turned to Thom, giving one last silent goodbye.

"High Street?" Wyn asked, referencing the overrun abandoned district of the city that we always Stuttered into, the place having been abandoned many years ago. After what the mortals did to it, there was no chance of recovery or resettlement. It was safe.

"Yeah, aim for the living room of that tilting house on the left side. The sun's been up for a few hours and I would rather not risk any more photographers," Jos said, holding her hand out to me and I winced.

"Photographers?" Wyn asked in confusion, but neither Jos nor I responded.

I was too busy bracing myself for being dragged into the tunnel of claustrophobic pain again.

"Take care of her will you?" I said to Thom, slowly lifting my hand to the girl in question, I could already feel my bones twist in pain of the coming Stutter.

Thom nodded once, "And you take care of her."

Wyn glowered, but said nothing, choosing instead to vanish just as I placed my hand into Joclyn's and she pulled me into the terribly twisting world of a Stutter.

I was never going to get used to this.

CHAPTER 24
RYLAND

The second we emerged in the remains of what used to be an immaculate townhouse the aroma of rot and smoke assaulted me, clinging to my skin and clothes and sending me gasping. I folded over, hands on knees in an attempt to keep myself upright, as falling to the ground in this place was not the smartest option.

The floor was littered with rubble, the broken remains of a well-lived life scattered over the once pristine wooden floor. Broken pieces of china, the cracked face of a child's doll, books... bones. You could still see the remains of the family who lived here in the corner, huddled together, screaming as the bombs dropped.

When everything first started, this part of London was considered a safe haven for those who survived the bite. Thousands lived here, in the one country that never issued an order to kill them. It was the other countries that dropped the bombs. The other countries that ended their safety.

Even though the remains of the UK government still hadn't placed an order to kill those bitten by the diseased

Vilẏ, they had all been forced underground, turning what had once been a growing and vibrant community into a graveyard.

"Breathe Ry," Jos whispered, her hand on my back as she tried to calm me.

"You know," I said between gasps for air, "I'd like to say that I'd give mastering Stuttering another try. But it's still going to be a hard no."

"Aww," Wyn soothed, taking her place on the other side of me, her bangles jangling as she placed her hand on my back. "It's not so bad once you get used to it, you'll need to master it once you are King."

That was all it took to send me standing, a deep glare firmly shot in Wyn's direction. Jos quickly stifled a laugh, which was good as I probably would have gone off on her otherwise.

"I haven't agreed to anything," I said, keeping my voice low as I drew a very heavy line in the sand.

My stern tone had no effect and Wyn's smile stretched into a Cheshire Cat grin, her eyes not leaving mine as she stared right into me.

"You sound just like your brother," she said, her voice a low prod as the corner of her mouth jumped even more, her eyes shining with all her playful nefariousness.

"Maybe he just sounds like me," I said in a quick retort that I knew at once had left too many holes for Wyn to poke through.

It wasn't my fault she had caught me way off guard, or that Míra had kept me up half the night. Even the thought forced me to stifle a yawn.

"Your brother, who was born nearly a thousand years before you... sounds like you..." She raised an eyebrow, her tone clearly mocking me. "I mean, I know you are both powerful... but time travel?"

"Us Krul boys have many skills..."

"Knock it off," Jos interrupted, stepping between us and putting a hand on each of our shoulders in a barricade.

"No prob, my lady," Wyn said, throwing her arm around Jos as the girl in question's face melted into a deep scowl.

"I said knock it off, Wyn."

"Sure, sure," she said as she released her, glass crunching under toe as she shifted her weight. "You know I just had to get one in before we left... my lady."

Jos groaned, doing her best to ignore Wyn as she gave her a clumsy bow.

"You have your mission," Jos stated, turning to me and choosing to ignore the woman who was now hyper focused on her tiny flip phone, texting Thom more than likely.

"I do," I said, choosing to omit the title that she hated almost as much as I did. "I will find her, Joclyn. Or at least figure out what is going on. Let us know what you find out from our prisoner."

"She should be awake today or tomorrow," Jos nodded once, our voices fading off as tension and stress began to strangle my muscles.

I hated leaving her. I hated not being able to be there, to protect her. Knowing that this woman who was obviously sent to kill me, to kill us, was still inside of Imdalind was making me uncomfortable.

"Everything will be fine," Jos whispered, obviously reading the look on my face.

"I know," I lied.

"Thom's got this, Ry," Wyn whispered from behind me, obviously having put her phone away. "Trust your brother."

I could only nod, carefully placing Joclyn back on the

floor as I turned to Wyn, "I do. Doesn't make me any less nervous."

"All the more reason for us to do this as fast as possible," Wyn said, shifting her feet in what was either anticipation or aggravation.

I couldn't tell which, and I wasn't about to ask.

Jos gave her a quick hug, whispering something to her before she pulled away.

"I expect full, and speedy, results," Jos said with a smile, pounding her fist against mine, and then Wyn's before she vanished; leaving Wyn and I standing in the destroyed house, drenched by the silent death that normally occupied this part of the city.

"Well, here we go," Wyn said brightly, sliding a glove over her holey hand before stepping toward what little was left of the poor family. "Excuse me, but do you have any hints for us?"

My stomach twisted, "What are you doing?"

"Following the dead," she answered simply, the toe of her chucks kicking at the bones of what used to be someone's foot.

"Wynifred," I snapped, using her full name and earning myself a glare in the process. "She said to follow the light..."

"And the dead," she interrupted me. I ignored her.

"Either way, I am sure mutilating the dead was not part of the plan. Nor should it be," I could barely get the words out.

Watching the charred bones roll over the floor was making my stomach turn.

"Don't freak yourself out, Ry," Wyn said, straightening her backpack and heading toward what was once a door, the heavy slab of wood now only hanging from a hinge. "You're acting like you have never seen a dead body before."

As much as I would like to fight her, this was not a pissing contest I wanted to get into, especially with her.

We walked along what had once been a street in silence, magic stretching from us as we looked for signs of life, signs of magic, anything that could spell trouble.

There was nothing but rubble and the smell of death. The shattered remains of the townhome we just left were all that was left of the once elegant line of red brick row houses. Not a single other thing stood, everything was piles of rubble.

"You getting anything?" Wyn whispered as she climbed over a large slab of asphalt, the jagged edge breaking off as she vaulted off the top and to the cracked remains of the road below.

"No," I returned, focused on traversing over the tiny caverns that had opened up between the pieces of road, or what was left of it.

When the bombs had gone off, everything had been torn to shreds, pulled into what was now a giant crater in the center of the high streets.

As we traversed another oversized pothole however, and crested the last rise of rubble and earth, 'crater' felt a little bit like an understatement.

The massive hole spread over at least four of the winding London streets in a space as large as a football stadium. A depression sunk into the ground, diving down past the sewage lines and opening up what had once been their underground subway system. The explosion had ripped through the world, left to fester like a canker, the wound still bleeding.

We moved toward the caldera, the ground sloping down before opening to the gaping mouth of the earth, the sides lined with the remains of the world. Houses lay in pieces, cars were shattered and strewn about as if they were nothing more than toys who made an unfortunate end with a violent toddler.

Dozens of fires dotted the landscape, pops and sparks of the brightest blue erupting every time the heat encountered a gas line, or some other accelerant. The entire image was like something out of hell. It never got easy to see, even a year after the bomb had dropped.

Everything still burned. The world still screamed.

"This is my favorite part," Wyn said, tightening her backpack as she shot me a grin.

"Your favorite part is the massive grave?" I asked, back straightening as the muscles there tightened, tensing against my bones.

Shooting me a disparaging look, she took off into the air, the strong pulse of her magic pulling at my hair and clothes as she spun and dove, clearly showing off.

"You are as bad as your husband," I called after her, letting my own magic swell as I burst into the air after her.

Instead of creating my own air ballet however, I set my sights on the dark opening near the bottom of the hole, the jagged entry to the former underground subway system waiting for us.

It should have been a straight shot, but the fires had shifted since the last time we had visited, their long tongues now licking around the dark opening. The sparks of flame erupted every few minutes, sending out long reaching fingers toward us, waiting to grab us.

"Wanna try it without magic?" Wyn hollered as she came up right beside me, her eyes focused on the twisting maze of flame.

"Ha!" The sound had no humor behind it. "Fire can't

touch you, Wyn. That is not a competition I want to find myself in."

"You scared?" she teased, her eyebrows wiggling comically as she swung around to face me, the action forcing me to stop mid-flight.

"Nope. I am also not stupid," I said, trying not to sound too much like a disgruntled third grader. I am pretty sure I didn't succeed judging by the way her lower lip pulled out. "Your magic is fueled by fire, Wyn. There is no way I could win."

"So you won't even try?" Her face was in full pout now, but the mischief in her eyes was clear, the light sparkling as she rolled onto her back, soaring through the air beside me like we were in a swimming pool.

"Get out of here Wyn," I said, unable to hold in the laugh any longer,

"Your loss," she said before soaring toward the flames, obviously intent on getting there before I did and needed to extinguish them.

Wyn danced through the air as she approached them, twisting and twirling in preparation to dive through the endlessly flickering abyss. She was just about to dive under the first wave of flame when I extended my hand, a bright line of white soaring from me and right to the burning fire, smothering it in one hiss of smoke.

"Ryland!" she bellowed, stopping in mid air to turn to me, humor and rage fighting for room on her face. "Gah! You are seriously no fun, you know that?"

"That seemed pretty fun to me," I teased, laughing at her as she rushed me. Her own smile was threatening to smother the anger she was still trying to hold onto.

"Jerk," she hissed, smashing her solid fist into my equally solid bicep and wincing.

251

I only laughed harder.

"You owe me a race for that," she threatened, massaging her hand in an effort to relieve what I am sure was a dislocated finger.

"A race I will gladly win," I bellowed happily, my voice echoing off of cars and trains and who knows what else.

It came back to us in an explosion of sound, a reverberation that turned into a deep haunting laugh. We turned toward the sound, Wyn's jaw tightening as the powerful warrior side she attempted to keep locked away inside her snapped into place.

"You hear that, too?" I asked, looking from her to the other side of the crater, to the houses and cars that were beginning to slide down the walls of the hole. Everything tumbled end over end as though a massive hand had pushed the remains of the city into an avalanche.

"Awesome," Wyn mumbled with a wide-eyed look toward me. "So, do we run and lead them right to the underground, or do we just chill here and wait for them to attack us?"

"We are less than an hour into this thing and already being attacked," I growled, tightening the straps on my backpack in preparation.

Not that having a fight while flying through the air was hard, but we hadn't even made it to The Draíocht yet and I had no interest in losing a good portion of my belongings in a fight.

"To be fair, it was just a laugh. Nothing has happened yet," Wyn said flippantly, waving her hand to the side just as a massive explosion rocked through the other side of the caldera, which sent another wave of debris cascading toward the graveyard at the bottom.

"Well damn it," Wyn growled, a spark of her magic

flaring in the corner of my eye. "That was magical wasn't it?"

"Considering that bright purple isn't usually the shade we see in a gas explosion, I would have to say yes." I scanned through the rubble that was close to a mile away.

I could already tell that this wasn't going to work. With as much destruction that covered the mountain I wasn't going to find anything, even if I was closer.

And I wasn't going to get closer.

"Do you sense anything?" I asked her, trying to push my magic ever closer.

"You know I need contact with the earth," she scoffed, her fingers sparking with bright red flame again. "This is ridiculous. If they haven't attacked us yet, they aren't going to. And I for one am not interested in walking into a trap. How about I just blow that side and we vamoose through the tube under a shield. Easy peasy."

I clenched my jaw. It was never that easy. Not with her, not ever. Besides, I was pretty sure that her 'blowing that side' of the caldera was only going to lead to far too many problems. Like a collapse, or reminding the world that magic exists.

"That is a bad idea, Wyn."

"Okay Mr. Second-in-Command," Wyn sassed, her magic carrying her through the air until she faced me. "What do you suggest?"

I gave her a stern look and looked around her to the other side of the pit, still searching for the sign of whatever had caused the explosion.

Needle in a freakin' haystack.

"Fine," I sighed, running my hand through my hair as my magic stalled, sending me down a few inches before I caught myself. "Hit them twice on either side of the explosion, give it about a hundred yard berth."

"Com'on Ry," Wyn whined.

"I'll hit above and below," I continued as though she hadn't interrupted me. "Then shield, circle twice, extinguish the flames there," I said, pointing to some particularly dangerous looking fires near the bottom, "and head straight for The Draíocht."

"Through the flames?" Wyn asked, the eagerness clear on her face.

"Yes, Wyn," I said, pushing her a bit and sending her soaring back a few feet. "But no racing. Just make it through safely, please. I'm not fireproof."

She gave me a look that clearly expressed that I wasn't in fact fireproof, a fact that didn't escape me, before soaring off, vanishing from my sight in the process.

"I guess we are starting?" I said after her, not loud enough that she could hear.

Working with Wyn had benefits, she never treated me like some kind of untouchable royalty, and only rarely treated me like I was even worthy of bossing her around. At least seriously.

Plus, she could take care of herself. That was the best part.

Not that Joclyn couldn't, but I wasn't responsible for Wyn.

I could just fight. I could just destroy.

The realization was an electrical jolt and I grinned, the evil laugh in my mind rising to meet it. I let my magic flare, the warm power flood through me as I vanished from sight, disappearing just as the first of Wyn's explosions rocked the pit and sent everything shaking.

A massive semi truck began to slide down the steep

slope, a burst of fire and smoke raining toward us as whatever it was carrying exploded.

I couldn't be sure, but I swear I heard Wyn laugh somewhere in front of me, her high pitched cackle drowned by the roar of fire and rubble.

Soaring through the air toward the explosion, I let my own magic ignite in two powerful jolts. They cut through the air in lines of the brightest yellow, sparking like lightning before they hit against earth and rubble in a massive ball of fire, exploding in flame and sparks of green.

A bang of a dozen cannons echoed around us, the sound increasing as Wyn's second explosion hit its mark. The racket of the detonation mutated to the roar of an avalanche as the long spires of fire below me extinguished with a hiss. The diversion was in place just as I arrived at the wicked tongues of flame that guarded the entrance to the cave.

The bright flames burned as I flew right into them. Even with the shield I could feel my skin begin to burn, I could taste the smoke on my tongue. Holding the last gulp of fresh air in my chest, I swooped and weaved through flames and smoke until I found myself at the other side, feet firmly planted on the twisted rails of the once popular underground train system.

Gasping for clean air and only finding ash, I fell into the crumbling cement walls of the tube, clinging to the cold wall as I let my magic rush through me, healing skin and lungs and everything that had been burned in my journey through the wall of fire.

"That was the dumbest thing ever," Wyn snapped from somewhere in front of me, her body still hidden behind a shield. "You are supposed to weave, Ry, not make Ryland shaped holes in the flames."

"I did weave," I snapped back between gasps, the retort sending her snickering.

"Well then you weave as well as an elephant doing ballet."

"It wasn't that bad." At least it couldn't be. I felt like I was avoiding the flames, of course I was fairly certain that clothes, skin, and lungs were going to say otherwise.

"Uh huh," Wyn began, her voice echoing with her steps as I assumed she began to move further into the dark tunnel, not that I could see her. "Either way you better move your elephant butt over here. I am pretty sure there are a dozen of them, and if they saw you cut through the fire like I did they are heading this way."

"There are actually more around twenty, but they aren't going to attack you."

The deeply accented voice cut through the loud crackle of flame and bending metal, and we both turned, ready to attack.

"Michel!" Wyn gasped, her voice caught in surprise as she burst into existence, her shield dropping only a moment before my own. "You should be more careful, I almost attacked you."

"I was counting on it," the tall dark-skinned man cooed as he walked into the flickering light of the fire, the red and yellows of the flames reflecting off his skin in beautiful shades of gold.

He was dressed in layers of jackets and scarves that at one point might have been stylish. Hell, I was dressed in an almost identical fashion. However, now they were covered in the remains of a war that he had been unwittingly thrust into. Layers for safety, layers for warmth, the dirt just helped us all to blend in.

"Then start counting on a few lost limbs," Wyn said,

popping her hip as she glared at Michel, but he only smiled deeper, flashing a row of perfectly straight, bright white teeth.

"Michel," I began, stepping between the two and extending my hand in greeting. The man took it easily, although he didn't quite break eye contact with Wyn.

It was the same every time we were here. The same weird game of cat and mouse, except with him it was more the pursuit of something he could never have. I was surprised Wyn put up with it as well as she did.

I squeezed Michel's hand, hard, the action sending him jumping and pulling his focus right back to me.

"Joclyn sends her regards," I quipped, my voice hard as I reminded him who he was talking to.

"And mine to my Queen, and to her second," he said, bowing his head just a touch, his dark eyes refusing to break eye contact with me.

It was the usual greeting for my position, but with him it just made me uncomfortable. The man was too full of flattery. I could never tell if he was telling the truth, or simply protecting his own ego. Today, however, there was a darkness behind his eyes that screamed danger, an untrustworthy ego that was making me question his intentions.

I knew he was safe. I knew he was trustworthy, he had done enough good in both Ilyan and Joclyn's name over the last few centuries. But it didn't change the fact that the man was greasy, and not only in the way he tried to seduce Wyn, but in the way he slithered in and out of existence.

I shook my head, I was probably still on edge from earlier.

"We didn't expect to see you here," I said, dropping his hand but keeping my wide frame between him and Wyn, a human barricade to the woman that he was far too interested in devouring.

I guess I couldn't stop the protective side of me from taking over. While it may not be a character flaw, it most certainly got me in a lot of trouble. Or at least made Wyn frustrated, judging by the sharp spine of her magic that she shot into my back, the warm hint little more than a warning shot.

Point taken.

"Nor did we expect to get attacked," Wyn added, stepping around me with one firmly placed side-eye.

"You were not attacked," Michel grinned, his eyes darting between Wyn and I as he spread his palm, a bright orb of silvery light appearing there before he threw it up to the ceiling.

Glittering light rippled over us as Michel stepped into the darkness of the tube, and led us down the winding path to their camp.

My own orb of yellow floated up to join his, the brilliant colors following behind us like a lost dog as they illuminated the twisted roots that were growing through the ceiling and trailing down the walls.

"That sure seemed like an attack to me," Wyn said behind me, she was clearly doing her best to not sound as exasperated as she did with Michel, even though she gave me a long side eye that instantly sent my guard up.

Wyn didn't like the man, yes, but the look was intense, even for her.

"Not from the men you sensed, they will not attack you, of this I promise my dear, Wynifred." He spoke with honey and fire, the use of her full name sending Wyn glowering even further. I couldn't even get away with using it, and this man was facing utter revulsion.

Knowing Wyn, she was already plotting ways to make him pay.

"Pardon me if I don't believe you," she growled, the response the closest she could get to reprimanding the man. "Because that explosion sure seemed like a warning shot."

"The men you sensed, Wynifred, are mine, they will not attack you," Michel said as he glanced back at us, the greasy smile that lined his face slipping away as though it could no longer cling in place.

I trusted nothing that he was saying, and Wyn's surly side eye was already begging us to get out of here. I just shook my head; she knew as well as I did that Michel was the best contact we had in the UK. He *was* slimy, which was kind of the point, he had the contacts and the rumors we needed to finish this job quickly.

"And the explosion?" I asked. "That magic was not healed. Was that yours as well?"

"The explosion was not ours, Ryland," he continued. "Although, I assume that after your display that whatever threat that was there is no more. It was Ryland's tactical ability I saw in that, yes?"

I nodded and forced a laugh, "Wyn just wanted to blow the place up."

The dark tunnel instantly broke out in a loud guffaw of a laugh; and I thought I had forced my laugh.

"I would expect nothing less from our little arsonist," Michel soothed, looking at her as though she was some desirable piece of meat.

"I don't know if I should be flattered or not," Wyn hissed, her voice deep as she postured him, popping her hip in the process. "That doesn't change the fact that your men tried to attack us."

259

"Not attack," he corrected again, still trying to laugh even though he was starting to sound more deranged. "They are guarding the north entrance for your arrival as we have not used it in many months."

This tunnel was one of the main entrances to their underground sanctuary. Coming from the rubble of what was still considered a dead zone practically guaranteed comers and goers safe passage. It was why he had chosen it, and why Joclyn and I had helped him build it out after the bomb had fallen.

Just the idea that they had abandoned it reeked of danger, the low tones of the man's voice only heightened the warning lights that were flaring in my mind.

"Why haven't you used it?" I asked, my voice just as tense as his, a mood that was only growing as he glanced back at us, coming to a slow, purposeful, stop.

My magic flared as he turned to face us, as the danger that was seeping off of him pasted itself against my skin. Every muscle was a wall of iron as I felt my hands heat, the floor under me growing warm as Wyn's magic began to spread.

"I think, for the same reason you are here."

"I'm sorry?" I asked, my voice stern and hard as I took another step toward the man, his smile only barely smothering the hard light in his eyes. "I said nothing about our visit other than..."

"A security issue," Michel interrupted, repeating the wording I had used when I had called him just a few hours before. "You have said it was a security issue and the Queen was sending you to get to the bottom of it."

There was something about the way he repeated what I had said that was unnerving.

"Yes," I said through the clench in my jaw.

"And then you arrive here ready for a battle. Ready for what was out there that did attack you." He was grinning, the smile sending a chill over my skin as he stepped closer. He knew he had won.

"You were attacked, weren't you?" Michel said when I said nothing, his eyes almost eager as he leaned into me.

"We..." I began, any response I had been about to give him trapped in my throat as Wyn gave me one sharp look. That was all I needed to know I was in dangerous territory. With her. With him.

With whatever game this man was playing.

I knew Michel as far as the war. Wyn knew him as far as the French Revolution, and everything about her was screaming warning.

I quickly pulled my cards closer to my chest, switching tactics.

"What do you know?" I finally asked, my voice harsh as his eyes continued to shift.

Michel's face fell even as his smile flickered. He stepped past where Wyn and I stood, back toward the flames. Even in the distance you could see them lick at the opening to the tunnel like a greedy monster waiting to devour us.

He waved his hand through the air, sparks shooting through his fingers as broken pieces of tile, twisted lengths of rail, and massive rocks danced through the air, creating a barrier that stretched from floor to ceiling and wall to wall.

While on this side the barrier was smooth, I could tell at once that on the other side it would appear as if nothing more than a cave-in had occurred during the year before.

Watching the barrier pull together so smoothly was unnerving. Not for the strength of the magic, but for the knowledge that he had done this before.

261

"Michel?" I asked, "I need you to tell me what you are talking about? What do you know?"

Wyn shifted her weight beside me; waiting, watching, and knowing she was monitoring the space for magic or danger. Judging by the hard look in her eye, most of that monitoring was being done on him.

Michel cowered a bit at the authority in the question, the greasy manipulator that I had always known him to be showing through briefly before his false confidence slid into place like a steel trap.

"The walls may have ears, my friend," he said, fixing me with a steely wink. "We must be careful what we say. As I said, the reason the north entrance is closed, the reason the city of London is bathed in dangers and the sounds of forgotten screams every night, the reason our numbers have dwindled to half of what we once were, is the same one for which we owe your visit."

He paused, looking from me to Wyn as his resolve slowly returned, the power I had expected in it fizzled away as he gasped the last few words into existence.

"We have been attacked as well," he finished, looking anywhere other than at me. "The SSU has come to play."

CHAPTER 25
ILYAN

The restraints were more comfortable than the handcuffs, but that was where the benefits stopped.

The straps were tight against my wrists and ankles as they held me against the bed in a tight spread eagle. The soft padding on the bands were only giving me the illusion of comfort, for the more they tightened them, the more they pulled at me. The more my joints ached, and the more the heat under my skin rumbled.

It was getting harder and harder to control it.

My muscles tensed as yet another needle was plunged into my skin, the short stubble on my scalp prickling as I twisted toward the nurse who stood beside me, filling vial after vial.

I watched her, recognizing her at once as the nurse from that very first day. Although her hair was streaked in grey and her face lined with wrinkles, the color of her eyes was the same as her daughter's. Katenka. The name on the badge was the same.

No wonder Kaye was Kaye.

I was desperate to ask. Desperate to know if Kaye was

okay and what had happened. The woman didn't look at me, however, and I didn't dare say anything with so many people in the room.

Detective Bondar and his companion stood anxiously at the foot of my bed, their feet shuffling as they stood closer to the wall than to me. For all that I had heard them yell about cases and propriety and a dozen other things that I couldn't place, they had been pretty happy about being here until a few minutes prior, when the man that now hovered over me had entered.

He wore a suit so dark it made his blonde hair appear platinum, both colors emphasizing his eyes so that they appeared to be little green sparks of danger. He glowered at everyone with those eyes, his expensive shoes crunching on bits of glass and metal that had been missed when they put the room back together.

Although the bodies of the Vilÿ had been swept from the room by a few blood covered nurses, you could still smell the blood through the strong aroma of the antiseptic. You could still hear the workers as they scoured the blood from the halls, talking of the way all the monsters had dropped dead around me.

Of the mystery of it.

Of the miracle.

The tapping of the man's shoes stopped as he bent over me, the low rumble of the television behind him making it clear it was turned to the news again.

"What is your name?"

The tone of the interrogator's voice was ice. It soaked the room with a shiver that ran down my spine, the same fear present even though he had asked the question before.

It was all he had asked. I still wasn't going to give him an answer.

I lay still, as if I had another option. Defiance spread through me as I met him head on, letting the warmth of my magic fill me as I once again tried to gauge my power and ability. My snarl faded when I caught sight of the embroidery on his lapel.

It was a tiny flare, an eight-point sunburst star with one long spire that stretched almost double the width above and below. It balanced on the point of his lapel like a top. The man so close I could clearly see the long threads in yellow and the brightest red that made up the insignia, the symbol the same as I had seen on the breast of The Cleaners' uniforms.

Then, it had been an ugly yellow smear painted on body armor and helmets. Here it was worn with pride. Like a warning.

A brand.

Judging by the reaction of those in the room, by the way Kaye had shivered with the sound of their boots, this group was feared.

This group was in control.

"I don't know." Forcing myself to look away from the star, I gave the interrogator the same answer I had before, the monotone response obviously not what he had expected. "I would like to know who you are, however."

The question seemed to be one that was not allowed. The moment I said it Kaye's mother jumped, the motion sending the needle she was manipulating painfully through my arm.

I restrained the yelp as I jerked against the restraints, all eyes turning from me to her as she stepped back, bloody needle held before her.

She cowered under the look the man gave her, the same one he then turned to me, his warning relayed.

"I am sure you would." His eyes narrowed before he clicked his heels against the floor. "Enemies of the State don't gain all of the information they want. That was how the old government operated. I am not part of them."

"So, you overthrew the government, then?" The interrogator smiled at my question, the look a dark smear of grease against my heart. The need to back down mixed dangerously with the need to plow ahead, to push buttons, to cause problems. If only the stubborn desire to challenge him wasn't so loud, if only it didn't buzz under my skin.

"*Overthrew*," he laughed. The sound made my muscles tense. "This is not the word I would choose."

"Nor I." The grumble came from the corner where Dr. Sirko sat perched behind the computer that had been brought in to replace the one I destroyed.

The response to the two words was instantaneous. The Detective shifted his feet and moved closer to the wall, the soldiers stepped toward Sirko, guns cocking as a few moved to aim. The guns were waved away by the dark-suited man. Not an interrogator, I realized, an Officer. The Officer turned toward my doctor with a scowl and a snap that even made me jump.

"What word would you use, *Doctor*?"

The threat was clear. A shadow of fear crossed the doctor's face, but he straightened his shoulders, his eyes unwavering as he faced the Officer. My magic sparked at the look in his eyes, that same protective need growing strong as my power rose up to meet it. I almost let it free, but it still felt out of control.

And surrounded by so many guns I knew it wasn't worth the risk. I didn't know if I could do anything against guns.

"I would call it murder." There wasn't a wave of fear in his voice, although I could sense it in the air around him.

"Murder?" The Officer choked out a laugh. "Murder to protect the people that the former government would not?"

The heat in my hands began to bubble as the Officer took a step toward Dr. Sirko. I tightened my hands into white-knuckled fists, determined to keep it under control.

"Murder to remove those that would rather see you bitten and writhing..."

Another step. The burn was moving up my arm now, the heat growing as the soldiers in the room began to re-aim their weapons, the motions deflating the elderly doctor's confidence.

The heat was a wave now, I could feel it wanting to explode. Was it worth it?

I tensed in an attempt to stifle it, the motion sending the restraints rattling and the Officer turned, his green eyes narrowing as he reached for the large gun that swung on his hip.

"It is murder to kill a family who would only..."

The Officer swung toward Dr. Sirko, a hiss of expletives and warnings streaming from him in Czech. It was only noise, my focus had been dragged away by a sharp jab in my arm and the scornful eyes of nurse Katenka. The danger was clear. I stared at her, trying to ask a thousand questions and glean a thousand answers. But there was only a warning of danger in her eyes.

"Is she...?" I began to ask, but even those two quiet words pulled the focus of the men, the bickering between Dr. and Overlord ending abruptly.

"Am I what?" the officer snarled as he misheard me, pushing the hair that had come loose from the slicked style back into place.

Katenka kept her head down, focusing on the new vial of blood she was taking and hastily grabbing gauze the moment she was done.

"Are you part of a military?" I lied without hesitation, the scratchy burn in my throat making my words blur together.

"I am here to assess you, sir." He avoided the question artfully, and although I could see Dr. Sirko shift behind him, the man said nothing. He only began inputting numbers into his computer and scratching who knows what on a pad of paper, his back now curled and shivering in submission. "I am here to determine who you are, what you know, and how you took down a fleet of the Chrlič on your own."

"I didn't..." I stalled, not knowing which lie I needed to give him first.

"I have told you, Commander," Dr. Sirko said, only faltering slightly when the tap of the commander's shoes gave warning, "he remembers nothing, and he was in a coma when..."

"I believe none of that," the now identified commander interrupted with a snap as he turned back to the physician. "You are a traitor to your country..."

"I am a hostage and the only competent physician in this facility..."

"Your hospital, and the local police," the commander continued with a nod to the two directors, who instantly stiffened. "The fact that they have been led into this guise only shows me further how inept you are to continue his case and his care..."

At that, both detectives and doctor erupted into revolt. Their voices ran over each other, combining with the low rumble of the television until the room was full of sound, full of anger.

The emotion pressed against me, heating and swirling until that same lightheadedness from before came over me, the edges of my vision pulling in and out of focus.

With a low groan, my body collapsed weakly, the metal clasps on my restraints clicking gently at the removed tension.

The anger in the room evaporated.

"Nurse," Sirko spoke over the still protesting detective, "I need you to dose him with cyclosporine. Make sure his blood levels are..."

"Don't dose him with anything," the Commander snapped, rushing to my side and hovering over me. "I need to test his blood."

"You have enough," Kaye's mother finally spoke, her voice so kind that the snap she tried to place in it felt awkward. "If he doesn't get this his body will reject his heart and he will slip back into a coma..."

"The coma never occurred..." The sound of the cleaning crew in the hallway silenced at the sound of his roar.

"Stubborn parasite," my nurse grumbled, a painful prick in my arm preceding the cool flood of foreign medication.

"The coma was a direct result of the heart transplant. His body is rejecting..."

"Heart transplant?" I asked in confusion, the sound swallowed by the Commander's hand slamming against the railing of my bed, the sound causing everyone to jump and cower back to the corners that they had been hiding in before.

I stared at the white-knuckled grip of the militant man

and listened to the echo of the impact, remembering my own fist slamming against a table in some other room.

Against a map in some other time.

The memory was no more than shadow overrun by the shout of the Commander's tirade.

"Stop this nonsense. They say you remember nothing. They say your heart is not yours. I do not believe them..."

"My heart...?" I couldn't stop the shock from bleeding out.

As well as I had put a lock on everything, this burst out of me, followed by the same image that had haunted me since the moment they had brought me back from the dead.

My blood, spreading over the stone. The pieces of my broken heart erupting from inside of me in an explosion that burst over rock.

My jaw dropped, a single sound dripping from my tongue before I clamped the betrayer shut. The Commander's smile spread wider, his knuckles growing whiter as he leaned over me, hovering like one of the Vilÿs.

"Your heart what?" he hissed, the tone making it clear he thought he had discovered something great.

"My heart is not mine?" It was more of a statement than a question.

I made an attempt to clutch my chest and all of those scars that crisscrossed over me, knowing full well none of them was big enough for a heart transplant.

The Commander smiled. The look only made the foreign object in my chest pump harder, my confusion growing with each throb.

My anger was rising. I needed to know what they meant, I needed answers. Pushing aside the desire to command them, I looked from the Commander to the Doctor, my eyes pleading for anything he could give me.

"No," Dr. Sirko said, the response was followed by manic chicken scratches at the foot of my bed, Detective Bondar and his partner coming back from the dead to take their notes. "We noticed it after you had been unconscious for a few months. Your condition had worsened and we had to intubate you. But all of our tests began to return... abnormal."

"Sir, I command you to cease," the Commander roared, another swath of his hair coming loose from its style.

"You bear no sign of transplant, but the organ itself bears signs of having come from the woman..."

"Doctor Sirko!" Another command was followed by the click of guns, no less than ten instantly trained on the man in question.

The snap of voices and guns sent poor Katenka into a tizzy as she began focusing on arranging her vials, putting as much space between her and the horrors of the room as she could.

"I will not advise you again," the Commander continued as he stepped toward the elderly physician, the man shaking as he attempted to hold his ground. "You do not share criminal information with wards of the Sovereign Sanctuary of the Ukraine."

Sovereign Sanctuary of the Ukraine.

The SSU.

Kaye had said the acronym once, but the fear and anger behind it had caused it to stick to my bones. Now I understood why.

Now, I understood the fear.

"He is my patient..."

"He is our property!"

The Commander roared louder as my magic jolted inside of me, the surge of power so strong that I jerked in an attempt to calm it, restraints pulling as half the guns turned toward me.

"Ugh," the groan twisted into pain as the magic did, the surge of aggression shifting to a warmth that stretched to bones and joints as I began to relax.

"I must see to my patient..." Dr. Sirko said, sliding from the chair as all of the guns trained on him, the few that had not loaded doing so with a faint click. "His heart... he needs attention."

"He needs nothing. You have been duped."

"I have not," Sirko snapped, his frustrations finally breaking free in a roar that sent the older man shaking in place.

"You will not undermine me!" the Commander roared in return, the room shaking as the eruption turned into a battering ram.

Soldiers flooded into the room, their guns already drawn as they pointed between me, the doctor, and the poor nurse whose tray of blood went flying, a few of the vials shattering and splattering against the wall.

Bright red streaks against the dark, striped grey wallpaper.

Blood against stone.

Blood against....

I jumped at the sound of the gun.

I jumped at the scream.

It was all I could do not to call out, not to let whatever magic was inside of me out and fight the soldiers.

I wasn't sure what good it would do even if I tried. I would be just like the doctor, blood pouring down my arms as I was dragged from the room.

CHAPTER 26

ILYAN

"What about that one?"

I felt her voice more than I heard it.

It came in a soft whisper that tickled over my cheek, hot like the sun that was burning our skin, but cool like the breeze. As confusing as a woman should be.

"I see a toad... or perhaps a prince." She answered her own question in a whisper, the sound almost lost in the waves that were not far from us.

The steady rhythm of the ocean was relaxing, almost as much as her fingers that trailed up my arm, the touch leaving a line of burning heat behind it.

"How about a toad prince?" I said lazily, lost in the sensation of her touch.

She giggled at that, the sound was the soft bell of chimes in my soul and I exhaled, letting the calm joy she was infecting me with take hold.

Finally, I opened my eyes to the blazing sun, the clouds that drifted over us looking like puffs of spun sugar moments before they melted.

There was not a toad or a prince in sight.

"It's called The Frog Prince..." She couldn't even correct me properly, she was laughing too hard.

"Where you were raised perhaps, but I met the author." Her giggles only increased at that, the sound off in my head as I tried to understand what was going on, and why I would lie about such a thing.

"He was a toad," I continued, my heart swelling as I shifted my weight in the sand, turning toward her bright smile. "So, I can't think of a more perfect way to describe him."

"Your life. It amazes me sometimes," she whispered, the soft touch of her fingers coming to a halt.

Yes. They were words I wanted to say, but they never came.

I knew the story, the fairy tale. Although why I knew it, and why I would lie about meeting an author that lived hundreds of years before made no sense to me. The words had poured from me with such an assurance of honesty, however, that I could not question them further.

Joclyn twisted in my arms as she giggled, shifting her weight until she hovered over me, the tips of her hair tickling my cheek.

I loved the feeling of it, the feeling of her so close to me, pressing against me. I loved the touch of the hair that smelled so divine. But I loved her more.

I loved her.

I wasn't sure if I controlled my hand as I reached out to her, as I swept her hair back and ran my fingers down her jaw, over her neck, around the mark behind her ear. The wind blew cold, pulling at her hair and the tall green grass that we were nestled in.

Neither of us noticed. She was too focused on my touch; I on the warmth of her skin.

Her eyes were fire as she watched me, her lips pressing into a tight line at the sensations. I had seen her so often in my dreams, I had seen her in flashes, and watched moments of a past I wasn't sure I would regain.

But this felt so real.

It was so different.

The way she looked at me felt real, the heat from her skin felt real, the pressure of her body against mine felt real. It wasn't a shadow of memory, it wasn't a moment that jerked and jumped in my mind like a dream. It was clear and perfect, right down to the feeling of her thunderous pulse underneath my fingers.

My body was heating on its own in a reaction that having her this close was doing to me.

"Joclyn..." I breathed, still unsure if I was controlling this dream or if it was just another memory.

She smiled at her name, her fingers lifting from the blanket to trail over my face, sending yet another wave of heated emotions through me.

"Jan..." The word was breathy and familiar in all the wrong ways.

Joclyn smiled from where she lay over me, her eyes closing as my fingers moved up her neck, combing through her flyaway lengths.

"Jan..."

The hiss came again, cutting through the serenity of my dream as everything began to freeze. Together we turned toward the sound, into the brush that lined the beach. Nothing was there.

"Jan..." The whisper came again as everything began to

grow dark, as everything began to grow cold. The mark behind her ear glinted at me as I looked back to her, her focus still on the brush, on something I couldn't see.

"You need to go," Joclyn said, her voice calm against the hiss as it came again.

"It's not my name, Jos." My tone was harsher than it had been before, the anger at being attached to that name bubbling up. "It's not me."

"It is right now." She turned toward me, her eyes sad as the clouds that had been so bright and fluffy before shifted to the dark grey that had smothered us.

"They aren't calling to me."

I wanted to snap at whoever was using that name and trying to pull me away from her.

"They are today," she sighed, her fingers soft as she ran them up my arm again. "And if you want to find me, you are going to need to listen to them."

"But you are dead…" The passion of the moment before had evaporated, leaving me with gooseflesh from the chilly air that drifted off the ocean.

She smiled, the light touch of her fingers leaving as she replaced it with the wide heat of her palm. "You don't know that for sure."

"Jan… wake up."

Anger, true anger, bubbled and rose up in me. It came so fast and so quick that I wasn't sure why I wasn't yelling. I wasn't sure why I wanted to. The words were there, waiting…

It is not my name. I am not leaving.

"You have to," Joclyn sighed, the response to my thoughts cementing the fact that it was a dream in my mind.

Her fingers were hot as they moved over my skin,

burning against the scars on my chest, her touch gentle as she traced them. Her breath was warm against my lips as she bent over to kiss me, but the pressure never came. It was only the sweet taste of her breath before it faded back into reality, leaving only cold air and painful restraints. The ever-present beeping of the machines I was once again connected to smacked against me just as hard as the hand across my cheek.

"Jan," the hiss followed the hit. "Wake up."

I groaned, opening my eyes to the low flicker of a television, the dim light only barely cutting through the dripping dark that drenched the room. The face that hovered over me was only partially illuminated by a soft light that should have been comforting, but the illusion was shattered by the look of fear that was penetrating her eyes.

"Kaye. You're alive," I gasped, trying to reach out to her. The only sound of welcome, however, was that of metal as I pulled against the restraints.

She glanced at the door with the loud clang, her body tense and ready to run. To hide.

I lay in the silence, nothing but the flash of the television and the ever-present pulse of my foreign heart.

"Yes, I'm alive," she hissed to the door, waiting an extra minute before turning back to me. "Thanks to you. If they had found me, they would have killed me."

"Were you bit?" I asked, the fear that I had expected to feel over the possibility melting away into an exhilaration.

I didn't understand where that emotion came from. The memories I have of the Vilỳ are of fear, what I had seen on the news was of fear...everything but that tiny raised mark on Joclyn's neck.

"Not that I can see, but it would have happened either way. I'm not registered."

I gave her a look, one eyebrow arching high as she shifted her weight, leaning awkwardly against the railing.

"You mentioned that before," I stated, my voice soft as I tried to glean any information I could.

From her or the television. "Does everyone need to be registered?"

"Now they do," she hissed, an obvious line of irritation coloring her voice. "And I'm not. My mom has hidden me here for years, and now I can't escape. Now that Commander Domor is here, everywhere is crawling with Cleaners. I don't know what will happen if they find me."

"Is that the man who was in here before?"

"Yes," she cut me off, her eyes drifting to the door again as if speaking of him would call him to us. "I don't have much time, my mother is making her rounds and told me you would be..."

"Kaye!" I hissed, pulling her focus back to me. "That man...I need you to tell me what happened. I need to know what's going on."

"I take it we are still in this together then?" she whispered, her eyes sparkling brightly as she leaned over me. "You trust me?"

"You are perhaps the only one I can." I shook my arms, sending the restrains rattling as I emphasized my point.

"Why? Because I am the only one who hasn't put you in handcuffs?" I could hear the tease in her voice and it rattled me, stomach twisting uncomfortably.

She should not be allowed to speak to me so casually. The thought was firm and cemented, and yet, here I was handcuffed to a bed. Completely out of control.

"Exactly why I need your help," I whispered, pushing my pride aside. "I need to know what is going on. Now, who is that man?"

She hesitated, taking a glance at the door before lowering herself to hover beside the bed. "Commander Domor is one of the Tykha Shist´, he was one of the six who overthrew the government three months ago."

"The Silent Six," I repeated the phrase to myself in Czech, the words sounding ominous.

I lay still, staring at the TV infused flicker of blue against the dark ceiling. "And 'The Cleaners'?"

"The loyal military of the Tykha Shist'. If you see the treacherous star, that sunburst looking thing they all wear, run the other way."

Kaye tapped above her shoulder to emphasize her point, but I only gave her a look, letting my restraints rattle again as I glowered at her.

"Forgetting something?"

"Well, maybe you just shouldn't tell them anything," she sighed. "The Cleaner, the military, they wear a yellow sunburst. There are orange for spies, grey for local officials, you get the idea."

"So, Commander Domor's red star..?" I asked, the question causing her to shift awkwardly as she again looked toward the door.

"He is one of the original six. There are five others. After that, only purple is higher. And there is only one of them."

She shivered, looking from the TV to the door as she pressed her lips into a tight line. Her knuckles tightened around the metal railing of my bed, posture tensing as if she expected the man with the purple star to come charging in right then.

I turned, expecting a man with dark hair and green eyes. I could see him now. The single memory sent my heart rate monitor into a haunted dance, the shadows that moved behind the hastily repaired glass only fueling the delusion.

Kaye ducked below the bed, the top of her head peering through the rails as she watched the door. The sound of her knife grinding against a sheath sent gooseflesh over my arms.

"So it was a coup?" I asked in a hushed whisper as she stood, slipping her knife back into the pouch at her waist.

"Worse. It was an execution," she nodded, the anxiety rising as she turned back to me. "It was aired live over the television network. Domor was the one who beheaded the prime minister. They showed it all. You don't question them. You don't disobey."

"So, Doctor Sirko..?"

"Is lucky to be alive," she interrupted with a determined nod, her jaw tight. "I saw them take him to the east wing, I don't know anything beyond that. He is the only surgeon in Kiev, though. They can't afford to lose him. Most of the other doctors escaped years ago before the SSU closed the borders. Now no one escapes alive, and no one enters unless they are certified pure."

"Pure?" I asked, that same familiarity making my stomach twist.

"Unbitten. Unscathed. No one has made it through yet. If you are involved with or near a Chrlič attack at any point, you don't pass." She hesitated, before sitting down in one of the ugly chairs beside my bed, the tiniest scrape echoing as she sunk into it.

"Sounds like all the other wars this planet has raged. Purification in the name of protection."

"And just as dangerous," she paused and I tensed, my physical restriction becoming nearly unbearable. "They don't take chances. Even a scratch from one of the Chrlič will end with a shot to the head. Everyone who was in the hospital yesterday is either dead or under surveillance."

"And me?" I said, letting the bands rattle.

"Well, you aren't like everyone else, are you?" she asked, the taunt she attempted to put in her voice seeming harsh. "Domor wants you. Or rather he wants the info you have. And now that you are awake..." She trailed off, glancing back at the door again. "He has been waiting for years to find out what you really are."

"I take it waking up when I did may not have been in my best interest," I sighed, my hand shifting as it attempted to drag its way over my head. I didn't even move an inch. Not that it mattered, I didn't have any hair to run my fingers through anyway.

"It wouldn't have mattered," Kaye swallowed, glancing toward the door before she leaned closer. "He has the pictures, he knows enough."

"What do they know? Those were so fuzzy there is no way they can know for sure," I sighed, the memory of seeing the fuzzy image of Joclyn feeling like yesterday to me.

"They have more, now," Kaye said, shifting her weight as she leaned closer to the bed. She peered at me through the bars of the bed, shadows distorting her face. "The Czech government released more images from that tent village in the Svarov ruins a few months after you slipped away. The images were on the news for one day before the SSU took control of the media. The former government fell three days later."

The timeline twisted in my stomach, having everything laid out so simply.

"So they are gone?" My disappointment was clear. "Do you remember anything about them?"

Kaye bit her lower lip, hiding a smile as she looked at the door again before pulling out her phone, the bright light reflecting over her face and revealing the deep lines of change I missed before.

Hours before I had seen the woman she had become, but as she stood over me now I saw what I had missed in the panic of battle. It wasn't just that I had been away for more than two years. It was that the world had changed and she had to change to match.

Her muddy eyes held a hard determination that was borne more from desperation than from courage. The loss of weight stemming from a lack of food rather than age.

I could tell she was brave, I could tell she was powerful, but it was for survival rather than by choice.

"Three years" I sighed, the time still feeling like a painful impossibility.

She froze, finger hovering above the phone as her focus flitted back to me with a piercing stare. She hesitated, phone dropping to her side, and it was only then that my resolve began to succumb to the pity she was throwing my way.

"Three years and four months," she clarified.

Her voice had taken a very quiet tone as if she was attempting to lessen the blow. I don't think anything could have made it less of a sting.

"Even my mother didn't think you would make it," Kaye continued with a whisper, the confusing realization vanishing to smoke. "I'm not sure how you did. Or how you woke up when you did."

"I heard you yelling at me in my dreams. Just like now."

"Nice, Jan," she said with a quiet laugh, the sound as unwanted as the name she had used. "You dreaming about me, then?"

"That's not my name," I growled just as I had before, the memory of the dream was a distant reality after everything I had just learned. "And you don't belong in my dreams."

She glowered at me, as if she saw the same anger in me, before she laughed, the sound lifeless and angry.

"What is your name, then?"

"I don't know."

"Hmph." She turned away, folding her arms over her chest as her focus returned back to her phone, the tapping of fingers against glass perfectly matching the gunfire on the television. "Figures. I spend months looking for your *Joclyn* and you wake up with no new information..."

"I don't believe I said I didn't have any new information." I cut her off, letting a smile play around the corner of my mouth, the same commanding tone taking control.

I moved to sit, forgetting that I didn't have the ability and sent the restraints into another orchestra of metal that set Kaye on the ready, her eyes shifting to the door as she prepared to run.

"Good," she said, eyes sparkling. "Because I wasn't idle."

She flipped her phone around to face me, the screen bright as it displayed an image of a man with a line of yellow light streaming from his hand, just like it had in this room. It was an image similar to what I had seen before, except that instead of the grainy pixelated imagery, this one was clean, pristine, and obviously me, right down to the massive scar on the palm of my hand.

I stood among the tattered tents in Svarov, Joclyn behind me, fighting in the same way. The yellow string I had seen before was now clearly a golden ribbon, the ends of the strand tied into both of our hair, connecting us as they tangled around each other.

Seeing her there, seeing the ribbon, sent my heart into a heavy bass of emotion, my stomach twisting in a powerful need. I tried to reach for the phone, desperate to see her better, to hold this tangible proof of her existence in my hand, but I was only met with pressure and an immovable force.

"Joclyn!" I gasped, my fingers aching with the need to grab the phone.

"Typical," Kaye sighed, sweeping the phone away from me and beginning to tap the screen again. "I show you an image that proves you're an alien, and all you see is her."

"I'm not an alien," I growled, although I was fully aware I had no proof of it. "It's magic."

I cringed at my own words, somehow saying it aloud while strapped to a hospital bed made it seem ridiculous.

"That's what you said after you killed all the Chrlič. Alien or not... you did something last night."

"It was magic," I said again, focusing on the warmth that always was present now. But instead of it rising to my fingers in a spark, it settled deeper. There was nothing but warmth.

As powerful as I was, as powerful as I felt at times, I still could not control it. Without control, I was nothing more than a prisoner.

"I'm actually starting to believe you," she said, looking at the phone with a subtle awe before turning it back towards me, the shot zoomed in on the woman I had dreamed of for years.

On Joclyn, and her determination. Her power.

My heart felt like it was going to beat out of my chest,

luckily the beeping of the machine I was connected to didn't agree, the beep stayed steady.

"The entire world wants these two because they can kill the Chrlič. And thanks to these pictures, and whatever stunt you pulled last night...Commander Domor has you. He wants whatever this is."

"What is he going to do? Cut it out of me?"

I asked the question rhetorically, putting the threat into the air with as much disdain as I could muster. Instead of responding in agreement and moving on, however, Kaye wilted. Her eyes grew wide as she swallowed, a worry I hadn't expected blasting through the dark flickers of the room.

"Can you 'cut it out' of you?" she asked, her fingers brushing the air in quotation marks.

"I don't know, Kaye," I said as she absentmindedly ran her fingers over the metal cuff that tied me to the bed rail. "It's magic, not an organ..."

"Are you sure?" Was it hope or disappointment I was seeing? I wasn't sure. Her reaction flared deeply and I cringed, suddenly doubting the trust I had freely given her.

"I'm not sure of anything," I said, choosing my words carefully.

The grinding scrape of metal against metal reminded me just how possible that was.

"I doubt that will stop them," she said sadly, the questions from before suddenly making sense. "It didn't stop them before."

She looked at me with pity and heartbreak. The emotions hit heavily, settling in the pit of my stomach like a rock as I narrowed my eyes at her, trying to ignore the thunder in my heart.

"What did they do to me while I was in a coma, Kaye?"

The question obviously caught her off guard and she leaned back, clutching the still illuminated phone to her chest as though it was a lifeline. She pressed her lips into a hard line, a look that I had seen enough just in this conversation to know it did not preempt good news.

"They know how fast you can heal, and they haven't found any magic to cut out of you. Not that they have stopped looking... Does that answer your question?"

She spoke fast, stubborn, defiant. But I only heard the horrors that I had been subject to, heard what she had refused to tell me before.

"I need to get out of here," I said, pulling against my restraints, fully expecting them to crumble under the force of my strength.

"So break your way out of here," Kaye hissed as she put her hand around mine, stopping my battle with the restraints. "I saw you..."

"I can't control it that well." I interrupted her with a snap. "It just kind of explodes."

Kaye flinched, an eagerness I had seen in her yesterday coloring her face, "Then explode your way out of here."

I cringed, she didn't know how close to the truth that was.

"It doesn't work when I want it too," I added quickly, the failure from before still stinging. "Last night... not now. And even then it can't stop bullets."

"How do you know," she countered, her defiance sounding like a playground taunt.

"That's just it," I said patiently, desperate for her to understand. "I don't. And it's not worth the risk."

"It is to me," she said, desperation bleeding through her as she grabbed my hand, her stubbornness turning into a plea. "You don't know what they can do..."

286

"Does it change anything?" I pulled my hand away with a jerk, sending the restraints rattling as my magic bubbled, her unwanted proximity igniting it in one single spark. "From what you have said about the government even if I was to break us out, we are trapped here. We have nowhere to go. I am not even sure who I am."

The hopelessness that lined her face vanished so fast I would have thought she was slapped if it wasn't for the eager smile that took its place.

"You may not remember," she whispered, tapping on her phone once before turning it back to me. "But I am pretty sure she does."

Her phone blazed with a black and white image from what looked like a news article, the headline a dark blank line amongst chicken scratches of text.

"Mother dies in firefight, daughter wanted for questioning."

Inset into the article was a picture of a joyful woman hugging a young girl with tangles of dark hair that were practically covering her face. The hood of a sweater was pulled down low and if it wasn't for the pale color of her eyes I would have never recognized her as the same powerful woman that was blasting her way through a dystopian wasteland.

Once again, I tried to grab for the phone, the clanging of the restraints even louder in my desperation. Kaye jumped at the noise, looking toward the door as she stepped into the shadow of the tattered window hangings. My own breathing picked up, both of us turning to stare at the door.

"The German government has been rumored to have fallen this last week..." The sound of the television was twice as loud as we waited.

The little light that filtered through the glass in the door dimmed in the shadow of one of the guards. My heart was a thunder, the ends of my nerves frayed as we waited; I looked at Kaye, her at the door.

"It is the fifth government to fall under the influence of the Japanese republic..." The television buzzed, the dim light returning just as Kaye lifted her phone.

"Angela Despain," Kaye whispered from the dark, my eyes wide as her shadow curled over the faint glow of her phone, "a forty-three-year-old single mother was found dead in her west-side apartment last night after neighbors reported a domestic disturbance between her and her daughter, seventeen-year-old Joclyn Despain."

I jerked again, the motion an uncontrolled response to the name, to the story. It was familiar. I stared at her, desperate for her to continue. I needed to hear more, to know more. Like a loose thread on a sweater, I knew this was leading to something I had forgotten. Something I needed to remember.

"The girl," Kaye continued, each word closing in around me and making the bed feel like the prison it truly was, "who was described as a loner and a destructive influence by the mother's employer, Edmund LaRue, is wanted in connection with the murder. The girl may be injured, as signs of a fall and a large amount of blood were found in an alley."

An alley.

The flicker of a broken street lamp, an old rusted dumpster overflowing with garbage. I could smell the sweet rancid scent, the aroma lingering with that of gunpowder and smoke. The scent was so strong I could smell it here, in this hospital room. It cut into my chest, the tension that came with the single image making the whole scene feel toxic.

I didn't see much more than that, but somehow I knew.

288

I knew it was where I found her, where I had saved her. A girl, dying behind a dumpster.

I half expected to find her blood covering my arms and hands right then, the memory was that strong. But there were only monitoring wires, irritated skin, and the gentle electronic beep of my pulse reminding me that that alley was only a distant memory.

"You found her." I could barely get the words out with how my throat was constricted.

"I found her," she sighed, taking a tentative step forward. "Except she's missing and hasn't been seen since this article was posted almost five years ago. No one who is alive remembers her, and as far as I can tell no one else has made the connection. You can't without a name, because this," she flashed a close up of the image attached to the article, "looks nothing like the image of the magical badass you are obsessed with."

"She's beautiful," I whispered, unable to stop myself.

"Obsessed is definitely the right word," Kaye growled, her irritation unable to break through the wall of awe I was currently wrapped up in. "There is something else..."

She was hesitant, cautious even. Like a child with a soap bubble. The warm blanket of awe I was wrapped up in evaporated, leaving me on the cold hospital bed, an ice cold dread working its way up my spine. I tensed, desperate to release this energy in some other way than the explosion I could feel brewing.

"That woman's boss, Edmund LaRue... his mansion was damaged the night Joclyn disappeared. And then the whole thing exploded about a month later, on the night of his son's graduation party."

"His son?"

"Yeah, Ryland..." she tapped her phone, turning it towards me again. "He was in Prague too."

It was the same tents, the same scene of battle, but instead of Joclyn and I standing back to back as we massacred the Vilÿs, it was a single man, his blue eyes raging as he screamed in an agonizing anger. Bright red light poured from him, the line of color dripping as though it was made from blood. The color was shocking, but not as much as he was.

The look on his face was pure pain, the skin crisscrossed with scars and fresh bleeding cuts. His hair dripped with sweat, lifeless curls hanging over his eyes and down his neck in wet tangles.

"He looks deranged." I didn't know how else to put it, although the words sounded harsh for some reason.

"And scarred. His face... It doesn't look anything like the kid in the yearbook that I found. That guy..." she sighed, "there is a newscast that is closer, however."

She tapped her phone again, turning it toward me as a video began to play.

"*I know it has been inferred that I may have been involved in her disappearance.*" The young man's voice was dead and flat as he stood before a bank of microphones, addressing what I assumed were multiple reporters. It was obvious he had been trained in public speaking, but his head and hand were continually jerking in awkward directions that were destroying the illusion of authority. While I could see some similarities from the pictures, looking at him here was more like a before picture from some drug rehabilitation program.

"*And I would like to state again,*" the video continued, the twitches increasing, "*that I was not involved in this tragedy in any way. I am proud to say that...*"

She turned the phone back to herself abruptly, tapping the screen so hastily that I half expected a soldier emblazoned with the yellow star to be standing right behind.

No one was there.

Kaye stared at me, obviously waiting for some flash of memory and more answers to go with the bombshell she had already dropped. But I didn't know him. There wasn't even a phantom emotion or image to go along with what she had shown me.

If I had known him, he was gone.

I shook my head no, and she plowed on, chatting away as she continued to tap on her phone screen.

"The images the Czech government released were only up for a day before the government began to cover them. I got these off the dark web about three months ago. It took some work, I had to teach myself how to access it on my phone, and without getting the attention of the SSU."

Another image, this of a woman with short hair and a man with long dark dreads.

Again, nothing.

"From what I can tell, and what I have heard while I was crawling around in the ceiling, everyone wants you, but no one in the world knows that the man from the images in Prague is in a hospital in Kiev. No one but the prime ministers of the former Ukraine, who are dead, The Cleaners, the SSU," she paused, "and me."

"All the more reason to organize some miraculous escape plan, I take it?"

I said it in jest, and part of me expected her to smile and jump into some master plan, but she continued to stare at her phone, tapping away before she again turned it toward me, this time showing a woman with a fan of blonde hair, with blue eyes that held more hatred and anger than I had seen in her before.

Because I had seen her before.

She was the same one who I had seen raped and beaten. The one who had stared out from inside me, as though she were part of me.

Here, in this image, she stood across from me, fighting me, hating me.

Just seeing it brought all those same emotions I saw in her face right into me. The restraints jangled loudly as I foolishly tried to grab the phone from her, the power that had been cycling through me for the last few minutes finally erupting in little sparks of lightning.

The jagged streaks of light jumped between my fingers. Kaye's eyes widened, fear and amazement pulsing in her jaw as she jumped back.

"If you are going to explode, you can at least warn me," she hissed, stuffing the phone into her pocket.

"I'm not going to explode," I growled, the chains rattling again as I fought against them.

Just like an animal in a cage. The realization was painful.

"Are you sure about that?"

No. I wasn't.

Not with her in my mind, not with this woman whose memory infected mine. Before, when I had seen her I had worried for her, I had felt for her. But in that image, in the spark of memory that followed it, there was only hatred, there was only pain.

"I know her," I gasped, the sparks of attack as we fought filling my mind, I saw her laugh, and I saw the streaks of blood against the stone wall.

My blood.

"Ahhh," Kaye sighed, glancing at her phone, "I guess I know who I need to find next..."

"I don't know if you can," I sighed, the same image of blood and stone haunting me. "I don't know if you should."

Kaye raised an eyebrow at me, clearly letting her curiosity overtake the fear.

"I think she is the one whose blood was covering me," I said. "I think it's her heart that is beating in my chest."

CHAPTER 27

RYLAND

When I was about twelve my father had taken me to Hong Kong. He called it a business trip, when in reality he wanted me to kill a Prime Minister who was visiting the city on a peace mission.

My father had given me specific instructions on how he wanted it done, and commanded Cail to record it. My father was ecstatic, it was to be my first true assassination. More than just the systematic killings he had had me perform on those he ruled as traitors, this was my first real test, and I wanted nothing to do with it.

I had sat up all night, watching the lights of Hong Kong flash, writing letters to Joclyn that I could never send, knowing I could never tell her about things I was seeing, and a city I wasn't going to step foot in.

It was sometime near one a.m. that I ran away, ran through the city after the lights and after the freedom they promised. I saw them first from across a busy city street, the brilliant green glowing from underneath a wide metal bridge. At first I thought it was magic, but the closer I got, the more I could see. Huge glass fans of green and blue spread under the bridge in a sculpture of illuminated ropes. The long snakes of glass spiraled through rails and skidded over the surface of the water like the sails of a fish. The color glowed from within the spun glass, reflecting in the waves and fanning through the dark like a beacon I could never reach.

A safety I could never find.

I stood there, crying, watching the colors, until Cail found me. He pulled me away by the crook of my arm to my father who waited in the limo. Cail held me down as my father broke one bone after another, screaming at me, demanding obedience. Demanding my service.

I was forced to kill the Prime Minister anyway, forced to watch him die.

But even as I watched the man gasp for breath, I remembered those lights, remembered the way the blue skimmed over the water's surface as though it was flying. Soaring to freedom.

I saw that again in the blue lights that shimmered over the ceiling of The Draíocht, the sails of clustered color danced on the ceiling, the pastel hues reflecting from sculptures of metal and glass that hung from the jagged roof of rock.

A massive cavern, bathed in light.

It was how Wyn had carved it when we first built it, and it was how Michel had wanted it. A magical sanctuary for the last magic in England.

As beautiful as the lights were, however, when we walked into the massive hall a few minutes ago I could tell everything about the magic had been stripped from this place.

It had once been full of life. Now, that same danger I sensed from Michel had infected everything. Beyond the glittering color on the ceiling there was desperation, fueled by a lack of food and clothing that made everyone on edge.

People sat in tiny huddles, tucked into corners or curled up on the dozens of makeshift beds that littered the space. They sat around low burning candles, heads bowed low as they whispered to each other, the side glances that peaked out sending me on edge.

The life that had lived here had vanished.

"The Silent Six stretched their border further this last weekend," a cool woman's voice buzzed through a radio somewhere behind me, the sound full of static and distortion as the few that were gathered around the repaired box tried to find a clearer signal. "The armies of the tyrannical leader stretched their borders into what had previously been known as Moldova. Many in the country rallied to join the SSU as their food supplies had begun to run dry..."

The sound of the BBC was drowned into a buzz as those that were listening broke into conversation, the sounds of chicken scratches bowling over the report that I only half heard.

"Not now, Lacey. We will talk about this later." Michel's voice pulled my focus as he shooed away a few more of the Chosen, sending what looked to be a mother and daughter scrambling away as they looked back at us with wide eyes.

Even though The Draíocht was considered to be a faction of Imdalind, and not tied to Joclyn's rule, everyone knew who we were. Massive wanted posters saw to that.

Wyn growled and leaned back into the armchair she was sitting in, the giant thing just as worn and tattered as the broken couch I had been offered. Both were set up in the very center of the enormous hall, something that I was sure Michel had done on purpose with how he dramatically shooed away two young men who were eyeing us with eager eyes.

"I don't like this," Wyn mumbled toward me, her mouth barely moving as she continued to eye Michel, giving instructions for someone to 'stand guard'. "Something's off. And more than Michel's ego."

"I know. We need information, then we need to move on," I returned, nodding toward Michel as he turned toward me and Wyn, saying something to a poor boy who looked equally excited and terrified to be this close to us. "Have you found anything?"

I barely let my voice get above a whisper, already knowing what she was up to. Her shoes were tattered, yes, but they were ripped to shards for a reason. With a sole full of holes, she could press her toes to the ground and give herself a direct line to the earth that fueled her magic.

With how warm the rock was I had no doubt that she was already searching for dangers, for magic.

For anything that Michel might be hiding.

She shook her head once, the motion slight enough that I wasn't sure anyone else would notice.

"Nah, nothing. Not in the tunnel on the way here. Not as far as I can sense. I would expect anything to be cleared out by now if there was too much wheat," she said as Michel hustled his way back over to us, his smile flashing toward me before lingering on Wyn again.

She just scowled at him.

"My apologies," Michel said conversationally, sinking into the large carved stone chair across from the tattered couch we sat in. "You are still as popular as ever it seems."

He spoke the words and I heard the attempt at apology, but when he instantly turned to wave to someone and pointed us out, I couldn't take him seriously.

"It's just Ryland," Wyn said, the seductress pouring out of her voice deeply as she crossed her legs, letting her hand drape over her knee, bracelets clanging loudly. "It's the curls that do it."

Michel laughed, the sound almost drowning out the quick double tap of Wyn's right foot.

Damn it.

Two taps. All clear.

I was hoping she would find something, some dark magic, some forbidden power, hidden in the man or the network of caves we were in. But he was clean. Not that I was surprised, he had stood by Ilyan for too long.

"He is quite the catch isn't he? If I hadn't already chosen my prize I would have considered having a go," Michel smiled at Wyn and sat back in the carved stone chair, looking very much the part of a smug King wearing a stolen crown.

We needed a change of subject before Wyn gave him a swift kick between the legs. Or I did.

"What has happened here Michel? First you say you have closed the North Entrance, and now we have walked into a damn mausoleum." I tried to keep my voice diplomatic even though I had no interest in mincing words anymore.

"You say you have been attacked. Did they get all the way in?" Wyn gestured to one of the metal and glass structures, the thing spinning wildly. They were all so twisted that I hadn't even noticed before; every pane of glass was cracked.

"You never miss a thing, do you Wynifred?" Michel's eyes widened before he sat back in his chair, the corners of his mouth pulling the smile from his face. "It has happened several times over the last few months."

"Several times? We haven't heard of any danger here?" I asked, the timber of my voice rising with each word. "Why haven't you told us?"

"Because we didn't know what was happening at first," Michel answered, leaning back against the chair, his fingers continually tapping against the edge of the arm rest.

The pace sped up, the sound hollow in my ears as the frustrated thump of my own heart vibrated against my rib cage. The guy was slimy, but now I was starting to think him a damn liar. Those warning lights were going off in my head again.

"How do you not know you're being attacked? There are explosions, usually people yelling at you. Don't be daft, Michel, and don't think we are," Wyn spat, her voice a solemn threat as the toes of her shoes slammed against the hard stone floor, a wave of heat washing through my feet as she did so.

Michel smiled, his bright white teeth gleaming as he shifted his feet against the heat. Although he was sweating enough he may not have even noticed it. "We didn't know what we were seeing, not at first. When we would go into the city to find those who had been bitten, to pull out the ones with powers and bring them home, they would be gone before we got there. We would never find them again. It was after that that my people started to go missing."

"Missing?" Wyn asked, the accusation in her voice replaced by confusion.

"Yes," Michel nodded once, that same tense look

pouring from his eyes before he clicked his tongue and leaned forward, teetering on the edge of his chair. Wyn leaned forward, eager. I, however, froze in place, watching everyone in the cave again.

I had thought they were scared of something else, but now I was starting to wonder.

"My people would go to visit the ones we would hear about, the ones with newly acquired magic, and never return," Michel said, his voice a mumble that struggled to rise above the sound of the radio in the background, the smooth female voice delivering some kind of bulletin. "We lost nearly a dozen, before someone escaped from her attackers, before she was able to make her way home." He hesitated, his eyes glazing over before they snapped back to me. "She screamed about rotted magic, about the magic that drips like liquid metal, the magic before Joclyn repairs the Chosen."

"You have been attacked by my father's men, and you chose not to say anything?" Michel flinched at my words, his jaw tightening before he straightened, his eyes narrowing.

"They are not your father's men." Michel's words were slow, calculated, his eyes were a bright spark of danger against the smooth ebony of his skin. "They are the Kyōwakoku."

The heavy pressure of desperation in the cave exploded, the weight pressing against my skin as a hush fell over everything, moving away from us in a ripple over water. Several people turned toward us at the word, their faces lined with fear as they quickly looked away, shuffling into the dark crevices of the cave like rats away from the light.

"The Japanese Republic," I provided. It was not a question, it was a statement. We had heard of them before.

Like many of the other tyrannies that had seen the world wide apocalypse as an advantage, the Kyōwakoku had taken control seemingly overnight, uniting many Asian nations under one flag. They promptly exposed their underbelly, building a stronghold to keep out any 'undesirables.'

They were not the only ones. The once great United States had done the same, only to fall when they were not able to provide resources to their people. The entire country was now in shambles, overtaken by dozens of cults and invaded by other nations that fought each other until they too fell. Just a few months ago the government in the Ukraine had fallen as well, their ruling party assassinated on live TV.

"I thought they were only in Asia," Wyn said, bangles jangling as she stood, hovering between Michel and I like an overprotective mother. "They are just like all the others, protecting their people..."

"Trying to take over the world," Michel cut in and sighed, leaning back against his chair. "They all are. I'm sure you've noticed."

"We have." I nodded, fighting the need to look at Wyn. Truth was, we hadn't noticed anything. Our focus was on saving those bitten, healing the Chosen, and finding Ilyan. The idea that we had missed something so huge was like razors against my spine.

"Religious zealots, the lot of them," he snarled, his voice heavy as it echoed over the suddenly barren cave, even the incessant sound of the radio had been extinguished. "I'm glad you know. We wouldn't have known they were here if it wasn't for the girl, and I wouldn't have known they were behind it if she hadn't gotten out of there and come running home."

His admission did little to calm my panic.

"Tell me about the girl," I demanded, my irritation growing at the awkward game of chase we were playing. "You say you were attacked, and now you say a child led religious extremists to your door. You could have just told them you weren't interested."

"Close the door? They aren't Mormons. Poor kid probably didn't know what she was doing," Wyn snorted, but Michel looked liable to erupt. His nostrils flared, making his nose look even wider as he lurched forward, leaning toward me.

"She was not a child," he snapped. "A woman, she was here on her honeymoon when Prague fell. Her new husband died, her friends died in the bomb. She worked by my side for nearly a year before she chose a different path. She wanted the men to pay for what they had done to her. I refused to help..." His voice faded away as the muscles in his face tensed and tightened, the deepened lines in his forehead making me wonder if she did more than just work for him. "She brought them here, all of them."

The tight balls of muscles that lined my back became even tighter, the knots digging into my ribcage as I waited for him to continue.

"The Kyōwakoku," he said, his voice filling with venom. "The girl, Hikari, she doomed us all."

He said her name like it was poison, each syllable dripping from him as he glowered into me as though I knew her, as though I had something to do with it. My jaw tightened at the devastation in his gaze only to have my whole body jump as Wyn gasped beside me, bracelets jangling as her hand flew to her mouth.

We both turned to her, Michel looking as confused as I

did, but Wyn only looked at me, her dark eyes so wide that I swear I could see through them.

"Wyn! What--?" I began, but she shook her head furiously, her hand still pressed against her mouth as she waved me off and pulled out her phone, her magic plunging into it and igniting the screen.

"Is everything okay?" he asked, his focus still drifting from me to linger on Wyn.

"It's fine," Wyn beamed as she spun back around to face us, phone already tucked into her pocket. "We still have business in Imdalind, Michel. You are not our only charge, nor are you the most important of our visits. However, it seems you have committed travesties here."

"Travesties?" Michel was affronted, Wyn ignored him.

"Your people are obviously starving, your position compromised." Wyn's accusations flew freely around the cave, each word gnawing at the ego of the man before me, each word sending him fuming. "You didn't tell us you were attacked."

Michel did not respond. He sat, fuming, on his throne, staring at us as he folded his arms over the barrel of his chest, long sinewy muscles flexing in the liquid reflection of the light.

"Why weren't we told?" I asked, following Wyn's lead as I leaned toward Michel, trying to keep both voice and body calm. It didn't matter, however, his walls were already up.

The man's jaw clenched, his eyes growing ever darker in warning.

I would have given anything to glare at Wyn just then, after all, she knew better than to attack Michel's ego. Not that she cared, Wyn jumped again, pulling her phone out of her pocket as she shuffled away.

"You know her better than to let her dig under your skin, Michel," I began, careful to keep my tone even. "She growls like a tiger, but you know she is a kitten."

"That is exactly why I want her." Michel's lip twitched, a tiny smile breaking free as Wyn scowled at me from behind him, obviously having heard what I said. Ignoring her, I mewed, clawing the air like an angry cat as Michel began to laugh, the low sound a deep rumble that cut through the tension like a knife.

Wyn looked like she was about ready to kill me. I just grinned brightly at her, well aware I was going to pay for that later.

"I, however, prefer her as a lioness," he continued, his voice dropping to a low husky whisper.

The grit of his mutter sent ripples of discomfort up my spine, the wild need to step between him and Wyn and keep her as far away from this low life as I could rising up like a steel trap. The way he spoke, the way his tongue tapped against his lower lip, the way his eyes glossed over; it created more than just an uncomfortable aroma of lust, it made everything around him reek of it.

Instead, I smiled, nodded my head as if I agreed and breathed deep when he sat back in his chair, satiated.

"Well, ignore her mews, Michel, and speak with me," I continued, hating every syllable. "You were speaking of Kyōwakoku, of how you fought off their attack on your own."

Patting his ego was always the best way to go, and lucky for me he played into it almost too perfectly. He sighed deep, his eyes darting around the large cave as though he was seeing if anyone else was watching.

"Hikari followed them, she worked with them. One day I received a letter, she wanted out. She had information to give me. We met several times working to pull her out of their trap, to hide her. One day, they followed us to our meeting space in the old town," he said loudly, speaking of his journey to the tattered remains of London as though it was a heroic war story. "I fought them off, and we sealed the north entrance."

I knew it was all important, that they followed the girl, that they saw the north entrance. You strip away his exaggerated tale and I was sure we could find something useful, but my mind focused on one thing, "Why didn't you tell us?"

"We didn't deem it necessary." The heaviness returned to his voice with a snap.

"I understand." I didn't, in fact, I was furious, but none of that mattered right now if I didn't get closer to whoever was attacking us - this Kyōwakoku.

"I know you are a talented Skřítek, Michel, I am not doubting that." I was careful, calculated. Feeding him everything he wanted to hear, but it didn't seem to matter, with every word his face fell deeper, his scowl slipping further and further into place. "But, we could have been of assistance. We could have brought you all home to Imdalind and pro..."

"I had it under control," he snapped, the loud punch of his voice as sharp as a razor's edge. "I protected my people and took the steps needed to ensure they were safe. We did not need your help, and we did not need to run away with our tail between our legs."

He jumped to his feet with a roar, hovering over me, posturing me. My magic flared at the danger, flared at the sound of anger. I was ready to attack, ready to beat him down to submission, and as much as I tried to control it, as much as I tried to stop it, I really didn't want to.

Jumping to my feet, I stood eye to eye with the man, bearing down on him as I made every attempt to remind him who he was talking to.

"It is not running away." I did not yell. I did not let my voice rise above a dull roar lined with a firm command that sent the man stumbling back a step, pulling Wyn from her phone call, whispering into the mouthpiece as she glanced between Michel and me. "It is what a good ruler would do. It is how a ruler provides for their people. You sir, are not a ruler. That is why, in the name of our Queen, I require you all to return to--"

"I am their ruler and she is not our Queen. These are my people, and I have protected them."

His tone matched mine beat for beat, although he did not step closer, his warning was clear. The depth of his delusions were even clearer. He may not accept Jos as his Queen, but he sure as hell wasn't the King he fancied himself to be.

The cave was a shadow of what it used to be, and even those who were left were sent cowering further into their corners at the sound of our shouts, peeking out from behind stone outcroppings with wide eyes.

Attacking him wasn't going to help. So much for feeding into his ego.

I needed to backpedal, and fast if this was going to work.

"I am glad you protected them," I began, speaking softly as I fed into his fantasy and attempted to pull him down from the ledge we were on. "We do not know much of the Kyōwakoku and it appears we have unwittingly walked into a war with them. I need your help if I am going to walk up to them."

Four words and he melted, that slimy smile moving back into place.

"You can't just walk up to the Kyō, Ryland," Michel said with his usual air. "Even if they will let you past their first checkpoint, they require certain sacrifices..." he paused, shaking his head as a mischievous smile pulled at the corners of his mouth. "Even with your fame amongst the Chosen of the world I am not sure if they will let you in."

"You may be right about that." I forced a smile, letting his barbs fall over me. Everyone wanted me and Wyn, I was pretty sure our faces alone would be our tickets in. Whether they were also our tickets to death I wouldn't know. "I know little about them. What can you tell me?"

I repeated the phrase and this time it seemed to satiate him. He leaned back, the darkness lingering on his face even as he settled into the heavy stone chair. The massive thing looked more and more like some throne he had created for himself.

"They are fanatics. They think magic is made to serve, and those who possess power should rule."

"Rule what?" I asked.

"Everything," he said with a smile so wide I couldn't be sure that he didn't agree with them.

"They wouldn't be the first to think this way," I growled, both my father and Joclyn's coming to mind. The parallels filled me with rage and I sat back, folding my arms over my chest lest I punch something.

"Hikari thought the same, after I refused to help her seek her revenge, she worked for them," he continued, "At first I think she just wanted to save more people, she came back asking for help when she saw..."

"Why didn't you come to us then?" I asked, without thinking, his eyes glossing over with the same darkness.

I only saw a flash of it before it faded to surprise, his whole body stiffening as Wyn draped her arm over his shoulders.

"Now, now boys," she whispered, her voice a seductive purr as she perched herself on the armrest of his chair. "We don't need to fight again, do we?"

Wyn leaned in towards Michel, her shoulder pressing against his as she let her fingertip trace the line of his jaw.

I heard the man's breath hitch, the sound a gasp as he closed his eyes pleasurably and Wyn's focus snapped to me, the gentle seductress pulled away with a tight clench of her jaw.

She didn't say anything to me, but she didn't need to; I heard the message loud and clear: stay out of my way.

We had played this game before. I gave her a nod and she shifted her weight, throwing her cell phone right at my head, the depth of her scowl making me question if it was intentional or not.

I caught it easily as she turned back to Michel, her fingers sliding down to cup his neck.

"Besides, you don't want your people to see you upset do you? Do you?" she cooed, her body pressing into him further. "You want them to see you as the powerful ruler you are. You want them to see..."

Her voice faded away as she leaned in closer, and I looked away, not interested in seeing more. I would be worried that Thom would be upset at the display unfolding before me, but this was the Wyn he fell in love with nearly three hundred years ago. When Wyn worked as an assassin for our father, this skill was one she perfected to lead people to their death.

Now she used it to get what she wanted.

I flipped the phone open, letting my magic run through

it and bring it to life. With limited power and cell towers remaining in the world, our magic served as both power source and receptor. It was a perfect combination for the dystopian spy movie we were trapped in.

The screen flashed once with an incoming message, Thom's name spelled out with a heart for the 'o'.

Hundreds of years old and Wyn was still a teenager at heart.

I tapped on the message, the phone opening to a screen with a short conversation that started with her demanding information on the Kyō, and Thom demanding she call him.

Questions about Wyn's call buzzed through my head like killer bees on steroids, but nothing was answered here. Not until I reached the last message, the one that had just come in from Thom.

The woman is awake. Will have more answers soon.

My focus snapped to Wyn, who was now leaning so far over Michel that she could very well have been sitting on his lap. The man was smiling, whispering something sleazy to her, but her eyes were only on me.

I turned the phone to her, the bubble of Thom's incoming message clear, even if she couldn't read the contents. Her eyes widened briefly before she pulled away, keeping her hand soft against his neck, and I am sure her magic a gentle lull inside of him.

"You are so funny," she cooed as she leaned into him, the forced tinkling of her laugh twisting through my gut.

Michel laughed with her as she leaned back in, "You know what would really show your people how amazing you are?" She paused, leaned in, and whispered in his ear loud enough that I could hear her. "If you help us track down these attacks, and stop them."

Darkness crossed his eyes at the suggestion, his focus

drifting toward where I sat across from him. Wyn pulled him back toward her before he got too far, her bottom lip placed firmly between her teeth as she pressed herself against him.

I could practically see him melt under her will from here.

"We need to see the Kyōwakoku," she whispered, letting her breath roll over him. His hand lifted to grab her, to pull her into him and I almost jumped up, needing to put a stop to this before it went too far.

Wyn however, didn't even seem fazed, she grabbed his hand and pushed it away, holding it against the chair in what I am sure he thought was a sensual embrace. Everything was under Wyn's control.

"They will destroy you," Michel whispered in return

"Will they?" Wyn countered, "Or will they too just know of your stature. Know of your power. After all, you will be the one who brought us to them."

His eyes widened, his breath hitched, and before Wyn could make another move he was struggling out from under her embrace, rambling about having to make a call.

I watched him step away, the seductress fading into oblivion as Wyn stood from the arm of the chair, shaking away the feeling as though it was sludge.

"Don't say anything," she growled as she snapped the phone away from me. "Also, you owe me twenty dollars."

"That was impressive," I whispered, earning myself a well-placed glare.

"I said don't say anything, Ryland."

"About that? Sure. But I really need you to tell me what the heck is going on," I hissed, double checking that he wasn't making a quick return. "First you gasp like you have seen a ghost, and now you are seducing Michel so that he will put us in touch with fanatics. I haven't seen you put on moves like that since..."

She silenced me with a look, her finger sparking dangerously as she held it up in warning. I stopped at once, I wasn't about to push it. I already had enough scars, thank you very much.

Wyn exhaled, casting a quick side glance to ensure he was far enough out of earshot. Even though I was sure he was, I had the distinct impression that he would find a way to hear. He was "uh-humming" too much for that to be an actual phone call.

"That woman's name... Hikari," she said in an almost silent whisper, her eyes an intense laser beam as she leaned into me, "it's Japanese for light."

Now it was my turn to freak out.

Instead of jumping and gasping like a teenage girl however, everything in me stiffened. I glanced at Michel, who 'hummed' his way out of being caught in a side eye and turned away from us, just as I grabbed Wyn by the arm. Towing her to the other side of the couch circle, I separated us from Michel by a couch and a few more feet. It still probably wasn't enough.

"Jeeze, Ryland," Wyn snapped as she pulled her arm away, her skin heating in warning. "Subtle much? And no, I am not kidding about her name, before you ask."

Something deep inside of me wanted to relax, to breathe deep that we had found it, that we had figured at least one piece of the puzzle out and knew exactly where to go. But I couldn't. Something about this about her name, it was too easy, too simple. Something was hiding, and I don't know if it was Michel who was doing it, or if we had inadvertently walked into a trap.

"Joclyn's sights have never been this exact," I grumbled,

my focus continually darting between Wyn and Michel, the latter not really trying to hide behind a fake phone call anymore.

"Jos' sights have also been under an emotional barricade," Wyn retorted.

"I do not think that would make it any better, Wyn." This time it was my turn to give her a look, she just shook her head innocently. I sighed, dragging my hand through my hair as I began to pace.

Joclyn had said to follow the light, and no matter how many warning lights were going off in my head, I knew better than to question her.

"Well," I said, pulling my pacing to a stop. "I guess we found the light we are supposed to follow."

"Yeah, and it sounds like it's leading us right into the dark."

"What do you mean?" I was almost scared to ask.

"The Kyōwakoku," she hesitated, taking one quick glance at Michel before she turned her back to him. "They call them the Kyō. I had Thom look them up just now. He says they invaded Australia last week. A blonde woman was leading them."

The monster inside of me threatened to break free, the sound of my father's laugh erupting in my ears.

"Ovailia." The word was snarl, it broke out of the clench in my teeth in a rampage, ripping itself from the cage I had placed it in. Shredding my heart and my stability in the process.

We had largely stayed out of the shifting governments since this all began, choosing instead to save who we could, and let the world figure itself out. We were safe underground, we needed to repair ourselves before we could fix the impending world war that was breaking out.

As Wyn relayed the news however, something became painfully clear.

The world had done more than change around us, it had grown beyond us, and Ovailia was ready to push down our door.

CHAPTER 28
RYLAND

Nearly an hour later, I closed the door to the large guest room with a smile, even though every part of me was ready to just slam the door in his face.

If Michel had glued himself to us for one more minute I may have lost it. I had more important things on my mind than seeing the new cavern he had carved out for the newcomers. The thing was miniscule and after Wyn less-than-enthusiastically grumbled about his handiwork, it became clear that we weren't going to pad his ego anymore.

It was only then he had shuffled us to the room Wyn had built for our visits, grumbling reminders about the meetings with the Kyō that he had secured for tomorrow after his mumbling phone call.

I heard him, I nodded gratefully, and yes, I slammed the door in his smug face.

"How safe is it?" I turned from the door to Wyn, letting my magic tumble through the wooden slab as I followed his retreat down the hall, making sure he actually left.

He didn't. He stopped a few doors down and leaned

against the wall, his magic bumping into mine as he scanned us and our movements in return.

Great.

I audibly growled and stepped away from the door, turning to Wyn who was already sitting on the edge of the bed, her legs swinging as she raised an eyebrow at me in question. Bringing my magic back from the hall, I let it spread through the walls, blocking him entirely.

The action was followed by a very faint curse that echoed through the door.

"Did you really think he would leave us alone?" she asked, patting the soft comforter on the bed beside her.

I sat without question, her fingers already flaring before her as faint ribbons of white seeped from her skin, they snaked through the air in wisps of dancing smoke, spreading and swaying until they covered us in a dome.

I was sure from the outside it looked as though the room was empty, an empty bed with two odd indentations cut into the comforter.

From where I sat it appeared as though we were smothered by a fishbowl. Thank goodness I wasn't claustrophobic.

"Safe?" I asked, grabbing the cell phone from her and letting my magic flare it to life as I flipped the archaic thing open.

"As well as I can get it," Wyn said, her eyes sparking with a secret. "Not that Michel is strong enough to sense a shield if it was looking him in the face. He isn't Joclyn, and two shields? Good luck, bud."

I turned to Wyn. "I take it your little flirting session was more than just pushing him to get us a meeting."

Her grin widened.

"He would have done that anyway," she said, not

breaking eye contact as I watched her eyes darken with the fire that always dwelled inside of her. "But when I heat his blood he can't tell when I infect him."

Her voice was a smolder that churned my stomach.

"Infect him?" I asked. "Do I want to know?"

"Little traces of magic, let behind," she held her fingers up in a pinch as though denoting the size, a tiny fire flaring between the tips. "Trackers. Bombs. Little demons of slow burning death. I haven't really decided what to use them for."

"That sounds horrifying," I spoke without thinking, my jaw dropping at just the idea of what Wyn would do with such a thing.

The horror was not shared and Wyn busted out laughing, letting the fire grow before she extinguished it all together.

"Wyn?" I asked, a sudden possibility flaring through my spine and gut. "You haven't done that to me have you?"

"No," she snapped, she actually sounded horrified that I would suggest it. "And even if I did, it was a long time ago when you were trying to kill everyone." She winked and my stomach dropped.

"Now," she continued before my frustrations could escape, "I need to talk to Jos, and only your magic can get me a direct line. Chop-chop."

She nudged her head toward the phone and I suppressed a groan. It was a tricky piece of magic that Ilyan and Talon, Ilyan's Second, had perfected, and one that Wyn had helped us figure out after Talon's passing.

At her insistence I pushed my magic into the phone and watched the display glow white. A shimmer of color rippled over the screen as I used the device as a receiver, connecting me right to her.

It only rang once before she picked up, I immediately pushed the speaker button, knowing that Wyn would have done it anyway.

"Ryland?" Her voice was calm, and I immediately felt the muscles in my shoulder relax. Just the knowledge that she was safe pulling me out of the stressful knot the last few days had placed me in. "Tell me what you have found."

"Shouldn't you tell us that?" Wyn cut in, her taunting snap resulting in a half-hearted chuckle from the Queen.

"Hi Wyn--"

"Thom said she is awake," Wyn cut her off again, the question followed by a sigh so clear I could practically see her throw a glare in Thom's direction.

"Yeah," Jos said after a moment, the single word more reluctant than I had heard from her in a while. "She woke up a few hours ago. She hasn't said much though, she just keeps mumbling in Ukrainian. Thom says it's mostly about some government."

The heavy weight on my chest came back with the impact I hadn't felt since my years on a rugby field. I was only barely able to catch my breath as I shot Wyn a look, the confused stare one that she was already returning.

"Joclyn," I began, gripping the phone tighter as my knuckles began to turn white, "do you know which government?"

"I'm not sure," Joclyn replied, her voice lined with a sigh as it scratched through the phone receiver. "If I had to guess it's the SSU, but she seemed to get quieter after Wyn called about the Kyō..." She faded off, her and Thom's voice muffled as they discussed something. "We can't get anything coherent out of her, even though she is very much alert, awake, and sane."

"Did she do something?" I asked, the hard growl in my voice already making it clear I knew the answer.

"I am fine," Jos sighed, skipping over one question and answering with the one that would have come after. "She can't control her magic enough to do anything. But she can sure as hell kick."

Thom laughed in the background, the sound making Wyn smile, but to me it was only ice. The cold slid down my spine as everything stiffened, my shoulder tightening as I brought the phone closer to my lips.

"Please tell me you have her restrained," I said, pressing my lips into a tight line.

"I haven't tied a pig in over two hundred years, Ryland, but I can tell you that even if you grease her she wouldn't get out of that," Thom cut in, the taunt clear even through the static in the phone.

Wyn rolled her eyes and opened her mouth to retort but I pulled the phone away from her. We had much more important things to cover than whether or not Thom had greased and tied a pig in his past.

"Well, I would use a bit more than rope," I warned, shooting Wyn a warning look. "There is something about the way Michel is behaving..." I hesitated, taking a deep inhale before continuing. "Something is up. I don't trust this."

"And when have I trusted anything this easily, Ry?" Jos teased, her light laugh was almost the exact thing I needed right then.

"And since when do you believe Thom when he says such nonsense?" Wyn chuckled alongside her, pulling the phone from my hand. "But anyway, back to pigs... Michel has bound his magic."

Three completely different curses rang through our

dome of silence; no wonder Wyn had been a little bit on edge all day. The ability to completely shield your magic wasn't new, but it also wasn't something that nice, upstanding, Trpaslíks engaged in. I looked at Wyn, shifting my weight on the bed as I resisted the urge to lean closer to the phone.

So much for everything being easy.

"He's restraining his magic," Thom provided, his gruff voice sounding like sandpaper through the phone. "It could be restraining anything from memories to magic to something he has done that he doesn't want anyone to find. Magic leaves traces, and he doesn't want anyone following the path he's left behind."

"I've worked with him enough that I have his magical fingerprint memorized. And what he is putting off ... well —" Wyn paused, her tattooed scars darkening in her scowl, "he's obviously bound a portion of his magic under a shield. Long story short, our fancy little friend is up to a whole lot of crap."

"So he's using his magic to hide something?" I asked, more to myself than to everyone else. "Or hiding the traces of what his magic has done."

"More likely the latter, considering how tightly he's wrapped it around his heart," Wyn provided, shooting me a side glance that bristled up my spine, turning the icy chill of fear into an immovable block.

"I felt the same in the woman who attacked us. I couldn't sense her magic before she spoke, and I almost missed several others that had traveled with her. They were hiding on the rooftops."

"It's hard magic, someone powerful had to have taught them." Wyn didn't need to finish, we all knew who she was talking about.

"So if Michel is restraining his magic the same way, does that mean he is working with whoever is behind this? Ovailia? The woman? All of them?" Joclyn asked, and I shot Wyn a look, her own face twisted in question.

"I think the safer assumption would be that Michel learned it from Edmund a couple hundred years ago," Wyn provided, her feet shuffling a bit against the stone floor. "Not that he's working for Edmund now. I mean, he's dead. But he could be connected to whatever is left of his army. My guess, is whoever is leading them now is teaching them how to do it, and there is only one person I know that can do that."

"Ovailia," Jos said immediately. I don't even think she was trying to hide the panic in her voice, and the static in the phone only made it sound worse. "I saw her multiple times in my sight. She has to be connected."

Wyn and I exchanged a look as I sighed, putting my hand out in request for the phone. Reluctantly, she provided it, knowing she didn't have much of a choice.

"So, what are the chances that Ovailia is leading either the Kyōwakoku, or the SSU?" I asked, scooting closer to Wyn as though both of us being closer to the phone would somehow drive my point home. "Has our prisoner said anything about either of them?"

"No, but the woman that looks like Ovailia was with them in Australia. Although," Jos added quickly, cutting off the question that I was seconds away from asking. "I don't think it's Ovailia, there is a picture online. It looks like her from the side. But..." She hesitated, exhaling with the tiniest hint of growl. "The magic is poisoned. I can see the soggy stuff dripping from her hands."

The knowledge hit against my chest like a ton of bricks. As much as I didn't want the woman to have been Ovailia, knowing that it wasn't her presented a complication that made it all the more dangerous.

"I knew it couldn't be that easy," Wyn grumbled under her breath, throwing herself back on the bed.

The movement caused the dome that covered us to expand, the swirls of white dancing through the air as it did so.

She had taken the words right out of my mouth.

"Well, tomorrow is going to be fun," I attempted not to groan.

"What's tomorrow?" Jos asked, the signal swaying as my magic sparked, causing her voice to distort.

"We get to meet with the Kyō," I whispered, not daring to open my eyes.

"You're right," Thom scoffed, his own brand of fury bleeding through the phone. "That does sound like fun."

CHAPTER 29
JOCLYN

"I still haven't taken torture off the table," Thom growled through gritted teeth as we stood at the foot of her bed, arms folded, staring down the woman who had only woken up a few hours ago.

She just lay there, grinning. She was clearly enjoying this, despite the fact that she was still pissed as hell at me for 'destroying her magic.'

It was part of the reason we hadn't moved her out of the main hospital hall; if something went wrong with this, we were surrounded by Skřiteks that could help take her down.

"And by torture, I mean give her a Black Water shower," Thom continued, grinning just as wide as our prisoner.

"I love it when you remind me why we don't have you in a higher role." I rolled my eyes, but he took that as an invitation. As he always did.

"Sounds like a missed opportunity, to me. Think of all the fun we could have." He was still staring at the girl but I was really struggling not to laugh.

We must have looked like we had lost it, because even the girl looked absolutely confused.

"What's so funny?" Curiosity killed the cat. I let my smile grow, just to drive her even more mad.

"You tell us about the Kyō, and I will tell you what's so funny." Seemed like a fair trade to me, but her brow was already knitting together.

"The Kyō?" She laughed, although the sound was notably more strained. "You know nothing about The Kyō."

"Yeah, we know. That's why we are asking you, kid," Thom was snarling, his hands slapping against the metal footboard so loud she jumped.

"Kid? I doubt you are much older than me." Poor girl thought she was prodding, but Thom's lip twitched as he gripped the rail, leaning into her until she recoiled.

"I'm over six hundred years old. How old are you?" Thom was trying to force a smile now, but the girl wasn't having it.

"Bullshit." She leaned closer, the old handcuffs that Thom had dug up from somewhere rattling against the metal frame. She had been fighting against the ropes so much she had burned her skin, so we had swapped them out for the handcuffs. Not that they were much better. We both knew that they were more for show than anything, but they did the trick after our prisoner realized she couldn't use her magic anymore.

Of course, she was blaming the 'enchanted' handcuffs, but we weren't about to correct her yet.

"You are both full of bull shit." She clearly seemed to think she had won. "Some Gods you are."

I gave Thom a look, but he looked just as confused as I did.

"So, we are Gods now?" I asked, and her smile stretched, that same stupid grin spreading over her lips.

"Didn't you know?" she taunted before she shook her head and set her scowl back in place. "I've seen the pictures. We all have. We aren't the only ones looking for you!" The handcuffs rattled as she fought against them, as though she was going to lunge at us.

"And who is *we*?" Thom asked, his tone the low purr of the French aristocrat he was born as.

Her face fell as she realized what she had done. Poor girl was even more trapped than she thought. I wanted to smile, but I clenched my jaw and stared her down instead.

"We know you are working for someone," I said leaning over the footboard again, but the girl leaned back against her headboard and went back to scowling.

So much for that tactic. My magic boiled as I stepped back, Thom swearing French as he stormed back over to me.

"Burn her," he snarled in French before switching back to English. "I am done with this. You want Ilyan, you want answers. She has them."

"I know." I spoke in Czech, the girls scowl furrowing into confusion as we switched languages. "Go get my mug."

"Finally!" Thom yelled, causing more than a few of the other patients around us to yelp in surprise. "I vowed to never touch that thing, but for this, it will be worth it."

He stormed off, rustling through the sheets that we had partitioned around us with a flourish.

The girl's dark skin colored slightly as she looked from the sheets to me, she was trying not to look scared, but her eyes gave her away.

"Do you know what a Drak is?" I asked quietly. I plowed on before she had a chance to answer, knowing that chances were slim that she knew what I was anyway. "A Drak is a branch of magic that can see into the future. Specifically the future of anyone who touches the Black Water, which is what Thom has gone to get."

I knocked my head back toward the sheets, but didn't look away from her. All of the stoic stubbornness was starting to slip away.

"I am a Drak. In fact, I am the only Drak." I expected panic, fear, shock. Instead, she laughed.

"That's impossible. You're a liar."

"Am I?" I laughed right back at her, which shut her up quickly. "I mean, they call me The Oheň for a reason don't they." I lifted my hand, palm up as I let the boiling magic that had been zooming under the surface of my skin out, letting the magic lift in a cylinder of water that shimmered and grew. "We can test it out when Thom gets back. But, I'll warn you, Black Water burns hurt."

I grinned as I let my magic flare, my eyes dipping to black as my sight pulled to the surface, and I cast the image of those marching armies that I had seen in my sight onto the water. The girl gasped and mumbled something in a language that sounded similar to Czech, and I dropped my hand, the water falling harmlessly to the floor.

"Believe me now?" I tried to sound smug, but I wasn't sure I had pulled it off.

Two years of this, and I still felt awkward when I threatened the people I was questioning. Of course, most of the time they just needed me to earn their trust so that they could realize they were safe enough to work with me. She showed up specifically to kill me.

This type of threatening I was no good at. I had tried to tap into my inner Wyn, but it didn't work and Thom had looked at me like I lost it.

Right now, however, this girl was looking at my hand in horror. She had recognized that army.

"Do you know them?" I tried to keep my voice light, calm, but everything in me was shaking, my soul rattling as though it was going to rip out of me. "Have you seen that army before?"

"The sinister star," she hissed, still looking at my hand. "You can see the SSU. You can spy on us."

Us. I almost jumped out of my skin, but kept it contained.

"I can." I was sure my voice cracked that time, but I continued on, trying to ignore the ache that was growing in my chest. "I can see anything, and once the water touches your skin I can see anything that I want about you."

It was a bit of a lie, but I didn't care, not with the way my soul was screaming.

I had seen that army after I had connected with his blood, and then I had felt his magic again for the first time, and now I was standing with a girl who knew those armies.

This was it, my connection to him. He was so close.

"Or, you can tell me," I added hastily, realizing that I was sounding a bit like a tyrant.

She shifted her weight, handcuff rattling as she sat up, her eyes darting from me to my hand, to the fabric that Thom could reappear through at any second.

"Tell me about the armies. Tell me about the sinister star. Tell me about the SSU, or how about the Kyō." Her eyes darted back to me, that gaunt horror that lined her face trying to twist back into a grimace and failing.

"No," she grit the word through clenched teeth, as though she was fighting against something to get the words out. "The Kyō are religious zealots, fanatics who would rather sacrifice themselves to you than fight you. They are nothing, and the SSU will wipe them from the earth."

And my heart had officially stopped beating.

"Who else is the SSU attacking?" I asked, but she just smiled.

"I don't care how powerful you are, you will never get past our armies." Once again, all of her vain ignorance settled on her face and she grinned, sitting back on her pillows in supposed victory.

I, however, could have flown through the ceiling with all of the electric excitement that rippled through me. The sheet fluttered as Thom rushed back in, mug held proudly before him.

"Now comes the good stuff," he was grinning, but I just grabbed the mug, filled it, and drank, never looking away from the girl before me.

"I've got all I need, Thom. Seeing as Ry and Wyn are visiting the Kyō, how about we go to the Ukraine? I would love to see what the SSU is planning." I sipped my water, smiling as the warmth flooded me, as my magic buzzed as though it knew just where we were going. Maybe it did.

Thom however, was gasping and sputtering behind me like a toddler. "What? You mean no torture?"

The girl looked even more smug at that, as though she had won in the end. I took another drink, smiling at her.

"Oh, I didn't say that."

I leaned forward, pouring a small stream of water onto her exposed wrist. She screamed, Thom laughed, and everything went dark as those armies marched through my sights again.

CHAPTER 30

RYLAND

T he center of London was a bustling mecca that was at once both awe-inspiring and terrifying.

It was amazing that a city could still contain so much life, that so many people could still exist in one place. But that awe was overshadowed by the scars that the city held.

I had been to London several times before. I had even stood in this exact spot in Trafalgar Square, watching people, waiting for information on a target my father had instructed me to kill. That was years ago; now the enormous public square didn't even contain whispers of its former self.

Unless you were comparing it to somewhere in the 1800s.

The ancient stone statues sat broken in praise to a fountain that no longer ran; what little water that made it through the pipes was quickly collected and sold off by more than a dozen soldiers who surrounded the now precious resource, the Union Jack on their back and the smoking muzzles of their guns on their front a clear show of strength and control. The statues wept, limbs missing, as they stared vacantly at the cracked stones and missing windows of the once pristine flats that lined the square and the shattered cathedral that had been reduced to rubble.

Now, the courtyard was filled with pop-up shops and tents of all kinds. Makeshift stores were set up on top of the debris in a maze of paths that funneled thousands of disheveled people through them like a cattle call.

People jostled each other as they hustled from stand to stand, voices fighting for focus as their owners screamed about fruit, or meat pies, or whatever it was that they were selling in an attempt to survive.

Through it all was the smell of sweat, the haunting aroma of death, and most of all of fear.

You could smell it in the rot and dirt that leached from the rubble. You could see that fear in the eyes of everyone as they moved between tents and huddled in the shadows, whispering as they looked to the sky, watching for the Vilỳ. You could feel it in the hundreds of soldiers that wandered through the crowd, eyes and guns pointed into the dreary grey clouds in expectation of an attack, shifting their attention to anyone on the ground who might look out of place.

The layer of fear was increased by the massive LED screens that stared down at the crowd. Bright flashing billboards had been hoisted onto what was left of the buildings, the lights pulling focus as they shifted to a new image every few minutes. Propaganda, warnings of war, and even my own face cycled through the last vestige of technology in the city.

London was possibly one of the safest places in the world, but that was only due to hidden tyranny in the royal family. The moment everything started to fail, they stepped in and controlled everything. The city was nothing near what it was, but it was nothing like the rest of the world, either. The city was the most guarded. They still allowed those who were bitten to roam free, but also had some of the strongest rules regarding safety and regulation.

It was more than most countries could claim, many having been reduced to militant rules and oligarchy. It was one of the reasons so many people lived here, that they braved the city and tried to rebuild a life.

With so much freedom, and so much security, it made me wonder how a group of religious fanatics had slithered into the city and begun to take control.

I darted around a tight cluster of women who were all carrying large woven baskets toward a bread stand and caught up to the deep purple and blue, waist-length curls that Wyn had transformed her hair into. The long lengths swayed over her back as she beelined toward the fruit stand Michel had told us about.

"This is one trend I could get behind," she said as I caught up to her, absently twisting one of the long strands of multicolor hair between her fingers. "I look like a unicorn. I kind of even feel like a unicorn."

She smiled brightly as she popped her gum at me, the sound a loud smack against the ever increasing sound of the crowd.

"You however..." she trailed off, pressing her fingers up her nose in a mockery to the glasses I was trying to use to hide my identity. That, along with the short buzz cut, wasn't cutting it. "You ain't no Clark Kent."

"I had very limited options, Wyn," I sighed as we were jostled away from each other again, the masses moving between us as a few teenage boys screamed about 'fresh pressed flour'.

"I'm a guy," I continued as the crowd brought us back together. "I can't have long green hair."

"Sure you could," Wyn said, throwing her hair over her shoulder as though she was a magical horse. "I don't see any rule that says otherwise. Besides, it would probably look better than..."

She faded off, waving her hand in front of me as her face screwed together. "Whatever this is."

"This is a disguise Wyn," I said, pulling her in closer to me as another throng headed for us. "No one is going to recognize either of us."

"I don't care if they do," Wyn asserted, removing my hands from her shoulders as we stepped up to the impressive display of fruit, and the mousy haired man who was already eyeing us as if he knew we were trouble.

"I would sign autographs if I got the opportunity," she continued as we moved within earshot, the man's eyes growing wider with every step we took. "I've never been famous before and I think it would be a nice change."

"A change from what?" I said with a laugh, no longer looking at her. "I am fairly certain I saw you signing a little girl's shirt in the infirmary last week."

I was the recipient of one well-placed scowl as we stepped further into the booth, the man's wide-eyed stare instantly replaced by a vacant smile. It was almost like someone flipped a switch.

"How can I help you two today?" he began, the falter in his voice picking up as he looked from us to the massive flashing billboard behind us.

I would be worried that he had recognized us, but he already knew exactly who we were.

"Our friend, Michel, says that you have the best peaches in London," Wyn began brightly, her voice mutating to the bubbly teenager that she so closely resembled. "It's been so long since I have had peaches, real peaches. I love peaches."

She ended her ramble with a sigh and a pop from her gum, leaning against me as her focus drifted away. The warm wash of her magic was so strong that just having her against me felt like a fever. The heat blazed hot as she placed her hand against my forearm, the heat dampened enough by the layers of the shirts and jackets I wore that it did little more than singe my clothes.

"Sorry, about her. She's a little excited. We haven't had fresh fruit in ages," I said, putting on a flawless British accent. The man looked taken aback by it, but Wyn didn't even react. She just wrapped her hand tighter around my arm and bounced a bit on her toes.

"No worries, no worries. Your friend is right, we have access to the last orchard in Britain, best peaches you will find," the man said with a smile, his eyes glancing above us again as I am sure the images of us battling Vilÿs and mortals in Prague cycled through the screens again.

This man worked for Michel, he was safe, or at least as safe as someone who worked for Michel could be. But it didn't stop the warnings from tumbling in the back of my mind. The way he continually glanced around, the way his fingers twiddled with the frayed edge of his apron and he shifted his feet. For a moment I was sure he could feel the ever increasing temperature of Wyn's magic as it coursed through the ground, but he seemed oblivious.

"Wonderful!" I said, letting my own magic spread away from me, this time in a shield, as I tried to keep my voice conversational. "We would like two of the ripest fruits."

Again the man shifted his eyes before he began to shuffle away, "Wonderful, wonderful, come with me."

His squat little body was more obvious as he began to weave his way through the crowd, his body moving awkwardly as he led us away from his cart with a nod to an elderly woman.

"Yeah," Wyn said with a glance at me, her eyes full of apprehension, "if we don't survive this, make sure Thom gets my boom box and all of my Styx tapes."

"Maybe next time we should get our information sans seduction," I said, under my breath as I reluctantly followed the man.

"Shut up, Ry," Wyn snapped, pushing her way through a group of disheveled looking teenagers in an attempt to stay next to me. "I didn't see you coming up with any better ideas."

"You mean like asking him?"

"Oh, is that why you two were yelling at each other?"

The man turned around, checking to make sure we were following. Wyn popped her gum and gave the man a false smile as he gestured to us one more time before he disappeared into a dark alley.

"Well, this keeps getting better," Wyn said, a laugh teetering on the edge of her words. "Make sure I get buried in a nice place, and tell Thom I love him."

"Shut up," I growled, holding her back as I let my magic run away from me, let the waves of my power peek around the corner and try to feel something, anything, that could be there.

I didn't dare close my eyes and truly look, but I didn't feel anything.

"Nothing is there, just that man, and his magic is weak," Wyn said, all business now. She was obviously just as concerned about where we were headed as I was. "I could probably breathe on him and take him out."

Well, at least as business as Wyn could get.

"Have you heard anything from Jos or Thom?" I asked, reluctantly dropping my arm as I took a few steps forward.

Wyn shook her head, knowing better than to pull out something as valuable as a phone in this crowd. "Not a thing."

I tried to ignore the heavy weight that was growing in the pit of my stomach, the knot was now so large I was pretty sure that it was going to be impossible to dislodge. I had hoped that we would hear something from them by now, but we hadn't heard a thing.

Pushing the rising panic aside, I gave one last glance to Wyn, her face a cross between panic and exhilaration, and stepped out of the crowd and into the alley.

The bright sun of the early morning vanished as we crossed over the cobbles and past the line of shadow. The buzzing noise of the crowd faded as the brick buildings swallowed us, the fear drenched dystopian city fading away into nothing.

"Do you have a pass?" the squat mousy haired man asked from where he stood in the middle of the alley, his stance making it clear he was intending to guard something, albeit poorly.

Wyn shifted beside me, her posture moving between an attack stance and a defensive stance as the waves of her magic rushed through the dark chill of the alley.

This time it was clear that he felt her magic, for the more it grew the more his hands began to shake, his stubby fingers continuing to fiddle with the edge of his apron. I was so used to being surrounded by powerful women, of feeling the ancient roar of Joclyn's ability, and the fiery heat of Wyn's that I may have forgotten how frightening feeling that strength for the first time would be, how daunting it would be to have the two of us stand before him.

"We come armed with Michel's word of our trustworthiness, our own reputation, and a promise of the safety of all innocent parties throughout this meeting." I spoke firmly, each word carefully calculated.

Michel had warned us of this, but he said nothing other than that we needed to assure them we weren't there to kill them all. I hadn't assumed it had begun with the man from the stand.

I had gone for a diplomatic approach, Wyn had a different idea.

"We aren't here to destroy you. But I can't promise it will stay that way," she sassed, a smirk smothering her face as the bright candy colors of her hair began to fade, shifting back to the usual dark auburn shade, if not a little redder and a little longer than it was normally.

The man seemed taken aback by that and he jerked, stepping closer to the wall on his left, right where the entrance to whatever he was guarding was hidden, I realized.

So much for a guard, he was no better than the teens outside of Imdalind that Thom liked to terrorize.

"Will you let us pass?" I asked, looking from him to the wall in obvious exaggeration.

The gaze gave the man a start, and he faltered, his own bewildered glance falling toward the hidden entryway, his jaw working.

"It is not my place to say," he finally said, the fear that had looked to grip him slipping away as he fixed us with a steely glare that ripped against my chest. I hadn't expected that from him.

"What do you mean?" My question was a growl.

"The man you have to convince is ahead," he whispered, "I can only show you the way. Do not mention it was me. I obviously value my life more than you value yours."

It was a dark warning that followed him out of the alley, both of our heads turning as the crowd swallowed him, no one in the crowd even noticing his sudden arrival, or where he had come from.

"Do you remember when I said this keeps getting better?" Wyn asked, the mockery dripping from her voice and increasing the tension that was currently occupying every muscle across my back and shoulders.

"Yes," I sighed, removing the glasses and slipping them into my pocket, my hair already returned to its usual curly shag.

"I take it back, this is going to be a freakin' disaster."

"Come on, Wyn," I sighed, a feral hiss snapping in the back of my throat as I dragged her toward what was obviously a false wall.

My magic rushed out in one last fan as I checked for any danger, any sign that we were about to walk into a trap, only to stop short. Spinning toward the high roof of the building behind me, an attack burst from my palm in one long stream of green. The light erupted through the alley in ribbons of acid that rippled through the air and reflected off the building in streaks of poison before it impacted against the edge of the roof, right where I had felt my father's magic.

"Ryland!" Wyn swore loudly as her own magic flared, a bright spark from behind me staining my shadow in the street as I assumed she shielded us in the alley, closing us off from the mortals and trapping us with whatever I had felt.

"What the hell, Ry?" Wyn erupted behind me, smacking me hard in the arm as I turned around, facing her and the wall she had created. The mortals rushing by on the other side were oblivious to anything having happened.

"I felt him. I felt it," I quickly corrected, trying to keep the growl out of my voice but failing. "My father's magic."

Wyn looked at me in panic, her jaw grinding as I assumed she tried to control her rage. It didn't work.

"We are heading into a fortress of people who have poisoned magic," she snapped, her eyes hard. "Magic that your father built and infected. Of course, you are going to feel his magic."

"This was different—"

"So barricade, restrain, tell me," she interrupted, her tone becoming far too motherly for me and I pulled away from her. "You have got to chill, Ry. We are going into the lion's den. Rein it in a little."

"Don't be so dramatic," I growled, but Wyn just looked at me like I was crazy, gesturing wildly toward the now scarred roof of the building beside us, proving her point.

"I'll control it," I snapped, her eyes growing wide as she looked at me, then past me.

"You better," she said, her voice dropping a solid octave as it died in her throat, "because things just got a whole lot worse."

I spun towards where she was looking, only to come face to face with an elegant Japanese man in a pinstriped suit.

"Hello," he said in heavily accented English, his eyes looking between us and only barely restraining the recognition. "We have been waiting for you."

Well, crap.

CHAPTER 31
RYLAND

I nstead of leading us into a dark tunnel or underground cavern as I had assumed, the wide doorway behind the false wall opened into an elegant, modern hallway.

The wide concourse stretched away from us in either direction; both design and layout reminding me of the mansion I had grown up in. Every few feet the carved wainscoting and striped wallpaper opened up to tall, floor to ceiling windows that flooded the beige hall with bright light. There was so much light that I almost missed the sconces between each window, the older brass fixtures were blazing with real, working light bulbs, and not the flickering lanterns that most of the world had reverted to using.

I stared at them, trying to wrap my head around how they had secured enough power to ignite this light, let alone a whole hallway of them. And all during the day no less.

Electricity was rationed, and anyone who still had access was limited as far as when and how they could use it. Decorative sconces used during the middle of the day would not qualify. Most of what was available was used by the government for the military, boundary protection, or the giant LED screens I could see staring at me through the windows. Wyn's face was screaming through the gauze curtains before it switched to Joclyn and Ilyan, fighting side by side.

"I see you are surprised by our access to power," the Japanese man interrupted, the depth of his accent making the words feel broken. "A gift from the government for our work with them."

Wyn smiled, taking the gum that she had been chewing out of her mouth and pressing it against the striped wallpaper that had been expertly placed along the hall.

She smiled at the man, never once taking her eyes off him. His plastered smile flinched as she stuck the gum to the wall, the silent conversation making the single tap of her foot against the plush carpet sound like an impatient tick.

It was a warning call that I didn't really need.

I was already on high alert, my mind rushing through every possibility, calculating every opportunity to escape. This was probably the only reason I knew that I needed to master stuttering. Then I could just pop my way out.

Something we were definitely going to need with the way Wyn was antagonizing the man. I wish I could tell her to knock it off, but I already knew it wouldn't do any good.

Wyn was exceptionally good at finding holes in pretty much every situation we found ourselves in. Right now, she was doing just that; aggravating him, searching for holes, monitoring his magic. Beyond being able to see in detail how many magical beings are in an area, Wyn could also sense the type of their magic, as well as the strength and any imperfections they might have.

It possibly gave us an unfair advantage, but seeing as we didn't use it to execute people, I wasn't too concerned. When going into a situation against a possible enemy, I had learned that holding back in the interest of playing fair was a sure way to get yourself killed.

"And what work would that be?" Wyn asked, wiping her sticky fingers off on the lightly colored curtains.

"I am sure you have many questions," he said calmly, deflecting Wyn's question as he stepped forward, his eyes digging into hers.

My magic flared protectively as he hovered over her, standing millimeters away as he reached toward the wall. His focus dug into hers as with one zap of magic the gum disappeared, the ashen remains drifting to the floor alongside the poisoned bits of his power.

He smiled, proud of his display, but Wyn only smirked as she watched the heavy spark of his magic drip down to the floor.

"What's wrong with your magic?" Wyn asked, her voice drawn out as though she was talking to a toddler.

The man smiled broadly as he turned away, making his way down the hall. "Follow me."

That wasn't anything close to an answer.

I shot Wyn a look. My glare ripped into her but she only shrugged and began to follow the man, already pulling another stick of gum out of her pocket.

"What are you doing?" I hissed at her in Czech, glancing between her and the man we followed in search of any sign he could understand me.

"Showing him some hospitality," she unwrapped another piece of gum and I reached out to stop her, but she batted me away, her bracelets spinning around her wrist. "Don't be an idiot, Ry. These walls aren't trustworthy."

The mischievous spark in her eyes faded at the last few words, her focus darting back to the man ahead of us as she once again began to pop her gum.

"How bad," I asked quietly in French, earning myself a glare.

"Shut up, Ry."

That bad.

It wasn't the first time I wished I could read her mind, she was obviously sensing something. Even as powerful as I was, I could only sense a wall of distorted magic and a heavy gloom that I couldn't quite place.

I would have to leave the plan of attack to Wyn, I trusted her. With what my magic could see, finding an escape route was up to me. The sooner, the better.

Letting my magic run through the building, I mapped every hallway and room out in my head, spreading them out in my mind. Even before the dapper Asian led us into another, nearly identical hall I had realized we had been brought into, or rather what they thought they had: a maze.

It really shows how feeble their magic was that they thought this was enough to stop us.

I turned to Wyn to say something, but her focus was already a million miles away, her finger rubbing over the side of the phone in her pocket.

Sending a text I assumed, not that she had any way to read whatever came back.

"Can you at least tell us your name?" I asked through the silence as I began to track my magic through what looked like a large meeting room on the second floor. The massive space was a cavity of nothing in the center of the building.

Yet another thing to set me on edge; if everything in this

mission kept sending me into a panic I was going to get an ulcer.

"My name is Tomi, and before you ask, I am taking you to see Suji." His voice was dead, flat, and he didn't even turn; he just looked straight ahead, turning to lead us down another hall and toward the large staircase at the end.

That large space on the next floor was feeling more and more like a possible destination.

"Who is Suj--"

"That is all," Tomi interrupted, his focus pulled forward as we followed behind him like dogs.

I was sure he was using his magic to verify that we weren't doing anything unsavory, but given the amount of tracking we were doing, I wasn't sure if his power was strong enough to gauge us beyond knowing that we were still here.

Taking a chance, I closed my eyes, supercharging my magic for one second as I used it to peek into the massive space above us. If there was any chance of there being an army waiting there, I needed to know. When I closed my eyes, however, my magic showed me only darkness. The massive space was drowned in black. Every few feet, faint lines of light shimmered over the floor, outlining the room in what I was sure were windows or doors. I would have to say doors given that the room was in the dead center of the building.

Just a hollow canker, like a tumor that had been removed.

Wyn placed her hand against my forearm and I jerked, eyes opening just as we began to ascend the stairs. Thank God Wyn was paying attention or I would have face planted right into them.

"Have a good vacation?" she asked in Portuguese, her

knowing eyes wide as she tried to relay her overly obvious code.

It was truly hard not to laugh. If we were in a spy movie we would probably be caught right away.

"Naw, we went to Alaska. It was too dark." Alaska, top of the map, above us. Dark, is well... Dark.

She wrinkled her nose, wrapping her hand around mine as the warm heat of her power began to wash over my skin, covering me like a warm blanket. A shield. A really powerful shield.

This was new. And horrifying. This was clearly so much worse than I thought. I gave her another look but she shook her head and released my hand, the warmth of her shield still clinging to my skin.

"And cold I bet. But I bet there were a lot of moose hidden in the trees," she whispered in Dutch, the response befuddling. I wasn't super familiar with Dutch, and although I understood the base of what she had said; I had a bad feeling that I had translated something wrong.

Tomi had stopped at the landing, signaling for us to take the last few stairs before changing his gesture to detail a door just to his right.

The door just opposite of the large hollow space on the floor.

I looked from the door he indicated, to the ones right across the hall and a dark weight of magic that was seeping from it. So, no empty space.

"As I said," Tomi said menacingly, "we have been waiting for you."

Tomi glowered at Wyn as she popped another bubble with her gum, sent a steely smile my way and then retraced his steps down the stairs, leaving us standing perplexed on the landing.

"Well then," Wyn said in clear Czech, the language she was raised with rolling into the air with ease. "Shall we see what's behind door number one, or behind door number certain death."

She gestured to the hallway lined with doors that we now stood in, each slab of carved wood identical to the one Tomi had indicated.

"I have a feeling you already know."

Wyn smirked at me, her eyes shining.

"Stay on your toes. The man with the chainsaw is waiting for you," she whispered, the humor in her voice vanishing as though it had been slapped out of her.

"Are they in the walls?" I hissed in Czech just as the door Tomi had indicated swung open, the creak of the hinges screaming in my ears as I peered into the dark space just behind.

"The moose are everywhere."

I gave Wyn one last look before I pushed the door open the rest of the way, letting my magic swell as I stepped through the entry and into a room so bathed in darkness I could feel it against my skin.

Close to a dozen people were waiting just on the other side, their tainted magic giving them all away. I could tell at once they were not what I should focus on, however, they were only a guard.

Whoever stood directly before us was who we were brought here to see. It was his magic that pulsed with a stronger beat, although it was just as tainted as the others. There was something different about it though, as if he was causing the darkness.

Or perhaps he was the darkness.

His darkness moved into me with each step we took, a humid weight clinging to it as stagnant air pressed against my chest. I tried to breathe, the aroma of wood and wet assaulting my senses. The whole room was something akin to a sauna sent straight from the depths of hell.

What little light filtered into the hallway behind us was swallowed by our silhouettes on the stained wood floor. They stretched before us like giants before they were sucked into the dark with the snap of the door behind us.

The sound echoed further by a single tap of Wyn's shoe against the floor.

As much I didn't need the reminder of the danger that we had walked into, this was not that. This tap was the start of a ripple of heat that moved through the heavy wood floor. The strong smell of campfire wafted through the air as the people who stood around the edges of the floor began to shriek and jump, the floor underneath them beginning to burn straight through them.

I expected to feel the burn rage through me, feel the heat snake around me, but there was nothing beyond the unexpected sounds of pain from the others.

Holding my ground, I stared in the direction of whoever stood in the middle of the room as the shrieks began to settle down. My magic swelled into my hands, ready for whatever was coming next.

"Are you going to turn on the light, or do I need to do it again?" Wyn snapped, the tips of her fingers beginning to spark into tiny flames.

The sparks of her fire must have been just as frightening as whatever she had done to all of them, because another round of shrieks filtered toward us from the far edges of the room.

"Don't worry, Wynifred, I can do it." My voice was a roar as I held my hand forward, palm up as I let my magic rush to it, let it swell and grow beyond the tiny orb that we usually used as a light source and created a ginormous fiery sphere the size of a beach ball.

The light spread away from me, hitting against the walls in waves as face after face came into focus, each one filled with the open mouthed awe we saw from many of the newly awakened Chosen we brought to Imdalind.

Whispered exclamations rippled through the room, whether it was in recognition of who we were or the clarity of the magic I now held, however, I wasn't sure. I wasn't about to ask.

I wasn't about to look away from the man who stood before me, either.

Dressed in a white suit, complete with an embroidered vest, his olive hands rested on a long carved walking stick. The man stood still, his almond eyes staring into me with a bright blue color so unnatural that it was clear he had used his magic to create the color.

He said nothing, he just stared, eyes burning into me as he focused his magic to move through the air toward us.

"No, thank you," Wyn said from beside me, the smell of burning wood growing as a faint black line appeared around us, the perfect circle burned into the wood from inside.

It took me only a second to sense the shield that Wyn had placed around us, her magic stopping the man and his power from getting any closer.

He, however, didn't seem to notice the change. I could still feel his magic licking the air as it made its way toward us, the intensity of his glare faltering a bit as his magic hit against her wall.

"You must be Suji," I said, repeating the name from before as his magic continued to bang against the shield like a shark against a tank.

I nodded toward him in greeting, but his lip only twitched, his magic flaring angrily as he continually tried to break through Wyn's barrier. He could try all he wanted, there was no way he was getting through, especially if the smile that spread over Wyn's face was any indication.

"My name is Ryland Krul, I am the youngest son of the original line of magic on this earth. This is Wynifred, the captain of our Queen's army, and head of the Trpaslíks. We have been sent on an investigation--"

"Your magic is very strong," he interrupted, as his magic finally faded away.

His voice was smooth and calm, I had expected an accent but there wasn't a hint of one, only the deep guttural phrasing that made the man seem a bit more ominous. I showed no surprise to his statement, I only smiled and let my power pulse through me in a strong wave, making the orb I still held in my hand pulse and glow.

"We are of the first," I said, knowing he didn't understand what that meant. "Our power does not carry the disease that yours does. It is strong and healthy, the way magic is meant to be."

Babbles of confusion rippled around the room, many of those who surrounded us looking to Suji in confusion.

It was clear they had never heard this, or rather that they had been told something different.

With that, I bounced the sphere on my hand, the orb breaking into a million tiny balls as it impacted with my palm, the tiny pieces soaring to the walls like they were flung through a slingshot. The men and women who surrounded us shrieked in fear, many dodging as the harmless balls of light soared around them to slam against the wall with faint pops.

Glowing in shades of blue and green, the tiny orbs

looked like bubbles as they congregated against the creases in walls and ceiling, traveling around window sills and sliding over the walls in search of their friends.

Strips of light fell over fearful faces as the emotion faded to awe, jaws dropping in differing levels of amazement.

I heard their chatter, but I refused to let my focus drift from Suji, his hand clenching around the handle of his walking stick as if the small rod was the only thing keeping him in place.

"Your power does not need to stay this way," I continued, speaking to everyone around me, even though I only looked at Suji, his stoic face drowning deeper in a scowl with each word I spoke.

"You speak of our magic as though you know of its strength and ability." He shook his head as though he was ashamed of me, the look producing a tiny growl from Wyn. "You speak as though you know all we have accomplished. As though you know who we are."

I resisted the urge to show him up, to smile at his foolishness. He may not be able to feel my magic, but I could clearly feel his.

"You are right, I do not know of your strength or accomplishments." I was careful not to let my voice raise too far, keeping my voice even and diplomatic, even though the rage of my magic under my skin did not match the tone. "I do, however, know of your power. For I know who created the creatures that have infected you."

Again, the room broke out in murmurs, only this time was different, this time was panicked. Even the elegant Asian man was affected, his eyes growing wide as he tapped his cane against the floor, the faint sound of the impact silencing everyone.

"You know who created us," Suji said, not a drop of a question enfolded in his words. The corner of his mouth ticked up nefariously, and I fought the need to step back, to step away from him and let my magic soar free. "Tell me, Ryland Krul of the first, was it your people who did so? Are you ashamed of your creations? Is that why you hide underground and steal the people who have been blessed with magic away, tucking them into that mountain, never to be seen?"

Ice washed over me, the chill moving over my spine as he stepped closer, every word he said hitting against me.

We clearly had not been as stealthy in our tasks as we thought.

He knew of Imdalind, and of our work to recover those who had been bitten. I had no idea how much he knew, but his knowledge, no matter how flawed, put him right in line to have orchestrated an attack not only against Michel, but against us.

I really should have listened to all those 'trap' warning alarms that had been going off in my head.

"We are not the ones who created the Vilỳ, nor are we ashamed of what has happened," I said simply, feeling Wyn stiffen beside me as the very air around her began to heat, something I was sure Suji could feel given the sweat that had begun to pool around his hairline. "We spend much of our time bringing those who were bitten to our home..."

"To your underground prison--" One of the men who lined the room interrupted me with a snap, the look on his face making it clear that he was sure of his answer.

Suji smiled at the man's outburst, chuckling softly to himself as he rocked back and forth against his walking stick.

Okay, so our usual negotiation methods were not going

to work. There was at least once a year that we found a pocket of survivors and had to convince them to come home to Imdalind. This group did not fall into that category. This group clearly thought we were some kind of jailers.

I smiled disparagingly at the man before turning back to Suji, his twisted grin only growing.

"It appears your reputation has arrived here before you could," he said, looking from me to Wyn as she took a step forward, her mind already set on causing a problem.

I held my hand out, stopping her before she could get too close, knowing full well that her magic had already infected each and every one of them with how the temperature in the floor had risen.

"Rumors and lies do not build a reputation," I growled, the full strength of my anger coloring my features as the red heat of my magic began to boil over my bulging muscles.

It did not go unnoticed, and while everyone else in the room took a wide step back, Suji held his place, his hand tightened against the walking stick.

There was a reason that many people feared me. The images that were released from that day in Prague depicted me as a war-crazed maniac. Wild eyes, bleeding cuts covering my face. I looked deranged. I looked dangerous.

I was sure that was what they were seeing now.

"We do not build our assumptions of you off lies," I continued before he could get a word in. "That is why we are here. We are searching for the group who has attacked us, who has attacked our Queen. It is our job to find them, and to destroy them."

"The two of you..." Suji said, pointing his finger between us. "You plan to take out all of us?"

I only smiled, "If we find that it was you who did this."

350

"And how do you plan to do that?" The tone of his voice made it clear that he did not believe I could accomplish such a feat.

Or perhaps that he alone could stop us. Both were foolish.

I hesitated, sending one glance to Wyn. She stood as stoic as I did, her focus drifting around the room as she slowly chewed her gum, slowly working her jaw as she kept her mouth open.

"Where is the girl, the one who came from a pocket of magic users near here; Hikari?" I asked, turning back to Suji.

The question caught him off guard and while he did not flinch physically, I could feel the pulse of his magic quicken. The heartbeat that he could not control, and that he did not realize I could feel, giving him away.

I didn't even try to restrain my grin.

"She is not here," he said after a moment, the pulse of his magic deepening as he stretched it away from him, infecting the air with the same heavy darkness I had felt when we first entered.

"That's too bad--"

"She was taken from us several months ago when we were trying to seek the return of some of our followers," Suji interrupted, his voice a snap as he drowned out my threat.

I opened my mouth to respond, only to have it snap shut again. My jaw tightened as my eyes narrowed in question.

"You have been attacked as well?"

"You are a fool, Ryland Krul of the first," he said, stepping toward us until he was right against the dark line in the floor, right against the barrier Wyn had surrounded us in. "You sit in your underground prison and *rescue* people, oblivious to the governments, and wars, and everything that is going on around you. You think we are the enemy, but you do not know us."

He stopped, the magical color in his eyes fading as he leaned forward, his breath spreading over Wyn's shield in blossoms of cold.

"You do not know who the true enemy is," he continued. "I will give you a hint. It's not us." He paused, his face darkening into a look so nefarious that if it wasn't for Wyn and her child-like gum smacking I would have taken a step back.

"Not yet," he finished, the low promise like a snake that wound down my spine.

Now I wanted to kill him. Just string him and his pathetic threat up and end him right then.

Calm.

The word was only barely enough.

"Tell him to sod off, Ry," Wyn hissed in her best British accent, still staring at the ceiling.

The exchange was not missed by Suji, and he smiled, obviously thinking he had found a weakness, and not just the switch to a bomb he could not stop.

"These two are our key," Suji said loudly, everything about him changing as he shifted to address the people who lined the room. "They will bring us above the SSU and everyone will see the power of our faith, they will see the strength of our magic and know that we are meant to rule over the lesser man. They will see that we have been ordained."

As one everyone began to murmur in what could only be described as a prayer, several bowing toward Suji as though he himself was the God. The thought was almost laughable. Well, it would have been if I didn't feel like I had walked in on a cult.

"Ordained. I'm not ordaining anyone," I said, letting my magic flare again in green sparks of warning. I wasn't even sure he saw, the man was now rampaging like a televangelist.

That was our cue to leave.

"The SSU may have captured their own God, but we have two right before us. Two of the same Gods from the battle in Prague. The SSU has grown strong from the strength of their God. And now we will have two of our own to grow our strength, to increase our worship and show the world the true order that has been designed for us."

"What the hell are you talking about?" It was hard to take this guy seriously, especially as he began to glow.

"There was a reason I never read the Bible," Wyn muttered, now focused on the mad man who was spouting nonsense.

"We have been waiting for you to join us. We have been praying for the Gods to return to us." Any more bizarre proclamations were cut off by Wyn's crystal clear laugh. The people that lined the space flinched, the calm zeal in their faces draining as she stepped around me, coming to face the man himself for the first time since we had arrived. Suji's lustful enthusiasm faded as her laugh continued, his eyes darkening as he scowled at her.

"Wait, wait, wait," Wyn prattled, shaking her gloved hand at him as she popped her gum again. "Are you saying that you want to worship us?"

She laughed louder, the sound more frantic than before, her distraction firmly in place. I stared at him, heart rattling in my chest as I watched his fury rise.

Just as she wanted it to.

This was her show now.

I would have loved to stand and watch, but I had work to do. I hadn't stopped monitoring the room since our arrival here, and now I pressed my magic away into the flimsy paper wall, watching those around me for any sign that they could sense my power.

No reaction, they were all too pissed at Wyn who was now slapping her knee. Poor Suji couldn't get a word in, everytime he tried, Wyn just laughed louder.

I kept my focus on him as I began searching for their magic elsewhere in the building, searching for shields and barriers and any weakness. Every window seemed to be barricaded, shielded with something that while not strong would take more than a minute to break through.

It wasn't worth the risk.

"We worship magic," Suji finally managed to get in, his voice deep as he extended his hand toward us, his palm toward the ceiling.

I barely saw the sparks of diseased magic that fell from his hand, I was so focused on finalizing the map for our escape.

"We worship the strength that was given to man to rule," Suji continued, as the sludge of his magic fell from his hand, dripping as though it was blood pouring from an open vein.

"I don't think you are going to get very far worshiping that," Wyn scoffed, the vowels drawn out in a clear effort to antagonize him. "Your magic is practically dead. You know, we know someone who can fix that..."

I moved faster, letting my magic pour through the building as I searched past their flimsy shields and barriers for an exit. I barely restrained the gasp as I found it. A window one floor above was open.

Once again, a path too easy for it to be true. I wasn't going to put any money down that we would actually be soaring through the one lone window; chances were higher we would break through one of the shielded windows. Or, knowing Wyn, blast our way through a wall, but at least we had some kind of plan.

Of course, every one of our exits also faced the busiest section of Trafalgar Square. I guess all the shoppers were going to get a show. Two of the most wanted people on the planet exploding through the building, right above them.

Perhaps, if we were lucky, we would take flight right as our pictures blazed over the LED billboards. I was sure Wyn would love that.

The image made me smile, something that Suji's sharp eyes did not miss.

His focus jerked to me, his eyes narrowing in question before Wyn pulled him back, her hand raising as if to reach out to him, only to stop millimeters before hitting against her barrier.

"What is he doing?" Suji asked, before Wyn could get a word out.

"You would be able to tell if your magic wasn't so trashed," she said with a shrug. "We can tell what you are planning, and where your weaknesses are. For example, that man there," she pointed, "has a heart murmur that his magic can't figure out how to heal. And the five... no six people in the room above us are only about halfway through that bomb they are trying to make. Not that it will do any good."

I began to pull my magic back as the room broke out in glances of shock and fear. Suji's prophetic facade slipped, the guy looking furious before he smacked his 'touched by an angel' smile back into place.

"Well, that was fun," I said as my power wound back through the hall just outside this room and passed every door that led to that large open room in the building.

Every door open, waiting to welcome us in.

It wasn't like that before. My heart sped up, an interesting mix of intrigue and terror practically begging me to leave this posturing match and go check it out.

I didn't know what it was about that space. There was nothing special about it, in fact there was nothing there at all.

Perhaps it was the dead feeling inside of it that made my soul want to explore, that made it feel like home.

Follow the dead.

Crap. We had to go in there.

"I was given this magic by the gods to rule..." And Suji the prophet was back.

"You were given magic that was created by a deranged man to create an army he could control," Wyn interrupted, her voice full of sass as she shrugged her shoulders flippantly. "Sorry to disappoint you."

Wyn flashed the man a bright smile, popping her gum as she stepped closer to me. Suji just smiled as he lifted his hands toward the sky, his walking stick clutched in his fist as though he was praying to some unseen god.

"My magic, and the magic of all of Kyō, was given to us by the Gods so that we can mold the humans into the servants they were born to be."

"No," I snapped, my magic traveling on the back of the single word as it ran through the room, the power hitting against everyone like a rubber band.

A few people who stood around the perimeter winced, but Suji remained still as my rage built.

"Your power was given to you by a mad man who

fancied himself a King. He was not a God, and in the end I was the one to kill him."

My shout increased with every word, my anger flaring as the yell in my mind grew. This time, however, Wyn did not try to restrain it, she let the monster take hold of me, knowing what was coming as clearly as I did.

Suji did not back down, he only stood before us as still as a board, his smile broadening.

"Perfect," he said, his voice as smooth as acid. "Then we will take the God's son and he will make us strong."

With a smile, he swung his walking stick up to point right at me. A bang erupted through the room as a bullet shot from the end, sparks of green and yellow sending the flash of metal streaming through the air, right to me.

I only barely saw the flame, saw the bullet soar my way when a scream joined the gunshot, and a blonde haired teenager burst into existence before me, her hand held out toward the man.

"Nice try," Míra said, just as everything around us caught fire.

CHAPTER 32
RYLAND

Fire enveloped the room, the tongues of Wyn's magic licking against the barrier of her shield as it engulfed a few of the men and women around us. With the bang and the shattering of glass against wood, Suji was thrown through the air, slamming into the wall with a smack, as his walking stick tumbled to the ground.

"I'll take that," Míra said, bringing the stick to her with one pulse of her magic.

I should have been glad for the small victory, but I was too angry at the little snake who stood before me. She was already giggling as I turned to her, holding the walking stick like a trophy.

"Míra!" I roared, rounding on the girl who stood within the lines of Wyn's shield, Wyn giving her a glare that was just as angry and confused as mine.

Míra gave me no response, she just grinned as fires and screams erupted around her, the whole effect making her look as though she had emerged straight from hell.

"Why am I not surprised?" Wyn snapped at her as the

fires began to die down, those who had survived the blast beginning to find their feet.

"You are so dead," I began, only to sputter uselessly as Míra grinned at me.

"No," Míra quipped, her smug smile spreading, "but you would have been if I hadn't followed you."

I wanted to rage at her, but all of that was cut off by one pulse of magic against the shield, the strong blast shattering the thing to the ground.

The survivors were already on us, caustic magic dripping from their fingers as they rushed through the flames in an attack.

"Do you really think one freaking bullet could take me down?" I snapped, sending one of the attackers to the ground.

I probably let out too much of my frustrations on that one.

"Oh, Ryland is going to kill you," Wyn said with a laugh, taking down another one of the ravenous cultists.

"You know, a thank you would be nice," Míra said just as one of Suji's men reached her, her magic already moving to make an attack. "I totally saved your butt."

Míra took them down easily, her face rippling with her usual mischievous smile. I probably would have been proud of her if I wasn't so pissed.

"Don't get too cocky," I warned, the last thing we needed was an overconfident mishap.

Defiantly, her smile stretched as she turned with me, fighting off the two Kyō who had rushed me.

I deflected the sparking yellow attack from one, pressing my hand forward and sending a rush of magic toward him. The man stumbled away, falling into the wall as Míra sent his counterpart directly after him, albeit with a bit more force. He slammed into the wall with a crack before sliding down the papered wall, leaving a trail of bright red behind.

"Whoops," Míra said, not a drop of empathy in her voice as she turned and smacked one of our attackers with the walking stick. "Too much."

"Get behind me and stay out of the way!" I yelled, shooting a bright red streak of stunning magic toward a woman with wild eyes, waving my hand through the air as I dropped her attempted attack to the ground.

Shoving the stubborn girl behind me, I turned to the next, magic already supercharged as I tried to move back toward where Suji was, not trusting Míra to stay by me, but not willing to lose our target either.

"Ry, I can do this. I saved you on the roof, too." Míra grinned again, light exploding from her hands as two men stumbled back, only to rush back to her with even more force, as she swung the walking stick she still held around, whacking one in the head as she attacked the other.

"See, I totally got this."

"Damn it, Míra," Wyn growled as she calmly walked by her, taking down every person she passed without a touch, each one screaming about heat and burning. "You know we don't need saving."

Míra grinned at her as if that somehow settled it, only to have two false doors on either side of the room swing open and lines of Kyō soldiers come barreling through.

"Great," Wyn growled, sending at least ten of the furious attackers soaring through the air, slamming into walls and windows as she reflected them back toward their entry. "I didn't see these guys."

Pulling Míra to me, I dropped to the ground, my palm hovering over the expensive wood as a wave of electricity streamed from my fingers, crackling and sparking through the air as it spread right toward them.

Like a row of dominoes, they fell to the ground, writhing in pain. Their screams grew as Míra jumped around me, sending a single barb of red hot magic right into each of their hearts. Their eyes grew wide as her magic attacked them, silencing their screams as they began to turn to stone.

With a glare to Míra, I left her there. As much as I wanted to reprimand her right then, it wasn't going to do anything. I had to remind myself that the girl had been trained to fight, she knew what she was doing. As long as her monster didn't take control we would be fine.

The risk was there for both of us.

Stepping away from her, I turned toward Suji, the man still recovering from Míra's attack as he attempted to lift himself from the ground. I needed answers, and it was now or never.

I wrapped my hand around his collar and lifted him into the air. I probably looked too much like a villain, but I didn't care. I was out of time. Blood stained teeth gleamed at me from behind his twisted smile, the magic in his eyes fading as the color did, leaving only bright blue flecks among the dark brown.

"I think we still have a few things to talk about," I growled, bringing him close enough that he couldn't see beyond the brilliant blue of my eyes; beyond the threat that was darkening them.

"Do we?" Suji asked with a twisted grimace as a loud crash rumbled through the room, everything shaking as Míra's 'sorry' was chased by Wyn's raucous laugh.

"Where is Hikari?" I yelled without turning to see what

had just happened, shaking the man and slamming him into the wall.

I could feel the madness begin to grow in the echo of my father's laugh, the sound mirroring Suji as his smile twisted further, a deep looming chuckle escaping from his throat.

"You really don't know, do you?" he said through the laugh, each word lined with a taunt that only infuriated me more.

"Where is she?" I screamed again, hitting him against the wall.

"She went to the border," he said, the blood dripping from the side of his mouth now. "She followed the attacks, just as you are. It led to her death," he taunted, his words spraying a fine mist of blood over my face. "Just as it will lead to yours."

I didn't have any time to react before his hand pressed forward, slamming into my stomach as his magic surged.

The diseased lines of his power exploded inside of me, the force sending me back as my clothing singed. The warmth of my blood spread over skin and fabric, the smell of iron mixing with that of magic and sulfur. Groaning as the pain spread, I pushed my magic toward the injury and worked to lift myself. Healing would be easier if this magic wasn't so toxic. I needed to fight back and this was making it frustratingly difficult.

"Join us, or join her," Suji roared as he stalked toward me, the taunt almost drowned by the explosions and screams as Wyn and Míra continued to fight the Kyō that were streaming into the room.

"I will do neither," I growled as I forced myself to stand, my magic already soaring towards the man.

He attacked as I did, the two streams of magic smashing into each other with a bang that shook the walls. The sound added to the already boiling room, fireworks showering over everything as attacks were either deflected or hit their mark.

"I am here to serve my Queen, to fight against people like you!" I roared as I lifted myself, air whooshing through the room as I towered over him.

I saw the fear on his face for the briefest moment before Míra's scream cut through me. I turned in a panic, only to face a blast ripping through the room. Everything rumbled in light and motion, wind and flame licking over me as everything, myself included, was picked up and slammed to the left.

The room filled with screams, fire, and pain as I was slammed into a wall. Pulses of pressure shot through bones and muscle as impact after impact pressed against me, until what felt like an entire building was piled on my chest.

Groaning, I attempted to roll over but found myself trapped by both building and what I was sure was at least a few cracked ribs. My magic flooded me in pockets of warmth around my torso, long strands of heat running in lines down my left leg and the completely shattered bone that was there.

Perfect.

I tried to shift myself out from whatever had landed on top of me, hissing and wincing as more bones cracked. I grit my teeth, my magic heaving against rocks as rubble and debris fell away from me, just as Wyn's enraged face appeared above, her hands clawing and throwing scraps of wood, drywall and segments of steel off me as though they were Legos.

"We have to move," Wyn gasped, heaving a large slab of stone off me and extending her hand.

"I wonder what gave you that idea," I growled, wincing as she pulled me to my feet. A sharp pain ripped through my leg and I went down again, the gleaming red on my pant leg giving a stark warning to whatever had happened underneath. I was sure you could see the bone if you looked. I wasn't going to look. "You didn't need to bring the roof down to get the point across."

"I didn't do that," Wyn growled.

"I did," Míra beamed, popping up behind Wyn and smiling behind an equally soot-covered face.

"Shut up, Míra," Wyn warned, throwing my bulky arm around her tiny frame when it became obvious I couldn't put weight on that leg.

She was more than a foot shorter than me, I was sure we looked ridiculous.

"Move kid," Wyn continued, lightly kicking the girl's shins and prompting her toward what was left of the door, just as the rubble behind us began to shift.

"Move faster," I prompted, kicking my one good leg like it was an oar.

Wyn took one glance behind before she began to hustle, practically throwing me through the collapsed door frame and sending me into a heap on the floor.

I groaned at the impact, twisting as I pulled myself up. Thankfully the bleeding had stopped, but I had a feeling I was going to need to reset that leg before it was going to be of any use.

"Want some help?" Míra asked as she crawled up beside me, displaying her palms as Wyn turned back to the door, her magic already ripping through the air.

What remained of the door, and the room, collapsed in an explosion that drowned out any chance at a response, so Míra just placed her hands against the exposed skin on my arm, her magic rushing through me to what I now recognized as a broken bone in my leg. Three places if I was finding them all.

"Ouch," she said, twisting her face into a grimace. "Hold still."

Míra scuttled over the tile floor, shifting her weight to hold my knee in place before with one kick she shifted the bones in both leg and hip. I heard a sharp crack before my scream took over, agony ripping through me as she set the bone without warning.

"There, that should heal faster." Míra beamed, placing her hand against my leg as she inspected her handiwork. "I wasn't even sure that would work."

I opened my mouth to rage at her, but before a single word could escape, Wyn rushed back over, hoisting Míra to her feet as they began to take off down the hall.

"Please tell me you found something," Wyn yelled behind her, as I employed my magic to work as a gurney. Lifting myself from the ground, I followed behind the two, my still broken leg dragging across the floor.

"One floor up, there is a window, but we can't leave without knowing..."

"One floor up won't work," Wyn interrupted me, having only heard about half of what I had said.

"I cannot leave yet," I snapped as I soared before her, stopping her in place. "We don't know enough."

"This place is swarming with magic, and not all of it is poisoned." Wyn roared, her fists clenching at her sides as she obviously worked to restrain herself. "You will have to make do with what you have. And based on what I heard, we have more than enough."

She pushed me to the side, sending me drifting into the wall as she streamed past.

"What do you mean it's not all poisoned," I asked, barely catching up to them as poor Míra was left looking between us in obvious concern; at least she was smart enough not to jump in that time.

"I mean that you have ten seconds before the next wave comes streaming down that staircase," she pointed at the stairwell that we were quickly moving away from, the sound of steps and shouts already bleeding through the air. "And if you don't find us a new exit, then we..." she paused, her rage turning to tears. "Get us out of here, Ryland!"

She screamed the last words at me just as the second wave of the Kyō's army burst into the hallway, their eyes widening in a hungry greed as they saw the three of us huddled together.

A punk teenager, an invalid and a crying woman. I was sure we looked like easy pickings.

"Now," Wyn snapped, the desperation and determination acting like a trigger.

The sound of the army rushing us blended with the slow burn of Míra's magic, her determination making it clear she was prepared to take them all on herself.

Seeing the look in her eyes was all I needed, to know what to do.

"Burn them Wyn," I instructed, as I steadied myself on the ground, my partially healed leg tentatively holding my weight.

Míra stepped behind Wyn just as the floor began to heat, the carpet smoking before it erupted in a ring of fire that stretched from floor to ceiling.

The line smoldered, before, with one wave of her hand it pushed away from us, engulfing the hall. Her fire swallowed the lavish decor, leaving behind a hall of black as it barreled toward the army. The men and women screamed, many of them turning to run, desperate to escape.

As Wyn attacked, I searched, my magic moving fast as I poked holes in the massive barrier that the building was covered by.

It didn't make sense. I had seen shields like his before, most recently in the cathedral in Prague. They had been strong, created by a singular power that left a residue that you could easily detect. You could tell exactly who made it. This was distorted somehow, twisted, and far more powerful than it should have been given the strength of the poisoned magic in the building.

It was trapping us in.

Pushing us in.

Toward the lines of open doors and the dead space.

"Okay Jos, you win," I mumbled to myself as I grabbed Míra by the arm and pulled her behind me, dragging her down the hall and around the corner to the wide open door, just sitting there waiting for us. I didn't give myself any room to second guess before shoving both the girls into the dark, hollow canker in the middle of the fortress.

The dark pressed against me in a wall of cold, the same smell from the other room assaulting my senses as we walked in. Usually, the smell of cedar was strong and meant to be relaxing, but there was an undertone to it that poisoned the effect. I couldn't quite place it, but I didn't have time to think about it either. The moment we entered, all of the doors that lined the space closed with a snap.

Well, shit.

"Oooh good pick," Míra taunted, a tiny orb of pure white appearing on her hand and illuminating her face. "You have chosen death by firing squad, Ry. I like this."

"Don't be daft, Míra," Wyn scoffed, her own orb, a clear

sphere with fire burning in the center, grew in her palm, the flickering light casting ominous shadows over the hills and valleys of her face. "This is obviously some kind of arena where we battle to the death. Any minute the stands will erupt in cheers and I will be handed a sword."

"And me, my ax," Míra countered in a rough voice I was sure was meant to resemble a dwarf in that movie she loved.

"You two clearly spend too much time together." Normally I would join in on the banter, even in battle. But normally we weren't locked into darkened halls, where floods of our attackers seemed not too keen to follow.

"Do you hear that?" I asked as their snickers began to die down, the sound of a low buzz, almost like an electric hum assaulting my senses.

The low metallic whir was just a murmur in the dark, but the more I listened, the more it seemed to infect me.

"Enough," I growled to myself as I threw my hands into the air, countless orbs of light taking flight.

The glowing blue lights spread themselves out in a wide net that stretched over the entire room. They stuck to the walls and hung from the ceiling ten feet overhead, the brilliantly colored lights illuminating everything.

Illuminating a room filled with people.

None of these people were standing however, I wasn't even sure if any of them were alive.

Wyn gasped and stepped back, Míra stepped closer to me as I stared in wide mouthed horror.

The room resembled the infirmary space back in Imdalind. A wide room filled with beds and people recovering from a bite. Instead of laughing people however, instead of healing and the growth of magic each bed contained a person in differing stages of decay, each one strapped to a machine that buzzed and whirled, sucking something out of them. It was as though the machine was draining their life.

"No," I gasped, realizing with a start what they were really doing.

They were draining their magic.

I didn't even know such a thing was possible. Now that I had seen it, however, I wanted to back my way out of this room and forget it. Perhaps emptying the contents of my stomach along the way.

"Well, well," A deep voice buzzed from the other side of the hall. "I didn't expect you would come running into your new home so fast, but here you are."

I recognized Suji's smooth voice immediately, but the once refined man who weaved his way through the beds toward us was nearly unrecognizable.

Suit tattered, walking stick stolen, and once stoic face now covered with deranged mania; I had a feeling we were seeing the real Suji for the first time.

The man smiled maniacally as he stepped closer, more than forty of his men filtering in behind him. Each one of their faces etched with something between disgust and discomfort.

Well, at least they all weren't as crazy as him. Not that it made it any better.

"What is this?" I asked, my voice hard as I nodded slightly toward the beds, refusing to look away from the deranged man that was now about thirty feet away.

"This?" Suji gestured to the hundreds that were hooked up to the machines. With a sneer, he lifted the arms of one of the bodies that was limp and rotting, the appendage falling to the filthy cot it lay on with a thunk.

I had thought them all to be dead, but the moment Suji

had arrived a few of them had begun to shift. With the sound of the hand against the cot, they turned, staring at us in wide-eyed horror. The looks in their eyes mirrored their pain as they silently begged for help; as they pleaded for death.

"This is the garbage that the reorganized government of the United Kingdom sends into our care." The mania in his face deepened, moving to the odd prayerful resonance I had seen before, as he looked to them, as if he was worshiping them.

No, as if he was sacrificing them.

"They are those that do not wish to join us and worship as we do. They have been resigned to bring light to the world in different ways," he said, confirming my suspicions.

A massive lump swelled in my throat, choking me, and making it hard to breathe.

"I don't understand," I asked, hating how childish the statement sounded. "You say the government gave them to you, but the United Kingdom protects those with a bite..."

It was his smile that cut me off, the greasy thing stretching over his face and sending a solid layer of ice over my heart.

"They have fallen," I gasped the statement to myself, finally recognizing the phrasing that he had used before. I wasn't the only one who had missed it; Wyn looked at me in confusion, her eyes narrowed in a demand for a response I could not give.

"Almost a year ago," Suji provided. "Right after we dropped the bomb on the district of Chosen in London."

"You dropped...?" I heard Wyn ask in shock beside me, Suji didn't even acknowledge her, he just plowed on, so lost in his own devotion that I wasn't sure he heard her.

"We removed our followers before the attack and with

the help of the United Kingdom took those that were unwilling to convert into our care. They now serve a higher purpose."

He looked at those around him as though he was some kind of loving father, his fingers gentle as he moved over a body so frail and grey I wasn't even sure they were alive anymore. The gaze twisted in my stomach.

"They have given us anyone they have found since then. And they have a choice to either convert, or to be used for the greater good."

I was going to be sick. I narrowed my eyes at him, trying to ignore the way my magic was boiling.

"What are you doing to them?" I asked through gritted teeth, distracting him as the floor underneath me heated, something which Suji and all of his men seemed oblivious too.

"We are taking the power that was given to them," he said, the same calm tone bleeding from him as he moved over the grey skeletal man to his left, his fingertips tracing over what looked like electrical cables that were taped to him.

I had somehow missed the large cables, the long lengths were taped to the arms and legs of each and every one of them, the heavy tubes leading to what appeared to be holes in their skin.

Their magic rushed to the injury, desperate to heal it, but instead of weaving the skin back together, some sort of current ran through it, sucking the power from them. Fed into the electric lines like they were nothing more than an outlet. An immortal battery.

"This is sick," Wyn said under her breath, her fingers tapping against her cell phone as I was sure she sent another message right to Thom.

"This is what was designed for us," Suji said, his dark eyes snapping to us at Wyn's statement, as though she had spoken blasphemy instead of the truth that it was. "If you do not follow, you do not deserve your gift. Your magic was brought alive just as ours was, so that we could rule over the pathetic humans."

"Yeah, we were born with our magic," Wyn said flippantly, everyone's eyes widening at her statement. "Oh!"

Shock colored Wyn's face alongside everyone else's, her exaggerated look appearing as though she had just been told a great secret, the irritating teenager returning. I was sure if she still had gum, she would pop it right then.

"You don't know," she continued, her voice airy. "You don't know just how inferior your magic is..."

Wyn stepped towards the man just as Míra lifted herself into the air. The movement was slight, the girl only lifting perhaps an inch off the ground, her position not deviating a millimeter. It was possible I only noticed it because she was standing right beside me. No one else even looked at her, Suji's focus did not shift from Wyn.

"You didn't know just how much like Gods we are," Wyn laughed, the sound full of a darkness that grew as everyone began to look around her, shifting their weight uncomfortably.

I was sure they felt the heat of her magic now, even if they could not place it.

It didn't matter either way, it was already too late.

"You know what they say about Gods," I said, as Wyn began to laugh. "They destroy their disobedient creations. And you are definitely a disobedient creation."

The words hung in the air as confusion ran through the army. It was Suji who understood first, his eyes darkening as he lifted his hand, intent on countering any attack that was heading his way.

It was too late, however, the attack was already there.

"Now," I said as I lifted myself into the air, three things happening at once.

A bright white sheen of Míra's shield surrounded us just as Wyn's magic exploded from underneath. The floor splintered and broke into the air, fire popping and crackling in the dark as the cots and tables the prisoners lay on fractured. Hundreds of limp bodies arched into the dark, the army screaming as they caught on fire from the inside out.

Their pain echoed louder as the web of lights I had cast earlier fell from the ceiling, slamming against what was left of the floor in a second wave of explosions.

Everyone was screaming as the three of us remained suspended inside of Míra's shield, the two women's eyes alight as they watched the world burn.

Remind me never to double cross those two, especially together.

"I need you two to Stutter out of here," I commanded, my voice hard as I forced my magic behind it. "I can move faster on my own under a shield and find a way out. I need you two to be safe. Get back to the Draíocht and wait for me there."

"We aren't leaving without you," Wyn growled, the hard line in her jaw making it clear she was fighting the forced authority I had put into my command.

"Don't worry Wyn," I heard Míra whisper from behind me, her hand tiny against the bulk of my bicep. "We won't have to."

I didn't even have a moment to protest, I had no chance to stop her.

Her hand made contact the moment the last word had

left her. Her magic flooded me, pushing to every side as she pulled me into a Stutter along with her.

Only two people in the history of Imdalind had the power to pull someone into the Stutter beside them - and the first time Ilyan had tried it, it had nearly ended him.

The pressure of the Stutter wrapped around me familiarly, the pressure an intense weight as I began to scream.

I screamed at the pain of the act, screamed at the pressure of the magic.

I screamed because I knew it would kill her.

CHAPTER 33

ILYAN

"Are you sure you are focusing on the right thing?" Kaye whispered from where she stood on Dr. Sirko's chair, the rickety thing squeaking loudly as she shifted the ceiling tile back into place like she always did. Every day for the three months since the Vilỳ attack, Kaye had snuck in through the roof while her mother made her rounds, leaving only when her shift was over.

Her mother glanced at her briefly before she went back to her work, her fingers deft as she continued to check my blood pressure and temperature.

"I'm not even sure how to focus," I said with a growl, my voice tense as I pulled against the restraints.

They would have normally flopped open by now. I could feel my magic spark, feel it flood the air. That's normally all it took, but today nothing was happening. Today it was only the warmth of my magic and frustration.

"You didn't dose him with anything yet, did you?" Kaye whispered to her mother as she came to stand right beside me, the loose sole on her shoe slapping loudly against the linoleum.

"No," the older woman said, gesturing to something that I couldn't see, something that I didn't want to. "I always wait until after you two finish whatever you do. There isn't anything new today, anyway. They were talking about a new truth serum..."

"They were talking about what?" I snapped, head turning toward her as my magic flared inside of me with agitation. With the angry spark of power, the restraints unbuckled, falling away from me with a soft flop against the bed.

"Why is it always anger that triggers your magic?" Kaye whispered as she jumped onto the end of my bed, leaning against the baseboard in the spot that had been occupied by my feet.

"Just because you know the trigger doesn't make me a reliable weapon," I reminded her, stretching joints and muscles for the first time today. The ache of the first movement was never my favorite, but today was worse after yesterday's test. I had run on a treadmill for three hours without water.

With Katenka's help, I was able to sit up and avoid the swirling nausea that usually came after I undid my shackles. Of course, how sick I got all depended on what drugs they were testing on me, drugs meant to force honesty, force control, numb senses. They all worked to one degree or another, Katenka and one other nurse tracking effectiveness. Katenka, of course, was fudging the numbers so they didn't overdose me and we still had a chance to get out of here.

"Thank you, Katenka," I whispered, handing her back the styrofoam cup so she could refill it. "Now will you tell me what I am on?"

Katenka smiled, the tiny look earning me a wide-eyed

stare from Kaye. I glared at the girl, not appreciative of the reminder that her mother thought I was *hot*. Unfortunately, Kaye's smile only widened at the glare I gave her. She looked so much like a teenager right then, you would have never guessed she was almost twenty-one. I fixed her with a scowl before turning back to her mother, the woman now preparing to draw blood from me.

More blood.

Every day they wanted more blood. One of these days she would only get dust.

"And what that is going to be used for," I sighed, hating the daily guinea pig routine.

"They have you on Midazolam," Katenka provided, casting one quick glance at me before she tied the heavy elastic around my tricep, the lean muscle flexing in agitation. "It's a sedative. Based on that, as well as the Serax and the Klonopin that you have been on for the last few months, I would say that they are trying to find a mixture that they can use to control you."

It wasn't necessarily new information, Kaye and I had surmised as much a few weeks ago when she had overheard Domor and another officer she hadn't seen before talking about 'breaking through' and 'taking control'.

It was sinister then and it was sinister now. Knowing that someone wanted to control you would never bode well.

I exchanged a glance with Kaye as Katenka plunged the needle into my arm, the tiny prick stinging briefly. I didn't flinch.

"And you know I can't tell you what the blood is used for, Jan, even I don't know that," I bristled at her use of the name, but let it go.

Kaye's brown eyes widened from where she lay, curled

up on the foot of my bed. Her lips pinched together as her nose wrinkled, the look one I had seen so many times before.

If I had to venture a guess, she knew what they were doing with my blood, and she didn't want her mother to know about it.

Not that I blamed her, the woman had a habit of getting frustrated and overly worried. Even though she knew who I was, and what we were doing here, she wanted no part, not until the actual moment that we would make our escape.

"I have one more spot check in the room at the end of my rounds," Katenka announced, pulling my focus as she set a third blood-filled vial on the metal tray. "I will wait to give you any medications until then, just in case..."

She stopped mid-sentence as she switched out the still full syringes with the empty ones from yesterday, placing the new ones on the ledge underneath the table that we had been utilizing.

The empty syringes hit the tray with a loud smack that caused Kaye to jump, the whole bed jerking with her movement.

"Katenka?" I asked, Kaye finally sitting up as the frustration of her mother hit her.

"Please be careful," she began, Kaye instantly opened her mouth to retort, as if she knew what was to be said after only three words.

I held up my hand to the girl in warning, the single finger one she had seen enough to know better than to defy.

I did, however, earn myself an eye roll.

"One of the orderlies," she continued, her voice growing stronger now, "a new one from a military village near the border said he heard voices in here the other day."

There was a pause, Kaye and I exchanging a look. While

'the other day' was vague enough that there was no way of knowing when it could have been, we knew.

Kaye's eyes looked right to the deep grey smudge on the wall where I had accidentally set it on fire a week ago.

"Everyone hears voices in here, mom," Kaye whispered, her voice strained as she tried to calm her mother down. "They all just think Jan..."

"Not my name," I mumbled under my breath, Kaye continued on.

"Talks to himself."

"I know," Katenka sighed, now holding the tray as she prepared to leave, "But new people talk more, and he's curious. You know they don't tell anyone who's in here, even many of the guards don't know."

"Ukraine's best-kept secret." I grinned, wondering for the millionth time if Joclyn was perhaps she was just trapped in another prison, in another country.

Another person's guinea pig.

My magic bristled, the heat running through me in a deep agitation that just the possibility gave me. I could feel the magic needing to escape, but I kept it restrained, only one pop of silver light erupting near my index fingers.

"Hey now!" Kaye interrupted, her perky response drenching my worry in sugar. "I like to think that's me..."

Kaye's mother visibly flinched, "I would like you to be a bit more serious about that. Be back to our dorm on time tonight or you are going to need to sleep on the roof. Last night was too close, and one of the doctors two doors down heard you..." She paused, her voice raising an octave before her emotions and frustrations burst out in the form of tears. "He heard the door. He could know Kaye."

I stood, legs shaking as I took one step toward the woman, towering over her as I pulled her into an awkward hug, the motion even more so due to the tray of blood and syringes she still carried.

"I'll talk to her about it," I whispered, sure the promise was gaining me another eye roll from the child in question.

"Thank you, Jan," she whispered, before, with a sigh and a glance toward Kaye, she shuffled away and out the door, the faint click of the lock the last echo of sound before Kaye turned the TV on.

It had been over three years since the attack in Prague, and while the news had shifted from that war and destruction, it had moved to another. Thanks to the still present plague of Vilỳs, the world was in disarray, people exploding, underground factions taking shape, governments falling.

We saw none of that. The only reason we knew was because of Kaye's illegal cell phone and non-registered existence. Everything outside of the Tor browser on her magic box was controlled by the SSU, and it showed.

Last month the morning news featured the report "Inside the Dictatorship: How America's Religions took Control to Protect their People." It painted a beautiful picture of how regimes and control can help a society. It was utter bull.

Today, Kaye was cranking the volume on some odd sitcom about teenagers growing up in an academy run by the SSU, *For The Love of Country.*

The whole thing was propaganda mixed with teenage angst and drama. It ground on me in a way that my magic would easily rise to. So, not only was it fodder, it provided the perfect audio cover.

"What happened last night?" I asked before Kaye could change the subject, her deep sigh turning into a grunt as she peeled herself off the bed.

"I got stuck in a wall," she said as she took my arm,

beginning the few tentative steps of our well-worn path around the room.

To anyone else that statement might sound purely ridiculous, but to Kaye it made sense. Years before she could wander through unused corridors, read books on the roof, steal food from the cafeteria. She was hiding, she wasn't supposed to be here, yes, but people knew.

They just didn't care.

Once the SSU took control things became more difficult. Now that the military was boarded in the old surgery wing, she was trapped in her own prison. Her existence now relied on crawling around through the ceilings and utilizing the old rooms locked off, after Vilỳ attacks, as places to hide. She slept on the floor under her mother's bed and would read in the old pigeon shack on the roof.

Her getting trapped in a wall literally meant she was trapped in a wall.

"They probably think there is a ghost with how much drywall I have had to rip apart to get out," she said, the image of her busting out of walls causing me to chuckle. "Maybe I can use that to my advantage."

"I think that might just worry your poor mother more."

She sighed, the truth was too much a heavy burden on her, as her mother, no matter how much she tried to fight it. She pulled us to a stop, her back tensing as she exhaled deeply, her focus on the stained and ripped wallpaper that covered my room.

"Kaye?" I asked, my fingers soft against her forearm as I tried to get her attention. "Everything okay?"

"We are trying to figure out how to get me papers," she finally admitted, as we began to pace the floor again, the sadness behind her statement confusing me. "How to get me registered."

"That should be a good thing, shouldn't it?"

She nodded once, "I have gotten through the last few years on luck... well, and a bumbling government. Once they moved the employees into the hospital I had no choice but to come here with my mother. It was that or go to the boarding school for survival children."

"Survival children?"

"Yeah," she stalled, swallowing hard as she pulled us to a stop again, her focus dropping to her broken and ripped shoes. "I've told you I've seen someone get bit before. I told you I saw him explode."

"Him." That information was new. "It was your father."

She could only nod.

"The school they tried to send me to was attacked only months after Prague fell. I was supposed to be there. We got a letter in the mail announcing my death and everything."

"And here I was thinking when you said you don't exist..."

She smiled tiredly.

"It got worse with the SSU, because they track everything."

"So you need to get registered."

"I at least need papers. We think we found a man that can make them, but we aren't sure. We get me papers and maybe I can get a job here, and then my mom can get rid of that ulcer."

She tried to force a smile, but the look was sad, broken. The failed joke only slammed harder against her, the impact setting the flood waters free.

I had only seen her cry once before, but then it was angry frustrated tears right before the Vilỳ had broken in. These were different. These were pain, these clung to her heart and dripped directly from her soul in little agonizing drops.

"Kaye?" I whispered as I turned to her.

Tears rolled over her cheeks as she looked at me, pain and heartbreak bubbling through as she shook her head in embarrassment, reaching up to wipe the treacherous things away.

"No," I whispered, grabbing her hand in mine as I stopped the progression. "It's okay to cry. It's okay."

"No, Jan, it's not okay" she sobbed, trying to break her hand away from mine, something I didn't fight. I let her go, the pressure in my chest expanding as she stepped away, wiping her dirty arm over her face, leaving smudges of grey behind. I could feel my magic heat and warm as it tried to break from me, as it tried to soar away from me.

The pressure, the warmth, there was something about my power that was different, a different feeling.

It wasn't angry.

"You're right," I said, taking a step closer that only ignited my magic more. "It's not okay. And we can't make it okay. But we can fight. We can protect ourselves, and..."

"No one protected my father," she interrupted, her voice so broken by a sob that I could barely make it out.

I longed to reach for her, to help her. The strength of my magic surged as I wrapped my arms around her, pulling her back into my chest. She spun in my arms in response, her own arms pulling me against her as her tears picked up.

"It will be okay," I whispered into her hair as the palms of my hands pressed against her arms, and my magic flooded into her.

Her sobs stopped with a gasp, her body stiffening in a way that made me sure I had hurt her. I tried to pull away, but she held on tighter, pressing me against her as she buried her face in my chest.

My magic continued to swell, the power strong as it filled her, as it felt her, as I began to understand her. The more magic that flowed into her, the calmer she was.

The more comfort my magic was able to bring her.

I was able to bring her.

When all of the emotions had ebbed, only one stood out, a faint whisper of pain that I didn't fully understand. My magic reacted on its own, flooding through her as it sought out the pain, sought out injury, and found it in a cut just below her shoulder blade.

I could see it clearly in my mind, the gash was deep and had obviously become infected.

Shock and confusion filled me as I pushed her away, her few words of gratitude stifled as I lifted the torn sleeve of her shirt to reveal the large gash, the angry red skin and puss only spelling danger.

"How did..." I asked, not sure if I was asking her how it happened, or how I knew.

Holding her sleeve up, seeing the angry gash flashed a moment that I had seen in a dream once before. Joclyn in a cave, blood pouring from a gash in her stomach.

"I'll be fine," she had said, her voice distorted in my recall. But it wasn't her voice that stuck with me, it was how my magic surged, just as it did now. It was my hand pressing against her skin.

A rock formed in my chest as I placed my palm over her cut; my magic surged at the contact, flooding through her. She gasped at the contact, the sound full of fear as she tried to step away.

This time I wouldn't let her.

This time I held her still as my magic moved, as I felt it

grow warm and hot against my palm, as I felt her skin begin to knit itself together.

I fought my own fear, fought my own need to pull away as I felt it, everything beginning to shake as an exhaustion I hadn't expected took over.

Falling back on the bed, the connection left as I gasped for air, my body physically unable to hold my own weight anymore.

Kaye dropped to her knees with a heave, hand fluttering over her shoulder in a reaction that I wasn't sure was done in pain or fear.

"Are you okay?" I asked, voice broken by my strangled breaths.

Her hand was flat against her shirt as she looked at me, breath held in her chest as she turned, lifting her shirt to reveal perfectly smooth and healed skin.

Only the dried blood remained.

"How did you do that?" Her voice was an amazement that I felt mirrored in myself, my own awe breaking free as I lifted my hands from where they were tangled in my short hair, staring at my palms, one smooth, one rough, as if they would show me what had happened, show me what I did.

"I don't know." But for the first time I wished it was a lie. I wished I could do it again. This, I wished I could control.

This magic was not done in death or destruction - it was beautiful. I wanted to master it.

"You healed me." Her awe was a wash of emotion as I tried to work through what had just happened, as I tried to understand it.

"I didn't know I could do that..."

"I'm starting to wonder what you can't do," Kaye said as she stood, glancing at the smoke stain on the wall before she stepped to stand over where I had collapsed. "We have got to get you figuring this out. More than just to get out of here, we have got to figure it out before they do."

Her hand reached to cup around mine, the soft touch one I would normally jerk away from, but this time I froze, eyes narrowing at the sudden change in tone.

The awe was laced with determination, her eyes taking on the far away look of a girl with a plan. No, a girl who knew something. It was the same look she had given me when I had asked her mother about the blood.

"Why did you get stuck in a wall, Kaye?" I asked carefully as I pulled myself to sitting. She flushed instantly.

"I heard Domor talk about you."

"You were eavesdropping on Domor!" All exhaustion left as my magic surged, the strong pulse sending me to stand as sparks erupted around my fingertips.

I knew I was too loud, but luckily so was the dramatic teenager on the TV who was now talking about 'those dangerous Hungarians'.

"Yes..."

"We talked about this Kaye," I interrupted her.

Her childish impulses were going to give both me and her mother ulcers. My magic flooded me as my irritation did, the warm power stifling the emotion, although just barely. "Listen where you can, but right now you need to find us a clear, gun-free, path out of here."

"Or you can just learn to stop bullets."

"I'm not even sure if I can do that."

"You just healed me, Jan!" she hissed, stepping toward me until she was inches away.

"Yes, but that's not getting shot at! I'm not even sure how we would test that."

"I could throw a chair at your head," she offered with

far too much malice. Even then it stopped me short, the ridiculousness pulling me back down to reality.

"Kaye. We need a gun-free path. I couldn't remove the locks on my restraints this morning, I'm not consistent, and I am not..."

"Stop with the lecture. It's not like you are that much older than me. Not like anyone could tell Mr. 'Always-look-fabulous-even-though-I've-been-locked-in-a-prison-hospital-for-years-and-still-look-twenty-two'."

She spoke very fast, letting the last of her irritation out in a rush.

"Are you quite done?" I asked, perfectly willing to side-step that conversation. It was one we had gotten in before and one I wasn't interested in repeating. Yes, I didn't appear to age, everyone had noticed, and I wasn't about to fight them on it. Nor was I about to share the memories that pointed to an entire other explanation.

From what little I had read on Kaye's phone, magic comes with immortality. While Kaye wasn't as apt to believe it, I wasn't going to dismiss it. I also wasn't going to entertain her lingering alien theory either. None of my memories occurred on another planet, as I had told her many times.

"Quite."

"Good," I sighed. "Now tell me what your journey into the wall revealed."

Kaye crossed her legs on the bed, her shoes leaving brown smudges over the white sheet, with her lips pinched together she looked up to me.

"They are using your blood to try to find a way to control your power. To replicate it."

Any response that I may have had washed away as what she just said hit me head on.

"How close are they?" The words felt distant, far away, as though they came from someone else.

"Not close as far as I can tell," she sighed, leaning back against my foot board as I stood up, thankful my legs had recovered enough that I could pace.

"It's not like I can ask questions though. But," she continued, cutting me off at the intense look I had given her, "from what they are saying they have identified a few things that 'slow down' what they think is the power in your blood. It's been hard work because of your transplant medication... I guess that has slowed them down for some reason."

I stopped pacing, my eyes drifting toward the movement on the screen and the teenagers who were laughing beneath a giant painting of the purple sinister star.

"So they have found what they think is my power," I spoke more to myself than to her. "But they can't get it out."

It made sense. As much as Kaye had told me they had experimented on me while I was in a coma, and as much as Commander Domor talked up his control, the last few months had been little more than weekly CAT scans, new medications, and odd interrogations that circled over the same information. What do you know of Prague? How would you get a new heart? Do you know who this is...

They were testing my resolve. Testing medications. Testing me.

"No wonder they always keep me restrained," I laughed, looking at the filthy restraints that still lay open on the bed.

"So they can test you?" Kaye asked, clearly not understanding.

"So they can control me." I clarified, still watching the characters on the television whispering in class while the teacher in the background spoke of proper extermination techniques for people bitten by a Chrlič.

"It makes them feel safer, thinking that they have control, that I can't break out." Kaye snorted a bit at that, the ridiculousness not lost on either of us. "They are scared of me. And like any good dictatorship, they control what frightens them."

"Do I frighten them?" she asked, she actually looked eager at that.

"Oh yes," I said, stopping my pace to look at her. "All of their people do."

"Does that mean it's time to fight back?" she asked, the eagerness expanding into a bubble that I truly hated to defuse.

For the first time, I wished I could agree with her.

"Once we have a way out, yes."

"I can't help but think that we are running out of time, Jan," she snapped, folding her arms over her chest as she sank back against the footboard.

"That's not my name."

"Does it even matter?" she snapped, her fists hitting against her things as she came to stand before me. "You may never know your name if we don't get out of here. We have to fight back."

"You can still fight even when you are in chains," I said, my calm response catching her off guard and she recoiled. "You are about to put your chains on too, Kaye. But I know you will still fight."

"My registration." The cruel reality smacked her hard and she sank back onto the hospital bed, any frustration vanishing as pure shock took over, widening her eyes.

"We will fight even in chains," I said as I knelt before

her, my heart constricting as I took her hands in mine. "We will get out of here."

She nodded once.

"You need to control that power before they do."

"And you need to find us a safe escape route," I responded, squeezing her hands before I released them, standing before her as the tower that I was.

"Do you remember the last two lines of the Ukrainian Anthem?" I asked after a moment, the images on the television sparking my frustrations.

"No one is allowed to sing that anymore," Kaye responded with a hiss. "It is forbidden."

"And for good reason," I said with a smile, turning back toward the girl who was slowly blossoming into a determined woman. "Ukraine is not yet dead, nor its glory and freedom..."

Her eyes welled with tears as I sang the song, my voice quiet as the last few lines of the song rang clear, even the television silencing to hear.

"We'll not spare either our souls or bodies to get freedom, and we'll prove that we brothers are of Kozak kin."

"Are you ready to fight?" she asked, her question honest as we faced a battle we had expected, with a timeline we had not.

"No matter the chains they bring."

CHAPTER 34

JOCLYN

The sight from the woman in the hospital hadn't revealed much, just flashes of that same army and her receiving directions to go recover more of those bitten throughout Europe. It had taken only a few more questions to discover that that's when she and her team had run into Ryland.

It had been more of a happy accident than them actually hunting us, but I didn't care as long as it led us to where I thought it was.

I had first seen the army when I peered into Ilyan's future, and now that the army was spread before us, I couldn't help but think that he was on the other side.

The sun was just coming up over the rolling hills, fog was still dripping from the higher peaks, covering the army that was nestled in the valley below where Thom and I were perched. We couldn't see them, but I could sure feel them; hundreds of Chosen milled around, that broken and fragmented magic humming through them.

It was more than that, though. Trpaslík magic weaved through the Chosen, commanding them. Ruling them. It was just as we had assumed, the rest of Edmund's army was here, and all of them were wearing those black uniforms emblazoned with that gold eight-pointed sunburst.

"Okay, so what now?" Thom asked as more of the fog broke away and revealed the length of the army. There were more of them than I had predicted, and not all of them were magic users. Although judging by the Vilỳs that were caged near the back they had plans to change that. I let my magic flare, feeling through each of them, but no sign of Rinax. Again.

"I think we found the tail, what do you say we follow it to the head?" I asked, eager to begin. My magic continued to weave through them, trying to find the strongest prick of magic, or at least someone who fancied themselves as being in control.

The more I searched, however, the more frustrated I became. The army was huge, and we had let it become this way.

I had been so focused on finding Ilyan that we hadn't done more than 'keep tabs' on the falling governments. It was painfully ironic that following the clues to Ilyan had led us here, but I was glad it did.

"If I had to guess, I would say the big tent would be the place to start." Thom pointed to the large white tent at the back, the canvas entrance that was flapping in the wind was emblazoned with red stars rather than the yellow the rest of the tents featured.

"Works for me, ready to play spy?" I grinned at him and held out my hand.

"You say that as though this isn't my first revolution."

"Stop sounding like such an old man, Thom." I gave him a grin and grabbed his hand, pulling us under a shield a second before I pulled us into a Stutter, and the tent.

Ribbons of color and time swirled around us as I focused on our destination, focused on the string that connected us to that tent on the other side of the camp.

With a yank we reemerged in the tent. The thing was much larger than I assumed it needed to be given the ornate furniture that was littered over the place. The space was completely empty save for a gathering of black-uniformed men near a desk at the far end. They were all yelling so loud that they were oblivious to the pop of our reentry.

Which was good, seeing as Thom was gasping for breath beside me. He hated that about as much as Ryland, but at least there wasn't a risk of Thom throwing up all over my shoes.

I gave him a look and he forced his breathing to slow before I guided us toward the group, his hand still wrapped around mine. Four men were yelling at whoever was on the other side of the desk, their voices raised as they shouted in what sounded like Ukrainian.

Thank god I had Thom with me, he was fluent and could fill in any gaps that I was missing. Which was a lot given how fast they were all talking.

I gave him a pleading look, lower lip pout and all, and he rolled his eyes and nudged us closer, both of us careful to drag our feet in an attempt to be silent.

"They are arguing over attack plans, I guess they are looking to expand their boundaries," Thom hissed, just as one of the men shouted a long string of what could have been expletives, slammed his fist into the desk and stormed off, giving us a perfect line of sight to whoever sat on the other side of the table.

A woman with a severe haircut and a scowl that was just as ominous sat in a chair twice her size as though she had a stick up her bum, nose wrinkled as she smelled some poo. She wore a black uniform like the rest of them, but with a purple star on her lapel instead of the red.

I had seen her before. In the sight in the cave. She was the one who had been with Ovailia.

I didn't know if this was worse, or better. We had come to find Ilyan but this goose chase had just exploded in our face. Feathers were everywhere. I gave Thom a look and he began tapping on his phone with his free hand, sending an update to Wyn who by the looks of it was doing the same from wherever she and Ryland had found the Kyō.

The woman on the other side of the desk cleared her throat and the other two snapped to attention. She was clearly in charge, although I had a feeling that was more to do more with how her magic hummed under her skin. Her magic was rotten, but stronger than the rest. If I had to guess, she had a decent enough control of the power to fight.

No wonder the girl in the alley had attacked instead of fled. Thanks to the remnants of Edmund's army here they had all been trained.

"Finally," the woman hissed in Ukrainian, my brain picking apart the words I knew, "I was starting to think that I would have to dispose of him."

The other two chuckled, but even she caught the quick glance the two exchanged and smiled. She was dead serious.

A trill of panic twisted up my spine and Thom's hand tightened around mine as though he was ready for an attack. This woman should be nothing. Her magic was broken, I doubted she had much training beyond 'how to kill'. I could take her, I had no question about that. Take her down, get some questions answered.

Thom's hand was a vice around mine as she stood, the large chair scraping against the ground.

"What would you have us do, Commander?" one of the men was asking, but she ignored them, grabbing a few papers before she moved over to the large map near the corner, the expanded boundaries of the Ukraine marked in red.

"Continue as we have planned. I have heard from Domor that our friend has awoken in a room full of dead Chrlič. Besides, I have a meeting in Moscow I can't miss."

Moscow, where I had seen Ovailia. If I had to guess, that was where she was headed. If I took her out now, I could get her to lead us to Ovailia. I could end this.

I took a step forward, ready to take them out and drag her out of there, but Thom pulled me back, head shaking.

"What? You gonna fight me on torture now? I thought you were ready?" I hissed, but he just kept shaking his head, finger over his lips. Of course, he was the responsible one now.

"I take it you are going to get him to remember," one of the generals said and all of them laughed with that forced sound of padding someone's ego.

"Yes, I leave for Kiev in the morning. They are setting up a room in the hospital there for me. Hopefully I will have a new weapon for you all..."

"A hospital," I spat as I remembered what Wyn had said the other day and Ilyan being in a hospital. "Where is the hospital in Kiev?"

I was half ready to Stutter us to Kiev right then when I turned to Thom who was staring at his phone and the text messages that were coming in earnest.

"What is it?" I asked even as I leaned over the phone, and the Czech that was panicking over the surface.

Surrounded.

Five in the walls.

Trapped off Trafalgar Square.

Michel has sent us into a trap.

All of the eager buzzing of my magic fell to my toes as our eyes met. Thom's face was practically screaming. He needed to get there.

I gave the woman who was still laughing with her soldiers one last look, before I squeezed Thom's hand, and followed his heart right to his wife and their unborn child.

CHAPTER 35

RYLAND

The cave echoed with my scream the moment we rematerialized.

Air rushed around us as the Stutter left, the dizziness and nausea that I was used to washed over me. I pushed it all away, forcing myself to focus.

I barely caught her as she fell.

Her limp body was tiny in my arms, her eyes rolled back in her head as a drizzle of blood began to seep from the corner of her mouth, from her nose, from her eyes.

The most frantic panic I had ever felt rushed through me; it swelled through every muscle as the world began to spin, as the fear of what she had done, of what had happened, slowly began to fade into my madness.

"No, no, no," I gasped, lowering her to the ground as gently as I could, the shake in my hands making it difficult.

Even before I could see straight, before I had been able to catch my breath, I pushed my magic into her, diverting it away from healing the remaining cuts and torn muscles in my own body and shoving it into hers. She didn't so much as flinch as the full strength of my power flooded her, swiftly running to every cell in her body and checking for injuries, checking for something that I could heal, something that would make her okay.

Everything felt fine, everything seemed fine, but just looking at her, I knew that wasn't right. There had to be something wrong.

"Míra?" I whispered, shaking her gently, something deep in my mind screaming that she was just sleeping. "Míra, you've got to answer me. Just say one thing, just move one finger..."

Every rambled word shifted my panic into a mind-numbing desperation, the emotion was a vice that felt like a rubber band around my heart, as though my lungs had filled with water and I would never be able to breathe past it.

Forget breathing, I could barely think. Mindlessly, I continued to flood my magic into her, searching for anything as I tried to see past my mental agony and figure out what to do.

When Ilyan had stuttered with Joclyn years ago, he was the first one to have done so, ever. It took an immense amount of magic and control not to hurt the other person, let alone yourself.

I had been there on that day, when they had made that desperate escape; I had watched them disappear into the inky night sky, unable to stop the monster I had become.

Joclyn had told me about the after, about how Ilyan was unconscious for days, about how Thom would wrap him in fabric embedded with his magic and cover him in herbs.

But I had no herbs, I had nothing to wrap her in - even if I knew how to do either of those things.

It was then that I looked up, expecting to see some

derelict cave in the middle of nowhere, only to see the faint glimmer of a cave that I knew all too well.

"Oh," I gasped in surprise, watching the faint lights flicker off the edge of the rough hewn rocks just ahead. "Good girl, Míra, good job."

Everything spun as I lifted her, holding her against me as my body ached in injury and exhaustion as I ran.

"Míra," I whispered as I stumbled through the cave, "wake up."

I burst through the narrow opening and right into the massive cavern that made up the Draíocht. I entered with a shout, but I wasn't the only one who was yelling, and my plea for help was swallowed by the darkness of the cave. A few of Michel's men turned at my entrance, pulled away from the verbal assault match that was currently exploding in the center of the cave.

Michel and Wyn stood head to head, screaming at full volume. The ornamental glassworks that hung from the ceiling rattled in their anger, shivering under the waves of their magic and sending waves of light through the room.

"You knew," Wyn roared as I began to weave my way through the onlookers, desperate to reach her. To reach them. "You knew what they were, and you knew what they would do..."

"I knew nothing of the sort!" Michel roared in return, stepping toward the smaller woman in an attempt at posturing. Wyn didn't even move, she just flared her magic in anger, a shimmer of flame moving over her skin and singeing her clothes.

Michel stepped back.

"You asked for a meeting with them, you assumed they had attacked your people," Michel continued as though

Wyn's flambéed warning had never happened. "I do not know what you expected to happen."

I watched them carefully, Michel's lies suddenly as clear as cellophane.

"You told us they had attacked you," Wyn attacked, her words forming the exact question I thought. "You told us you had sealed the entrance because they were after you."

"They were," Michel stuttered. "They did." He paused, shuffling his feet as he tried to move away.

He didn't get far. Wyn let her magic burst forward, popping through the air and reappearing right where he had been headed; he needed a better escape plan.

"Excuse me," I whispered to one of the Chosen who called this cave their home, my quiet formality drowned out by the yell that came after.

"What was it Michel?" Wyn's voice filled every inch of the cave, the few who had not come out to watch the show now gingerly peeking their heads around the stone outcroppings that concealed their living quarters. "Did they attack you, or did you feed your people to that killing machine?"

"I had to protect my people from them. You saw what they do to our kind! You saw what they have done to so many of us," Michel boomed in return, the anger in his voice faltering as an emotion I hadn't expected from him roared to life, his eyes filling with treacherous tears. "I had nothing that they wanted. I had to protect my people..."

I froze the moment I had stepped onto the lifted outcropping of stone. While I was sure Wyn could sense me there, she didn't move. She was as frozen in place as I was, her jaw working as though it was on a hinge.

"You gave them us," she finally said, her shock melting into fury. "You used us."

She slammed her hands forward, magic shooting from her palms and sending him soaring a few feet away from where they stood on the raised stone outcropping.

The cave erupted at her attack, soft screams of surprise followed by murmurs and whispers of both shock and fear. The hushed gossip seemed truly torn between the possibility of finding safety with us, and of what the Kyō would bring. No one, however, seemed ready to attack Wyn for what she just did to their leader.

Some leader indeed, he was more like a tyrannical overlord.

"Wynifred," I said, stepping further onto the raised stone, her name drawing her focus immediately.

She turned on me in a rage, her anger thankfully drifting away as she caught sight of me, and the limp girl I carried.

"No," she gasped, running from Michel who was barely starting to recover from the attack, his body shaking as he tried to lift himself, only to fall down again with an attack from Wyn, her hand thrown behind her as she ran to me.

I dropped to my knees, pressing Míra tightly against me before I lowered her to the ground, her hand and limbs lolling as though they were nothing more than rags.

"I was worried... I didn't know where you went..." Wyn said, her voice choking in her throat as she placed her hands against Míra's limp arm.

Wyn's magic swelled through the girl, rumbling alongside mine as she made the same checks I had, as she searched for something, anything, to heal. I withdrew my magic at the burning heat of Wyn's, finally letting my power do what it wanted and heal my own injuries.

Warmth enveloped me as my magic spread over me, rushing to fractured bones, cuts and pulled muscles in a rush. Everything began to repair and I closed my eyes for one second, determined to recenter myself before I focused back on the traumatizing scene.

"Everything seems fine," Wyn gasped, shifting her hands to another bare swatch of skin, as if it would give her a better angle.

I was ready to follow when Michel pushed himself up from the floor, shaking his head as he looked for an escape. With what little I had heard of his conversation with Wyn, I knew I could not stay here.

Michel, and his despicable actions, were my responsibility too.

"I've got her," Wyn whispered to me, wrapping her hand around my wrist as she pulled my attention, having obviously seen where I was looking.

Or perhaps she had just seen the deep scowl on my face and knew what was about to happen.

I nodded once to her and slowly stood, rising to my full height just as Michel did. The dark-skinned man stood an inch or two taller than me, but where I lacked against his height, I more than made up in muscle. A fact that I made painfully clear as I folded my arms over my chest.

"Is she correct?" I asked with a boom so loud the man jerked. I didn't even bother to nod toward Wyn; I could see just by the frantic look in his eyes that he knew exactly what I was talking about. "Did you deliver us to them?"

"I... I only wanted to..."

"Do you know what they are doing to our kind?" I roared, interrupting his stammer. My voice reached every inch of the cave before it began to echo back to me.

I had everyone's attention now, every eye was on me as I stared at Michel, the guilt clear on his face as he began to wilt.

"They are draining the magic from them. They are killing them for just a little bit of power."

A gasp rose from the floor of the cave, but I didn't dare turn, I was already having trouble controlling my breathing. It was taking everything in me to remain in control, to keep my anger in check.

I could feel it growing with each word that I spoke, the memory of all those people being *sacrificed* for the Kyō's cause spiking the emotion even more. My magic flared over my skin in a faint blue spark of power that rippled over the surface like a wave.

Michel stepped back at the eruption of magic, his eyes narrowing as his own hands began to shake.

"Did you know this, Michel?" I asked him, watching him for any tell, any sign of the truth, already expecting him to lie.

Instead, his shoulders sagged, his eyes dropping as he said, "I did."

A gasp of shock and pain rippled through 'his people,' their eyes full of betrayal as they looked at us. While a few of them had clearly heard of this before, so many of them had not, the pain of the lie etched into their shock.

It made me want to scream.

"Instead of doing something, instead of asking us for assistance, you let them suffer." I spat the words with all the malice and anger that they deserved as I dropped my hands to my sides, fingers flexing as I tried to keep an attack at bay. "You betrayed us all."

His focus snapped back to me, his eyes hard again as his pride began to bristle.

"I betrayed no one." His response was a growl, his magic was a feral wave as it filled with his hostility.

I opened my mouth to respond, ready to rage, ready to scream. I never got the chance.

"You betrayed me."

The voice echoed through the cave in a calm rage, the deep voice of the man I recognized at once. I slowly turned to it, Wyn already unwinding herself to stand as she stepped between Míra and the invaders in an obvious attempt to protect the girl. I wasn't sure if it would help.

I wasn't sure anything would.

More than a hundred Kyō stood clustered around the main opening of the cave. Suji stood in the center, leaning on a brand new walking stick, his face hard as his cuts still oozed red over his handsome face.

Time to see how much more I could mess that up.

With a snap of his fingers, his cluster of minions scurried away from him, extending themselves until they made a wide circle around everyone. Surrounding us. Presumably trapping us.

The man was determined to win; he clearly assumed himself impossible to kill.

He had changed his suit, the trashed one from before replaced by a steel grey three piece. It reminded me of something my father would wear, as it blended him perfectly into the stone.

At his appearance and the quick movements of his people, the cave broke out into a panic. Screams rumbled through the air as Michel's untrained followers began to rush the dais, swarming us in an expectation of protection.

Suji glared at me from behind a still bleeding cut, a smile spreading over his lips before he looked away, his dark glare boring not into me, but into Michel.

"You have betrayed me, Michel," Suji said, a hint of an accent peeking into his voice. "You promised me followers, you promised me magic, you promised me Gods. I expected all in return for your people's safety. You have given me none of that."

"I did nothing..." Michel began in the same pleading lie he had given me.

Suji stopped his plea with a wave of a hand, a deep booming laugh spreading from him. The sound rumbled over the stone, multiplying in an echo until his demonic laugh was all we could hear.

Many of The Chosen who had run to the raised rock with us began to cower at the sound, a few even stepping behind me as though just my bulk could protect them.

I looked from Michel, to Suji, and then to Wyn only to see the same confusion furrowing her brow.

Michel was an ancient. He was born with the power of a Trpaslík hundreds of years ago. He had worked for Edmund, spied for Ilyan, double crossed everyone... We should have seen this coming.

Wyn kept herself close to the still unconscious Míra as she shifted to the two men in an attempt to guard her.

"I have changed my mind, Michel," Suji said, the faint echo of his laugh still rippling around the cave, igniting the echo of my father's in my mind. "I do not want these Gods."

"I don't understand," Michel began to sputter, waving to Wyn and I as though we were inanimate beings. "I brought you two of the people from the images in Prague. I brought you two Gods."

He practically choked on the last word. Suji clicked his tongue and shook his head, the action causing Wyn and I to exchange another look, both of us maintaining our silence as we watched this play out.

"I don't want these Gods," Suji said again, the guards he brought shifting their feet as they stretched their lines.

Considering we had barely escaped last time I was going to have to pull out all the stops this time.

"I want *her*," Suji qualified. "I want the Oheň."

The silence stretched before it was broken with the sharp crack of Wyn's laugh.

The sound broke like a whip, Suji snapping to her as his momentary triumph was sapped from him.

I shook my head. Wyn always did make these things more interesting.

"You are a fool," I said, as Suji took a step forward, his brow furrowed.

Every member of his army followed his motions, the uniform smack of their boots against the stone sending a rampaging thunder through the cave.

"I am not a fool," Suji said as they all took another step. "I am righteous." Another step, another boom, this time louder. "I am ordained." Another step, another boom, and this time the makeshift chandeliers shivered under the force. The one near the far entrance crashed down to the stone with a sound that made several people jump and scream, sure the battle had begun.

Each time Suji stepped, the army would follow, and each time the army smacked hard against the stone the rumble grew.

Michel's fear grew, what he had mistaken for power suddenly made sense.

"Resonance," I heard Wyn whisper, and then I felt it.

A faint ripple of his poisoned magic traveled on the back of each step, moving with the sound much the same way I could inject my magic into the voice of my command. He took that simple magic and magnified it, the magic growing in power as it echoed back to him. Each step, each sound, it all made him stronger.

He had done the same thing in the dark room by Trafalgar Square. It was why the darkness felt so heavy, and why that feeling had left when Wyn had cast her shield. With no echo, with no resonance, there was no power.

It was an old skill, and a simple one. With the time it took to create the strength in the magic it was not suitable for combat. I had never seen it used so effectively before.

"Stop," I said, lifting my hand and sending my magic in a high arch through the cave.

A shimmering wall extended from one end of the cave to the other, stopping the flow of his power with a snap. The impact of the shield as it snapped against the stone sent many of Suji's men to the ground. They writhed in pain as my magic sliced through them, the last of Suji's magic falling to the floor like pebbles.

Suji's eyes narrowed, realizing what I had done, and that I knew what he was doing.

"Your tricks are as foolish as you are," I taunted, stepping past the swarm of Michel's followers so I could face the man. "Your power is not great, and your request will only end in your death. I can guarantee you that setting your eyes on our Queen will be the last thing you do in this life."

The words were powerful, they were lined with my magic. More importantly, they were lined with truth.

Something Suji obviously didn't understand.

His lip twitched in disdain, a tiny laugh attempting to force itself past his clenched teeth.

"Is that why you sent your people to attack us?" I asked as I stepped through the last of the Chosen, passing by Wyn without a glance.

"I have told you that was not us," he said, his eyes boring into mine as he leaned on his walking stick.

The buzz of noise and voices from the group behind me picked up as I stepped toward him, but I didn't dare turn, I didn't dare remove my eyes from the man.

Whatever it was, Wyn could take care of it.

"If you would like, however, I can take you to them. They already have one God, I am sure they already know what to do with you," his voice was a soft threat, the fear in him only shown by the tight grip he had on his walking stick, if indeed that was what it was.

I wasn't going to risk another bullet to the chest. Casting a shield before me, the invisible thing stretched to cover myself and all of Michel's people who stood behind me.

"Oh, that won't be necessary. Just give us their name, we can find them ourselves," I said confidently, even as the corner of his mouth twitched.

"Fine by me. I hate that bitch, anyway," he said as he lifted his walking stick, slamming the tip into the stone floor and sending a ripple through the cave.

The floor shifted, the ceiling rattled, and with a groan of thunder a massive crack began to split through the stone, right down the middle.

Wyn swore loudly behind me, instructing Michel and his people where to go as Suji's smile spread.

I steadied myself against the still shifting floor, refusing to look away as I brought my magic to my hands, letting the flood of warmth and color slam against my skin in preparation to attack.

"Do you really want to do this?" I asked, knowing exactly how outnumbered we were.

Taunting him may not have been the best idea, but I wasn't going to try to stop myself either.

I let my fingers spark freely, expecting that foolish smile

to fall from his face. It didn't. Instead, it grew deeper, if that was possible.

"I do."

Without another word, every single one of his men lifted their hands, poisoned magic dripping from them.

It didn't matter, I had already let the madman that my father made me take control.

CHAPTER 36
RYLAND

My magic intercepted theirs in an explosion of light, the sound of the impact rippling over the cave and sending the already fragile cavern quivering. Rocks shifted above me as the floor jerked in the opposite direction. The motions were enough to send the Draíocht people into a mob.

Shifting my feet, I balanced against the motion in an attempt to keep myself upright. Suji and his men, however, weren't quite so lucky.

They fell like cans shot off a fence, the wide circle of our attackers shifting as one after another they collapsed; the pandemonium barely hidden behind the smoke and fire that rippled over the surface of my shield.

Panicked shouts warbled into nothing as the cave began to calm. Suji's men quickly regained themselves, while Michel's untrained people whimpered in panic; Wyn's exasperated voice barely carried over them.

"Oh, for cripes sake," she snapped. "You babies! You, Michel, come here. Take her. You need to get everyone out of here. Go to Vienna. Now. And if you put one toe out of line I will remove your heart. You know I can." She sounded far too excited for that threat.

Her commands fell away, swallowed by the bustle of an escape as I stepped toward my newfound enemy.

My magic spread away from me in an invisible wave, pressing against the dust, as it began to dance and swirl around me. Suji's men reformed their circle, unaware of the way my magic was twisting around them, creating a web that was locking them in place.

Suji still stood across from me, the smug look on his face now painted with shock.

"You really shouldn't have done that," I said, my voice a hard snarl.

Fear darkened his eyes in a flash, the deep color fueling me on, as I stared him down. As frightened as he appeared, he did not look away.

He should know better.

I should know better.

Good thing, neither of us were better.

Kill him.

I didn't need to be told twice.

Hand slamming into the air before me, the cave filled with the sound of an explosion. The roar slammed against the stone, echoing back to us with a boom. An impenetrable wall of green spread from me, the emerald flames licking the air as it rushed right toward Suji.

His men screamed and rushed away from the attack, their quick Japanese mixing with the panicked yells of Michel's men in a weird mesh of sounds.

The fools had obviously not quite made their escape, no matter how much Wyn prodded them on. I could hear her yell at them, her sharp tone making it clear she knew exactly what I had done, and what was in control.

Suji screamed from behind the wall of magic, many of the men around him scrambling to return the attack. Their weak magic streamed from them, only to fizzle into smoke as my magic swallowed them. Suji flew around the side, leaving the attack to collide with the cave and sending the cavern into another serious rumble.

"If you don't knock it off I won't be able to stop a collapse," Wyn's exasperated shout was obviously meant for me, but I didn't turn.

I just continued forward, a laugh that didn't belong to me ripping from my chest.

"Damn it, get out of here now. Before it's too late." Wyn snarled, her voice all but swallowed by the sound of my father's voice that had taken over.

Make him hurt.

Magic sparked from my fingers in ribbons of electric flame before I threw another attack at the haggard man. He barely moved fast enough to block it, pressing his cane forward and using it like some kind of shield. My attack slammed against it with a crack, the bright yellow flame turning to smoke as whatever barrier the stick created destroyed it.

Staring at the stick, I arched my brow. My confusion was not lost on the man.

"A powerful lord," Suji snarled, his voice twinged with a pride that barely overshadowed his fear, "and yet you obviously know nothing."

Show him what you know, my madness said in a deep growl, *show him what you are.*

"I know nothing?" I scoffed, any sign of a taunt lost in the threat that carried in my voice. My magic continued to spark over my fingers, rings of electricity running up my arm as Suji's minions watched.

412

Poor little bastards had no idea what was coming.

"You know nothing about this world. Who are you to tell me of my knowledge?"

My words were meant to silence the ego driven maniac, but he only smiled, twirling the carved stick between his fingers. Sparks of grey light emitted from the end, dancing in the air like a child with a sparkler.

The sparks that flew from the end were magic, that much was clear, but it was not the poisoned magic that dripped from the man himself, it was clean.

Perfect.

Pure.

As though Joclyn had healed him, even though I knew there was no chance in hell that was possible.

"I know enough," he returned, the response ripping at my obvious confusion.

My lips curled as I took another step forward, many of Suji's men stepping along with me as the man I kept in my sights began to hiss at them in frantic Japanese.

Make him bleed.

Magic stick, confident jerk. I didn't care, he was still an enemy, and I had a job to do.

Swinging my left arm wide, I let my magic rush free. A ribbon the color of a sunset with an edge as sharp as a knife rushed from me. Screams echoed over stone as the magical blade hit my attackers, cutting into their skin and filling the cave with the aroma of damp blood. The monster inside of me smiled in relief.

Suji glanced at his fallen men, the look on his face gaunt as he turned back to me. Our eyes locked as he hit his walking stick against the floor, magic erupted as the floor shivered over to me. A line of silver moved closer, sliding like a snake. I lifted myself into the air just as it reached me.

I didn't soar high, choosing to lift myself up enough that he wouldn't notice.

Whatever he had been trying to do had failed, the poor guy didn't seem to know what to do next.

"Maybe you are right. Maybe I am a God," I taunted as the ripple of magic intersected with his minions. Most jumped moments before impact, terrified for the wave of magic to make contact.

One, however, did not. The ripple of silver electricity smashed into him, moving up his body in a jolt that sent him writhing, sent him screaming. Until, with one last gasp, the man turned to a pillar of glittering stone.

Okay. That was dangerous. Don't touch the silver electricity.

Swallowing the lump in my throat, I turned from the stone man to Suji, forcing the hard anger to remain in my eyes as I taunted him.

"Oh, is that what it was supposed to do?" I was amazed I could keep the warble of panic out of my voice.

Suji looked like he was about to explode, the rage clear in his eyes. Instead of responding, however, he hit the walking stick against the stone again. This time, instead of a ripple of silver, everything rumbled in an explosion of magic.

Red and yellow sparks filled the air, the poison of his power mixed with whatever pure magic he held in the stick, the combined force swirling through the air like a fractured snake. It bobbed and weaved in jerking motions as though it was undead. Swiping my hands through the air, I sent my magic after it, letting one single arrow stab through the demonized magic with the force of a bomb.

The collision bounced through the cave and rumbled through the stone, sending the walls and floor shifting once again. This time, however, it was too much. The massive crack spread over the wall behind Suji, the fiend unaware as he sent another attack toward me with a smile.

We couldn't keep this up. His magic was too volatile, too erratic. While I could face and defeat him easily, the cave would not survive. I could still hear people scream as they tried to escape.

Hands pressed before me, my magic swallowed his as I soared higher into the air. Making a beeline right for him, I purposefully taunted him off the ground. I needed to get him away from the stone before he caused more damage.

"Wyn!" I yelled, as I soared past where she was trapped, herding the practically hysterical Chosen out of the cave, her face enraged as she shouted at two younger women. Michel flinched from where he hovered behind Wyn, Míra thrown over his shoulder. I didn't like that, every ounce of me wanted to yank the girl away from him, but Wyn's response dashed any possibility of that happening.

"I can't fix it!" She was practically screaming at me.

The answer was not the response to what I had been hoping to ask, but it told me enough. Too much rock. Too big of a collapse. Even if she hadn't been attempting to shuffle the throng of panicked sheep out the door, her powerful magic couldn't stop the downward spiral the cave's structure was taking.

Why wouldn't this bastard just die already.

"You seem to think you are superior to me. To my people," Suji yelled at me from across the cave, his magic sparking with each syllable. "But all I see is a whiny little man. A child, who plays at being a god."

Really? He was going to try to taunt me? Still?

Grinding my teeth together, I quickly changed trajectory back to him, and sped up. Poor Suji hadn't expected that, he looked like he was about to wet himself. Spinning around him, I landed, grabbed the man and pressed his back to my chest. My wide arms held him as I pressed my palm against the flesh of his neck. I let my magic flare against my hand as I held it there, sending sparks of an unfiltered attack right into him. He didn't even tense underneath me.

I guess I spoke too soon, this was too easy.

I shot us twenty feet into the air, towards the high ceiling of the cave as my magic flared again. He jerked, the motion almost sending him through my arms and to the stony ground far below.

He wasn't fighting me now.

"Think you are a big boy?" he hissed, the pain in his voice coloring everything.

"Tell me where the girl went." I ignored his poor attempt to provoke me and plowed on, sending a spark of my magic into him in warning.

"I told you," his voice was strained now, the strength of my magic against his neck almost too much, I didn't care. "She was taken from us--"

"By who?" I snarled.

The man smiled at me with blood stained teeth. "The SSU."

"The ones who captured a God?" I repeated his weird phrasing from before back to him.

"The Tykha Shist´ will have your head," he snarled with a demonic laugh. "Or rather, your magic."

The phrase was confusing, but before I had a chance to ask, his hand slammed into my gut, his magic infecting me with a single pulse that sent me tumbling through the air and right into the rock wall yards behind with a crack that rattled my skull.

416

I swore, Suji screamed like a mad man, and I was only barely able to move fast enough to catch myself before I tumbled to the ground.

My 'getting away', however, was overshadowed by the sound of his magic smashing into the wall of the cave right above my head.

Damn it. Rein it in, psycho. I don't want to die today.

Everything groaned, stone groaning with a low roar as the massive crack that had split down the wall widened. The fissure of broken stone spread over the floor in a jagged line of black that shifted and heaved as the floor began to pull apart.

Sound filled my head, the creak so loud that I could barely think. It was as though the cave was screaming.

The floor jerked heavily to the side, the crack widening into a crevice that began to swallow everything whole. Ripped couches tumbled into the black, followed by the tangled bodies of Suji's men as they lost their footing, their magic not enough to catch them.

Air whooshed past me as I soared down to the huddle of Michel's followers who were screaming in panic around the now caved in exit. Thanks to the constantly shifting floor I landed, stumbled head first into two of them and found myself in a huddle on the ground.

"Get up," Wyn shouted, the strain in her voice making it unclear if she was talking to me or one of the dozen Chosen. "Don't you dare move."

Definitely not talking to me.

"Get your ass over here," Wyn continued on, her voice fading in and out over the sound of the tumbling rocks. "If you so much as lift your grubby hand I will cut it off."

I heaved myself back to standing, bones and muscles screaming as my magic strained to heal me. A hot line of fury burned through me as I turned back to Suji, the now disheveled man glowering at me from across the wide cavern. His eyes burned a bright red as he stared at me, standing still as rocks the size of small cars tumbled from the ceiling.

He didn't even flinch as one hit mere feet from him; I barely moved as the floor shifted again. The two of us were frozen there, staring, glaring.

Waiting.

"This is pointless, it's like herding cats. I don't even like cats," Wyn's voice was a snapped whisper in my ear.

"Then stop wasting your time and let's finish this guy," I growled, a maniacal smile spreading as I took off, Wyn right beside me.

We weaved through the forest of falling rock as smoke and dust erupted from each impact against the collapsing ground below us, the sounds of screams echoing from the ever growing cavern.

Bombs from the ceiling.

Mines from the ground.

Rip him apart.

Gladly.

Dust and dirt exploding around me, I attacked again, one single stream of my magic rushing right toward him. We were almost there.

"Let's end this."

Boulders broke apart into thousands of tiny jagged bullets at Wyn's command, each one soaring right toward Suji and the few of his men who were brave enough to stand beside him.

His face paled as he realized what was happening, his magic sparking against his fingers. A wicked smile distorted his face as his eyes flashed dark.

"I always get what I want." I barely heard him. Hell, I wasn't sure if I had heard him correctly through all the rumbling noise of the cave.

I didn't get a chance to ask either way.

His eyes were still locked with mine as Wyn's daggers began to crash into the stone around him, exploding like tiny landmines. I forced myself to fly faster, desperate to be the one to end him, just as I watched a shard of stone plunge itself into his chest.

The blood was so thick I could barely see him fall, I could barely see his face as he went down, still staring at me.

I could have sworn he was smiling.

CHAPTER 37

ILYAN

"How about this one?" Detective Bondar spoke in English, his Slavic accent thick and burly against the familiar language.

His dark eyes pierced mine as he slid an image across the scratched surface of the table I was handcuffed to. It was the same image he had shown me every day in his vendetta to find The Oheň.

Every day they would walk me down an older wing of the old hospital, chains grinding against the cracked floor as The Cleaners yelled and smacked the butts of their guns against the doors, igniting yells from the other patients.

No, from the prisoners who had thought they were coming to a sanctuary, a country without war, without The Chrlič, only to find themselves locked in a purgatory.

A prison, posing as a hospital.

We would walk to this room, the only other room I saw, as Detective Bondar showed me pictures. The same pictures. As though seeing them so often would spark a memory.

Of course, I knew exactly what this image was, and exactly what he wanted me to say.

He would get neither.

"There is a green baseball cap near a dumpster. A door is ajar in the background..." I rattled off the memorized details without looking. I didn't even look at him. I just stared at the double mirror that covered the dark wall behind him and what I was sure was officers behind it.

"What else?" the Detective said, the low rumble of his voice pulling my focus from the glass, although I would still not look at the image. I would look anywhere else, even at the ugly green of the sinister star that graced his lapel.

It was that that I landed on.

"A pile of cloth, it looks like..."

"What else," he interrupted with a snap, tapping his finger against the portrait.

That was new, he very rarely lost his temper.

Perhaps I could use this.

"Where is Commander Domor?" I asked in Ukrainian and Detective Bondar sighed, bristly mustache dancing in agitation as he snatched back the photo, shuffling it with the others.

This was new. He had never given up so quickly. I had only been chained to the desk a few moments ago.

I had rattled him.

I had upset him somehow, but why? Something had changed. Something was different, it made my stomach twist.

"Is he here?" I asked, the chains around my ankles clanging loudly as I shifted my weight, feigning an attempt to see through the glass.

Except this time I wanted to.

My magic bubbled through me, stretching through air

and floor to reach the glass as I had mastered before. The wall of glass began to melt away in my mind, my vision shifting as my magic revealed the tiny room just behind. The same men stood there every day, the insignia of the red and yellow spark embroidered on their lapels. The Tykha Shist´. They would stand in circles, smoking as they talked, as they yelled at their prized prisoner as time and again I foiled them.

Today, however, they stared at me in frightening eagerness, their bright eyes and smiles clear from behind their large smoking pipes. Commander Domor paced to the side of the other five, each one stiff as they stood around a woman in a large black cloak, the five of them looking like ladies in waiting against the powerful confidence that was bleeding off this woman.

Her aura saturated the air, and although I had never seen her before, although I knew nothing about her, I found myself growing just as agitated as the Commander was. The way she was looking at me, right at me, made me twitch. The movement was slight, but I was sure she had seen it with how her lip twisted into a demented half smile, the wicked grin growing as she began to remove her black leather gloves, mouth moving in some command I couldn't hear.

"How about this?" The snap of the detective's aggression was gone, replaced by a careful phrasing and an eagerness that pulled me right from those behind the glass and to the smiling man before me.

Detective Bondar slid another picture across the table, even from my peripheral vision I could tell it was part of the beautiful city I had seen destroyed in my dreams for the last few months.

"The blood filled river," I began, still focused on him, "the ruins of..."

"Look again." The man interrupted me sharply, the nefarious humor in his eyes was making me bristle.

His finger tapped loudly against the table in an attempt to get my attention, the tap continually growing louder, until I finally looked from him to the large square image that lay flat against the scratched surface.

"How about this," he repeated, the tap-tap-tap of his finger slowing.

It was the sister of the image I had seen for months. The same scene. The same part of the city.

A murky river ran along the bottom, the bank lined with the remains of the white stones and red roofs that had made up the heart of Prague. Except the remains were gone, they had been cleaned away. The ancient bridge that had previously fallen into the river was being rebuilt, the old sections blending seamlessly with the new. I could clearly see where The St. Vitas cathedral had once stood.

The few buildings that had been spared in the destruction, were clustered in the bottom corner, a few people milling around as life slowly began to return to the city.

This was not the picture of the ruins from years ago. This was now; this was recent.

And there, under his ink-stained fingertip, was her.

My magic sparked as I leaned closer, the power rolling over my skin in waves as I kept it restrained, albeit barely.

A girl in a blue tank top and jeans ran along the river banks with a boy who could have been her brother judging by the dark curls they both had.

I could barely make it out, but I knew it was them. I knew it was her.

Joclyn.

The word. The name. It was dying to escape, to explode out of me, but I restrained it - keeping it safe inside. Keeping my reaction safe inside.

"I am glad to see the rebuild is going well." I kept my voice even, letting my vowels roll out in my thick Czech accent so that it made the Ukrainian sound garbled.

The man glared at me before returning to his pile of photographs. My heart raced as he shuffled through them. I needed to see her again. I needed to see the image. To see the boy, to memorize everything. But I could say nothing.

The SSU was too dangerous now, and while I had mastered quite a lot of my magic, I wasn't ready. Sitting here I could feel my magic press against my heart, where I had learned to hold it, the slow steady beat keeping my power calm. It was waiting to explode, ready to react, but here in this room was not the place to start a war. The truth would only end in death.

Detective Bondar mumbled to himself before he slammed the next image down, this one a magnification of the last. I expected it to be an out-of-focus mess, but it was clear, perfect.

My heart relaxed at the tiny freckles over her nose, at the way her hair bounced as she carried herself confidently. The relaxation was short-lived, however, the emotion followed by pain at the look of devastation in her eyes. She was angry as she rushed away from the boy, his image clearer - and definitely the one Kaye had found months before.

Ryland LaRue.

The plea on Ryland's face was evident as he followed her, his hand held forward as he tried to give her something. A golden ribbon wound into a nest.

The ribbon from her hair. I had seen that before. In the

images from Svarov, in my dreams.

Only weeks before I had watched my memories replay as I weaved it into a braid, twisting ribbons into roses and designs that I could never hope to replicate. The meaning was still unknown to me.

"How about now?" he hissed, his victorious tone making it clear he thought he had caught me. That he thought he could break me.

But I still knew nothing more than her name and that she existed...

She existed.

The city was being rebuilt, his eagerness giving away that the image was recent enough it may have been days old.

And there she was.

Existing.

She was alive. I hadn't killed her.

Heat rumbled through me, a joy swelling so fast that it was nearly impossible to keep the emotion restrained; to keep myself in this chair and not fight my way toward Prague.

"Is that the girl you have shown me before?" I asked, desperate to keep the shake out of my voice. "The Oheň? Dark Fire, right?"

His knuckles tightened, the skin discolored in his anger.

I could feel the emotion mirrored in myself, but in joy, and in triumph. My magic echoed the strength of the feelings, everything in me suddenly feeling very alive.

The electricity was ready to explode.

I shifted my weight, trying to hide my hands, but instead, the chains and handcuffs only rattled loudly, creating the opposite effect.

The man before me, and I am sure those behind the

glass, glanced down in expectation.

As if they were waiting for some eruption of power.

Perhaps they wanted it. Perhaps they thought this picture was the key.

"So, she is alive then?" I spat, purposefully making my voice loud so as to pull their attention.

"It appears so," the man growled, leaving the magnified image on the table as he riffled through his folder. "We assume she is working with this man, helping to decrease the Chrlič."

"And is it working?"

Detective Bondar didn't look up, his focus remained on the folder, a tiny twitch playing around his lips as he finally found what he was looking for.

I tensed. For once, he was pushing buttons.

"Of course, they could also be looking for you."

One after another he began to lay images down, far enough away that I couldn't reach them, close enough that I couldn't ignore them anymore.

Even if I had tried I couldn't look away.

Some of the images Kaye and I had already found, some of them were new. Each and every one pulled at my heart, making it harder to breathe. Shot after shot of Joclyn and I as we fought through the Svarov ruins, battled against both Chrlič and a wide array of battle-worn soldiers. Images of my hand around hers, images of me standing before her in protection.

One after another they came, the knot in my chest rising to meet the tension of my magic, the hot boil pushing everything up and out in a threat of release.

I breathed deeply and clenched my fists, more concerned with keeping everything restrained than with keeping my emotions hidden for the moment.

Bondar's face turned up in a wicked grin as he slid another image across the table, this one facedown. Its white back winked at me as he pressed it underneath my fingers, his eyes dancing as he nodded toward it in invitation.

Heart pounding, I attempted to swallow the massive lump of fear away as my magic continued to flare and bubble. Slowly everything began to ease. I knew at once it was not enough.

One glance to the mirror and my magic flared, letting my eyes peer through it once again to see the men behind it, their exhilaration flooding the space. The woman, however...

"Go ahead," Bondar prompted, his eager voice pulling me from the Six and back toward the photograph.

I knew I had no choice.

Twisting my wrists against the heavy cuffs, I fumbled with the image, turning it towards me.

It was her. In my arms. She looked up at me, her hands clenching my shirt as I held her against me, the world exploding around us as I protected her, as I cradled her.

I remembered this.

I remembered this moment.

I remember feeling her against me, and the feeling of her magic inside of me, the heat of her skin.

And not just from the dreams of us on the beach every night, I could feel it now, feel the warmth, feel the power buzz inside of me. Feel the way our magic would combine, the way my power longed for her.

I couldn't stop it from exploding.

The photo turned to ash in a flash of red, the pieces shimmering to the table like snow. I watched them fall, the facade I had built tumbling right beside them. Power surged over the surface of my skin as I looked up to the man, his face a mixture of horror and exhilaration.

I had one second. One second to decide what to do and what card to play.

I could attack. I could run. I could escape.

Even with all the work I had done over the last few months, however, even with all Kaye and I had learned, I already knew it wasn't enough.

It wasn't enough to get out. It wasn't enough to escape.

I had one choice.

I had to keep the lie intact. I had to play the game, and if I was lucky, get more information.

"What in the world..." I stammered, forcing as much confusion as I could into my voice. I jerked away, sending the chains rattling as I pressed against my restraints in a need to move away from the still smoldering remains of the photograph.

"Is this a joke?" I roared, my voice breaking as my magic continually tried to break free.

I tried to restrain it, tried to lock it inside, but it broke free. It sparked from the tips of my fingers in flames of red and yellow, the electric charges bounced over the surface of the table. I screamed at the appearance, even though it was something I had done every day for months. It was then that I realized, while I couldn't control the slow leak, I could definitely control the explosion.

"What's happening to me," I yelled as I twisted my hands toward Bondar, sending him screaming and diving to the side.

His yell joined my fake one as I pushed my magic out, sending the charge rumbling through the air and right into the mirrored glass.

The screams of the commanders joined ours as the glass

shattered, the walls shook as the handcuffs broke free as I easily popped the lock. Holding my hands before me, I continued to scream, ready to fire again when each of the Six began to yell in Ukrainian. Their threats became clear as their guns were drawn, several warning shots going over my head before each of the dark barrels were aimed right at me.

"Another one and you die," Commander Domor yelled, his own gun lifting as he stepped right up to where the wall had been.

"I can't control it," I said, attempting to push out a sob as I aimed my hands to the ground. "Please, I don't know what's going on."

"You seem to be controlling it quite well, to me." The voice was silk drenched in acid. It burned through my soul as the six men parted, letting the woman I had seen with them before step forward. "I wonder what else you can do."

Her face was plastered with pleasure and triumph, the dark ink of her eyes glinting with it.

The look alone was enough to stop the flow of my power, but it was the sinister star on her lapel that turned the world to ice, any hope of fighting fading away as my power recoiled. The colors were one I had never seen before and knew I would never see again.

'Only purple is higher, and there is only one of those.'

Kaye's words repeated as I froze in place, my magic dead inside of me. This was the leader. If I was to kill anyone, it would be her. But I couldn't. I couldn't even move, something in the air was telling me it was a lost cause.

With one greasy smile, she raised her hand. Her own fingers sparking with magic before, with a flick, a needle plunged into my neck.

CHAPTER 38

ILYAN

The world was swimming.

Everything around me was moving so fast I couldn't tell which way was up. As the world spun, so did my mind. Fuzzy thoughts rotated as I spun through the air. One moment I was sure I was standing up, the next I was lying down.

Everything blurred, swimming.

Swimming.

Breathing out in a shaky exhale, I attempted to stabilize the world in order to figure out what had happened and where I was, but I only spun more, the oxygen not quite reaching my brain. It felt like something was stopping it, blocking my nose and mouth.

No matter how many breaths I took, it didn't seem to do any good, everything spun like a Catherine Wheel, sending my vision into a blur of light and confusion.

Like a star.

The Sinister Star.

The sparkling tips of a purple and gold star winked from above me, the embroidery the only clear thing in the wobbling world. It taunted me, promising danger and death in a flash. I tensed, hands flying forward in an attempt to push away the star and run, but every movement was hindered. Panic rose up as I tried again, metal clattering as I fought, as I convulsed, but still nothing. My fight was stopped by a gentle tinkling laugh, the sound like broken china against my being.

"My, my, aren't you a feisty one." The woman's voice was a low grind, the sounds as garbled as my vision. But I couldn't mistake the low drawl of fascination, the undertone of cruel domination. The warning of pain.

The way she spoke was familiar, like a memory that couldn't quite come. Something from my past screaming at me to run. To escape. To fight. I could do neither. I could only push against my bands, but these were more than just the ankle and wrist straps from the past few months, these wide padded restraints ran over the entire length of my body, restricting arms, torso, legs, even my head.

"They said you were a boring charge," the woman drawled, the joy in her voice growing as the wobbly shape of her hovered above me. "It seems that you just needed the right motivation."

Motivation. Is that what they called this, taunting me with her picture? Stealing the last fragment of my humanity?

I fought again, but the strength of my fight was turning into a shadow. I wasn't even sure my body had received the command my brain had sent it.

"You could never..." I tried to get the words out, only to have the edict stolen by slurred speech and a large plastic disk that was wedged against my teeth.

I truly was trapped.

"Interesting," the woman snarled with false concern as she ran her fingertips over the short strands of my hair.

I attempted to jerk away at the touch, but no movement came, only the low moan of lost love, only the slurred speech of a name I had kept hidden inside of me for years.

"Joclyn."

My own fear rose up at the slip and I fought against the restraints. The faint beeping of what I was sure was my heart rate echoing behind my mournful screams. Between whatever was lodged in my mouth and the panic that followed, however, the single word remained unheard.

"I suppose this dose is too high," she said with false concern, the raised pitch of her voice grating on me. "It appears that you can't speak."

The wobbly outline of the woman moved toward something behind me, the sound of her shoes a hollow explosion in my head.

Out of the corner of my eye, a wide wall of glass lay ominously, the window and the people behind it didn't even try to hide. There was no double-sided glass, there was no prelude. It was only a clear window into a viewing area where the Tykha Shist ´ stared openly, the shadow of a reflection mirroring the old bed I laid on.

The room was new to me, although something told me I had been here before. Glancing at the walls of glass and blood-stained cement, it suddenly became clear as to what this room was, and why it felt so familiar.

I may have been in a coma, but I was sure I was no stranger to torture chambers. Even without the memory, the emotions rang clear.

"That should do it, Ma'am," a man spoke in an emotionless echo. "You should have greater control now."

"Wonderful."

The blur of the woman slid into focus, the waves of light and dark transforming into the same woman I had seen standing behind the mirror of the interrogation room.

Nothing about this woman was welcoming. I had heard the threat in her voice before, but now the tone was echoed in her lifeless eyes, in the icy scowl she fixed me with. I saw the threat; saw her exhilaration of what was coming, of what I was here for. The hunger chilled me more.

"Hello, Jan," she smiled, the same wicked taunt clear in her voice.

"That's not my name." Although each word came easy, the garbled drawl was gone. Every syllable was broken by whatever was in my mouth, the plastic disk turning my defiance into humiliation.

"What is your name, then?" she asked, her eyes piercing deep into me. "My name is Nastya."

She whispered as though it was a secret, or rather like it was something I should fear. Something everyone else did.

I could tell she expected the reaction. I gave her none of it, even though I could feel a shadow of it roaring up my spine. She did not deserve the emotion.

"You don't know who I am, do you? You think all these burly men are in charge, don't you? Hmmm.... I was once a spy for the Security Service of Ukraine," Nastya continued, her voice dropping lower as she leaned closer, both voice and body so low I was determined to ignore them. "Now I rule the SSU. I rule you."

"No one rules me," I mumbled past the disk, the retort more to myself than to her.

With a sneer, Nastya stood, nodding to the man behind me before she returned her focus to me, her fingers moving back to my skin. Another rush of cold, another rush of anger and I knew exactly what she was doing.

She was seeking the reaction, she was showing her control.

"I rule you, Jan," she repeated, the use of the name agitating me more. "You can't escape. You can't leave. Not unless you give me what I want. Now, will you tell me your name?"

My lips flared around whatever was lodged in my mouth, my eyes shifting to my own defiant glare. The joy in her eyes grew at my determined stare, the lack of power I had making itself clear.

I may be able to keep my secrets locked inside, but I was playing with more than fire.

I was playing with pain.

My father had done more.

The words came on their own, pulled from a memory I couldn't fully recall, the drugs making everything slow and confusing. I flinched at the weight of the statement, at the knowledge it held, and continued to sneer at her, knowing that even without context, this survivor was me.

This fight.

This defiance.

She could bring death.

I would still fight.

"They said you couldn't be broken. They tried to convince me you weren't The Oheň's partner," Nastya's taunt pulled me from my memory as she began to pace alongside the bed, leaving me to look at the water-stained ceiling above her as the bed lowered me back down to lay flat. Or, at least, I think I was. "They were wrong, weren't they? I showed them that."

"You showed them..." Once again the words were swallowed, no doubt a large amount of drugs still making everything move twice as slow.

434

"Oh no," she cooed, "I showed them you could be broken. You showed them what you really are."

My heartbeat was thunder in my ears, the fateful organ giving me away as the machines beeped faster. Nastya's smile grew, and yet the once familiar buzz of my magic never picked up. I could feel the warmth, but it was sludge inside of me.

Whatever they had given me was doing more than slowing my thoughts and speech.

It was slowing me.

It was stopping me.

They had figured it out. They had found their drug before we could make our escape.

They had won.

"Now," she continued, "The question is who will be right this time."

She paused as if waiting for me to question her. Her focus was not on me, but on all of those who stood behind the glass, their figures still blurred in my peripheral vision.

"Will Commander Domor be right, and now that we have been able to take control, you will give me the power?" She paused, her pace slowing as she hovered over me again. "Or will I be right, and I will have to find a way to use you. To create you into exactly what I've always wanted. The perfect weapon. My weapon."

Rage broke past the drugs, the world beginning to spin again as the sludge of my magic bubbled. Although I knew it was in desperation, I fought. I pushed against the bed with everything that I had, head and hands barely moving as I screamed through the disk in my mouth, suddenly realizing what it was, and why it was there.

"No," I yelled through the mouth guard, continuing to fight against the bands as she came to sit beside me.

The bed sagged under her weight, springs creaking loudly as the archaic device I had been strapped to groaned and threatened to collapse.

"No?" she asked, the single word sounding like a nail in a coffin.

"Will you give me the power then?" She ran her hand over the skin of my arm, and I flinched, the angry magic alive for that one moment as I tried to get away. Before I could control it, however, it was gone; crawled into some hole inside of me.

Even if I could control the magic, even if I could give her this power.

I wasn't going to.

"No," I said, firmer this time.

While I saw her flinch from where she sat beside me, the motion was small and quickly overshadowed by the wide joy that spread over her face.

"Does that mean I am right, again?" she said with a laugh, the false sound grating against my bones. "Am I going to have the pleasure of creating you into my own personal weapon?"

Fear gripped me, but I couldn't look away. I wouldn't.

"No," I growled, knowing the word meant nothing. Not really.

"Oh, yes," she cooed, her voice as soft as the fingertip that was running down my jaw bone.

I bit down hard on the mouth guard, fighting against the touch.

Instead, with a nod from Nastya, I was faced with fighting something even worse.

Cold metal bulbs were placed on my temples, echoes of current sounded in my ears as the bulbs began to heat, the sound a warning for what was about to happen.

"I found this machine years ago, in an old auction. I always thought it was beautiful, aggressive. I can't wait to use it on you."

Still, I did not look away from her. I did not close my eyes. I glowered as she smiled, the buzzing heat beginning to grow against my skin.

"I saw the electricity pour from you," Nastya whispered as she leaned over me, her hand flat against my bare chest. "I have seen the pictures. You have lightning inside of you, and the way I see it, lightning loves a party."

"No," I said again, making the word as clear as I could.

"You will become my weapon, a creature I can use. Or you will tell me who she is - and then I will take it from her instead. Either way, you will give her to me."

"No!" The defiance faded as panic took over, the emotion smashing against me as I hit against the restraints. The buzzing grew to a charge that ricocheted inside my head, that split my bones. I shook against the restraints, no longer fighting them, no longer in control of my magic. No longer in control of myself.

I was only a painful fire.

The pain lasted for a minute before it ebbed, the room swimming and sparking as something smoked from nearby.

"Go again," I heard Nastya whisper, "go higher, and someone bring me a scalpel."

The words felt far away before the pain returned, everything shaking and burning as I willingly let the black take me, only faintly wondering if I would be gone for hours, years, or if I would be gone for good.

CHAPTER 39

RYLAND

The sound of Wyn's arsenal exploding around Suji was cannon fire against the already feral groan of the cave. His blood sprayed as he smiled, falling to the ground as the air quaked with the scream of rock breaking apart.

"Okay, so that may not have been my best idea." Wyn rubbed her nose as she twisted in the air, jaw pressed into a tight line as she stared at the ceiling.

"One of these days we will stop bringing down caves," I said, not wanting to think about how many we were up to now. At least four that I knew of. It was becoming a bad habit.

"One of these days we will stop hiding underground. Although, I blame my people for that." Wyn had a point, but before I could tell her that, screams rang from the floor far below, both of us spinning in the air as the rock groaned and everyone left on the floor was sent to their knees.

"This place doesn't have much time." Wyn twisted in the air, toward the new crack that was forming there. "I'll get this. You get that Suji bastard and get them all out of here. I'll keep the roof up as long as I can. Stutter out if needs be."

"I can't Stutter!" I yelled after her, but she was already gone, soaring to the large crack in the ceiling, hands already burning red. Air rushed behind me as I headed for the crumpled mass of stone, blood, and limbs. If he was alive, he was coming with us.

Sure, we could leave him, a tomb of stone would be fitting, but not when I still needed info from him. I was sure Jos would have a few choice words as well.

He lay among the shards of rock, covered in a layer of grey dust that made him look like a ghost. His eyes widened as I landed, and he opened his mouth with the obvious intent to taunt and belittle, but the only thing that came out was a cough and a thick drizzle of blood that pooled and ran down his cheek.

I didn't even try to restrain the smile.

"I would say sorry, but..." I shrugged my shoulders, and grabbed him, lifting him from where he lay on the ground and pressed him against the wall, his legs crumpled on the ground beneath him. "I'm not sorry, not even a little bit."

Suji opened his mouth to scream as I slammed him into the wall, but the sound barely registered above the blood that had pooled in his mouth, the bright red fluid now pouring over his chin and painting the front of his ruined suit. Even holding him like this, I could tell he didn't have much time.

None of us did. Wyn was yelling, people were screaming, and the floor continued to rasp out its dying groans.

I wrapped him tighter with binds of my magic until he couldn't move. He just coughed up more blood, his magic sputtering as it tried and failed again to heal him from the giant stone dagger that still protruded from his rib cage thanks to Wyn's attack. There was no way he was going to heal himself with that in there, and no way he would survive if I took it out.

If I wanted answers, I needed to get them now.

"Tell me where the girl has gone? Where is Hikari?" I asked, as his blood-stained smile spread.

"You think..." he coughed up more blood. "Tell nothing."

I reached for the dagger, knowing I didn't have enough time. Was it worth it to remove it? Was it worth it to try?

Instead, I slammed him against the wall again, grateful when the cave didn't creak. Wyn must have been successful in stopping the cave in. I was going to owe her a million favors for how often she saved me from falling rocks.

"Where is the girl? Where is Hikari?" I asked as I wrapped my hand around the grey stone and he winced. "Who is attacking us?"

"Why would I tell you?" he gasped, his smile all but gone as his eyes began to slip in and out of focus.

"Tell me!" I yelled, wrapping my hand around the stone in what I hoped he saw as a threat. He called out in pain, slamming his own head against the stone wall as I held him there.

Okay, maybe I had grabbed it too hard.

"Why?" Suji yelled through his pain, the scream echoing awkwardly in the sudden calm that had filled the cave. "They will... they will find you anyway..."

Every word was laced with pain as he began to gasp, the blood that ran out of his chest and down my hand beginning to slow.

I was out of time.

"We are only the beginning." I could barely hear him over the blood that dripped between his lips, the sounds rattling in my ears as Suji began to laugh. The sound was deep, and almost identical to the roar of my father's madness. I twitched, trying to push it away, but it just grew, until Suji became my father and all I saw was red.

"Fine," I snarled, letting my magic flare in sparks of crimson that rippled down the edge of the stone dagger and right into him, "then I will make you the beginning of the deaths."

I didn't give him a chance to respond, I didn't even want to hear what he had to say. I let my magic surge as my father's laugh did, another scream echoing behind me as I watched the life drain from him.

"No!"

Suji shook violently as my attack crippled him, sucking the last of his life away. My father's laugh echoed loudly, pounding against my skull as it grew into a maniacal chuckle that poured from my own throat.

"Stop!" The shout behind me was louder now. The panicked voice broke through the sound of my deranged laugh, my body shaking in my own madness.

Rough hands wrapped around my shoulder, pulling me away from Suji as a sharp zap of magic surged through me. Back arching, fire ripped apart my muscle and I fell to the ground, a loud crack echoing in my ears as I slammed into the hard stone.

"Damn it, Ry," Wyn screamed as she rushed toward the slumped shape of Suji. "Don't you die you bastard! Where is she?"

"Wyn," I groaned, shaking my head as I attempted to banish both the laugh and the spinning/ Neither left, the world was still a smear. "Wyn, the cave..."

"Shut up, Ry." Another spark of magic shot into me. "Where are they! Where did he take her?"

Who was she talking about? What was she talking about?

I fought through the haze as I turned to her, the two of them barely coming into focus as Wyn shook the man. His limbs and head flailed like he was a rag doll. I would have thought he was dead if it wasn't for the smile, for the last gasping breath that shuddered through him.

"Good luck."

I could barely hear him, Hell, I didn't even understand.

But Wyn did, and Wyn screamed. The sound was feral as it ripped from her, the power of her scream echoing across her skin as her magic erupted. Waves of flame ran over her, singeing hair and clothes as it began to ripple over her arms; the shadows of her scars darkened as Suji burst into flame, the lifeless man turning to ash.

"Holy shit, Wyn!" I yelled, back tensing in shock as the debris that was once a man fell from her fingers.

It wasn't the first time I had seen her burn someone to a crisp, but it was the first time I had seen her do it like that, with so much pain.

So much anger.

Instead of responding to me, however, Wyn just clenched her fist and let out an almighty scream that sent me jumping. A few yards away, a few of Suji's men who had survived the onslaught flinched, eyes wide as they began to scuttle away.

"What in the world--" I mumbled to Wyn, wrapping my arms around her tightly as I pulled her away from the sudden crematorium.

"She's gone."

Her words slammed into my chest and sucked all the air from my lungs as I instantly went into the worst case scenario.

"Joclyn?"

"No," she gasped, turning to face me, the pain in her eyes darkening in her anger. "Míra."

Heart thundering, I spun towards where Michel's useless sheep had been herded, expecting to see some kind of funeral pyre or keening circle. But they all looked like nothing had happened, well nothing beyond almost being crushed to death by a cave.

One thing, however, was instantly clear, Michel was not among them - and he had held Míra.

Wyn had asked where she was, not who had killed her.

Casting a single glance at Wyn, I stepped toward the group, ready to soar over there and rip my way through them, as though she was just hiding behind them, cloaking in a shield as she always was.

The pain at the fear of having lost her instantly transformed into a formidable wall of anger, the emotion burning through my veins as I silenced my madness and let the purity of my own rage take control.

"Damn it," I growled, slamming my fist into the already damaged rock with such force that I left a near perfect imprint of knuckles behind.

Rugby muscles don't do that on their own.

I wanted to remind myself to breathe, to restrain my temper and magic, but I couldn't. She was gone and the only man who would know where she was, was now glittering particles of ash.

No.

That wasn't true.

I spun from Wyn, taking two quick steps toward where the few survivors of Suji's men sat propped up against a large rock. The one closest to me was folded over, his chest and throat bleeding profusely from what appeared to be several large holes. Wyn's stone daggers had obviously plunged right through. I was amazed his magic had been able to keep him alive this long. He didn't even try to move from where he was slouched, covered in a fine layer of dust, staring at me with wide defiant eyes.

I focused on him, stubbornly ignoring the shadows of pain that still ripped through my bones as I stalked toward him, as though I was the feral one.

"Where would he take her?" I snarled, narrowing my eyes at the man in a look that I was sure was more madness than menace. "Where would he take the girl?"

Judging by the way the man flinched, he knew something. Two of his comrades that lay equally as incapacitated behind him turned toward us at the sound of the interrogation, their faces a mix of pain and foolish defiance.

"Where is Michel?" I repeated, enunciating each syllable as I turned to each of them, not really trying to restrain the growl.

Wyn came up behind me, her heat permeating the air, sending ripples of flame and magic over the stone just above the men's heads. They stared at it in panic, attempting to shift away from the flames. The first man, however, only sagged against the wall, a deep chuckle rattling through him. The wet sound bubbled at the corners of his lips, bright red lines of blood beginning to trickle over his chin.

"You will never find them. They will never let you," his voice was filled with a dampness that made every word sound like it was spoken underwater.

It was obvious he spoke of a threat. Wyn, however, just laughed.

"Don't be ridiculous," she said, leaning against the stone wall and letting a single line of fire shoot out from her finger to caress the rock; it looked like a dragon's tongue. "I stopped that. It wasn't that bad. We only *almost* died." She sighed and rolled her eyes. "You guys are just lucky someone with real magic was here."

Wyn returned the smile in that 'I-didn't-think-I-could-but-clearly-saved-us-all-anyway' way of hers.

I laughed which only freaked Suji's men out more.

Using it to my advantage, I leaned closer, as my fingers sparked in a menacing warning. There was no recoil, however, only a hard light in his eyes.

"We will die with honor," the man returned, his stare full of pained stoicism.

I should have assumed as much. No matter, I could play with this.

"Who said I was going to let you die?" I said, keeping my voice in that low, menacing growl that I wasn't very good at. "I have questions. I have a girl who was stolen from me. I have a woman I am trying to find. I am confident that you will give me answers."

The threat was met by a blood-filled chuckle and a cough. "This girl must mean a lot to you, if you will kill the blessed army of the Kyō to reach her."

I ground the back of my jaw as I stood, my heart and soul screaming at that. Screaming in panic that she was gone, and I needed to save her. I could feel myself becoming uncontrollable again at just the thought.

"Where did he take her?" I asked, I was growling again, hands shaking as I tried to control my anger. Although, with the way Wyn was smiling I would say she didn't want me too.

"I really wouldn't ignore him." Wyn was still leaning against the stone as she flicked her fingernails one against another, watching as tiny sparks of flame erupted with each strike.

"We will die with honor," he repeated, and I lost it.

Snapping my fingers, I threw my magic away from me, grabbing one of Suji's men from far behind the group and pulling him through the air towards us to intersect with the wall beside their heads.

The impact of his flesh against stone echoed through the strangely quiet cave, sending the last man jumping as my victim's crumpled, lifeless body tumbled down, limbs and appendages almost detached.

Of course, the man had died sometime before, but they didn't need to know that.

"We will die with honor," the man in the middle said, his voice quivering even though the defiance in his eyes did not, he just stared straight at me, as if daring me to make him the next victim. "Our magic is stronger than yours, we have what we need, and you will find your end at the hands of..."

Now it was my turn to laugh, the deep rumble cut him off as it echoed over the walls of the cave, rippling over everything like oil over water. I let it take me, aware of how much the laugh was in my head as it was out. Aware of just how much I was letting my father's madness take control. I didn't even try to stop him, not after what they had taken from me.

No one knew what she was to me. But my magic knew, and my magic was going mad.

I was going mad. I would get her back.

"You truly believe that nonsense don't you?" The man at the end was practically wetting himself at the power behind my voice, while the other two were still stubbornly presenting themselves to the slaughter.

Fine.

Living or dead I heaped them together, binding them with my magic as they began to scream in pain, the barbs of magic digging into them like hot wire. I let them hurt, I let them scream, my father's laugh echoing in my head as my magic screamed for more. Screamed to find her.

It was the one at the end who broke first.

"He will have taken her to them" he said, his voice broken in a sob. "Just like Hikari, just like the woman from the train."

I could tell by the way the other two were looking at him that he had revealed some massive secret. I stepped forward, towering over the three, letting the screams of the prisoners behind me darken everything.

"Who are they?" I asked, this time all three of them shook their heads.

"Ry, you are letting him get too loud," Wyn hissed as she stepped up to me, sliding her hand to the side and slamming the three men into the orb alongside the screaming men and women. "You know I will never say no to a good bit of torture... but not when he is in charge."

She faded off, shaking her head and glancing toward the writhing Kyō.

"Shut him up, Ry," she pleaded, squeezing my arm once.

"I agree," a voice said from behind me, the soft-voiced woman barely audible over the screams. "You are better than this."

Wyn and I turned in unison, facing a woman with a hood pulled so far over her face I probably wouldn't have recognized her.

I wouldn't have, if it wasn't for a very nauseous Thom standing behind her.

"We will find her." Was all she said.

CHAPTER 40
RYLAND

Although all of the Kyō were still restrained under the liquid snakes of my magic, all of them staring at Jos and I, the look in their eyes made it clear that they knew exactly who she was. The Oheň.

The one they wanted more than anything. I had a feeling, looking at the anger in their eyes, that attempting to capture her would lead to an honorable death. I wasn't even going to let them try; every time their magic sparked, the binds I had covered them with sent it right back into them. They all kept yelping and jumping as though I had trapped them in a bug zapper.

Wyn and Thom might be guarding them, but they were more for show until more Skříteks from Imdalind could get here and transport them to the underground prison.

"You shouldn't have come here," I spoke low as I turned back to Joclyn, placing myself firmly between Joclyn and the restrained prisoners, as if I alone could serve as adequate protection, or as if Jos couldn't take care of herself.

I knew both were foolish.

"My sight said otherwise," she returned, giving me a sidelong smile before taking a drink from the mug she held. "You are the one person they are looking for, Jos, showing your faces to these nutcases was not smart." I reached towards her, placing my hands on her shoulders.

"Right now, it is not my safety that I am worried about," she looked at me with a twisted grimace, the same one she would give me when we were kids and I started complaining about silly things, like only getting five thousand dollars in allowance money that month. I dropped my arms and sighed.

"I know I lost control, but..." I hesitated, my heart pounding as I stared at her, wondering if I should tell her. No, that wasn't going to help anything right now. "They have Míra."

She nodded, "How did you get her here and how on earth did you lose her."

"I have no idea how she got here, Jos," I said, trying to keep my voice level as I ran my hand through my hair. More sparks erupted from the prisoners, the sounds followed by screams and snickers from both Wyn and Joclyn.

"You must have seen something..."

I gave her a look, "You say that like I'm the one that can see into the future, Jos. You know that no one can control her. We didn't see her until suddenly she was there in the middle of a war. I have no idea how she followed our Stutter, the girl is an enigma..."

"The power she holds makes it that way," Joclyn interrupted, as if I needed the reminder. "It's amazing she hasn't just Stuttered back here."

"She can't." I hesitated, resisting the urge to run my hand through my hair again. "She was unconscious."

A shadow of anger crossed through the light silver of

Joclyn's eyes before it faded into concern, and I was sure I looked the same. My heart felt as though it was going to beat out of my chest just thinking of her like that.

"Do I want to know?"

"Yes actually," I glanced back at the pile of prisoners, the way they were arranged suddenly reminding me of the alley in Prague, of all the dead soldiers my father had reanimated, and the little girl we had thought we had rescued from them. The child who had just vanished.

That was before we knew she was working for my father. Before I had felt her magic for the first time. Before she had killed...

I stopped the thought like one would a freight train, the emotions rolling over me as I pulled my focus from the smug desperation of the prisoners and to Wyn, the woman clearly losing her patience with having to play prison warden.

"She pulled me through a Stutter," I finished, looking back at Joclyn as her jaw slowly began to drop, her eyes going wide.

"But that's..." Her shock swallowed her words, a glazed look taking over her features; I half expected her eyes to dip to black.

"Impossible," I finished for her, shaking my head once.

I took another glance back to everyone behind us but this time Wyn gave me a look that was pure worry. While the prisoners didn't seem too fussed one way or another, Mr. Smug-Smile was still looking right at me, the gleam in his eyes enough of a warning to start a war.

If we weren't already in one.

Grabbing Joclyn's arm, I gently guided her away, moving the two of us deeper into the cave and toward the large crack that had broken through the floor. Our movements gained some curious looks from Michel's Chosen as they packed up what was left of their belongings to go to their new home.

Was there no privacy here?

"Screw it," I grumbled, casting a shield around us and dropping us from view.

"Do you think she is gaining control?" Jos asked the moment the shield had snapped into place.

She didn't need to say anything more for me to understand what she was talking about.

"Whatever was separating her magic from Edmund's is definitely slipping, but we already knew that would happen. His magic is too strong, and her emotions are too volatile, they ignite against each other like gasoline and an open flame." I forced myself to look at Joclyn, no matter how much I wanted to look away. "We have seen signs of this for a while. She doesn't realize it, I think she just thinks she is getting older and therefore getting stronger. She isn't around the other Chosen her age enough to know the difference."

"So we have an unconscious little girl who holds some of the most wicked magic in the world, taken by a group who may or may not be attacking us in some sort of bid for power," she twisted her face up in confusion. "Does that about sum it up?"

"You are missing a few key elements," I began, looking up to see Wyn and Thom strolling towards us, hand-in-hand.

The security detail from Imdalind must have arrived.

"First," I said quickly, dropping the shield and widening it to allow Wyn and Thom to join us. "It's a bit more than just some bid for power. The Kyō think they are chosen..."

"But they are," Jos said, looking between Wyn and I.

"Not Chosen like we call it, chosen by God or something."

"Yeah, except Edmund's the God, and the four of us are some kind of angel Gods," Wyn said, filling in the gaps in one quick breath. "Did you get to the part where they want to worship us and harvest our magic?"

"Harvest our magic?" Both Jos and Thom erupted in unison, their looks fanning between confusion and disgust.

"Don't ask me how they do it," I said, just the image of the room we had almost been trapped in twisted my stomach, the memory of greyed bodies fueling me with both anger and disgust. "It's some kind of electrical system. They are pulling magic out of unhealed Chosen, turning it into energy."

"Like his walking stick," Wyn whispered as we slowly pieced it together. I nodded, the waves of silver magic that had rippled from him suddenly made sense. That, along with what I had assumed was nothing more than a bullet, was more like concentrated magic.

Pulled from hundreds of Chosen.

It was all I could do to restrain the shiver.

"So, we have somehow lost the last vestige of Edmund's magic to a bunch of freaks who are going to harvest it and turn it into a weapon?" Thom always had a way of summing things up.

"Yep," Wyn replied, any attempt at sounding positive about the whole thing fell flat and she sighed. "Best case scenario they will just worship her for a hundred years."

No one found the joke funny, and it even gained her a look from Thom.

"No," I said, crossing my arms over my chest as though the action would release some of the tension that was tightening through my shoulders. If anything it just made it worse. "They are going to use her to get to Joclyn. It's you they want."

"Explain," Jos commanded, and without missing a beat, Wyn plunged into it, rambling about everything that had happened.

I stood still, my heart thundering in my chest as I watched the Kyō slowly being removed from my bind. The powerful Skříteks debilitated each of them as they removed them, clipping both magic and mind as they led them out of the cave in a line of crippled religious zealots.

They all looked so defeated; they all looked ready to give in.

All but the man I had tried to speak to. The man who would rather *die with honor.*

He looked right at us.

Well, not right at us because he had no idea where we had gone, but he stared toward where we had all vanished, his eyes narrowed as if he was just waiting to make his move.

"They are going to use her against the SSU," I suddenly said loudly, unsure if Wyn had even gotten to the part about the Kyō and their need to capture a god. "What has the woman we captured said?"

I turned around to face them, Wyn glowering at me, obviously upset at having been interrupted.

"Still nothing valuable," Thom said, his deep voice rolling as he stepped closer to where Wyn stood. "She still just keeps mumbling in Ukrainian, something about the Tykha Shist´, although I have no idea who they are," he clarified, the phrase sparking through me familiarly again. This time, however, I knew where I had heard it before.

The man on the riverbank. The Kyō's warning just hours before.

"The Silent Six," I translated quietly, turning back to the man who still stared at us. "I heard about them on the radio. They lead the SSU. Which, if I am putting this together, is who the Kyō is gearing up to fight. It's why Michel sold us out."

Everything was falling like dominoes, and the more they fell the more everything seemed to shatter.

"Explain," Jos commanded, but I didn't turn. I was still staring at the man, my horror building.

"It wasn't the Kyō who attacked us in the alley, or on the riverbank," I said, still looking at the man. "That was the SSU or the Tykha Shist ´ or whatever they are called."

"What does this have to do with Míra?" Wyn asked, and I turned again.

"Because the Kyō are going to use Míra to attack the SSU, they told us as much in their house on Trafalgar Square. They wanted to use us against them 'to destroy their enemies' they said. They wanted to capture their own God... because the SSU has one."

Everything was growing tighter as the words kept tumbling out of me, as everything kept fitting together. I stared at Jos, her confusion growing as my heart threatened to explode.

"They have their own God?" Wyn whispered, her eyes wide as she looked from me, to Joclyn. "The Gods from the photos. From the wanted posters."

Joclyn's eyes widened as everything clicked into place, even Thom's hand flew to his mouth in shock.

"The SSU has Ilyan."

I barely caught her as she fell to her knees.

CHAPTER 41

JOCLYN

This time we had brought everyone to Imdalind for the council.

It was always a risk to have everyone come here seeing how many people were still in the city rebuilding, and reporting, or just wandering looking for signs of aliens. But given the current situation bringing all of the 'aliens' here was worth it.

We had found him.

We had found Ilyan. I had even heard that woman talk about him hours before. We had been so close. I guess, in a way, we were even closer now.

After years of searching, he was within my grasp. If I knew exactly where, I would just Stutter in and save his ass, but I didn't. Besides, he apparently was behind an army of Trpaslíks and Chosen. We were going to need help.

"Are you sure we have to wait to get Míra? She's just a kid," Ryland hissed to me through the corner of his mouth from where we stood on the dais, the crowd still filtering in.

"I'm not sure of anything, Ryland. I would have thought

you would have picked up on that by now." I grinned at him and pulled back my sleeve to pick at the ribbon on my wrist. It had been itching a bit lately. Maybe it knew we had found Ilyan, too.

Okay, no, that was just weird.

"Oh good, does that mean you are going back on your attempt at a reverse coup?" Ry's eyes flashed dangerously, but I just smiled at him.

Okay, I grinned, and maybe I chuckled a bit. It was ridiculous how light and free everything felt all of a sudden. All of that power and determination to save my mate had cracked away the last of my misery.

"I stand by what I said before. You would make a great King." I was still grinning, but he just rolled his eyes at me.

"You're right. You really don't know anything." Leave it to Ry to know just how to push my buttons.

I slugged him in the arm. "Hey! I said I wasn't *sure* of anything. Not that I didn't *know* anything."

"I don't see any difference," he laughed and slugged me in the arm right back. If this had been six years ago we would have been racing to his closet for nerf guns right about now. Maybe I still would.

Except Ryland didn't look quite as light and airy as I did. He didn't have to tell me why.

"We will find Míra, Ry," I said, weaving my arm through his and pulling him into me. His brow furrowed as he looked down at me before looking back at the far door, so fast he might as well have given himself whiplash.

"My sight is clear that everything is connected. Míra. Ovailia. Ilyan. The SSU. We find one, we will find the other. We know more about where Ilyan is, so we are starting with that. With the Trpaslíks and trained Chosen on their side it's going to take all of us to go in against the SSU. We need to convince them today, and then we can move." None of this was new information, and I hoped it would have calmed Ry down, but he just stiffened underneath me, his eyes still focused forward as the last of the stragglers entered the large hall.

"I sure hope you are right," Ryland sighed, the sound laced with panic, "because it sure feels like we are opening Pandora's box."

"We probably are," I shrugged and he spun to me, eyes wide. "Calm down. Míra will be fine."

I made sure to use a grandma voice for that, patting his arm the way my grandmother used to do. Now he was really looking at me as though I had lost it.

"She will be fine," I hissed at him, turning to where Wyn and Thom were closing the large doors to the room. I guess everyone was here. "But it wouldn't be the first time that we collapsed something and threw the world into disarray."

"That is really not very reassuring, Jos."

I knew it wasn't, saying it aloud was already turning my previously good mood into a topsy turvy roller coaster ride. Maybe we needed to slow this ride down a bit. We didn't know enough about the SSU to just barge in and rescue him though. We had to be careful. If I sent in people first--

"Are you guys ready?" Wyn asked as she jumped onto the dais in front of me. "There are a few people from the American districts that would prefer not to stay long. I guess things are getting bad there."

"They are getting bad everywhere," I mumbled, looking over to where the Americans had clustered in the corner, heads down as they tapped the screen of a cell phone. I would have to track them down later and get a detailed account of what was happening there.

It's not like I had gone into my ivory tower to mope, but we had been so focused on saving the Chosen that everything else had gone to shit around us.

I had a bad feeling that the time for me to 'fix it' was here.

"Go ahead, Ry," I said with a wave of my hand, still focusing on the Americans as Ry went through the usual sayings, and everyone bowed and clapped and accepted me as their Queen and Ry as my second.

"No surprises this time, okay?" Ryland whispered as I took his hand, finishing the ceremony and initiating the start of council.

"No promises." I grinned at him and stepped away, already raising my hands, ready to make my plea for us all to head in after the SSU when a soft gasp echoed from the corner of the hall, the sound instantly followed by hissed conversations and what I could have sworn was crying.

I looked back, but Ry and Wyn seemed just as confused as I did.

Another gasp, and a swear that I didn't often hear anymore. The Americans.

My heart dropped.

"Everything okay over there?" I called in English, knowing full well I sounded nothing like a Queen.

"No, I'm sorry my Queen," one of the Americans scuttled forward, bowing as tears fell down his face. I knew I was supposed to stay up on the dais and be a Queen and all that, but right then I could care less. I jumped off the raised platform and ran right to the guy who was already pushing his cell phone towards me. A single word text was at the top, followed by what looked to be a news story.

'Run!' Was in all caps, followed by the story 'Kyō takes White House. Extermination order given.'

My heart was in my throat, my stomach in my toes as I turned to Ry, our eyes locking as everything inside of me broke.

There was no way I was going to convince everyone to go after the SSU now. We had bigger wars to wage, and we couldn't put it off anymore.

CHAPTER 42

ILYAN

"Don't try to speak," Kaye said, her voice soft in my ear as I moaned and rolled over, the cool slab of cement I lay on painful against my joints. "It will just hurt more."

"What happened," I moaned out, the words burning so much I almost screamed.

"I told you not to speak, I'll explain..." Kaye was firm, angry even, as I lay on my back, blinking myself back into existence. Blinking my brain on...

Everything ached, my head most of all. It buzzed as though it had been set on fire, my temples pulsing as I stared into a hard cement ceiling. This wasn't my room...

Kaye's face was lined with worry as she and her mother stood by my side, focused on my arm and a minor burn there. I watched them curiously, my drugged thoughts trying to piece together what was going on.

"We have to be gone before she gets back. My mother is prepping you..." Kaye began, giving her mother a look before she turned back to me, pushing her hair out of her eyes.

Hair that was shorter than the last time I saw her.

The panic swelled again and I grabbed her arm, pulling her closer as my eyes screamed for answers.

"You've been out for a week, we've been trying to lower your dosage, to get you to wake up. Looks like it worked," she sighed, gently squeezing my hand, her thumb rubbing against my skin.

"I still don't know how smart this was. You might be better off sleeping through this," Katenka said, her voice more pained and haggard than I remembered it.

"Sleep through what?" I asked, throat still burning.

Her sad eyes dug into mine as she rubbed what looked like an alcohol pad over my arm. I tried to shift to see what was going on, but the drugs made it hard to move, everything around me swimming in an awkward dance.

"Don't worry about that. We will be getting you soon, and we need you awake for that," Kaye provided. "I am working to learn all the skills a nurse has, so I can make my papers official and we can get out of here."

"Do you have a plan?" The burn was so bad I began to cough, sending them both into a panic.

"I can't..." Kaye began, looking between me and her mother as some internal battle raged. "We can't stay here."

I wasn't sure if she was clarifying or including.

She sighed and tapped her foot. The motion wasn't in frustration, however, I could see her eyes narrow in contemplation, trying to decide something.

"We don't have time, Kaye," her mother whispered, now moving to clean up an array of knives and needles.

"I can't just leave him..."

"You have to," her mother snapped, talking about me as though I was not here. The tone filled me with agitation and I slammed my hand against the floor, the loud noise making both women jump.

"You need to be careful," Kaye pleaded, wrapping her hand around my tight fist. "I don't know what they are going to do to you now that you are awake. I can't take the risk of you telling them..."

"She's coming," Katenka hissed, my arm pinching as she inserted a needle.

"Who..." I gasped, even as I heard the progression of feet, the stomping of boots. I already knew.

"Nastya Klotz," Kaye hissed as she pressed herself into the shadowed wall. "You need to stay strong," she whispered, her bright eyes digging into me. "I will tell you everything later. But now, stay strong. Don't use your magic. Don't let them break you, Jan."

"That's not my name..."

Before she could reply, several loud alarms went off at once, a bank of machines near where Kaye's mother had been working firing up as she flipped them back on. Lights flashed, buzzers sounded, and the ever present beeping of my electronic heartbeat sped into overdrive as more alarms began to echo to me from the hall.

'Code Red, Room E, Code Red, Room E.'

Women and men yelled in Ukrainian before the door slammed open, a severe-looking man with a yellow star on his chest barging in, gun already pointed right at me. Confusion painted his face as he caught sight of me, hands wrapped around the rail as I attempted to sit up, eyes wide as I stared at him.

"Komandyr!" he yelled behind him as he cocked his gun, threat and warning screaming from the tip of the barrel. "Get Ms. Klotz! He's awake!"

The Cleaners announcement sent more panic through

the halls, the sound of voices and feet overwhelming the alarms of the machines.

The man kept his gun trained on me as he stepped forward, looking down the sight in a clear willingness to shoot me if I did anything out of the ordinary.

I couldn't even if I tried. My mind still spun under the influence of the drugs that pumped through my veins, my magic feeling like a slow-moving sludge; the muck bubbled with each step he took.

"Well, well," Nastya snarled as she walked right up to me, hands wrapping around the rail of the bed as she leaned over. Hovering above me like a fly.

Her face was pinched together in joy, the look accentuated by the way her hair was slicked back into a severe bun. The look complimented her posture, the way she moved. The way her eyes glared at me with both lust and murder.

Nastya.

"I am so glad to see you alive. I have been waiting to have some fun. To get some more answers," she sneered, the devil peering from behind her eyes before she turned from me, rushing past Kaye's mother who still cowered beside the door.

"You have 5 minutes," Nastya said before she vanished, leaving five soldiers to rush into the room.

The soldiers stood in a line, guns drawn, the tips aimed at either myself or Katenka.

"Move!" one of the soldiers said with a snap, pressing the tip of his gun into the small of her back.

No wonder Kaye hadn't wanted to tell me anything. She was protecting her mom as much as she was protecting me.

My magic gurgled as she walked toward me, her hands shaking as she opened my shirt, quickly removing the monitors from my scarred chest and arm. She said nothing as she moved my IV bag to the tall stand on the bed, and covered my aching arm with some foul smelling brown liquid. I only caught a whiff of iodine before I saw her push a syringe into my IV, the same cold rushing through my hand, my arm, spreading all through me.

The sensation was more intense than before and I gasped, my body sagging under my own weight as I collapsed into the pillows.

"I'm sorry, Jan" Katenka whispered to me as the soldiers came forward, the sound of their steps sounding far away in my now spinning confusion. "Be strong."

The words sounded like a broken memory as the hands of the men began to wrap around me, rough fingers hitting hard against my wrists and ankles before they were replaced by familiar padded bands.

The pressure on my joints increased as the straps were tightened, the sensation pulling as something cold was placed against my temples, the same bulbs from before immediately following.

I jerked at the addition, looking to the woman who I was now being wheeled away from, a deep apology in her eyes.

"No," I growled, the word a burn as it slurred past drugs and the raw skin of my throat. "No."

Attempting to fight, I pressed against the restraints, trying to call my magic to me, to awaken the deep tar that had settled in my heart. Nothing happened. Refusing to stop fighting, I pulled against the bands, watching the hospital lights above me flicker on and off, just as they had on that very first day.

And then they were gone.

The clean walls and the smell of antiseptic were gone. The hospital was gone.

A strip of fluorescent lights hung from the ceiling by fraying wires, swinging and swaying as the entire space flickered in movement and shadow. Paint peeled off of walls in large chunks that dipped down toward the floor, large cobwebs running from them to the wall, to the ceiling and back again.

A scream and a cackle echoed through the hall, the sound sending more fear through me as I jerked, fighting against the restraints.

"What is going on," I attempted to demand, the man I was in my memory attempting to break through. He didn't get far. My words were slurred, the tone so deranged that I sounded more like the laughing woman and less like the powerful man I was.

"There he goes again!" the cackling voice sang, the tune grating against my paranoia. "Goes to burn. Goes to bleed."

I attempted to turn my head to the sound. The halo I had been attached to restricted my movement but I still saw the lines of windows, the dirty panes smeared with streaks of red and brown. Seeing them only added to the smell that was assaulting me.

Windows sped by, each one filled with a glimmer of maniacal eyes and crying victims. Their faces pressed against the glass, begging for food and water. Screaming for help. Men, women, I even saw a flash of the sad eyes of a child.

They all pulled at me, pulled at the deep sludge of magic inside of me. I felt the heat in my skin, felt the pulse of power in my hands, but nothing came. Any ability to control it was gone.

I didn't have the power, I didn't have the control to get out of here.

Not yet.

My heart constricted as we turned a corner, two of the soldiers falling back as the other two continued on, pushing me through one set of double doors and then another. The space grew darker as the swinging lights were replaced by the flicker of a lone light bulb.

Even that disappeared as more doors swung behind us with a heavy thunk, taking me right into the room that I was sure I would die in.

I recognized the large wall of glass, the room behind still filled with black-suited men, their lapels sporting a rainbow of stars now. But beyond that, everything was unrecognizable. I hadn't been in here long, but I didn't remember there being so much blood. I didn't remember the smell of bleach and iron being as assaulting.

"There he is," Nastya cooed, as though she was speaking to a long-lost nephew. "My little pet, right on time."

The bed came to a stop, and with an electric whirl, the entire thing rotated on a point as it lifted me to face her. The wide bands were so tight I could barely move.

She was so close I could see the tint of red in her eyes, smell the tobacco and mint on her breath. She smiled again, showing me a straight line of white teeth before another white-clad nurse began shifting tubes and hoses around, placing new monitors on my chest. The room filled with the accelerated pulse of my heartbeat as the bed began to twist, the room rotating as I was moved to face the wall of people.

"What is going on?" I asked, the words slow and slurred which only made the woman smile more, the purple star glinting at me.

"Why, we are going to have a little fun," she cooed, the voice and smile not fitting her as she played with me.

466

"No." I tried to yell, tried to fight against the bands, but again nothing happened.

"Now, now, don't fret. You are my little pet, Jan. You've been so good for me. I want to show you just how good."

She smiled, the muffled sounds of laughter coming from behind the glass as Nastya turned to the audience, the men looking thoroughly entertained by the conversation.

They stood there, as close to the glass as they could without pressing themselves against it, all dressed in the same black suits, with the rainbow of sinister stars on their lapels. It was the only color amongst them, between the white and browns of skin and hair and the black suits, there was nothing else. It was as flat and dead as the rest of this place, as what was waiting for me.

"We have developed a way to use your power. To use you as a weapon," Nastya said, her tone filling in some nefarious plot that I wasn't sure I wanted to hear. I no longer had a choice, however. "I have made that magnificent body of yours do the unimaginable."

Nastya paused, the same look of lust and need coming into her eyes. But it wasn't me that she wanted. It was whatever was inside of me.

"I wonder," she continued, her intent focused on skipping over my outburst, "if you want to see what your body can do? I wonder what will happen if you are forced to see…"

She smiled at me before nodding again to the nurse behind me, the bed twisting and lowering as everything drifted in and out of focus until I was left staring at the ceiling, the peeling paint splattered with blood, dripping with water and who knows what else.

The electrodes attached to the halo began to buzz with

electricity, as she smiled, snapping bright blue gloves onto her hand.

I tensed, fighting again, even though I knew it was a mistake.

"You can't do this," I yelled, glad my voice had some force behind it. The drugs must be wearing off. I wasn't sure if that was a good or bad thing.

I could speak, but I would be feeling everything. It was something I didn't want given the large scalpel Nastya had just been handed.

"I assure you I can," she said as she inspected the tip of the tiny knife, the dirty silver glinting dangerously in the dim light. "I told you before, I own you, and whatever is inside of you is mine. I will take control of it. Whether you are awake or asleep means nothing to me. At least when you are asleep you don't fight."

I pulled against the restraints harder as she stepped closer, the knife at the ready.

"I would say I hope it doesn't hurt," she teased, running her gloved finger over the dark brown fluid Kaye's mother had put on my arm minutes before, "but I really hope it does."

The point of her scalpel dug into my arm, bright red blood pouring over my skin before I began to scream. The same pain as before overtook me as she ran the knife toward my elbow in a straight line of widening red that poured over my skin and splattered against the floor.

"Watch this," Nastya growled, grabbing my chin as she pulled my face toward my arm, my screams turning to whimpers as the pain began to leave, as I watched the skin slowly knit itself back together.

I couldn't look away, I couldn't look past what I was seeing. I had dreamed of healing Joclyn, I had healed Kaye.

Now it happened on my own flesh. I could feel my magic, I could feel the heat pool around my arm, but I didn't control it. Whatever ability was inside of me did it all on its own.

"Now," Nastya growled, clearly not talking to me as the electricity buzzed and pulsed through the electrodes.

Little pops of electricity made me jump and jerk as they ran through me, a new pain joining the first. A scream ripped from me at the agony, my eyes shifting into the back of my head as the same darkness threatened to take me.

She wouldn't let it.

"No! Look!" she screamed in my ears as she shook me, the same spurts of electricity continuing to pulse through my body, through my bones, and sparking in my arm.

In my arm.

She cackled in my ear, my eyes widening in confusion as the power I had seen so often in dreams began sparking from the open gash in my arm. Fireworks of color sparked between the still open ends of my flesh, zig-zagging like bursts of lightning until they erupted into the air in a burst of painful color.

"You see," she hissed, moving my focus to her, her fingers rough against my jaw as she caressed it. I jerked away at the touch, but she held tighter, refusing to let me look anywhere else. "I have already figured out how to control your power. If you won't give it to me, then I will just use you. Awake. Asleep. I do not care. I own you. I control this beautiful weapon.... I control you."

Her words drifted away as her hands did, shifting down my neck and over my bare chest. Her cold unwanted touch moved over my scars, tracing the lines as Joclyn had done...

Joclyn.

I jerked at the touch, but my exhausted body barely moved. Instead, I sagged against the bed, my mind filling with thoughts and dreams of her. Thoughts that created an escape that was so very wanted right now.

"Now, are you ready?" she asked, her question grabbing my focus as much as the glint on the scalpel she once again twirled before me.

"Ready for what?" My confusion was dead, my mind already drifting away to something that wasn't rooted in so much pain.

"Ready to fight for me? Ready to bend yourself to me," she clarified, pressing the tip of the scalpel into my arm again. I winced at the pain, but this time my scream never came, only a soft whimper as tears began to roll down my cheek.

I was crying. From everything I had seen about myself, I was not the type to cry. I was not the type to just give in. I was trapped, but I knew I had been in a position like this before, that even with the drugs and the torture, I could control my magic.

That I could destroy her.

I knew I could.

I knew I had the power.

I couldn't give in so easily.

Even if right now it was only a glare, only a heavy jaw and the choice to take the pain.

"No." The word broke out in a snap, loud and confident, and obviously just what she wanted to hear.

"Wonderful."

She nodded to the nurse as the scalpel plunged into my body, the electric shock turning up to eleven.

CHAPTER 43

ILYAN

Nastya's machine buzzed, electricity bursting through my veins, and running over my skin in waves that made me convulse. Even in my dreams, the torturous energy ran through me in crackles of lightning that melted my memories into a blur.

A teen falling from a cliff face as we climbed, his haunted face screaming up to me as he plummeted.

A woman in a forest, dressed in an elegant gown as she seduced me.

Myself tied to a tree as Ryland sobbed before me, a man who could have been his much older twin yelling at him before Ryland plunged a dagger into my side. Ryland's mournful scream followed me in an echo before the memory faded to the same woman from before. A joyful laugh painted her youthful face as she sat with the towering man that I had seen follow me before, all signs of the seductress gone.

The seductress returned with a bright flash of red, the same woman clinging to me as she begged, her words nearly indiscernible over the sound of electricity and magic that rumbled through the dreams.

"He killed her!" Her sobs exploded as she fell to the ground, the embroidered tunic I wore shifting under the change in pressure.

One after another they came, moving in double-time as my tortured mind released them, each one growing more and more twisted and terrified. I tried to hold onto them, to slow them down, to remember. But my mind was caged. Trapped with the electric explosions of magic and torture.

Forced to watch confusing moments of my own life.

"No!"

Desperation clung to the word, the emotion lingering against my soul as the new memory came, that of myself sitting next to the same green-eyed man I had seen destroy the blonde woman.

The same man I had seen chant inside of the cave.

The dark-haired man sat beside me, twisting his hands in agitation as he bounced on the edge of the cement fountain. The town square stretched before us, but everything about it had changed. The cathedral was built, the long spires towering over us in their journey toward the sky. The surrounding buildings were the same, but the architecture was different, there weren't as many rough-hewn rocks. If it wasn't for the familiarity of the place, and my mind whispering a million other memories I couldn't see, I wouldn't have recognized it.

"Perhaps he will not grant me her hand," the man said, his voice distant and far away as my tortured mind distorted it.

"I believe he will, Sain." The mention of his name sent a jolt of anger through me that didn't quite match the memory.

I felt the emotion, but I only continued to sit in eager anticipation, watching the man's hands writhe together. "My father is a man of reason..."

"And I am a worthless Drak," he cut me off, the word known to me, although I did not know why.

Anger mixed with the electricity until my magic sparked in a pop and everything shifted.

"Please, no." My own voice again, the sound distorted. I wasn't sure why I was begging. Shouldn't I be laughing?

Something told me I should be laughing.

Instead of my own defiant chuckle, however, another laugh responded to my plea, the sound followed by a touch that pulled me right back to reality.

"Please?" Nastya sneered, my vision leaving the flashes of memory as she slid back into focus, her three heads shaking and jumping around in front of me. "Are you begging me to stop, Jan?"

"Please," I gasped again, the taste of blood in my mouth. I spit it out, attempting to let the glob fall right on her face, but I couldn't get enough strength and it instead dribbled down my chin. She laughed as it slid over my skin.

"My, my," she cooed, the false concern barely clear through her mockery. "Do you need some help there, Jan?"

"That's not my name..."

"What is your name, then?"

Attempting to avoid her and the blood-stained cloth she held, I pulled to the side, head rocking violently as everything began to spin. Windows, door, muck-covered walls, they all blended together and for one minute I thought I saw her.

There, standing in a corner.

I saw her, ready to save me.

"Silnỳ..." I began, needing to call out to her, needing her to protect me this time.

She was right there. She could protect me. She was the Silnỳ.

No, she was just Joclyn. I didn't know what that other name meant, I didn't know what any of it meant.

"Silnỳ?" Nastya asked, the beautiful name sounding like poison as it dripped from her. "What is that? Is that your name?"

She asked the question and I cried as the electricity that surged through the bulbs at my temples made the emotion worse. I jumped in expectation of another jolt.

Luckily, one of the three Nastya's held up her hand, stopping whatever was about to happen as she stepped right up to me, her face inches from my own.

"Is it what you are? Is it where you are from? A city? A planet?" She asked the questions in turn, watching me intently with each one before she stopped, eyebrows arching high before she vanished, leaving me staring at the hundreds of men who were swimming behind the glass.

"Now," she said from behind me, and the electricity from her machine exploded.

I screamed at the pressure, at the pain, my spine twisting as it threatened to break, my mouth filling with blood as my teeth clamped down on my tongue, leaving me to writhe.

The torture chamber faded as the electricity pulled me back into a memory, an image of Joclyn and I walking hand in hand over the beach, followed by that man, Sain, from before. An unwanted joy washed over me as I stood beside the two of them. Joclyn turned toward me with a smile, her body flickering to her covered in blood and back again.

The scent of iron and salt followed me back into reality

as the electricity stopped, my heaving breath shaking my body as blood dripped from my mouth and onto my bare feet.

They had moved me again, put me on display.

"No more," I pleaded as my head flopped to the side, giving me a perfect view of the corner of the room, and the beautiful woman who stood there.

My heart pulsed as I heaved in air, the need for her was so strong, but the pain of knowing it wasn't her was stronger.

"Silnỳ," I whispered through my heaving breath, and she smiled, the use of the name confusing me. It wasn't her name. It wasn't who she was. She was "Jos..."

"Is it her?" Nastya snapped, interrupting me as she shoved one of the many images at me, the photograph of Joclyn and I fighting together beautiful to me now.

Beautiful because she wasn't just a mystery that I longed for. Beautiful because I knew her. Because I knew her strength. Because I knew her soul.

I stared at it as her joy and determination filled me, listening to my breath, listening to my heartbeat. The tortured organ pounded against my chest, screaming that I couldn't stay here.

I couldn't put up with this anymore. It wasn't me, and even though I didn't know all of who I was. I knew that.

I could feel that in the way my muscles tensed and my magic flared, the slow sludge barely responded, but still, it was there.

"Silnỳ."

Nastya's smile spread wide as she stepped back, looking from me to the photograph as if she had won the jackpot.

As if she had won her prize.

The slow drudge of my magic dripped into my fingers at

that look, it swelled and buzzed, wanting to explode. Trying to. I kept it there. I held it in, heart pulsing from the effort as I willed it to grow.

"Hello, Silnỳ," Nastya cooed to the photograph, her fingers running over the image gently.

Caressing her face.

The slow sludge of my magic sparked in its own anger. In its own need to protect her.

An angry flood of power was expelled from me in one prompted burst of white light. The restraints turned to ash, a shower of grey falling to the ground as I did, my legs barely able to hold my weight.

Screams echoed around the room, the men, the technician, everyone erupting in panic as the weapon Nastya was perfecting escaped. Their anger fueled me in a way I hadn't expected, the power roaring underneath my flesh.

Releasing the power in a rush, everything began to shake as a strong wind circled the room, my magic erupting around me in fireworks of color. The wind grew into a torrent, explosions firing alongside my magic as light fixtures broke the bed, machines slammed into walls. With a twist of my wrist, the wind shifted, my magic picking up the demented woman, lifting her off the ground and sending her into the glass wall with a slap. The windows cracked beneath her at the impact, the men behind the glass ran for the exit, eyes flashing between me and the door in obvious fear.

With one pulse, I flung her around to face me, limp body sagging in the air as I held her there. The genuine fear I had expected to see was replaced by a mask of pure joy.

"Beautiful, Jan," she said as she smiled, her response only fueling my eruptive magic more. "Beautiful."

Before she could even get the final word out, I let my

power fly free, the magic shooting from me in a ribbon of purple that slapped against her face, knocking the smile from it and sending her screaming to the ground.

Her pain blossomed through me in an exhilarated joy and I hit her again, this time in the chest. The colors of my attacks sparked in the tiny room, casting the dark corners in colorful shadows that only made it, and its blood-stained walls, that much more sinister.

"Leave her alone," I screamed as I attacked her again, and again. The dark strips of my magic cut through her like knives, the action causing more screaming. More yelling. Until it didn't.

Until there was only silence.

My magic froze in expectation, ready to see her dead on the floor. My heart swelled at the possibility, only to shatter as she began to laugh, the delirious sound echoing hauntingly around the space.

Ice ran through my veins as she began to pick herself up, joints twisting as her head snapped to me. I lifted my hand to her, ready to end her. To end all of this and get out of here.

The magic never came, however, it stuck inside of me like sludge, held back by the ice that ran through me. It was not the ice of fear as I had thought it was. It was not the cold chill I would get before death.

It was the ice of her control, of the chill of her power as it ran through me.

As it controlled me.

Her magic.

The icy power surged as I crumpled to the ground, realizing just how much of a fool I had been.

"Did you really think you would escape," Nastya

sneered as she crawled her way over to me, a wide trail of red left behind. "Did you really think you could end me?"

She was inches from me, the tiny cuts on her face healing over as she stared at me, specks of blood flying over my face with every word.

"Yes," I hissed, the word slurred behind my destroyed tongue. "I will."

"You foolish man. You have only made things worse for yourself," she taunted, the acid in her voice making my heart seize. "You gave me her name. Now I am going to find her, and kill her in front of you."

I was sure she expected the same reaction she had gotten before, but instead of the outrage, instead of the panic, I only laughed. The sound had the same effect on Nastya as it had on me, and her anger grew. It grew past the awed fury and became a torrent.

"Destroy him," she hissed as her magic rushed me, electricity surging through me as she clamped her hands against my head.

Although I tried to call my magic up to numb the pain, nothing responded. Nothing came, and all of her magic hit me like a live wire, destroying me. Everything shook and rattled as I screamed, jolts of fire moving through me.

Her laughter followed me into the dark, to a tiny girl with long hair and the darkest eyes I had ever seen. She ran down a beach, her feet working hard as she sprinted through sand and brush, laughing as a man with short brown hair chased her. The woman I had seen before followed behind them, smiling as her bright red dress blew in the wind.

"What do you wish to do, my lord?" A hushed voice buzzed behind me from where we hid in the brush, the hulking form of the man who always seemed to be following me only slightly recognizable in the shadow. I didn't turn to him, I remained focused on the family, my heart constricting painfully.

"There is no sign of loyalty from my brother?" I asked, that same regal sound resounding through my voice.

My focus shifted to the man on the beach as I spoke, the same bright blue eyes I had cementing the familial relationship. The tension in my heart grew, and I got a distinct impression that something bad was about to happen. That these three were in trouble.

"None, my lord." the man beside me whispered, shifting his weight in obvious discomfort. "And none from Wynifred either."

"You are sure your intel is correct?" I hissed, my heart restricting more as I saw the little girl's eyes.

I had known they were black, but this close they were clearly as dark as her mother's. I was amazed she was as old as she was, that he hadn't destroyed her yet.

It could only mean two things; Wynifred was protecting her daughter, or my father was using them all.

It was the latter that brought us here.

"We don't have anyone on the inside, this came to me by pure coincidence," the man said, ducking lower in the brush as they got closer.

"She is a child; it is worth the risk, either way."

My magic stretched away from me, although I knew it was dangerous. If they moved much closer Wynifred would sense us. No matter how well we were hidden she would feel us. I wasn't interested in being burned to a crisp today.

The thought confused me until her eyes snapped to me, her anger clear as she scowled right into the brush we were hidden in.

"Fly, Talon," I hissed to the man, his bulky form disappearing.

I, however, stayed still, my magic surging as I lifted myself from the ground, heat beginning to radiate from the sand beneath me.

I smiled at the woman before she rushed to me, reaching the brush just as I too vanished, moving into a black nothing with the slightest pop. The hollow sound echoed as my scream did, rippling from a life so far away I wasn't sure what was real anymore.

I opened my eyes to the same beach I visited every night. It was so similar to the one I had seen moments before. Except the laughter of the child was gone, everyone was gone. It was only the sound of the waves as they crashed nearby, only the hot and cold feel of the breeze, only Joclyn's fingers as they brushed over my face.

"Wake up, my love," she soothed, her voice a calm whisper.

I shivered at her touch, shivered at the breathy whisper of her voice.

"My love," I repeated the phrase with a sigh, reaching up to place my fingers over hers. A desperate part of me wished that she would say my name, that she would give me that tiny piece of who I was, the piece that I was missing.

Hearing myself spoken about in such a way was enough of a treasure. I sighed again at the name, at the touch, and with one swift movement I swept her up, rolling over in the sand as I held her against me.

Nuzzling her neck, I sent her into a fit of giggles as she squirmed, the motion making me laugh right alongside her. Sand was everywhere as we tangled, the joyful laughs ending in a sigh as she lay down on top of me, her head nestling into my collarbone.

"I love you, Joclyn," I whispered, running my hands up and down her back as she settled into me, her breathing moving to match my own.

"I love you," she responded, her fingers moving to run through the stubble of my hair. "Not just in here, either. I love you out there. Your memories show you that. You know that."

"I do."

Joclyn propped herself up to look me in the eyes, so close that for a moment I was sure I was going to get the kiss I had dreamed of for so long, that I was going to feel her lips against mine.

I prepared for it, ready to make the move and steal the kiss I had longed for.

"Then wake up, and find me," Joclyn teased, leaning towards me as my heart accelerated.

"I will," I promised, every nerve ending alive as the sand vanished into hard stone, the sound of the waves faded into screams, and the bliss shifted to agonizing pain.

My deep sigh of relaxation became a shuddering breath of the purest sorrow as the dream left. Although I felt a hand run over my back, I knew it was not hers. It was not the one I wanted.

"Wake up, Jan," Kaye whispered above me as the soft touch turned into more of a shake, the motion hesitant.

"You need to wake up." Her voice broke with desperate tears as the shake became a little more abrasive, the movement a rough rocking now. "Please don't leave again. Please don't give in. We will find her, I promise."

Her tears were falling in earnest now, I could feel them on

my face as the sobs broke her voice up in little gasps. The sound was heart-wrenching, but it was only barely distinguishable from the sound of sobs that were echoing around us.

"Please, Jan," she pleaded, abandoning her focus on my back to clench my hand as she tried to rouse me.

It took all my strength to squeeze her hand back.

She gasped at the pressure, still holding tight to my hands as she shifted her weight, slowly moving my exhausted body over the impossibly hard surface.

"You're alive." I was sure the use of the word was incorrect. "Please be okay. Please."

My head moved as she shifted it into her lap, the odd positioning making my already pained bones twist further and I grunted.

"You're here," she gasped, running her fingers through the short lengths of my hair. "You're alive."

I wasn't sure if she spoke more to me, or to herself, or to whoever was sobbing in the room, but it didn't matter, and right then I didn't care. Her joy at my existence was enough.

My face ached as I slowly began to force my eyes open, the subtle motion sending agony through every tiny muscle from the crown of my head through my neck.

"Hi there, Mr. Blue Eyes," she whispered, her fingers continuing to run over my buzzed hair. I tried to smile at the words, at the exact phrase her mother had used so long ago, but I couldn't make the motion come. I couldn't even drum up enough emotion to do so.

It was only agony, it was only hot tears as they rolled down the side of my face.

Even though my eyes were open, I saw next to nothing. The world that drifted above me was a mass of color, splotches of red obscuring most of it. I could see the shape of Kaye, I could see a stream of light from somewhere above, a blinking light of what I assumed were my monitors off to the side, but everything was a faded mass of color.

"Where am I?" I could barely get the words out, each one stung and burned as the warm sludge of my magic attempted to react.

"They moved you to the north wing," Kaye said, her voice choking with something I didn't recognize. "I don't have much time. They are still trying to get the cameras online after we cut them. I can't be caught in here."

"I don't understand..."

"The north wing. The hall before Nastya's torture chamber," she hesitated. "It's where they keep the ones they use."

She didn't have to elaborate, I already knew. I knew from the hard floor and the smell of urine and mold. I knew because I had heard the sobbing child echo through the halls as I was wheeled by them, same as now.

"I need to get out of here," I groaned, trying in vain to lift my body from her lap.

My agonized body screamed with every attempt, the sound beginning to seep from me as bones and muscles began to twist in threat of breaking, my entire body erupting in waves of electric aftershocks.

I lay back, staring at the peeling paper and swinging light of a new misery. The box in the corner that I had thought was monitoring equipment was only one large box, a grey IV tube trailing from it-- right to me.

"What have they done?"

"You are severely drugged, Jan," Kaye whispered, my head jostling as she shifted her weight, looking at something behind her. "It's something different than what they were using before. A mixture of several different drugs; ethanol, morphine and a few others that have no place in a hospital. I don't know what it will do to you. It has done different things to the others."

She faded off, her words losing some of their power as the honesty behind them dug into me.

"I need to get out of here," I repeated, the words firmer as my vision continued to focus, the red slowly leaving. "We need to get out of here."

"I am working on it," Kaye reassured, placing her hands on either side of my head, looking down at me from above.

"How?"

"I'm working in receiving and I've met some people there," she hesitated, looking around as if she expected someone to be behind her. "They have a plan. Now that you are here I will try to get transferred. I won't be able to come back here until then."

"Until you get transferred?" I asked, she only gave me a single nod in response. "How long? A month?"

She shook her head, "I don't know when I will be able to come back, Jan. It could be a month. It could be a year."

The phrase caught in my chest, swelling into a panic that sent the world spinning. I froze, letting my agonized body sink back into the hard floor.

"I will get back here," she said, squeezing her hand around mine. "I just don't know when. There are some things I need to do first..."

"But you will return." I cut her off, the strength of my voice rising to meet hers.

"I will not leave you behind, Jan," she promised, her eyes determined.

"That's not my name."

"You let me know when you figure it out," she teased, a light joy leaping from her eyes before a loud noise from the hall caused both of us to jump.

The sound repeated itself in another loud jump before the sounds of sobs and screams followed behind. Doors. Someone was opening doors.

"I have to go." Kaye groaned as she began to shift her weight, carefully placing me back on the floor again. "I am out of time."

"Kaye..." I pleaded, knowing that there was nothing I could do to stop her.

"Stay strong, don't give up." She said as she stepped toward the door, the rhythmic thunk-thunk of doors opening and closing growing closer. "I will come back."

"Promise me we will find her," I gasped, the words choked with tears as I lay on the cement, watching her disappear behind the heavy metal door.

"I promise."

It was the last thing she said before she left me alone.

Before she was gone.

CHAPTER 44

MÍRA

SOMEWHERE OUTSIDE OF WARSAW,
POLAND

"I did not expect you to contact me so soon. Was the intel faulty?"

The woman's voice was sugar sweet, like candy that you can't stop eating, even though you know that it's not good for you.

That's exactly what her voice reminded me of, something not good for you. That could have been because she just pulled me out of a deep sleep to experience the world's worst headache, or it could have been because everything about my situation spelled trouble.

Biggest of all being that my magic appeared to have been turned off. Weird.

A second woman responded to the louder one, her voice sounding like a dog's whine as I carefully tried to bring my power up and just Stutter out of this mess. But nothing happened.

Not even the low buzz that always ached near where Edmund had placed his Štít. I felt like I did years ago, a boring mortal.

Except this time I was a powerless teenager tied to... a chair? I wasn't sure.

'You are powerless, you always have been.'

Damn it. Now was not the time for that bastard to make an appearance.

I worked hard to keep my heart rate even and my eyes closed, no matter how much I wanted to snap them open and figure out what the heck was going on. I remained still, listening to the low murmur of voices, and a consistent chug-chug that was way too familiar.

That one I knew immediately. A train. An old commuter train to be exact.

Father had taken Jaromír and I on one when we were about seven, he had a business meeting in Poland and mother was too sick with her pregnancy to take care of us.

It was a good memory, but being here, tied to the chair, was tainting it. It wasn't just the sounds of the train that were familiar, it was the smell.

Dust, sweat, and old rotting wood. The train reeked of it.

When I was a child, I had breathed in the aroma and declared it to be something out of a fairy tale. Now, it was blended with something out of the worst kind of horror movies.

All that dust and wood was nearly overpowered by the smell of blood.

Add that to the fact that the last thing I remember was trying to get Ryland out of that exploding room...

'Perhaps you killed him. Perhaps he abandoned you because he doesn't care about you.'

Edmund, you freaking bastard. Get out of my head.

Forcing the thought, and the demented voice of the

madman away, I shifted my focus to pushing my heart rate to slow. I had no idea if this woman and whoever she was with had magic, or if that magic was strong enough to gauge my heart rate. It so wasn't worth the chance.

Figure out who they were and where the heck I was, and then I can get myself out of here and figure out what happened to Ryland. He had to be okay.

"So I must assume that you have something to trade?" The sugar sweet woman's voice roared over the train as everything rocked to the side.

My body tried to combat the movement before I remembered that I was supposed to be unconscious and let myself lean into it, trying to be as much of a ragdoll as possible. I was sure I overdid it, the motion so big that the long sweaty strands of my hair flew over my face in a sheet. I went from being in a somewhat comfortable position in a squishy chair to being draped over a hard wooden armrest, the worn down corner poking into my rib cage uncomfortably.

At least I knew where the restraints were. An old seatbelt over my lap, and either zip ties or handcuffs around my ankles and wrists. Flimsy, dumb, foolish... at least it would be if I had my magic. I still wasn't sure what happened there, but I had a feeling that the weird tape that I felt pull against the crook of my arm, and the cold spot near my elbow had something to do with it.

To them, with whatever they had done to me, I was little more than a dumb kid.

Even as a dumb kid, however, I was pretty sure I could break out of this.

"Intriguing," the woman said loudly, the sugar in her voice fading somewhat as she responded to the other woman, her voice indistinguishable murmurs to me. "I have heard you speak of Edmund before, I did not think any part of him survived."

All of my confidence turned into ice. Little shards of fear that pricked in my gut like that one time I ate a rancid apple on a dare. Everything twisted uncomfortably, it was all I could do to hold still. My eyes on the other hand flew open, unable to stay shut any longer.

It was a train alright, in fact, it looked almost identical to the one father had taken me on. Well, identical in the way that this one had been part of the apocalypse and barely survived to tell the tale.

Seats were torn out of the floor, wood splintered and broken at their rough removal. Beautiful lamp shades had hung over the chairs, but now, only one remained, and even then it hung from a single chain, the light blinking lamely as it swung back and forth. The cracked shade and busted light flickered over everything in a weird haunted dance that made everything look even more twisted and broken than it was. It probably didn't help that I was seeing it all through the long greasy clumps of my blonde hair. The light swung wide, flickered once and illuminated others that were just as restrained as I was.

Talk about a horror train.

There were about ten others, and not all of them were unconscious. Most of them were restrained the same as I was, seat belts and zip ties. Some even had bands around their foreheads. Each one of them had heavy grey tubes running from the crook of their arms. The wide tubes weaved through the disheveled train to a large box in the middle of the floor, a tiny red light steadily beating. Well, that explained the pain in my arm and the lack of magic.

Step one, kill the box.

I looked from the box to the others, half expecting them to be glowering at the box with as much anger and disdain as I felt.

None of them even gave it a side glance however. They just looked straight ahead, as if the devil was sitting behind them, ready to attack.

Maybe she was.

From where I lay strung over the side of my chair, I could see the woman sitting in a chair that looked like it belonged in a Jane Austen book. The high-backed, deep red upholstery made everything about her pop, her perfectly cut taupe business suit and blonde hair looking almost ethereal against the crimson. I would say she matched perfectly if it wasn't for a weird purple star on her lapel, the embroidery was almost black in the dim light.

She smiled at whoever she was talking to and sat back in the chair, looking like she was posing for a portrait. All she needed was a cat.

Her companion sat in an equally massive chair, their back to me in such a way it was no wonder that I couldn't hear them. I was sure the fabric alone was enough to swallow the sound.

"Interesting." The candy-voiced woman said with a smile that made her voice even more haunting. One of the restrained women that sat in the aisle opposite of me stiffened, her lips pressing together, almost as if she was expecting a hit.

Awesome.

Could I just have my magic back now?

Carefully, I began to pull against whatever was holding down my left ankle and wrist. I was going to need some freedom if I was going to get out of here and destroy that box.

"How do I know she is who you say?" Candy-woman asked, still sitting back in her chair.

The train rocked again, but this time I resisted the motion, keeping myself in my hurting-more-by-the-second position as I watched the woman, only to be rewarded by the appearance of the other.

Blonde hair as long as mine leaned forward, perfectly manicured fingers stretching forward to wrap around the arm of the chair, tapping so ferociously that even against the thick upholstery I could hear the tips of her nails make contact. The ice that had prickled against me before turned into a freaking thunderstorm. Warm and cold, fear and relief. It all washed over me as the recognition set in.

It couldn't be her...

"I am sure you could ask her," the second woman said, confusion joining the tirade of emotions that were running through me as she turned to face me. "She has been awake for the last few minutes."

Outed or not, I still didn't move, I just stared at the two women, eyeing the newcomer with disbelief.

So much about this woman looked like Ovailia. The way she held herself, the way she did her hair, heck even her fingernails and ridiculous heels reminded me of Ovailia.

But it wasn't.

She wasn't. I had no idea who she was, but it wasn't Ovailia.

The two women stood, Candy stepping in front of the Ovailia-imposter as they slowly made their way down the aisle of the train.

They looked ridiculous in their business suits and heels,

although they didn't so much as lose their footing as the train rocked swiftly to the left.

I, however, was thrown roughly aside, slamming painfully into the broken chair beside me. I gasped at the pain that shot through my shoulder. I needed some kind of plan, and I already knew the simpering teenager act wasn't going to work. Looking down from my awkward position I stared at the zip tie that was around my wrist, at the long tube that was inserted into my arm, and at the odd grave-yard of metal and wood at my feet, an especially jagged looking piece protruding right near my foot.

I shifted my weight, catching the tube with my toe as I shifted my ankle towards the large shard of metal. I wasn't sure if I had gotten it close enough, but I didn't have time to check. I rocked back in my chair, disguising my movements as I forced out an overly fake groan and let my head sway back and forth.

The woman closest to me obviously wasn't buying it. Many of the other prisoners jumped as the woman snatched a large handful of my hair, pulling me up to look at her. Refusing to give into even a yelp of pain, even though the crown of my head suddenly felt like it was on fire, I let her pull me up to look at her, finding myself face to face with a woman so severe that calling her candy seemed like an insult.

Her blonde hair was pulled back, her narrow lips painted red in such a way that it made it almost impossible to look away from her twisted smile. But I did. If she was going to kill me, if she was going to hurt me, I was going to look her right in the eyes.

Right in her dead grey eyes.

As much as I hated to admit it, it was possibly one of the best lessons Edmund had ever given me.

"What is your name?" she asked, the sweetness in her voice seeming like a joke now.

"Pretty sure you already know." I probably could have tried to keep the sass out of my voice, but I didn't. I just let it flow, the snark resulting in a few gasps from the other prisoners, a laugh from the Ovailia doppelganger and an almighty jerk of fist against hair from *Candy*.

I practically screamed out in pain as she rocked my head around, the sharp stab ripping through me - but not from her hand against my hair. From the quick kick I had given the jagged piece of steel.

Warm droplets of my own blood ran down the back of my ankle, pooling in the heel of my shoe. I could feel each drop, I could smell the salt and iron. I could also feel the zip tie press against my ankle, still firmly in place.

Darn it all.

I plastered a smile on my face as Candy brought my head back up to look at her, her erroneous smile twitching as she edged herself a bit closer to me.

"What is your name?" she asked again, the dark madness in her eyes spelling dangerous.

Hmmm, maybe I shouldn't push her quite so fast. "Míra."

Her smile blossomed. "And where did you get your magic?"

I guess we weren't beating around the bush.

The train heaved to the right as we began to turn, and although the two women barely moved, I felt myself shift, my head held still by the almighty fist of the woman. I hissed as hair and scalp pulled, pressing my ankle into the shard of metal again. More pain. More blood. Unwavering zip tie. I needed to be careful, too much and I was going to sever my Achilles or something. I was sure there was something down there I didn't want to hurt, especially without magic to heal me.

"From the Vilỳ," I said simply.

They may have been familiar with magic, and apparently had found some way to control it, but Vilỳ they did not know.

"The flying bats things..." I amended, speaking to them like I would a child. It seemed fitting given the way they were both looking at me like I had spoken gibberish. Neither of them seemed to like that.

My head rocked again as she jostled me, screaming something in what I recognized as Ukrainian. Even though I didn't speak it, I had traveled there enough to recognize it. It was similar to my home language, but different enough that I only made out a few profanities from her tirade.

"The Chrlič give everyone their magic," she hissed, bringing me closer still, I didn't have the heart to tell her how wrong she was. Even if she deserved to know. And she didn't. "Who trained you?"

The woman was bordering on psycho and I really wasn't interested in battling her, at least not until I had a foot free to kick her in her smug little face.

Might as well give her what she wants.

Please do.

Shut up, you psycho.

"Edmund LaRue, the Krul." I said through gritted teeth even though a dozen other names deserved that honor more than he. Ryland. Wyn. Heck, I would even say Jos.

But Edmund, I grit my teeth and slammed my heel into the metal again, letting my hatred for the bastard fuel my masochistic tendencies.

This time the zip tie broke free.

I didn't even try to restrain my smile, the grin was

equally as wide as the woman's, who looked like she had hit the jackpot with my answer. Maybe I shouldn't have been quite so honest.

"What is your name?" I asked, as I carefully tried to move my foot into position without being noticed. "Where did you get my magic?"

I was sure the question would result in insolence, but instead she smiled, released my hair and wiped her hands against the back of the seat before me as if she had just touched the most disgusting thing. I was sure the chair was dirtier.

"My name is Nastya Klotz," she began, her tone changing swiftly. From torturer to teenage beauty Queen. "I received my magic from the Chrlič in a cave in Poland about three years ago. I now rule the Ukraine."

I had the perfect plan of attack, I was ready to go, right up until she said those last few words.

"You *rule* the Ukraine?" I asked, not quite sure what she was going on about. I had had about enough with the fake kings and queens, and sometimes even the real ones. I wasn't a fan.

"Yes," she said, a vein of pride slithering into her voice, as if I was supposed to be impressed. "Myself and my team of six overthrew the Ukrainian parliament."

The woman behind her smiled broadly as Nastya leaned in, her breath smelling about as falsely sweet as her voice.

I kept up my facade as best as I could, face passive if not almost awed, even though somewhere in the back of my mind I was laughing. She had perfectly lined up the shot.

8-ball corner pocket.

"So you are like a Queen or something?" I really hoped that would feed into her ego. It did.

"I guess you could say that," she beamed, "I beheaded the former on live TV, so yes."

I smiled broadly at that, but not for the reason that she thought.

"Cool," I said, my stomach twisting in excitement. I obviously hung around Wyn too much if I was getting this excited for what was about to happen. "I always wanted to kick a Queen. You're not really a Queen, but you'll have to do."

I swung my leg up as I jolted my arm to the side, feeling the burn of the IV as I ripped it from my arm just as I heard the sharp crack of her jaw. Warm droplets of her blood sprayed over me as screams and hollers erupted in the train.

Dislocating my thumb with one hard jolt, I pulled my hand out of the restraint, ready to grab her hair and slam her face into the chair back. It would have been a great ending just as my magic returned and I Stuttered myself the hell out of here.

But my magic didn't return, and hers intercepted mine before I could even reach her perfect blonde bun with my outstretched fingers.

Nastya's magic hit me firmly in the chest, a blast of ice and fire moving through my bones and I slammed back against the chair.

It hurt like a mother and I screamed, but I could tell at once that she either didn't have good control, or was worried about hurting me.

Edmund had done worse when he was training me. This was almost like a slap on the wrist.

Of course, without my magic to heal and combat the pain, it was significantly different.

I sat against the chair, gasping for breath before she

grabbed my shirt, her long nails cutting against my skin as she lifted me to look at her.

"You have got some fire in you, girl," she said, all sweetness gone from her voice now. Now, there was only a hunger, only a desperate need to own me. The thought made my stomach twist.

I had never seen anyone look at me that way, like they wanted to cut me open and see what made me tick. Even Edmund just looked at me like I was some kind of toy. This was different, and I sure as hell wasn't going to stand for it.

"Do what you want, bitch, but I can promise you that in the end you will regret it and I will be the one to remove your head."

I smiled as her anger smoldered in her eyes, her breath picking up as she heaved angrily. The smell of burnt fabric assaulted me as her magic sparked, flaring against my skin in embers of pain before she began to scream, her eyes wide as she roared, as her magic plunged into me igniting my own.

It flooded me, roaring to life as she felt my power.

"Ohhh, you're just like The Oheň's partner," she grinned, and all of my magic froze at what she was saying. "I wonder if you spark the same way?"

Her magic sparked in an attack again, racing through me as my mind worked in overdrive. She had Ilyan, she was taking me to Ilyan.

He was alive.

I could fight her, or I could follow her. I already knew what I was going to do.

"Oh, you're going to be in so much trouble," I laughed before I screamed, the false sound running through everything as I let her think her attack worked. I sagged in my chair as she stepped back, clicking her tongue in that condescending way that always ground on me.

"Well, that was easy," she said before stepping back to her chair.

Strange, I was thinking the same thing.

TO BE CONCLUDED...
Finish the story with **Flare of Villainy**.
The Imdalind Series is complete, so you can get your binge on.

ALSO BY REBECCA ETHINGTON

THE WORLD OF IMDALIND

The Imdalind Series (complete)

Kiss of Fire, Imdalind #1

Eyes of Ember, Imdalind #2

Scorched Treachery, Imdalind #3

Soul of Flame, Imdalind #4

Burnt Devotion, Imdalind #5

Brand of Betrayal, Imdalind #6

Dawn of Ash, Imdalind #7

Crown of Cinders, Imdalind #8

Spark of Vengeance, Imdalind #9

Flare of Villainy, Imdalind #10

THE LAST FAE KING

Crimson Stained Catalyst

Gold Branded Requisite

Ash Burned Sypher

THE DARK WORLDS

The Through Glass Series (Complete)

Book One: The Dark

About the Author

Rebecca Ethington is an internationally bestselling author with over a million books sold. Her breakout debut, The Imdalind Series, has been featured on bestseller lists since its debut in 2012.

Born and raised under the lights of a stage, Rebecca has written stories by the ghost light, told them in whispers in dark corridors, and never stopped creating within the pages of a notebook.

Find me online
www.rebeccaethington.com
contact@rebeccaethington.com

THE IMDALIND SERIES